PRAISE FOR NE...
BESTSELLING AUTHOR
RAEANNE THAYNE

'Emotional and deeply satisfying. I savoured every page.'
Sunday Times bestselling author Sarah Morgan
on *The Sea Glass Cottage*

'RaeAnne Thayne gets better with every book.'
Robyn Carr, #1 *New York Times* bestselling
author of *Virgin River*

'[RaeAnne Thayne] is a rising star in the romance world.
Her books are wonderfully romantic, feel-good reads that
end with me sighing over the last pages.'
Debbie Macomber #1 *New York Times* bestselling author

'RaeAnne Thayne is quickly becoming one of my favourite
authors.... Once you start reading, you aren't going
to be able to stop.'
Fresh Fiction

'RaeAnne has a knack for capturing those
emotions that come from the heart.'
RT Book Reviews

'Tiny Haven Point springs to vivid life in Thayne's capable
hands as she spins another sweet, heartfelt story.'
Library Journal on *Redemption Bay*

**Also available from RaeAnne Thayne
and Mills & Boon**

The Path to Sunshine Cove
Christmas at Holiday House
Summer at Lake Haven
The Sea Glass Cottage
Coming Home for Christmas
Snow Angel Cove
Redemption Bay

For a complete list of books by RaeAnne Thayne,
please visit www.raeannethayne.com

Sleigh Bells Ring

RaeAnne Thayne

MILLS & BOON

Mills & Boon
An imprint of HarperCollins*Publishers* Ltd
1 London Bridge Street
London SE1 9GF

www.harpercollins.co.uk

HarperCollins*Publishers*
1st Floor, Watermarque Building, Ringsend Road
Dublin 4, Ireland

This paperback edition 2021

First published in Great Britain by
Mills & Boon, an imprint of HarperCollins*Publishers* Ltd 2021

Copyright © 2021 RaeAnne Thayne LLC

RaeAnne Thayne asserts the moral right to be
identified as the author of this work.
A catalogue record for this book is
available from the British Library.

ISBN: 978-1-84845-891-8

MIX
Paper from
responsible sources

FSC
www.fsc.org
FSC™ C007454

To Leslie Buchanan, Terri Speth and Angela Stone
for the late-night laughter, treats, tears and joy.
I love you all.

Sleigh Bells Ring

1

THIS WAS WAR. A RELENTLESS, MERCILESS BATTLE for survival.

Backed into a corner and taking fire from multiple fronts, Annelise McCade launched missiles as fast as she could manage against her enemies. She was outnumbered. They had teamed up to attack her with agile cunning and skill.

At least it was a nice day for battle. The snow the night before hadn't been particularly substantial but it had still left everything white and sparkly and the massive ranch house behind her was solid and comforting in the December afternoon sunlight.

A projectile hit her square in the face, an icy splat against her skin that had her gasping.

At her instinctive reaction, giggles rang out across the snowy expanse.

She barely took time to wipe the cold muck off her cheek. "No fair, aiming for the face," she called back. "That's against the rules."

"It was an accident," her six-year-old nephew, Henry, admitted. "I didn't mean to hit your face."

"You'll pay for that one."

She scooped up several more balls as fast as she could manage and hurled them across the battlefield at Henry and his twin sister, Alice.

"Do you give up?" she called.

"Never!"

Henry followed up his defiance by throwing a snowball back at her. His aim wasn't exactly accurate—hence her still-dripping face—but it still hit her shoulder and made her wince.

"Never!" his twin sister, Alice, cried out. She had some difficulty pronouncing her *R*s, so her declaration sounded like "Nevoh."

Alice threw with such force the effort almost made her spin around like a discus thrower in the Olympics.

It was so good to hear them laughing. In the week since they had come to live with her temporarily, Annie had witnessed very little of this childish glee.

Not for the first time, she cursed her brother and the temper he had inherited from their father and grandfather. If not for that temper, compounded by the heavy drinking that had taken over his life since his wife's death a year ago, Wes would be here with the twins right now, throwing snowballs in the cold sunshine.

Grief for all that these children had lost was like a tiny shard of ice permanently lodged against her heart. But at least they could put their pain aside for a few moments to have fun outside on a snowy December day.

She might not be the perfect temporary guardian but it had

been a good idea to make them come outside after homework for a little exercise and fresh air.

She was doing her best, though she was wholly aware that she was only treading water.

For now, this moment, she decided she would focus on gratitude. The children were healthy, they all had a roof over their heads and food in their stomachs and their father should be back home with them in less than a month.

Things could be much, much worse.

"Time out," Henry gasped out during a lull in the pitched battle. "We gotta make more snowballs."

"Deal. Five-minute break, starting now."

Annie pulled her glove off long enough to set the timer on her smartwatch, then ducked behind the large landscape boulder she was using as cover and scooped up several snowballs to add to her stash.

The sun would be going down in another hour and already the temperature had cooled several degrees. The air smelled like impending snow, though she knew only a dusting was forecast, at least until the following weekend.

She didn't worry. Holly Creek, Wyoming, about an hour south of Jackson Hole in the beautiful Star Valley, almost always had a white Christmas.

Annie's phone timer went off just as she finished a perfectly formed snowball. "Okay. Time's up," she called. Without standing up, she launched a snowball to where she knew the twins would be.

An instant later, she heard a deep grunt that definitely did not sound like Henry or Alice.

Annie winced. Levi Moran, the ranch manager, or his grizzled old ranch hand, Bill Shaw, must have wandered across the battlefield in the middle of a ceasefire without knowing he was about to get blasted.

"Sorry," she called, rising to her feet. "I didn't mean to do that."

She saw a male figure approach, wearing sunglasses. The sun reflecting off the new snow was hitting his face and she couldn't instantly identify him.

"No doubt," he said, wiping snow off his face with his sleeve.

She frowned. This was definitely not Levi or Bill.

He stepped closer and Annie felt as if an entire avalanche of snow had just crumbled away from the mountain and buried her.

She knew this man, though it had been nearly two decades since Annie had seen him in person.

It couldn't be anyone else.

Dark hair, lean, gorgeous features. Beneath those sunglasses, she knew she would find blue eyes the color of Bear Lake in summertime.

The unsuspecting man she had just pummeled with a completely unprovoked snowball attack had to be Tate Sheridan.

Her de facto boss.

The twins had fallen uncharacteristically silent, wary of a tall, unsmiling stranger. Henry, she saw, had moved closer to his twin sister and slipped his hand in hers.

Annie's mind whirled trying to make sense of what she was seeing.

Tate Sheridan. Here. After all this time.

She shouldn't be completely shocked, she supposed. It was his family's house, after all. For many years when her father was the ranch manager, the Sheridans had trekked here annually from the Bay Area several times a year for the Christmas season, as well as most summers.

His younger sister had been her very best friend in the

world, until tragedy and pain and life circumstances had separated them.

She had wondered when she agreed to take the job if she would see Tate again. She hadn't truly expected to. She had worked here for nearly a year and he hadn't once come to his grandfather's Wyoming vacation ranch.

How humiliating, that he would show up when she was in the middle of a snowball fight with her niece and nephew—who had no business being there in the first place!

"What are you doing here?" she burst out, then winced. She wanted to drag the words back. It was his family's property. He had every right to be there.

"I might ask the same of you. Along with a few more obvious questions, I suppose. Who are you and why are you having a snowball fight in the middle of my property?"

"You don't know who I am?"

Of course he wouldn't, she realized. And while she thought of him often, especially over the past year while living at Angel's View once more, he probably had not given her a moment's thought.

"Should I?"

It was stupid to feel a little hurt.

"Annelise McCade. My dad was Scott McCade."

He lifted his sunglasses, giving her an intense look. A moment later, she saw recognition flood his features.

"Little Annie McCade. Wow. You're still here, after all this time?"

She frowned. He didn't have to make it sound like she was a lump of mold growing in the back of the refrigerator. She had lived a full life in the nearly two decades since she had seen Tate in person.

She had moved away to California with her mother, struggling through the painful transition of being a new girl in a new school. She had graduated from college and found success in her chosen field. She had even been planning marriage a year ago, to a man she hardly even thought about anymore.

"Not really *still* here as much as here again. I've been away for a long time but returned a year ago. Wallace…your grandfather hired me to be the caretaker of Angel's View."

She saw pain darken his expression momentarily, a pain she certainly shared. Even after two months, she still expected her phone to ring and Wallace Sheridan to be on the other end of the line, calling for an update on the ranch he loved.

The rest of the world had lost a compelling business figure with a brilliant mind and a keen insight into human nature.

Annie had lost a friend.

"I'm sorry for your loss," she said softly.

"Thank you." His voice was gruff and he looked away, his gaze landing on the twins, who were watching their interaction with unusual solemnity.

"Are these yours?" He gestured to the children and Annie was aware of a complex mix of emotions, both protectiveness and guilt.

The children shouldn't be here. She had never asked permission from anyone in the Sheridan family to have the twins move into the caretaker's apartment with her.

She deeply regretted the omission now. While it was a feeble defense, she hadn't really known whom to ask. No one in the Sheridan organization seemed to be paying the slightest attention to any of the goings-on at a horse ranch in western Wyoming that represented only a small portion of the vast family empire.

Annie knew she was in the wrong here. No matter what uproar might have been happening during Wallace's illness and subsequent death, she should have applied to someone for permission to bring the twins to live with her here.

Instead, she had simply assumed it shouldn't be a problem since it was only a temporary situation and the children would be back with their father after the first of the year with no one in the family knowing they had been here at all.

"Not mine. They are my niece and nephew. Wes's children."

Tate and Wes were similar in age, she remembered, and had been friends once upon a time, just as Annelise had been close to Tate's younger sister Brianna. The McCades lived on the ranch year-round while the Sheridan children only visited a few times a year, but somehow they had all managed to have a warm, close bond and could always pick up where they left off when the Sheridans came back to the ranch.

She could only hope Tate would remember that bond and forgive her for overstepping and bringing the children here.

"Henry and Alice are staying with me for a few weeks because of a...family situation."

"Our mommy died last year and our daddy is in the slammer," Henry announced.

Annie winced, not quite sure where he had picked up that particular term. Not from her, certainly. She wouldn't have used those words so bluntly but couldn't deny they were accurate.

Tate looked nonplussed at the information. "Is that right?"

"It's only temporary," she told him quickly. "Wes had a little run-in with the law and was sentenced to serve thirty days in the county jail. The children are staying with me in the caretaker's apartment through the holidays. I hope that's okay."

Tate didn't seem to know how to respond. She had the impression it was very much *not* okay with him.

"We can talk about it later."

Annie frowned, anxiety and nerves sending icy fingers down her spine. She didn't like the sound of that.

What would she do if he told her she had to find somewhere else for the children to spend Christmas? She would have to quit. She didn't want do that as she enjoyed working here. But what other choice would she have?

"Why don't we, um, go inside," she suggested. "We can talk more there."

"We won, right?" Alice pressed. "We hit you like six times and you only hit us twice each."

Her priority right now wasn't really deciding who won a snowball fight. But then, she was not six years old. "You absolutely won."

"Yay! That means we each get two cookies instead of only one!"

Annie had always planned to give them two cookies each, anyway. She was a sucker for these two. The twins knew this and took full advantage.

"Kids, why don't you go change out of your snow stuff and hang out in your room for a few moments," she said when they were inside the mudroom. "I'll be there soon to get your cookies."

The twins looked reluctant but they went straight to her apartment through her own private entrance, leaving her alone with Tate.

Drat the man for somehow managing to seem more gorgeous in person than he looked on-screen.

A few years earlier, Tate had appeared in a public television documentary. Annie must have watched that clip of him at least a dozen times, seeing him help villagers dig a well in Africa.

He had looked rugged and appealing on-screen, even tired and sweaty. Seeing him now, dressed in jeans and a luxurious-looking leather coat, made her feel slightly breathless, a feeling she wasn't happy about.

"You obviously weren't expecting me."

The understatement of the month.

"No. I'm sorry. Maybe I missed an email or something."

Earlier in the year, Wallace would text her about once a month to tell her and the housekeeper/cook, Deb Garza, that he would be flying in for a few days, when he was arriving, what time to pick him up and how long he would stay.

That had been his pattern early on, anyway. Then he caught pneumonia in late spring and never seemed to bounce back. He seemed to be a little stronger the last time she spoke on the phone with him in October and he had been planning to come during the holidays but a heart attack had claimed him out of the blue only a few weeks later.

"We must have had a miscommunication," Tate said with a frown. "I thought my grandmother was sending word we were coming and she must have thought I would inform you."

"We?" Was someone else here that she hadn't seen yet?

"The rest of my family. I'm the advance guard, so to speak, but they're all showing up by the end of the week."

Annie gaped at him. "The rest of your family?"

"The whole lot of us. My grandmother Irene, her sister Lillian, my mother, Pamela, and her husband, Stanford. And my two sisters."

"Both of them? Even Brianna?"

"Yes. That's the plan. You were always good friends with Brie, weren't you?"

"That was a long time ago. Another lifetime. I think the summer we were eleven was probably the last time I saw her."

The instant she said the words, she regretted them. Both of them knew what had happened that terrible summer.

Brianna and Tate's father, Cole Sheridan, Wallace's son, had fallen down a steep mountainside to his death while horseback riding with his children.

The tragedy had lasting ramifications that rippled to this day.

"Yes. Everyone is flying in Friday. I offered to come out early to make sure the house was ready for company. Things have been so hectic I guess I just assumed my grandmother would have informed the staff, like my grandfather used to do."

"What staff?" Annie could hear the slight edge of hysteria in her voice. "There is no *staff* except me, Levi Moran, the ranch manager, and a ranch hand, Bill Shaw."

Tate frowned. "What about the housekeeper and cook?"

"Deb Garza used to fill both of those roles, but after Wallace got sick and stopped coming to Angel's View, she decided to retire. She moved down to Kemmerer to live with her sister. Your grandfather told me to hold off hiring anyone to replace her for now. We have a cleaning crew that comes a couple times a month to keep the dust bunnies under control but that's it. I take care of the rest."

Tate sighed. "That's going to be a problem, then. I have four days to get the house ready for Christmas and no idea how the hell I'm supposed to pull that off."

2

COMING BACK TO THE ANGEL'S VIEW RANCH was turning out to be even more difficult than Tate had anticipated.

He had not wanted to come here in the first place. The very log-and-chink walls of this massive home, beautifully appointed as it was, seemed to seethe with memories and pain.

From the moment he had driven under the carved arch across the road up the long, winding drive to the sprawling ranch house, with its gleaming windows and river rock accents, ghosts haunted him.

His father. His grandfather.

Men he had loved and admired, both inextricably linked to this place.

Both gone now.

If he could have figured out some way to avoid it, he never would have returned to Angel's View.

How could he argue with his grandmother, though? Irene insisted they have a private family memorial ceremony here in addition to the lavish public memorial held for his grandfather in the Bay Area. She wanted to sprinkle a few of Wallace's ashes in the mountains he had loved so very much, to join the ashes of Wallace's son, who had died in those same mountains.

He knew his grandmother well enough to know that when Irene made up her mind about something, no one could dissuade her.

You know this is what Wallace would have wanted, she had declared. *Your grandfather loved that ranch. It was his favorite place on earth, even after your father died. Don't you think some of him should spend eternity in his own little corner of heaven?*

Tate had known she was right. Wallace was never happier than when he was here at Angel's View, riding his horses, walking with the dogs, hanging out at the café in town with the locals.

Even after Tate's father died here, Wallace seemed to find even more solace and peace in the solidity of the mountains and the wind whistling through the pines.

His grandfather was a different person after spending time here in Wyoming. More focused, more relaxed. More comfortable in his own skin.

Tate and most of the rest of his family, including Irene, had stopped coming to Angel's View after Cole Sheridan's death. Wallace never had. At least once a month, he would fly in from California for a long weekend or sometimes longer.

Tate could only think his grandfather must have found some kind of connection to his son in riding the same trails they had traveled together, fishing in the same waters, seeing the same stars overhead.

This was the most appropriate place to memorialize his

grandfather, even if Tate personally would rather be any-where else on earth.

Now, as he gazed down at the unexpectedly lovely Annelise McCade, Tate wasn't sure where to start.

On the flight to Jackson Hole and the hour-long drive through the twisting canyon along the Snake River to Star Valley, Tate had expected things to be relatively easy.

He would walk into the ranch house, give the staff instructions about what his family would need and then find a room where he could closet himself with his laptop and his phone so he could continue the gargantuan task of taking over as president and CEO of all the various family enterprises.

Obviously, that wasn't going to happen, if Annelise was the only house staff.

She was the first to speak after his grim pronouncement. "Four days. That doesn't give us much time."

He still couldn't quite get over his shock that Annelise Mc-Cade had taken a job as caretaker of the house and he hadn't known a thing about it. Or that the cute little girl he remembered with freckles and braids had grown into a breathtakingly lovely woman with auburn hair, a full, delicious-looking mouth and green eyes the color of aspen leaves in springtime.

What other surprises were in store for him here at the ranch?

"That's the plan. All but my great-aunt's son and his family, who have school obligations until next week."

"The house is always kept ready for guests," she said briskly. "The rooms are cleaned and the linens are changed weekly. That's the good news. The bad news is that nothing has been decorated for the holidays except my own rooms. It didn't seem appropriate to put the usual Christmas trees up in all the bedrooms or the public spaces when I didn't expect any of the family to come for the holidays."

"Christmas trees. In every bedroom," he said faintly, beginning to grasp the enormity of the task ahead.

"You certainly don't have to follow tradition. There's no law governing how to decorate the house, but that's what Wallace did last year and what Deb told me has always been done. Smaller trees in the bedrooms, then a huge live tree in the great room, as well as greenery on the mantel and the stairs."

If he closed his eyes, he could smell his childhood Christmases spent here with his family. A fire in the huge fireplace, cinnamon simmering throughout the house, the sharp tang of the pine sap from a towering tree he and Brie would cut with their father and grandfather in the forested foothills above the ranch.

His grandmother wanted that slice of memory again and he had promised to deliver it, no matter what.

"It should only take a couple of days to take the Christmas things out of storage and decorate the bedrooms, but we'll have to find a big tree for the great room," Annelise went on. She reached into a drawer in the kitchen and pulled out a notebook, flipped a page and started scribbling a few things down.

"And we still don't have a cook," he pointed out.

"We still don't have a cook," she said, just as the pint-size snowball throwers came into the room, this time without their winter gear.

The girl, who had dark-blond curls and big blue eyes, marched straight up to him and gazed up with curiosity. "Are you a movie star?" she asked him with a pronounced lisp. "Henry says he thinks he saw you on TV once."

Tate wasn't quite sure how to answer that question. At sea, he glanced at Annelise, who seemed to have turned a rather adorable pink.

"He's not, Alice," she said quickly. "Remember that nice

Mr. Sheridan who owns the ranch? You met him once when he was here. This is his grandson, Tate."

"You said he died. The man with the white hair like Santa Claus," Alice said with a frown.

Tate felt the familiar ache of loss. Even after two months, he still could not believe his indomitable grandfather was gone.

"He did, sweetheart." Annie looked sad, too, if Tate wasn't mistaken. The boy—Henry, she had called him—slipped a hand into hers as if to offer comfort. The sweet generosity of the gesture made Tate's throat feel tight suddenly, especially when he remembered the children had apparently suffered their own recent losses.

"How long have you been working at the Angel's View?" he asked as she reached into another drawer and pulled out a couple of coloring books and crayons.

She handed the art supplies to the children. "Nearly a year now. I needed to find a local job so I could come back to Wyoming to help my brother. Somehow your grandfather found out that I needed to relocate back to Wyoming. I still don't know how he knew. He reached out to me and said his current caretaker was retiring and asked if I could help him out by keeping an eye on things here. It seemed the perfect solution."

That seemed so much like Tate's grandfather, who had a reputation for running his business interests with compassion and fairness and an insight into people that Tate knew he could never come close to matching.

Before he could sift through all the questions running through his brain to figure out which one to ask, she turned her attention to the children. Her niece and nephew. He wasn't quite sure why he felt this odd sense of relief at learning they weren't hers.

Why were they there? The boy had said his father was in

the slammer and their mother had died. What was the rest of the story?

"Auntie, I'm hungry," the little girl said.

Annelise flushed. "We had peanut butter and jelly sandwiches and ants on a log right before we went out to play."

"I'm still hungry."

"I'll fix dinner for you later," she said. "Right now I need to talk to Mr. Sheridan."

"Go ahead and do what you have to, " Tate said. "I'll grab my bags from the car. What room should I use?"

"That's really up to you. You can take your choice of any of the ten guest rooms. If your grandmother is coming, she will probably want to use the room your grandfather always stayed in."

"Good point. I'll start with my bags."

"Do you need help? I can text Levi to meet you at your car."

"I travel light. It won't take long."

He grabbed his duffel and backpack out of the small SUV he had rented at the airport and carried them back through the artistically carved front door.

So many memories hit him as he walked through the house, familiarizing himself again with the layout. Kitchen and living area in the middle of the house and two large wings with bedroom suites fanning out from it.

He had forgotten how much he had loved it here once. He had spent many happy childhood times at the ranch.

The closest ski resort was in Jackson Hole, about forty-five minutes away. In between trips through the winding canyon toward the slopes, they would snowshoe, cross-country ski, ride horses on groomed trails into the mountains.

This had been their paradise, a place of peace where his busy family could be together.

Tate finally dropped his bags in the same room he used

when he visited here with his family, remembering he had always enjoyed the small gas fireplace, private patio and lovely view of the mountains and the creek.

He returned to the kitchen to find Annelise distributing granola bars and juice boxes to the twins.

She looked up. "Hi. Did you find a room?"

"My old one. All the rooms have had a refresh since I was here. It's very welcoming."

"That was before my time. I think your grandfather had everything redone about five years ago."

She left the twins and met him at the kitchen island. "I'm really sorry I wasn't better prepared for you. I did a quick scan through my emails and messages and couldn't find anything about your family visit but I easily could have missed it."

"Please don't worry. As I said, the mix-up was probably on our part, with everyone presuming the other person had reached out. I assumed my mother or grandmother would let you know and they must have assumed I would, as I was coming first. I'm the one who should be apologizing to you for dropping in without warning."

"It's your house. You don't have to warn me you're coming."

"None of that matters, really. Right now, the important thing is making sure we can get the house ready in time for everyone."

"Christmas, with all the trimmings."

"That's what Irene wants."

He wasn't sure why it was so important to his grandmother this year, of all years. In his memory, while she had always enjoyed the holidays, she never seemed as obsessed about making sure Christmas was perfect, whatever that meant.

No doubt it was connected to Wallace's death. Maybe his

grandmother was feeling her own mortality and feared this might be her last holiday with her family.

This would be the first time they had all been together in over a decade, between Brie's restless wandering and his work for the Sheridan Trust. Irene obviously wanted to make it count.

"It will be lovely. You'll see. The decorations are all stored in a building on the property. I can talk to Levi and Bill about bringing them in first thing in the morning and get straight to work decking all the halls for you."

She paused, looking toward the children, then back to him. "Sorry. That's presumptuous of me. I suppose I first should have asked if you're going to fire me."

He gaped at her. "Fire you? Why would I do that?"

"I moved Henry and Alice into my apartment without permission. I should have asked someone. I could have at least reached out to Wallace's assistant to let her know the circumstances. It was an egregious lapse in judgment on my part."

He wasn't completely thrilled about having the children underfoot, for his grandmother and great-aunt's sake, but he also didn't want her to angst further about it.

"It sounds as if you were backed into a corner. Er, Henry said their mother died and Wes is in jail?"

He hadn't seen any of the McCades in nearly two decades but Wes had once been a good friend. They had ridden together, fished together, hiked. He remembered the man as having a quick temper, a wicked sense of a humor and an honorable character. Finding out he was incarcerated was a shock.

Annelise looked at her nephew and niece, busy coloring and not paying them any attention.

"My sister-in-law died unexpectedly a year ago. Cassie was six months pregnant and had complications. A pulmonary embolism caused a stroke. The twins were in kindergarten at the time, and when she didn't meet them at the bus after school, a neighbor came to the house and found her. Neither she nor the baby survived."

"Good Lord," he exclaimed. "I'm so sorry."

Through his work with the Sheridan Trust, he had seen plenty of tragedy around the world. He certainly knew how many complications could happen to mother or fetus or both during pregnancy and childbirth. While not much surprised him anymore, he was deeply saddened for Wes, for Annelise and for those two adorable children.

She acknowledged his sympathy with a grateful nod. "Needless to say, it's been a rough year. That's the reason I needed to return to Wyoming. Wes had no one else to help him. Our mom came out to stay for a few weeks right after Cassie died but she has teenagers herself, my half brothers, who have school and other activities in California, so she couldn't come permanently."

"So you did."

Annelise shrugged. "Wes needed help. He was a hot mess. He's *still* a mess, if you want the truth. Right now he's in jail on drunk and disorderly charges, his fourth offense in the past year. The judge had enough and ordered him held for one month, hoping it will straighten him out. Unfortunately, that left the kids with nobody else but me to take care of them."

"I get it. Exigent circumstances."

"I didn't know what else to do. I could have stayed at Wes's place with them but my job as caretaker here requires me to live on-site. Moving them here seemed the easiest solution."

"I'm sure it will be fine," he assured her. "They seem well-behaved."

She looked over at the children with a doubtful look that made him wonder what he might be missing. He didn't have time to worry about that now, when his family would be arriving in only a few days.

"It's Christmas," he said gruffly. "I might be a Scrooge about the holidays but even I wouldn't toss a couple of children out into the snow at Christmas."

Her eyes lit up with relief. "Thank you. I'll do my best to keep them out of your family's way, I promise."

"What do you think my chances are of hiring a cook and housekeeper between now and Friday?"

She snorted. "Slim to none."

"You could be a little more encouraging."

"The job market is tight around here. I can call Deb Garza and see if she would consider coming back for a few days but I wouldn't count on that. We keep in touch and I know she just had a new grandson who is a preemie and I think she'll want to stay close to help her son and his family until the baby is out of the NICU."

"That's only to be expected. Maybe I can hire a personal chef from Jackson."

"It's possible, though this is a busy time of year."

"I need to find someone to feed my family. Considering I'm pretty helpless in the kitchen, that's got to be a priority."

"In a pinch, I can cook."

She looked as if she regretted her words as soon as she said them. "I'm not a gourmet chef by any measure, but my food is passable. I might be able to muddle through for a few days."

"I doubt that's in your job description."

It hardly seemed fair to show up without warning and then force her to feed them all, like the worst sort of houseguests.

"Your grandfather hired me to take care of the house and any guests who might be staying here. I don't think he would be happy with the job I was doing if I let you all starve to death."

"We would hardly starve. We can fend for ourselves. And we could always do takeout for a few days, until we find someone to cook for us."

"You won't find many take-out places around here, other than pizza and sandwich shops."

"Well, we don't have to worry about that for a few days, when my family arrives. I have a little time to figure something out."

"As far as a housekeeper goes, I can talk to the cleaning company and arrange for someone to come in every day to keep things in order while your family is here."

"That would be terrific. Thank you."

"You're welcome."

She smiled at him and Tate wanted to bask in the glow.

Annelise McCade worked for his family, he reminded himself. That made her completely off-limits.

3

THAT NIGHT AFTER THE KIDS WERE FINALLY IN
bed, Annie worked at her sewing machine until her eyes
burned and then decided to take a walk down to the barn to
stretch her legs and also check on Luna, one of the ranch dogs.

The Australian shepherd, great-granddaughter to one of
her father's favorite cow dogs, was due to deliver her first litter of pups and Annie felt a bit territorial about her progress.

The children usually slept well, save for the occasional
nightmare. Just in case one of them might wake up and need
her, she turned on the security camera she had bought online
for this very thing and the app on her phone that would alert
her to sound and movement inside her apartment.

The evening was lovely, clear and cold. The moon and the
vast blanket of stars overhead gleamed on the new snow.

She drew in a deep breath, rotating her neck and shoulders

as she tried to center the chaos that had consumed her thoughts since she turned around and found Tate Sheridan standing in the snow in front of her earlier that afternoon.

It seemed a losing battle. Even working at her sewing machine, which she usually found cathartic and calming, hadn't spun its usual magic tonight.

Annie sighed. His entire family would be there in four days.

On a purely selfish note, the timing could not have been worse for her right now. She still had orders to fill in her online store, not to mention the thirty items she had promised to deliver a week from tomorrow to a local charitable organization.

How was she going to meet all her obligations without having a nervous breakdown? She had no idea.

One step at a time. That was how Annie managed all the stressful things in her life.

Right now, she decided to focus on this lovely winter evening. She pushed open the door to the barn. It was warmer than outside, though still cool, and smelled of her childhood—hay and leather and animals.

How many hours had she spent inside this barn when her father was the ranch manager? She would come here the moment the school bus dropped her off at the end of the drive and usually not leave until bedtime.

Scent memories crowded in and she suddenly missed her father with a fierce ache. Scott McCade had been gone for five years and it was still a shock to walk into this barn and not find him there, going over ranch accounts or working with one of the horses.

A light was burning in the office in the front that also doubled as a tack room. She wasn't really surprised. In fact, she would have been more surprised if Levi Moran *wasn't* there.

She knocked softly on the door and pushed it open when he called for her to come in.

Levi was sitting at his computer while three of the ranch dogs dozed in front of an electric space heater that had an artificial flame like a woodstove.

Two of the dogs, Jock and Pep, barely acknowledged her presence but Luna slowly rose to her feet and waddled over to Annie.

"Hi there, baby. How are you?" Annie crooned, scratching between the dog's ears.

Levi smiled, leaning back in his office chair and stretching, much as she had done earlier after rising from her sewing machine.

"She's hanging in there. I think we're getting close. Maybe another week. Maybe less. I have her sleeping in the whelping box we made and she seems to be settling in."

"That's my good girl," Annie crooned. She loved this dog and wished she could sit here for an hour, simply petting her.

"So," Levi said. "There goes our quiet Christmas, I guess."

"Yes. I'm sorry."

Not that either of them had been looking forward to the holidays that much. While she struggled to provide the best possible Christmas to two motherless children, poor Levi had to spend the holidays without his own son, even though it was technically his turn for custody.

The injustice of it made her burn. She was still half tempted to call Levi's ex-wife and have words with her for the harm her selfishness had caused a good man.

"It would have been nice to have a little warning about the family coming home for the holidays."

"Right. Shocked the heck out of me when you told me Wallace's grandson was here. I've worked at the ranch going on five years and never met a single other member of the family except Wallace. I figured the rest of them would be selling the place the moment he breathed his last."

His words made her stomach hurt. She didn't want to think about the Angel's View passing out of Sheridan hands.

"I'm sure it's going up for sale eventually." As much as she didn't want to think about it, she had known her days of working at the Angel's View were likely numbered. She didn't see other options.

"I've decided I'm not going to worry about that now," she delcared. "I've got enough on my plate, having the twins here for Christmas."

"Including sewing about a hundred blankets. How's that going?"

Annie made a face. "That is a bit of an exaggeration. Not quite a hundred. Only ten more to go for my Etsy shop and then thirty more for the Family Connection."

"No problem. Just forty fancy blankets in a week, along with catering to a bunch of spoiled rich people. You got this."

"The Sheridans aren't like that," she protested. "At least they never were when I knew them. And Wallace certainly wasn't."

"He wasn't. You're right. As for the rest, I'll have to take your word for it."

"I remember the Sheridans as always treating me and my family well. Even Irene, Wallace's wife. She's a tough old cookie but was always kind."

Annie's mother had been the housekeeper and her father the ranch manager but they had never been treated as employees, more like members of the family.

Maybe that was her ten-year-old brain speaking. As a girl, she hadn't seen any differences between her family and the Sheridans with their vast wealth, other than to feel sympathy for them that Tate and Brie weren't lucky enough to live at the prettiest ranch in Wyoming year-round.

Levi didn't look convinced. "Tell me what you know about the rest of the family. Who's coming? Did Tate tell you? Also, why don't you grab a chair? You don't have to sit on the floor."

"I'm good here." Annie shifted into a more comfortable position, with Luna's head on her lap. The space heater seemed to soothe her achy muscles and she drew comfort from the unconditional love of the dog.

"Wallace and Irene only had one son, Cole. He was a great guy. Everyone loved him. I remember him always laughing."

His death that summer she turned eleven had cast such a pall over the ranch, as if everything colorful and bright had leached away. It was around that time her parents had started fighting. A year later, she and her mother moved to California to be near her maternal grandparents, leaving Wes behind to stay here with their father.

"I think Wallace wanted him to take over the family business," she went on, "but Cole preferred managing the family philanthropic arm, the Sheridan Trust. This is probably all information you already know. You've worked here five years."

"Most of it, but I appreciate the refresher. I'm familiar with the trust. I watched that PBS special about their work."

To her dismay, Annie could feel her face heat. She told herself it was only from the heat of the electric fireplace and the warm dog, not anything to do with her own embarrassment at how many times she had watched the same thing. Or about how she would pause on the part about Tate to see if she could find any trace on his features of the boy she had once considered a friend.

"Cole and his wife, Pamela, had two children. Tate and Brianna. Brie is my age and we were friends when we were kids, but I haven't talked to her in years. We lost track of each other after my parents divorced and I moved to California."

Annie wasn't exactly sure why they hadn't stayed in touch.

They had each texted the other often for the next year and had talked about all the fun things they would do at the ranch when Annie came back for summer visitation with her dad.

She had returned but Brie never did. Annie waited that summer and the next, then one day when she was about thirteen, she realized that she had texted a half dozen times with no response. After that, she stopped trying to reach out.

She was only realizing now what a void that missing friendship had created in her life.

After she had come back to work for Wallace, Annie had asked him about Brianna. He had become uncharacteristically closemouthed.

She's walked a hard path, that one, he had told her gruffly. *We just want her to come home but she's as stubborn as her father was. I think she worries she's not welcome, which couldn't be further from the truth. Breaks her grandmother's heart.*

She had the feeling by his tone that Irene's heart wasn't the only damaged one in the family. Annie had chosen not to press Wallace, though she was intensely curious about what he meant.

"Is it hard for you, to see the Sheridans parading around the land like it's always belonged to them?"

Levi's question dragged her back from worrying about her friend. "No. Not at all," she assured him. "My grandfather sold Wallace the land more than fifty years ago. It hasn't been ours for a long, long time. Long before I was born. I think maybe it bothered my father sometimes. But not me and not Wes."

Sometimes she wondered if that discontent somehow had contributed to her parents' divorce, if her father perhaps could not get over his father selling what Scott considered the McCade legacy. The ranch had been in her family for five generations, going back to some of the earliest settlers in the area. It had been floundering, though, like many small ranches.

Instead of fighting a losing battle and working the land into bankruptcy, her grandfather had chosen to sell the ranch to the first stranger who came along with a deep enough pocketbook.

If it did bother her father, he never said. In fact, he and Wallace had been dear friends to the end.

Still, dissatisfaction with one's circumstances could seep into every area of life, especially a relationship.

She would likely never know the answer to that question. Her father was gone now and her mother had been remarried for years, so there was no point in dredging up the past.

"Back to the family," she said. "Pamela, Cole's widow, eventually remarried and they had another daughter, who is a teenager now. Catherine. I've never met her but Wallace dropped a few hints that she was a bit of a handful."

Levi looked less than enthused at this information. "And they're all coming?"

"That's what Tate said. Along with Irene's sister Lillian and Lillian's son and his family, though they're coming out later."

"I suppose it could be worse. They could be bringing a dozen of their friends."

She smiled at him, wishing not for the first time that she could feel something more than brotherly affection for him. He was a good guy and a dear friend but they didn't click romantically.

She knew Levi had suffered a broken heart from his divorce. It wasn't something they ever talked about but she could see the pain in his eyes at random moments, especially when he talked about the darling son he didn't see nearly as often as he would like.

Levi dated here and there but nothing serious, which saddened her. He was a guy who definitely deserved someone terrific.

"What kind of help do you need from me up at the house?" he asked.

She didn't want to think about the logistics of having the Sheridans there until Christmas. "Tomorrow I'm decorating. It's a holidaypalooza. Would you and Bill mind hauling the decorations up from the shed?"

"All of them?"

"I'm sorry."

"That's a pretty tall order. I might have to borrow Nick Dawson's big sleigh and Percherons."

"I'll help you. We can load up the horse trailer, as long as it's clean."

"It's always clean," he retorted, as if she was presumptuous to think otherwise. "What are you going to do with it? Drive it straight into the great room of the big house?"

She laughed. "I'm only trying to save you a few steps. I was thinking you can pull to the house and unload but if you want to carry everything all the way from the shed, that's your business. I'll let you and Bill figure out the logistics."

She rose, feeling better after talking to him. Levi always had that effect on her. "However you do it, we've got a long day tomorrow. I'll leave you to your accounts. Good night. Bye, Luna-girl. Be good."

The dog flopped her tail on the wide-plank flooring in the tack room and Annie zipped up her coat, prepared to brave the cold night and her sewing machine once more.

4

H E WAS COMPLETELY IN OVER HIS HEAD.
Tate stood in the great room with red and green plastic boxes scattered everywhere, overflowing with sparkles and bows.

The entire house now looked like this. The ranch manager, Levi Moran, and a grizzled old ranch hand named Bill Shaw had brought all the boxes and bags inside first thing that morning while Annelise oversaw the operation like a traffic cop, directing them to drop various boxes in certain bedrooms.

She seemed to know what she was doing. So what the hell was *he* doing here?

Tate didn't know the first thing about throwing a traditional family Christmas. How could he? He had only spent a handful of Christmases in the same country with his family since becoming an adult and had mostly felt like a bystander during those times.

His fault.

He knew it was. Contrary to what he had told Annelise the day before, Tate didn't really hate the holidays, though he did sometimes find the weight of his family's expectations on him too onerous.

One reason he didn't like them was that he was constantly aware at family gatherings that at least one important seat was empty. His father's, of course, but also Brie's, as she had usually been off doing her own thing, moving from place to place and project to project, usually because of her current relationship.

As for his father, seeing that empty place at the table always served as a harsh reminder that Cole would never share any more holidays with them.

For the past decade, Tate's guilt had driven him to avoid traditional family gatherings. Instead, he had spent nearly every Christmas visiting a different spot on the globe where the Sheridan Trust was engaged in some kind of philanthropic activity.

The year before he had been in the Congo, building a flour mill. The year before that, a tiny village on the Amazon, where he had helped construct a schoolhouse.

The year before that had been one of the 'stans, Uzbekistan, he thought, doing more of the same.

Tate considered himself a fairly handy guy. He could dig a well, could drywall a medical clinic in an afternoon, could make bricks out of mud.

Despite all his disparate skills that had served him well, Tate had no idea how to decorate a house like this for the holidays. At least not in a way that would meet Irene's approval.

The magnitude of the task ahead left him feeling overwhelmed and out of his depth.

He wasn't alone, though. He supposed he could find some comfort in that.

"Where do you want to start?" Annelise asked.

She was asking him? He had no earthly idea. If it were up to him, he would start by walking out the front door and taking a hike along Holly Creek all afternoon, but he didn't think that's what she was asking.

"What about in here?" he suggested. "We could get the main room out of the way."

Instead of answering, she smothered a yawn with her hand, then seemed to turn a quite adorable shade of pink.

"Sorry," she said quickly.

"Don't worry on my account. I take it you're not any more thrilled than I am about the task at hand."

"That's not it. Not really. I just had a late night."

He had caught a glimpse of her walking down to the barn the other night. Were she and the rugged-looking ranch manager a thing?

Tate wasn't crazy about that idea, though he wasn't exactly sure why. It was none of his business if the ranch caretaker and the foreman were seeing each other.

"The problem in here is that we don't really have an artificial tree tall enough to look good. The big space needs at least a twelve-foot tree and we've only got seven-foot trees for the bedrooms."

He craned his neck to look at the two-story room.

"Even a tree that is fifteen or sixteen feet would work."

"Possibly."

"Last year, Wallace had a real tree in here. It smelled heavenly."

Now that she mentioned it, Tate remembered the Sheridan family tradition of riding horses into the hills above the ranch and cutting down a tree for this room. "We always had a real tree here for the main family tree," he said.

"I think that's why there's no artificial tree among the decorations that would be large enough to fit the proportions in this room."

"Any suggestions? Could we still go up and cut one down that might work?"

"Oh, sure. You own a whole forest of pine and fir."

He could handle that. Using a chain saw was more his speed than hanging tinsel and shiny ornaments on a tree.

"Maybe we ought to take your niece and nephew with us when they get home from school and they can help us cut it down. Do you think they would like that?"

He wasn't sure why he made the suggestion, other than he and Brianna had always enjoyed the outing.

Whatever the reason, Annelise's features softened and she gave him a look so filled with gratitude he didn't know how to respond.

"What a wonderful idea!" she exclaimed. "They would love that so much."

He probably shouldn't feel this deep sense of accomplishment, especially when they both still had so much to do. "What time do they get home from school?"

"Not until three, by the time the bus brings them here and I meet them at the end of the driveway."

"That only gives us a few hours of daylight. Will that be enough?"

"It should. They'll just have to do their homework after dinner."

"Meanwhile, maybe we can try to finish as many of the bedroom suites as possible."

"Sounds like a plan. Why don't we start with your grandfather's room? That's the largest space to decorate."

"Good idea."

Annelise smiled again and he found himself fascinated by the way the expression lit up her whole face.

She led the way down the hall to the large three-room suite his grandfather had always used. Inside the room Wallace utilized for an office while he was here, several boxes had been stacked neatly next to an artificial tree.

The room, dominated by a massive carved oak desk, smelled of his grandfather's custom aftershave: a mix of leather and pine and sagebrush that Tate only now realized seemed to encapsulate everything about Angel's View into one appealing scent.

Tate felt a sharp pang of loss again, missing Wallace dearly.

He had a sudden memory of coming into this room, with its wide windows and massive stone fireplace, after his father's death. His grandfather had done his best to comfort him but even then, as a boy of fourteen, Tate could sense that both of them were ravaged by the loss.

Still, he remembered finding some comfort in being with his grandfather on that long-ago day, sitting quietly in this room, drawing what strength he could from him.

Cole Sheridan had been such a force of nature. The most decent, kind man Tate had ever known, lifting the lives of everyone who came into his orbit.

His death had left a deep void in their family, as if the heart had been yanked out of them all. Twenty years after Cole's death, his absence still resonated, even as life had marched inexorably onward.

His mother had remarried a decent man, even having another child. Tate admired and liked his stepfather and knew the man adored his mother, which mattered.

In the years since Cole's death, Wallace had managed to grow the business by diversifying into new tech and aerospace arenas.

The work of the Sheridan Trust, which Cole had built from the ground up, had moved forward, as well, with Tate at the helm for the past decade.

Tate loved the work he did there, even as he had been aware that following in his father's footsteps only made him miss the man more.

How many times had he wished he could call his father and ask him how to work out some thorny supply chain issue or diplomatic tangle?

Now the two most important men in his life were gone and Tate didn't know quite how to handle the loss.

"I love this room," Annelise McCade said softly, coming in behind him. "It always feels so peaceful."

He turned around, embarrassed that he had been so caught up in the memories evoked by his grandfather's office that he had completely forgotten she was there.

"The last time your grandfather was here, I could tell he didn't feel well. He went out to see the horses a few times but spent most of his time in here, sitting in that chair by the fire where he had a good view over the ranch."

Tate wished he had known Wallace wasn't well. He had tried to spend more time with his grandfather after his bout of pneumonia, canceling several trips overseas. When Wallace seemed to recover and returned to his regular activities, Tate had resumed his travel. He had been in Indonesia when Irene had called to deliver the news of Wallace's sudden death.

He was further dismayed to feel a lump in his throat and did his best to clear it away. He had a feeling Annelise could sense he was feeling emotional but she said nothing, only gave him a sympathetic smile that somehow did actually make him feel better.

"That area next to the window might be a good place for the Christmas tree in here. I think that's where your grandfather had it last year. What do you think?"

He didn't really care one way or the other. It had to go somewhere, though. "Good idea."

"The window is big enough your grandmother will still have a view out."

The prelit tree was easy to put together and came on as soon as Annie plugged in the cord.

"You're right. That's a good place," he said, watching the lights twinkle in the window. "I remember a tree always being in that spot when I was a boy. I think my grandfather liked to be able to see it from his desk."

He caught Annelise giving him a careful look, which made him wonder what he might have revealed by his tone.

"I don't mind doing this by myself, if you would rather not be here. It is my job."

He couldn't let the ghosts chase him away when he had work to do. Otherwise, he would be running the rest of his life. "No. It's fine. It shouldn't take us long, right?"

"Depends on how good you are at decorating Christmas trees."

He managed a smile. "Uh-oh. What if I'm lousy?"

She laughed, a light easy sound that reminded him of chiming bells ringing out across a December morning.

"Then I'm afraid we're in trouble. The tree in my sitting room looks like it was thrown together by a couple of first-graders up past their bedtime. Oh, wait. It was."

This time, his smile was more genuine. He liked this woman. He always had liked her, he remembered. He had forgotten how much.

Annie had always been good at making him laugh. She had been silly, funny, clever.

Yes, she had been several years his junior, but when there were only four young people at the ranch, they always seemed to hang out together.

Annelise had been game for anything, whether that was watching meteor showers on an August night, going for an early-morning hike or jumping into the cold swimming hole at the creek.

That spunky little girl had grown into a lovely woman who seemed to make the entire room feel brighter by her presence.

"Lucky for both of us," Annelise went on, "Deb Garza and I came up with a system last year when we put away the decorations. We took photographs of how each room looked and stuck them into the boxes for that room. Our job, should we choose to accept it, is to find the picture for each room and do our best to match our efforts to that."

"Genius," he said with an admiring look.

She gave a modest shrug. "I am pretty sure that was Deb's idea. She claimed the decorating gene passed her by and that she struggled every year trying to figure out how to make the decorations look good. I don't think she knew she would be retiring this year, but maybe she had a premonition or something. Either way, it works out great for us."

She dug through one of the boxes until she found several snapshots, which she perused for a moment before handing over to Tate.

"Here we go. Last year's Christmas decorations in this room. We can match that, can't we?"

He saw photos of a warm, welcoming room decorated with ornaments and greenery. "I'll let you lead the way," he said, handing them back to her.

"I hope we both don't come to regret that decision," she said with another smile that made his pulse seem to accelerate.

They started opening boxes, comparing contents to the photographs, then Annelise went to work on the Christmas tree, twisting the garland on first.

He watched her for a moment, enjoying the little frown between her eyes as she concentrated on the task. He was supposed to be helping her, not gaping at her, Tate had to remind himself. He stepped forward to help her with the garland, earning a grateful look in response.

"So," he said, after they moved from the garland to hanging the baubles. "Tell me what you've been up to for the past twenty years."

She laughed, her cheeks turning that same adorable shade of pink he had seen the day before. "Do you want the long version or the condensed one?"

"We'll be at this awhile. You can give me the long one."

"I was born on a rainy April night in a hospital not far from here to Scott and Jeanette McCade," she began with a teasing look.

He rolled his eyes, completely charmed by her. "Okay, I suppose you can condense it a *little*. As long as you promise not to leave out any juicy parts."

"Well then, this won't take long since there aren't all that many juicy parts."

He had a hard time believing that a woman as vibrant and appealing as Annelise hadn't left a string of broken hearts behind.

"Let's see," she finally said. "My parents divorced when I was twelve and I moved to California with my mom. I didn't want to go. In fact, I believe I may have thrown a royal fit about it, but my parents didn't give me a choice."

Poor thing. That must have been so difficult for her, to leave the ranch she clearly loved. "Did Wes go to California with you?"

"No. He stayed with our dad. He was already in high school by then and played on a couple of sports teams here so that seemed to sway them into letting him stay, which I thought at the time was highly unfair."

Tate thought it unfair, too. Divorce could be so hard on children.

"Where did you move in California?"

"Sacramento, near my maternal relatives." She sighed a little as she hung a gleaming red ornament on a bough. "About a year after we moved away, my mom remarried and we moved again, this time with my new stepfather to the San Jose area."

"That's a lot of moving around."

"It was a hard few years," she admitted. "I missed my dad and Wes and the Angel's View like crazy. I would come back for a long weekend a few times a year and then spent summers here with them but it was never enough, you know?"

She colored. "I'm sorry. That was insensitive. I could at least text or call my dad."

In contrast to Tate and Brie, who had lost their father completely. He knew what she meant just as he had known it was inevitable that he wouldn't be able to escape constant reminders of Cole here at the ranch.

Was it any wonder he and the rest of his family avoided coming back here when they could help it?

"What did you do after high school?" he pressed, mostly to change the subject.

"I ended up going to school in California and studied both business and hospitality. I wanted to open a B and B somewhere back here in Wyoming. That was my dream, anyway. After college, I was lucky enough to land a job at the Lancaster San Francisco."

He knew the luxury hotel chain, based out of Silver Bells, Colorado. His company used them exclusively for their travel.

"Fancy. Their San Francisco property is not far from our corporate offices."

"I know." She reached into the box for another ornament but not before he thought he saw a little more color climb her cheekbones.

"My job wasn't very exciting. I worked the front desk for a

few years but eventually worked my way into becoming one of their concierges."

"Interesting. That takes a complex skill set."

"Yes. I have to be part confidante, part social secretary, part research librarian."

"What led you to that career path?"

"I didn't think I could make it as a professional cowgirl, I guess."

He smiled as he hung an intricate crystal icicle on the tree. "You never know until you try. Dream big, Annie Oakley."

She made a sound of amusement. "I actually really loved my job as a hotel concierge. The pay wasn't fabulous but the tradeoff was that I got to help people for a living. I loved nothing so much as recommending an out-of-the-way restaurant to someone and having them come back and tell me they had discovered a new favorite place."

"But you walked away from all of that to come look after Angel's View for my grandfather?"

"Wes needed me, " she said simply. "What else could I do?"

He knew her words weren't intended to make him feel guilty but they had that effect, anyway. His family had needed him often over the years and he had always chosen other priorities. How could he give up helping supply an entire village with clean drinking water, simply because his sister was going into rehab for the fourth time?

He should have known something was going on with his grandfather beyond the pneumonia he had suffered earlier in the year. Tate would always regret missing those extra months with Wallace, learning from him and absorbing more of his wisdom.

"Do you miss the city?" he asked her.

"Sometimes. I miss the nightlife and meeting friends for

seafood at our favorite place. I don't miss the ridiculous rent or the pollution."

"Probably not much nightlife in Wyoming."

"Not unless I want to go hang out with the tourists in Jackson at the Million Dollar Cowboy Bar. Which I certainly don't."

With a pensive look, she hung up another ornament, moving closer to him to fill in a bare spot. "I haven't really minded, if you want the truth. There's a peace and balance here I never found when I was working twelve-hour days."

She smelled of vanilla and peaches, an irresistible combination. Tate held himself still as the scent seeped through him.

She was close enough to kiss.

The completely irrational thought popped into his head out of nowhere.

"There. That's the last ornament I have," she said, apparently oblivious to his sudden turmoil. "What about you?"

He took a hasty step backward. When he looked down at his box, Tate was more than a little surprised to find it empty. "I'm out."

"The tree looks great. Let me take a look at the photograph to see if we're missing anything."

She crossed to Wallace's desk, where they had laid the images out in a row for reference. "There are pine boughs above the mantel. If I remember right, those were real, which helped make it smell like Christmas in here. Maybe when we cut down the tree for the great room, we could save some extra branches to use as greenery on the mantel."

"Good idea," he said gruffly.

This would be a very long day if he didn't figure out a way to put the lid on his growing attraction to her.

He helped Annelise set out various-size candlesticks on the mantel as well as an exquisite sculpture of an angel with its wings spread wide that Tate guessed was an actual art piece his grandfather had purchased somewhere and casually stored with the other Angel's View holiday decorations.

"Looks great," he said when they had matched the images from the previous year to the best of their ability.

"It does," Annelise agreed. "That wasn't so bad, was it?"

"I suppose not."

He had to admit, it wasn't the worst morning he had ever spent, talking to a lovely woman who smelled delicious, in a room lit by a cozy fire.

She was completely out of bounds, he reminded himself firmly.

"We should probably move on to the next room," she said.

"Right."

He would be better taking that cold walk next to the river. Maybe then, he could work out of his system this attraction for someone he shouldn't want.

5

THAT WAS ODD.

Annie gave Tate the occasional look under her lashes as they started setting up the Christmas tree in the second bedroom suite across the hall from Wallace's, the one his parents always used.

For a moment there, she had the weirdest idea that Tate Sheridan actually wanted to kiss her.

Ridiculous. Impossible.

Perhaps all the late nights in front of her sewing machine had finally ruined her eyesight. Or at least made her start having hallucinations.

She was an awkward, bookish, nearsighted geek who had barely had time to pull her hair back into a braid that morning and who could stand to lose about fifteen pounds. Why on earth would a hot billionaire like Tate Sheridan even dream about wanting to kiss her?

She most certainly had been imagining that sudden heat in his eyes.

Better to focus on decorating the house and pretend he was no different than Levi.

No, he was definitely different. She worked for him, which put him in an entirely separate category.

The stupid dreams that had made her toss and turn all night and had awakened her with a strange sort of restlessness filled her head again but she firmly pushed them away.

She had absolutely no business having sexy dreams about Tate, even if he did have those killer blue eyes, broad shoulders and a smile that seemed to make everything inside her go soft and gooey.

She had to put all this crazy nonsense away. Okay, she might have once had a crush on the man but she had been eleven years old! That was also the era when she'd had crushes on various members of her favorite boy band and her biggest dilemma had been choosing which one she liked better.

Tate Sheridan had been kind to her at an impressionable time in her life. He had been sweet and friendly to an awkward girl who would grow up into an awkward woman.

Nearly twenty years had passed. She would be thirty in May and was a completely different person from that girl who used to write his name in her notebook and wait anxiously for the days when his family would come back to the ranch.

She was hardly recognizable from that girl. So was he, a man she barely knew.

As they worked to unwrap the ornaments, she admitted to herself that while that crush had begun when she was only a girl, she had nurtured it over the years.

Tate Sheridan—or the idea of him, anyway—had become her ideal man. She compared every other guy she dated to him and somehow they always came up lacking, which she knew was completely ridiculous. She didn't even know what kind of a person he had grown into, other than what she had seen in that PBS documentary.

She sometimes wondered if she took the job at Lancaster San Francisco because of its proximity to the gleaming office building that housed both the Sheridan International company offices and the Sheridan Trust headquarters. Maybe she secretly hoped that she might accidentally bump into Tate in front of the building on her way to work. She thought she had seen him once going into the building, surrounded by a group of people, but she had been too far away to be sure.

She was a grown woman, for heaven's sake. It was time she put all that behind her so she could focus on the job ahead of her.

"This shouldn't be that tough," Tate said after unpacking the last box. "Looks almost the same as my grandfather's room, only with different colors."

Where the Christmas tree they had set up in Wallace's office had been decorated with mostly gold and red ornaments, this one had a silver and blue tone, which matched the cool, elegant mood of the room.

A few of the guest bedroom suites in the house were set up similar to Annie's own apartment, with two en suite bedrooms and a bathroom off a main sitting room. In her case, she had a small kitchenette as well as a dining set, currently covered with her sewing machine.

One of the great perks of taking this job had been the private apartment, with a door to the outside she could use instead of coming through the house.

The bedroom alone in her apartment here at Angel's View was larger than her entire studio apartment in the city, for which she had paid an arm and a leg.

"I love the colors in this room," she said as she started winding the garland around the tree.

"This was always the room my parents stayed in."

He said the words casually, without inflection, as he reached for the garland from her to wind it around the tree.

She gave him a close look to gauge his reaction but couldn't read anything on his features.

"We loved when your family would come to the ranch," she said quietly. "You just seemed to belong here."

"We always loved it, too. When we weren't here, we were talking about it. This felt like a place where we could simply be a family, you know? Without my dad's work or my mom's social obligations or school or whatever."

They had all lost so much the summer his father died. Not only the man they loved and respected but the solace and peace they found together here at the ranch had been taken from them, as well.

She could only hope maybe the family could regain a little of that while they were here for the holidays.

"I know it's none of my business," she said after a few more moments of decorating. "But can you tell me if your grandmother is planning to sell the ranch?"

He paused in the act of hanging a silver snowflake, then gave her an apologetic look. "Yes. She's already had a few offers. I suspect that's one of the reasons she wanted to come here this year, to spend one more Christmas at the ranch. I imagine by next year, someone else will be figuring out where to put all the blasted Christmas trees."

She had been expecting his answer but hearing him confirm her suspicions so bluntly still hurt. "I see."

"I'm sorry. I know you have a deep connection to the ranch."

"Yes." She forced a smile. "You could say this land is part of the McCade DNA."

He looked startled. "I was thinking about when you lived here during your childhood while your father was the ranch manager. I had completely forgotten your family originally sold the land to Wallace."

"It was a long time ago. Long before either of us were born."

"I'm sorry."

"Please. Don't be," she said. "It's your family's ranch. Any claim we might have once had to the land died when my grandfather sold it to Wallace. You have the right to do what you want with it."

Annie tried her best to keep her voice level, swallowing away the ridiculous quaver she could feel building in her voice.

She was a grown woman, she reminded herself again. She certainly knew that people didn't automatically get what they wanted out of life, simply because they willed it so.

She had learned that lesson early. She hadn't been able to seal up the cracks in her parents' marriage nor convince them she belonged here on the ranch with her father.

"Whatever we do with the ranch will be a tough decision. Nothing is set in stone and I'm sure we'll have more discussion about it moving forward," he said.

"Right." She had known this was the likely outcome the moment she had learned of Wallace's death.

"It really makes no sense to keep it in the family when none of us intends to use it."

"I understand. You don't have to justify anything to me, Tate."

His mouth pursed and he looked as if he wanted to say more but his mobile phone rang, breaking the suddenly awkward silence of the room.

He glanced at the caller ID, then gave her an apologetic look. "I'm sorry. This is the chief operations officer of one of our companies and we've been playing phone tag for two days. I need to take it."

She waved him off. "Do what you have to do. Now that I know what is involved, it shouldn't take me long to finish the next few bedrooms on my own."

His phone rang again and he gave it an impatient look.

"This shouldn't take that long. Maybe a half hour. I'll catch up with you."

"Sure."

He could take as long as he needed. She might be able to work faster if she didn't have to spend so much effort and energy trying to pretend she wasn't so attracted to him.

"I'm still planning on cutting the main Christmas tree this afternoon, if you think the twins would enjoy going with us."

"Sounds good."

He picked up the phone and she heard the comfortable tone he had taken with her change to brisk and businesslike.

She continued decorating the tree but Tate seemed to have taken any hint of festive joy with him.

Annie tried not to be too glum. She hated to think about the ranch being sold. Even in the years she had not lived here, the Angel's View had been a sanctuary in her mind, the happy place where she always escaped.

After her father died, when she had been mired in both grief and guilt for the cracks that had grown in their relationship over time, she had remembered all the happy times they had spent together here. Riding horses along the fence line, sledding down the hill above the ranch, fishing Holly Creek for rainbow trout. Those memories had brought her deep comfort.

She still had those memories. Nothing would change that, no matter who eventually ended up with the ranch.

It was silly to be upset about something she had always

known was inevitable, especially when she had only been back at the ranch for a year, after being gone nearly twenty.

Still, she couldn't help thinking the Sheridans belonged here, maybe even more than her family. Wallace had given his heart and his soul to this ranch. His son had died here.

Perhaps this holiday might convince Tate and his family of those roots. If they had a wonderful experience during their visit, perhaps they might reconsider their decision to sell the Angel's View.

She had no idea how she could make that happen, but as she continued decorating the room, she was determined to try.

6

WHY, AGAIN, HAD HE EVER THOUGHT THIS WOULD
be a good idea?

Tate stood outside in the crisp Wyoming air, listening in bemusement as Annelise's niece and nephew chattered non-stop about their day.

Who knew two six-year-old kids could have so much to say?

"And then we had recess and I played on the hill with my friend Maria and my other friend named Sam," the girl, Alice, was telling her aunt, who appeared to be absorbing it all patiently, even as Tate tried to wade through the lisp and the way the little girl used *w*'s for *r*'s.

"And then, guess what? My friend named Sam wanted to play Outlaws and he said Henry and me should be the out-laws since our dad is already in jail."

Annelise looked askance at this no-nonsense statement.

"That doesn't seem very fair," she said. Though her tone was mild he could see fire in her eyes and suspected she might be making a phone call later to this Sam person's parents or guardians.

"I know. That's what I said. I said we don't have to be outlaws if we don't want to be and I said if I wanted to be on the posse I would. But Henry wanted to be an outlaw."

"Why was that?" Annelise asked her nephew.

The boy shrugged. "Because Cody and Javier said they wanted to be outlaws and I wanted to do what they did."

Annelise didn't appear particularly thrilled about that, either, but made no comment. The children continued on about their day as the big dual-tire diesel easily climbed the road, packed with only a few inches of snow.

"Is the truck doing okay?" she asked.

"Seems to be."

"I think we just made it under the wire today. Any more snow than this and we probably wouldn't be able to drive up here this time of year, unless we took the snowmobiles or the tractor."

The truck was warm and comfortable and smelled like Annelise. Tate tried not to pay attention to his sudden craving for peach cobbler, focusing instead on the children as they chattered about what they were going to do during their upcoming school vacation.

Tate didn't feel as if he were particularly good with children, though he always enjoyed being around them when he was doing work for the Sheridan Trust. Their enthusiasm and creativity always astonished him.

His sister Catherine, now fourteen, was the youngest person he interacted with on a regular basis—*regular basis* being a slight exaggeration, considering he traveled so much and hadn't lived with his mother since he was eighteen.

When they were still only about halfway to the forested area where his family usually cut trees, Henry started wriggling in the back seat of the crew cab pickup.

"Are we almost there?" he asked, an odd look on his face. "I gotta pee."

Annie gave an exasperated wince. "You were supposed to go before we put on your snow pants and boots, kiddo."

"I didn't have to go then. Now I do. Really bad."

"Want me to pull over?" Tate asked, keeping a wary eye on the boy in the rearview mirror, who was now all but dancing in his seat.

"You can just stop here in the middle of the road. This is all private Angel's View property. No one else should be up here. Come on, Henry. We're going to have to unzip everything."

Henry unbuckled his own car seat and opened the door to hop down and Annelise turned to Alice, whose car seat was directly behind the passenger seat. "What about you, Al? Do you have to go while we're stopped?"

The little girl shook her blond curls. "No, because I did what you said and went to the bathroom before we left."

"Are you sure? If you don't go now, you won't have another chance until we're back at the house."

"I'm sure."

Her aunt didn't look as if she completely believed her but she walked around the front of the truck, anyway, to help the boy. They walked behind a large rock that was just off the road.

"Hey, Mr. Tate. Do you like to sing?" Alice asked him. "I do."

"Um. Sure," he answered. What else was he supposed to say? It wasn't exactly a lie, though he usually only occasionally sang in the shower and along with the car stereo if a familiar song came on.

"I love to sing," she informed him. "My mom used to say I have a voice like an angel."

Poor little thing. The reminder that she and her twin had lost their mother tragically was sobering. "Did she? That's nice."

"Yes. Want to hear?"

He looked out the window a little helplessly, where he could just see Annelise trying to help a now-dancing Henry out of his parka and bib snow pants.

"Um, sure," he said. "Why not?"

She broke into singing "Away in a Manger" in a sweet, pure voice that unexpectedly made a lump rise in his throat.

"Wow," he said when she finished. "That was very good."

"Want to sing with me? We should sing 'Rudolph the Red-Nosed Reindeer,'" she went on, without giving him a chance to answer. "Do you know that one?"

Didn't everyone? "I know it but it's been a while since I sang it. I'm not sure I remember all the words."

"I'll start."

She began singing and then paused, obviously waiting for him to join her. Glad no one he knew could see him, he sang along with her as best he could.

After the last phrase about Rudolph going down in history, she made an impatient sound. "You didn't sing all the words," she accused him.

He felt an absurd twinge of guilt. "I forgot some of them. I told you I haven't sung it in a while. Plus I wanted to hear you. Your mother was right. You do sing like an angel."

She beamed at him, making him feel about ten feet tall and strong enough to tear down their Christmas tree with his bare hands.

"What should we sing next?" Alice asked.

His carol repertoire was regrettably limited. He looked out the window, where Annelise was helping Henry zip back up.

"I can sing you a song I learned in South America about a donkey," he said on impulse. "It's in Spanish."

"Okay!"

He wasn't sure why he said it, other than some of the children at a remote village in Colombia had insisted on trying to teach him the words to one of their favorite holiday songs, "Mi Burrito Sabanero."

For some reason, the words to this one came more easily than "Rudolph" and he was just starting the "tuqui tuqui tuqui tuqui" part when her brother and Annelise climbed back into the pickup.

He stopped but Alice protested. "That didn't sound like the end. Sing the rest."

Yeah. He should never have started this. Feeling his face heat, Tate sang the final part of the song, at least as much as he remembered, aware the whole time of Annelise trying to hide her astonishment.

"Wow. Sounds like we missed a concert, Henry," she said when he finished.

"Mr. Tate was teaching me a song about a donkey."

He cleared his throat. "A few years back I spent Christmas working on a new schoolhouse for a village in Colombia and the kids all insisted on teaching me the song about the burrito going to Bethlehem. *Belen*."

"A burrito going to Bethlehem!" Henry started laughing uproariously.

"Fun fact, the word *burrito* actually means little donkey," Tate said when the boy's laughter stopped long enough for him to get a word in edgewise. "So the Burrito in 'Mi Burrito Sabanero' is a little donkey going to Bethlehem."

"Ew. Does that mean when I eat a burrito, I'm eating a donkey?" Henry asked.

"No," Tate said quickly. "Not at all. They're just called that."

"Can you teach me the song?" Alice asked eagerly.

He again didn't quite know what to say. "I could teach you a verse or two, if you want."

"But I can't speak Spanish," Henry said with a glum note to his voice. "My friend Xavier can, though."

"This song isn't too hard. I can teach you one verse and the chorus, if you want. That way if you hear it on the radio, you can sing along."

He should have found an excuse to turn their attention to something else. Tate wasn't sure why he didn't, other than singing the song with them brought back good memories of the trip and the sweet kids he had been trying to help.

"I like that song," Alice declared, giving it her stamp of approval. "Maybe you can teach us the rest of it later."

"We can work on it. I might have to double-check that I'm singing the right words. It's been a few years since I was in Colombia."

And he likely would not go again any time soon. Tate felt a pang. He truly did love his work for the Sheridan Trust. He had a feeling nothing else he did in life would feel as satisfying or useful.

He pulled the truck over to the thickly wooded area where he remembered finding a tree with his father and grandfather when he was a kid. "We can work on it later. Right now we have to find a Christmas tree before it gets too dark."

"Yay! I'm gonna find the best one," Henry said.

"No, I am," his sister said.

"You both need to stick with us and don't wander off," Annelise insisted. "If you can't see one of us, stop where you are and stay put. We'll find you. Got it?"

"Got it," they said in unison.

They all climbed out of the truck in the afternoon sunlight, scaring up a couple of magpies who cackled at them before soaring away.

"This is one of my most favorite places on the ranch." Annelise lifted her face to the pale sunshine. "It smells like I think heaven probably does."

The heady mix of pine and sage did smell delicious.

The twins followed her lead, lifting their faces and sniffing in an exaggerated way that made him smile.

Annelise caught his gaze and smiled in return, something that made him feel far warmer than he should in the winter sun.

He had been a little worried that she would be angry with him after he told her he and his family planned to sell the Angel's View Ranch within the year. She hadn't exactly concealed her dismay and disappointment at the news.

How could he blame her for being upset? She loved this place and had deep family roots growing down into the soil of the ranch.

He didn't see any other option, as he had told her. He certainly couldn't imagine anyone else in the family stepping up to say they should keep it. The painful memories were too strong for all those left.

As far as he knew, Brie hadn't been back since they were kids. His grandmother didn't want to hold on to it, either.

Wallace had stipulated in his will that the ranchland should have a conservation easement that would prevent any future commercial development. The ranch and the surrounding acreage had to be sold intact to a person or organization that would protect it for generations.

Any profit from the sale, Wallace stipulated, should go directly to the Sheridan Trust, which would allow them to provide more schoolhouses and health clinics and clean drinking water to communities that needed it.

Tate knew selling the ranch was the right decision; he just didn't like having to disappoint Annelise McCade.

"What about that one?" Alice asked, pointing to a giant spruce that was probably sixteen feet too tall for the space they had available.

"We should probably look for one a bit smaller," Annelise suggested gently.

There were only a few inches of snow on the ground, which made it relatively easy to walk through the grove of trees.

While the hillside was covered in pines and spruces, finding the perfect tree turned out to be more challenging than he would have expected.

Other than the first giant one Alice had chosen, the twins seemed to have problems with every tree Tate or Annelise picked out. One was too sparse, one had a branch missing on one side, one was too fat.

Finally, on the edge of a clearing not far from the road, Henry found a tree the twins deemed exactly right.

Tate and Annelise stood shoulder to shoulder, studying their choice.

"It looks good to me," she finally said.

"Same here," he said, gauging the height at about eleven feet. "Stay here and don't move from this spot so nobody else cuts it down and I'll go grab the chain saw."

"There is nobody else," Alice said with a giggle.

"Wait. You have to cut it down?" Henry looked upset.

He gave the boy a wary look. "Yes. Sorry. That's the way it works."

His sister frowned suddenly. "Won't that kill the tree?"

Tate glanced at Annelise for help, not sure how to answer them.

"If you cut it low to the ground, another tree can grow in the same place," Annie told them. "My dad and my dad's dad—your grandpop and great-grandpop—planted a bunch of trees here just for Christmas trees. And every year, more are planted so some are always growing in this forest."

"We should plant another tree to replace this one," Henry said.

"We can plant a dozen, if you want," Annie assured her nephew. "If I'm still working here, you guys can come back with me in the springtime and plant several trees up here to take the place of this one."

That seemed to soothe their ecological worries. He couldn't disagree with them. Cutting Christmas trees seemed wasteful, though he knew they could be recycled into mulch and also wildlife habitat.

He moved the truck a little closer so they wouldn't have to carry the tree as far, then carried the chain saw to the waiting trio.

"I'm sorry, tree." Alice patted the trunk.

"Okay, you two. We need to step back." Their aunt drew them far enough to be out of danger but still within view as he cut down the tree quickly.

It was heavy but he managed to pick it up and smack it down a few times on the nearest hard surface, a large flat rock about four feet wide.

"Why do you have to shake it like that?" Henry asked, his eyes wide with curiosity.

"Two reasons," Tate told him. "One, we need to make sure any creepy-crawlies or forest creatures who have made the tree their home know it's time to move on. Two, this way all the loose needles stay here in the forest instead of coming out in the living room."

He had a flashback of being the twins' age or maybe a little older and coming into this forest with his father and grandfather in search of a tree for the great room when a small western screech owl had flown out suddenly, startling all of them.

Brie had burst into tears, distraught about the owl losing its home, he remembered now. She had always had a soft spot for creatures.

He had completely forgotten until this moment. Something about the flash of sun on the snow, the scent of pine sap and the crisp Wyoming air brought it back in vivid detail.

He could remember his father taking Brie in his arms, telling her what a good and gentle heart she had and assuring her the owl would find another home.

Cole Sheridan had always been so wise. Tate had spent his entire adult life trying to measure up.

He smiled now at the twins, who were watching his every move just like he used to watch his father. "Okay. That should do it. I think we've managed to get rid of all the loose needles and hopefully any bugs still around this time of year are on their way somewhere else now. Who wants to help me load it onto the sleigh we brought to carry it to the truck?"

"Me!" they both exclaimed.

He was grateful Levi Moran had suggested they take the long toboggan Wallace always kept for the job. He would have completely forgotten that and would have had to carry the heavy tree to the truck with only Annelise's help since the twins were more hindrance than help, as he suspected they would be.

They did try, each taking a branch as he and Annelise did most of the heavy lifting onto the sleigh.

"I want to pull the sleigh!" Henry insisted.

"No. I do," Alice said. "I'm stronger."

"How about you both help me? I'm not sure I'm strong enough to pull it without both of you."

He thought he heard Annelise snort, but she covered it with a cough. When he met her gaze, she smiled, looking so bright and lovely he wanted to go cut a dozen more trees with her.

One was more than enough, he told himself as he and the twins pulled the sleigh the twenty yards to the pickup truck.

He managed to lift it himself and slide it into the bed, though he was sweating by the time the tree was secured.

"I'm beginning to think it would have been easier to get an artificial tree," he muttered at one point.

"About a hundred times easier," she said. "And we haven't even started stringing lights on it yet. That's the fun part."

He groaned at her reminder.

"But artificial trees don't smell nearly as delicious. Life is all about trade-offs."

He couldn't disagree. "Do we need pine boughs for other areas in the house? You talked about that this morning. We might as well cut down a few while we're up here."

"Oh. Yes. Not too many, just enough for some of the fireplace mantels in the bedrooms and down the staircase."

They wandered through cutting a branch here and there from trees that seemed to have an overabundance, then Tate carried them to the truck and loaded them in on either side of the tree.

"I hope Irene appreciates all this work," he grumbled.

"I'm sure she will."

He wasn't so sure.

Right now, that didn't matter. Even if she didn't, Tate wasn't sure he would have traded this afternoon with Annelise and the twins for anything.

7

ANNIE LISTENED TO THE CHILDREN SINGING "The Little Drummer Boy" as Tate drove with care down the snowy road toward the ranch house.

How had they learned the song? She didn't think it was one of the numbers they would be performing for their first-grade program the next week and she seriously doubted they had picked up the words from her brother.

Wes wasn't exactly the type to listen to Christmas carols anytime, especially during the past year since his wife and baby died.

Cassie used to have a lovely voice and would sing to her children all the time. Maybe they were remembering their mother singing to them.

Her throat ached at the thought. Her sister-in-law had been a wonderful mother and had doted on their twins. She and

Wes had both been over the moon with excitement about bringing another child into their family.

Life could be so unfair. Cassie had her whole life ahead of her. Instead, a twist of fate, a blood clot, came out of nowhere and snatched her away from these children who needed a mother.

Every time Annie wanted to curse and yell at Wes for the choices that had led him to this place, in jail for the holidays, she had to remind herself of everything he had endured. The man was stuck in purgatory, grieving the wife he adored and the baby they had eagerly anticipated.

She wished she could help him somehow, even as she knew this was a road he had to travel his own way.

He would get it together. She was sure of it. She had every expectation he would be able to work through his sorrow and once more be the father his children needed.

Meantime, she was doing her best to help them all.

"That was very good," Tate said.

"What else can you sing?"

"How about 'Jingle Bells'?" Henry said, their perennial favorite. He and Alice launched into a rousing rendition that took them almost all the way back to the ranch house.

For a man who had been so reluctant to have a couple of children underfoot during the holidays while his family was here, Tate was being wonderful with the children. Clearly, they both liked him, which she found surprising. They weren't usually so quick to take to someone new. They liked Levi well enough but they had known him for months, since Annie came to work at the ranch.

When Tate pulled up in front of the house, Levi came out of the barn with Bill close behind.

"Good to see you. I was afraid you might get stuck up there in the snow and not be able to make it back down."

"The truck did just fine," Tate said. "The chains were a big help, but I kept it in four-wheel low the whole way down."

"Smart." The ranch manager gestured to the tree. "Looks like a big tree. Kind of bushy, though."

"We cut some boughs for wreaths and garlands," Annie explained. "That's probably what you're seeing. Kids, why don't you help us carry the branches to the house? You can leave them next to the porch."

With all of them working together, it only took a moment to carry the pine branches up to the house, then return to the truck.

"Can we help you carry this guy inside?" Levi asked.

"That would be great," Tate said. "I don't think this old toboggan would go very well on the hardwood floor."

Henry and Alice both laughed as if that was the funniest thing they had ever heard.

"You can't sled inside. You would get in so much trouble," Henry told him between giggles.

"Good to know," Tate said, giving him a serious look.

"We wouldn't want you to get in trouble," Levi said, hiding his own smile. "We can carry it in, no problem. Henry, Al, you want to help us?"

The twins jumped eagerly at the task, always willing to help. They might have an overabundance of energy and a tendency to push all her boundaries, probably because of an absence of strong parenting right now, but Annie had to remind herself they were truly sweet at heart.

Just as their father would figure out his way without Cassie, the twins would, too. She had to believe that.

"The tree stand is already set up inside," she told Levi. "I made sure it would be ready to go when we returned."

"Thanks. That helps."

Levi, Tate and Bill pulled the tree out of the pickup bed and thumped the trunk a few more times on the driveway. She was relieved when only a tiny number of pine needles fell out.

Levi inhaled deeply. "Looks like a good one and it smells great."

"Nothing like a real Christmas tree to get in the old holiday spirit," Bill said. "Reminds me of Christmas mornings when I was a kid at our place in South Dakota."

Annie raised an eyebrow. The old cowpoke hardly spoke. She never would have expected him to wax rhapsodic about a Christmas tree.

That was why the holidays were magic, she supposed, that chance to recapture moments of joy and peace again, even briefly.

Levi corralled the children into holding a branch each so they felt like they were genuinely helping while he, Tate and Bill actually carried the weight of the tree into the house. Annie followed behind, feeling superfluous.

The tree turned out to be perfect for the space, not so huge as to overwhelm it but big enough to command attention, even from the second-floor balcony. The three men had it in place easily.

"It's beautiful," Alice declared. "The most beautiful tree I ever saw."

Annie smiled. "But it doesn't even have any lights or ornaments on it."

"I don't care," Alice said fervently. "I like it just the way it is. I wish we could leave it this way and then take it back to the forest."

Annie hugged her close. "It is a beautiful tree. You're right, I'm not sure we can make it any better."

"It's dead now," Henry said, a little sadly. "We killed it when we cut it down."

Alice's delight in the tree seemed to seep away and she

looked heartbroken as she reached out and touched one of the boughs.

Oh, it was hard trying to navigate these difficult waters with them.

Annie chose her words carefully. "We can't take it back to the forest. But when Christmas is over, we can either use it for firewood or we can find another good way to recycle it."

"I promise, we'll find a good use for it," Tate told them.

"And meanwhile, we can enjoy it every day during the holiday season," Annie said. "We can take lots of pictures of it and, especially, we can keep it alive in our memories. Remember what Bill said? This tree reminded him of the Christmas trees he had when he was a little boy."

"And that was a *loooong* time ago," the old cowhand said with a raspy laugh.

Alice sighed a little sadly but seemed resigned to the tree's fate. "We can help you decorate it, though, right?" she asked.

Tate answered before Annie had a chance. "Of course you can. We wouldn't think of doing it without you. That might be a little while, though. It might not even be tonight. We should let it dry out a little and then I still have to string the lights, which will take time."

The twins both looked as if they wanted to protest but Annie redirected their attention. "We wouldn't be able to do it tonight, anyway. You have chores to do and reading practice."

"Plus, we have to go visit Luna and see if she's had her puppies yet," Henry suddenly remembered.

"I can save you a trip to the barn. She hasn't," Levi assured them both. "As of about an hour ago, she was still as big as ever. I think we're still looking at a few more days. Maybe a week."

"Promise you'll tell us as soon as she has them?" Alice demanded.

The ranch foreman grinned at the little girl, looking so rugged and handsome Annie again wished she could feel something for him other than brotherly affection.

"Cross my heart, darlin'. You will be the first to know."

She supposed she shouldn't be surprised Tate had been so good with the children all afternoon. The twins were easy to love. They had managed to win over everyone at the ranch, even the taciturn Bill.

"Go take off your winter stuff and grab a snack from my refrigerator. I'll join you in a few minutes."

The twins traipsed off, probably to turn on the lights of her own small Christmas tree inside her apartment.

"We've got to get back to the barn," Levi said. "We've got a delivery from the feed supply store coming shortly."

"Thanks for your help," Tate said.

"We did the easy part. Now you get to decorate it."

He and Bill were still chuckling as they walked out of the house again, leaving her alone with Tate.

"The soup I made this afternoon is in the refrigerator and there's a salad in there, too. Is there anything else you need from me tonight?"

Tate blinked a little, looking a bit taken aback at the reminder that she worked for him.

Annie hadn't forgotten. She couldn't let herself forget he was her boss and she was simply the hired help, trying to make it through until Christmas.

"No. I don't think so. Thank you for your help today. The tree really is beautiful."

"You picked a good one."

"*We* picked a good one." His smile held warmth and approval and left her feeling slightly giddy.

She wanted to stand right here and bask in it, let it soak through all the cold and empty places.

She pushed away the yearning, annoyed with herself.

She couldn't afford to let her childhood crush grow into anything more, no matter how good he was with the twins.

As soon as her brother straightened out his life again, she would be leaving the Angel's View and returning to a world where she could only hope to catch a glimpse of him on her lunch hour.

"Good night. You know where to find me if you need me."

She turned around briskly and walked back down the hall, determined to once more put up all the necessary defenses to protect her heart.

Tate watched her go, not sure quite what he had said to put that steel in her spine.

Annelise McCade was a fascinating, intriguing conundrum. He couldn't believe he hadn't given her more thought all these years. Okay, he hadn't given her *any* thought. Now that they were together again, it felt as if all the years between them had melted away, reminding him of just how much he had always enjoyed her company.

That afternoon had been the most enjoyable time he'd had in a long time. Henry and Alice were characters, funny and inquisitive and empathetic, even toward the plight of a Christmas tree.

Poor things, to have lost their mother. He wished he could figure out some way to help them.

And their aunt.

He had loved her company, as well.

His mind kept going back to the time he had spent decorating the tree in Wallace's office, how he had ached with the urge to kiss her.

He had to put that out of his head right now. Annelise was a fascinating woman, but the truth was, he had enough on his plate. His family would be here in three days, bringing his grandfather's ashes along with all their expectations of Tate.

He was just heading into his room, where he had created a makeshift office, when his phone rang.

He glanced down and was surprised to find his sister's number appearing.

Brie rarely called him. They did communicate, especially more the past year, but it was usually via email or a quick text exchange. Sometimes he suspected those methods were easier for her, not having to speak to him one-on-one.

Their relationship had fractured over the past decade. He wasn't sure how to fix it.

He answered swiftly, concerned something might be wrong. "Hey, Brie."

There was a slight pause on the other end, almost as if she had forgotten she had dialed his number or hadn't really expected him to pick up.

"Tate. Hi. How are things at the ranch?"

He frowned, quite certain she wouldn't have called him just to chat about the Angel's View. "Good. Not much snow this year, but I understand a big storm is forecast for next week, after you're here."

"Great. Something else to look forward to."

While her tone was bland, he didn't miss the edge of tension underlying it.

Why did everything have to be so difficult with his sister? He loved Brianna deeply but had no idea how to reach the contained, slightly defensive woman she had grown into.

"It's beautiful, though," he went on. "I had forgotten how crisp and clean the air feels here. I was up in the forest today above the ranch cutting down a Christmas tree. I thought of you actually. Do you remember that time an owl flew out of a tree after we chopped it down and you cried and cried?"

She was silent for a moment and then he heard a slightly rusty chuckle. "Wow, that was a long time ago. I'd forgotten about that poor owl. I hope he found another house."

"I'm sure he did. You'll be glad to know, we double-checked that there were no creatures living in this one before we brought it down to the house."

"I'm having a hard time picturing you chopping down a Christmas tree."

"I used a chain saw and everything."

"I'll look forward to seeing it," she said, sounding a little less prickly, before changing gears. "I won't keep you from the tree chopping but I wanted to ask if you might know anything about what's going on with Mom."

"What do you mean?" he asked with a frown. "Nothing's going on with Mom, as far as I know. What makes you think otherwise?"

"I just hung up with her and it was a very strange conversation. I was only calling to double-check if there's room on the plane for me to take more than one bag this week and she was really weird about the whole thing."

"Weird, how?"

"She sounded like she had been crying and she couldn't hang up fast enough. Do you think something's going on with her and Stan?"

His mother and Stan had been married for sixteen years, since Brie was nearly fourteen.

Their stepfather was a good man with a caring heart who had taken on a wife and two troubled teenagers. Pamela had grieved for Tate's father for a long time. He was happy she had found someone else.

The two of them had always seemed to have a loving, healthy relationship, as far as Tate was concerned. He wasn't sure he had ever even heard them fight. He couldn't wrap his head around the idea of them having marital troubles bad enough to make his mother cry.

"I'm sure it's nothing. Maybe she was just having a bad day. Or maybe she read something upsetting. Or maybe she's not looking forward to coming back here, after all this time."

He couldn't blame her for that and neither could Brie. Neither of them had wanted to come to the Angel's View for the holidays. They wouldn't be here if Irene hadn't insisted.

"Maybe." Brie didn't sound convinced.

"If they are, it's really none of our business, right?"

"Other than she's our mom and I don't want anybody to hurt her."

In the interest of diplomacy, he didn't point out that over the past decade Brie had been the one to hurt their mother more than anyone else had. At one point, she had almost completely cut herself off from the Sheridans, living off dividends from the one trust fund she had been able to access and working odd jobs to support her and whatever freeloading boyfriend she had found this time.

Tate caught the direction of his thoughts, annoyed with himself. His lingering resentment always made him feel small and selfish.

Brie had rejoined the family a year ago and was working diligently on her recovery from the drugs and alcohol she had turned to when she was younger.

She was doing her best to put the pieces of her life back together, to move forward and become the person she wanted to be. Tate was happy about her progress and should be able to celebrate with her, not feel these random moments of residual anger at the pain she had caused those who loved her.

"I'm sure everything is fine," he repeated. "One phone call doesn't necessarily mean anything. She could have been upset about something completely random. But if you're worried about it, we can both keep a careful eye on her while they're here at the ranch."

She seemed to sigh over the phone. "You're probably right. I think I spent too long not caring about how I was breaking her heart. Now that I do care, I seem to be hypervigilant about her moods these days."

He suspected Brie had been through more than he either he or his mother knew. He needed to show more empathy and compassion for the effort she was making to turn things around.

"Don't worry. When you all get here, I'm sure we'll see that everything between Mom and Stan is just fine."

"I hope so."

Because he thought it might lift her mood a little, he added, "You're never going to guess who's working here at Angel's View."

"I have no idea."

"Remember Annelise McCade? Her father, Scott, was the ranch manager here for many years."

"Annie!" Her voice lit up with delight and she sounded like she was smiling. "Of course I remember Annie. She was my dearest friend. That's so funny. I was just thinking about her the other day and wondering where she was! I can't believe she's been at the ranch the whole time!"

"Not the whole time. Only a year. Wallace hired her to be the caretaker of the ranch. She lives in that small mother-in-law apartment off the kitchen."

"Wow. It's been years."

"I thought you might be happy to have an old friend here when you come out."

"That will be nice actually."

They spoke a few more moments about their family members before Brie cut off the conversation. "I've got to run. I ordered takeout and the delivery service just texted me that they're here."

"All right. I'll see you in a few days."

"Ready or not," she said, before ending the connection.

After she hung up, Tate gazed out the window at the dark river winding through the snow and the trees. Brie was worried about their mother, while Tate was mostly worried about *Brie*.

What was he going to do about her? Now that she was clean and sober and had worked so hard at her recovery, she had started working in public relations at Sheridan International. All reports were that she was a hard worker and good at her job but he kept getting hints that she wanted more.

He didn't know what that might be and couldn't begin to guess.

While he loved solving problems when it came to his work for the Sheridan Trust, he wasn't good at being the unofficial head of the family.

Wallace had been so good at that. He had been the one encouraging Brie to come home and make her peace with all of them, had helped her through rehab, had found a position for her at the corporate headquarters.

Wallace was gone now and Tate felt the weight of responsibility to carry on for him, even as he knew this was one more area where he would never measure up to his grandfather.

Brie ended the call with her brother and placed her phone back on the charger, then stood at the French windows watching rain plop down on the café table on the tiny balcony of her apartment.

She didn't have much of a view from here, only a tiny slice of the city through the trees, but she didn't care. She loved this old house, with its quirks and weird layout. She was paying entirely too much for a one-bedroom apartment on the third floor of a decrepit old Victorian, but she was happier these days than she had been in years.

Except for her relationship with her family. Everything else seem to be coming together but that.

Tate thought she was overreacting in her concerns about their mother. She should have known that would be his response. Her family did not exactly trust her judgment. Why should they? She had spent a decade giving them every reason to question her.

Maybe he was right. Maybe their mother was fine and Brie was imagining everything. It wasn't out of the realm of possibility that she was so nervous herself about returning to Wyoming that she was projecting her own mood on everyone else.

No. She wasn't wrong. Her mother had definitely sounded distraught on the phone. When Brie had asked if everything was okay, Pamela had said she was absolutely fine and there was nothing to worry about.

Brie wasn't buying it. There had been a false, thin-sounding note to her voice that sounded painfully familiar. She recognized it because she had often been the one with the roles reversed, trying to assure her mother she was fine when she was anything but.

Brie didn't want to go to Wyoming. That much was true. She had a sudden wild urge to stay right here and spend the holidays alone in her apartment. Maybe she could babysit her downstairs neighbor's cute little cuddly mini poodle and spend the entire holidays holding a dog, watching Christmas movies and eating far too much.

She sighed. No. Irene wanted the whole family to go to the ranch, whether any of them wanted to or not.

She closed her eyes, memories stirred up from Tate's description coming sharply into focus. She could almost smell the pine, hear the creek that twisted through the aspens above the ranch, see the wide expanse of blue sky.

Oh, how she had loved it there. Their family trips to the Angel's View had been the highlights of her childhood, a time of laughter and family togetherness and peace.

And then her father had died and everything changed.

The ranch came to represent everything they had lost—a good, honorable man who had loved his family and was trying to help the world.

Her fault.

Guilt could be such a powerful thing, like a cancer spreading across the mind, damaging everything in its path.

She had been running from it for a long time, which meant staying away from the Angel's View. The ranch had come to represent pain and sorrow, not only because of what they had lost there but because it represented a time of joy she could no longer recapture.

Brie's grandmother wanted them all to gather at the ranch to remember Wallace and maybe say a final goodbye.

A big family Christmas, whether any of the rest of them wanted it or not.

If that would help Brie work on rebuilding her fractured relationships within her family, she would figure out how to endure it.

8

"I DON'T WANT TO GO TO BED," ALICE COMPLAINED. "Why do we have to? I thought we were going to decorate the big tree tonight!"

"It's not fair. You promised!" Henry chimed in.

Annie closed her eyes and prayed for patience. The twins had been on a rampage all evening, ever since they came home from school and she had told them the tree wasn't ready to be decorated yet.

They complained about dinner, they whined about having to do their reading time with her, they didn't want to practice their addition.

Everything she did seemed to be wrong. The crowning complaint centered on the news that they would not be able to decorate the tree they had cut the day before, a treat they both apparently had been eagerly anticipating all day.

"I'm sorry," she said again. "I wish we could decorate it, too, but it's impossible tonight. I told you that. Some of the lights for the tree didn't work right and some of them were old and not safe to use. Tate decided to drive to Idaho Falls to look for some new ones and he didn't make it back in time to put the lights on the tree. He will be working on it in the morning, so the tree will all be ready for us to decorate with ornaments when you get home from school."

She had only seen Tate briefly that day, a quick conversation while she was finishing the decorations in the last of the bedrooms his family would use. He had come to tell her about the malfunctioning lights and that he planned to run errands all day and would be back after dark.

She didn't want to admit how colorless the day had felt as she worked to ready the house for his family with wreaths and garlands in the rooms and on the front doors. Or how many times she had looked down the driveway to see if he was on his way back yet.

She was completely ridiculous.

"It's not fair," Henry said again.

"Why can't we hang the ornaments right now?" Alice whined.

They were tired, disappointed and overexcited, she told herself.

She knew that was part of it, but Annie also sensed that the closer they drew to Christmas, the more discontented the children seemed with their situation.

It was only natural, she supposed. They were staying with their aunt at Christmastime, sharing a bedroom in a small casita of a house that wasn't even theirs. Their mother was gone and their father was, as well. Wes hadn't been much of a father for a year and was now absent literally as well as figuratively.

Annie couldn't fix those things for them, much to her deep regret. No matter how she tried to give them a good Christmas, she couldn't change that they didn't have their mother or that their father was in jail.

"You have to put the lights on a tree first, honey. That's the way it works."

"The way it works is stupid," Henry said.

"I'm sorry."

"You're stupid, too," Alice said, and then promptly burst into tears.

By the time she calmed them both down enough to sleep, she was emotionally drained.

"Good night, darlings," she said after they were tucked in bed.

"We can decorate the tree tomorrow, though, right? Pinky promise?"

"I swear on Santa's beard. Tate's family is coming the next day and we will definitely have to be done by then."

"Okay," Henry said.

"I'm sorry I said you were stupid," Alice said, her voice a little sleepy. "You're not stupid. You're the best auntie in the whole wide world."

The girl threw her arms around Annie's neck and held tight. Annie hugged her back, her throat aching. Above all, she was so grateful that she had been able to step in and help them keep some semblance of normalcy in their life. The situation wasn't perfect but it could have been so much worse.

"Good night. I love you guys."

She closed the door behind them and rotated her shoulders, feeling like she'd just wrestled one of the ranch's prize steers.

This parenting thing was hard.

She took a minute to do some yoga stretches in her bedroom to work out some of the kinks from decorating all day and corralling cranky twins all afternoon and evening.

Her phone rang when she was in Rabbit Pose, with her head lowered to the floor and her arms outstretched behind her.

Recognizing the ringtone, Annie sank down to her mat, rolled over to her back and answered. "Hi, Mom."

"Annie, darling. Hi. I'm past the kids' bedtime, aren't I? I lost track of the time difference. I just looked at the clock and realized how late this is on a school night. I'm sorry. I wasn't thinking."

"Yes. They've been down for about fifteen minutes. They might not be asleep yet, if you want me to go check."

She held her breath, afraid her mother would say yes. Since Henry and Alice came to stay with her, Annie truly had come to treasure the evening hours when they were finally asleep and she could have a moment to herself.

Those hours between their bedtime and hers had become sacred, when she could finally tackle her own personal to-do list.

Did all parents feel this guilt about savoring that golden time when the children slept? she wondered. Maybe that was only aunts.

To her great relief, her mother only sighed. "No. It's fine. I wouldn't want to wake them. I was just checking on them. How are they holding up?"

"Their mother is dead and their father's in jail at Christmas. How are they supposed to be holding up?"

Apparently the yoga hadn't quite done enough to take the edge off her mood. She heard her sharp tone and immediately regretted it.

"I'm sorry. It's been a rough evening. They had a tantrum over a Christmas tree."

"Oh, I remember those days." Jeanette chuckled a little. "Didn't matter if it was you and Wes or your half brothers. Christmas always makes kids act a little manic. Happy one minute, crying the next. It's like going to Disneyland. They can't wait to get there and then they throw a tantrum the minute they walk down Main Street USA. Sometimes I think it's just too much stimulation for little brains to handle all at once."

"You can call back tomorrow. Or they can call you. I can have them reach out right after school, if you want."

"That would be good. I really was only checking to see if my presents arrived. I bought them online and had them shipped. They should be wrapped."

"They're not here yet. I'll keep watching."

"I always forget it takes longer to get things to Holly Creek."

"I'm sure they'll arrive in time. I wouldn't worry."

"You know me. I'm a mom and a grandma. Worry is what I do best." Jeanette paused. "Are you sure you and the kids don't want to come here for Christmas? You know Jeff and the boys would love to see them."

"No. I don't think so."

"I can send money, if that's what you're worrying about. Or you could always drive."

Annie wasn't about to spend all that money on plane tickets when she was trying so hard to save so she could help Wes. And she certainly wasn't going to brave a fourteen-hour drive on her own with six-year-old twins.

What a nightmare that would be.

"We're looking forward to spending the holidays here," she said gently. "It will be nice. I've got some special things planned for them and Wes had already bought a few things, too. They have enough turmoil right now. I think it's better if we stay close to home."

She didn't add that her mother could always come here for the holidays. That was out of the question, as both of them knew. Jeanette had walked away from Holly Creek after the divorce and didn't seem at all interested in looking back.

"All right. But if you change your mind, you know how to reach me."

"I will. Thanks, Mom."

They chatted about other things for a few moments, then Jeanette was the first to end the call. "I've got to run. We have a homeowners' association meeting in a half hour. Give the twins my love and I'll try to call them tomorrow after school."

"I will. Bye, Mom."

She sat up, wishing she had the energy to go back to the yoga poses but she knew she needed to get going on her sewing or she might fall asleep right there on the floor.

If someone had told Tate a week ago he would be decorating a Christmas tree with a couple of cute blond twins—and, more, that he would be *enjoying* it—Tate would have questioned their sanity.

But here he was the night before his family was to arrive, listening to holiday music on the house sound system while a fire flickered in the big rock fireplace and the scent of pine and cinnamon mingled to create a festive scene.

"Can you lift me up so I can put this ornament on the bare spot right there?" Alice asked him.

He started to suggest she point to where she wanted the ornament and he could hang it for her but she was gazing up at him with an expression filled with so much anticipation he changed his mind.

"Sure thing." He hung the ornament in his hand on a random bough. "Ready?"

In answer, she held up her arms. He scooped her up and positioned her on his shoulders, high enough that she could hang the shiny red bauble.

"Are you sure that's where you want it?" he asked.

He couldn't see her face but could almost picture her scrunching up her nose, studying her work. "I think so. What do you think?"

He tilted his head in order to grant the appropriate level of scrutiny. "Looks perfect to me. Want to hang more ornaments while you're up there?"

"Good idea," she said happily.

"No fair," Henry glowered. "I want a piggyback ride."

"This isn't a piggyback ride," Alice retorted. "We're working."

"On piggyback," her brother replied.

Tate could see a battle brewing so he swiftly stepped in to head it off. "How about Alice does four or five more ornaments, then you can have a turn hanging the same number of ornaments?"

"Good idea," Annelise said, giving him an approving look.

"Meantime, maybe you can hand us the ornaments so I don't have to bend down with this big load on my back," he suggested to the boy.

"Okay."

Over the next few minutes, they developed a system, amid many giggles from the children. Henry would choose an ornament and hand it to Tate, who would hand it up to the boy's sister. She would then instruct him which side of the tree was looking empty and he would move there, with her on his shoulders, for her to hang the ornament.

Much to his shock, it was the most fun he'd had in a long time.

Tate had never given much thought about having a family of his own. He was too busy traveling the world with the Sheridan Trust, immersed in trying to make a difference.

He loved his work, and while he dated here and there, Tate hadn't yet found anyone he cared about deeply enough to give that up.

Maybe he had sacrificed too much.

Having a woman by his side—a confidante, friend, lover—seemed enormously appealing suddenly, not to mention having a few of these little rug rats of his own.

He had always figured he had plenty of time to settle down

but now Tate wondered. He was not quite thirty-four years old and on the cusp of taking over a high-pressure position helming an international conglomerate of business interests.

He wasn't going to have time to *breathe* for the next few years, let alone get serious about dating and marriage.

For now, he would simply enjoy this moment with these cute kids and worry about the rest later.

"Is it my turn now?" Henry asked after a moment.

"I think so. Ready to get down, Alice?"

"No," she said with a pout in her voice. "But I guess that's fair."

Tate lowered her to the couch, then hefted Henry onto his shoulders. The boy weighed more than his sister but not by much.

"You get to pick the ornaments now," Henry told his sister. "If you want, you can still tell us where we should put them since I don't know."

"Okay."

Alice clearly liked to be in charge. She handed Tate each ornament, then marched around the tree looking for bare spots and ordering them exactly where to put it.

A few moments later, they were running out of ornaments.

"That should do it for the higher branches," Annelise said. "Why don't you two give poor Tate a break?"

"Oh. Do I have to get down?" Henry complained. "I don't want to. I'm tall up here."

"*Mr. Tate* is tall," Alice told him. "You're not."

"He's as tall as our dad, I bet," Henry said.

Poor things, having to spend Christmas without their father. He couldn't imagine the kind of grief that had driven Wes to such self-destruction. He must be in a bad place if he put himself in a situation that led to him being away from these cute kids over the holidays.

"Looks like we have about six more ornaments," Annie said. "That's three each for both of you to hang."

She handed them three baubles each and the children took great care hanging the final ornaments onto the tree.

When they were done, both children stepped back to admire their work.

"I love it!" Alice declared. "It's the prettiest tree ever."

"Prettiest and best," her brother claimed.

"And it smells *sooooo* good," Alice declared, drawing the pine scent deep into her lungs.

"You both did a great job. Thanks for all your help. I couldn't have done it without you all," Tate said.

"It's snowing!" Henry declared.

The twins raced to the big window and peered out. Giant snowflakes fluttered down.

"Doesn't that look pretty?" Annie said.

"It's like the North Pole," Henry said.

They all watched for a moment, listening to the Christmas music and watching the swirling flakes. It was probably the single most festive moment of his life.

"I say two expert tree decorators deserve some hot cocoa. What do you think?" Tate asked.

"Yay! Please, Auntie!" Alice asked.

Annelise bumped Tate's arm with her shoulder. "Sure. Because more sugar is what you both need right now," she said with a rueful smile.

"Sorry," he mouthed.

She shook her head. "It's fine. You guys want to stay here or come keep me company while I make it?"

"We'll keep you company," Alice said.

The four of them traipsed into the kitchen. While she heated the milk, Tate was entertained listening to the twins tell him about the program they were preparing for school.

"We've been practicing and practicing. I get to sing all by myself for one part," Alice said. "Want to hear what I'm singing?"

"Sure," he said.

"We should sing together the part that everybody sings, then you sing your part by yourself," Henry said.

"Okay."

The twins then sang a song he'd never heard, a cute, jazzy number about getting ready for Christmas. Alice's line was five words, "I won't sleep all night," but she delivered it with emotion and verve.

When they were done, he clapped with enthusiasm.

"Excellent job. You're both going to be great."

"You can come watch, if you want to," Henry said.

"You can bring your whole family," Alice said. "Everybody can go, not just kids and their moms and dads."

He looked over at Annelise, who gave him an apologetic look.

"I'm sure Tate and his family are going to be really busy," she told them. "I'm not sure they'll have time to watch a first-grade program. But we can see."

"What day is it?" Tate said. "We can certainly try, if it works with our schedule."

"It's next week, the day before Christmas Eve. That's our last day of school."

"All right. I'll make a note of it and talk to everybody else. I can't make any promises but we'll come if we can."

He again caught Annelise giving him that same warm look before she quickly turned back to the hot cocoa.

"This is almost done," she said. She poured it into mugs, then topped each one with whipped cream from a can.

"Mmm. This is the best hot cocoa I ever had," Henry told her.

She gave the boy an amused look. "You say that every time I make it for you. I'm glad you like it."

"It is pretty good." Tate would usually prefer a beer but had to admit this wasn't bad. "Thanks for making it."

"You're welcome."

"Maybe you could make it for my family when they come."

"I'll leave that for your chef," she said. "She'll be here to-morrow before they arrive, right?"

He had spent most of the past two days trying to track someone down and had finally found a personal chef who could fit them in. She was planning to come from Jackson Hole, starting when his family arrived the next day.

"Will Santa put our presents under that big tree?" Henry asked.

"No," Annelise said. "He'll put them under our own tree in my apartment, the one you helped me decorate a few weeks ago. That tree is for Tate and his family."

"Do you think your family will like our tree?" Alice asked with a big hot-cocoa mustache that made Tate smile.

"How could they not like it? It's a beautiful tree."

"It is. I wish our daddy could see it," Alice said.

"And our mommy," said Henry. "She would really like it, especially the ornaments we hung up."

"She can probably see it from heaven," Alice told him. "That's what Daddy said last year, that Mommy could see our Christmas tree from heaven."

These poor kids. How could they smile and sing about Christmas and presents after such a chaotic year?

"Okay, it's almost reading time and then bed," Annelise said after the kids finished their cocoa.

"Can we look at the tree one more time?" Henry asked.

"Okay. For a few minutes. But the ornaments look just fine the way they are. You don't need to rearrange anything every night, like you do on our tree."

The twins gave her a look that didn't promise anything, then raced into the great room together, chattering about their program.

"They're adorable." He took one last sip, finishing off his own cocoa.

"A little energetic and mischievous but I guess that beats the alternative."

"Agreed. You're doing a good job watching over them. Auntie."

She rolled her eyes. "My family calls me Annie, as you probably remember. When they were little, the twins never could say Aunt Annie, which is a mouthful, or Aunt Annelise, so they have always called me Auntie."

"I like it."

He liked more than her name. He liked her. She was warm, funny, sweet.

And so lovely he couldn't seem to look away.

He gazed at her, knowing she would be embarrassed if he told her she had a tiny spot of whipped cream on her lower lip.

Tate suddenly had a fierce, overwhelming urge to reach across the space between them, pull her into his arms and touch his tongue right to that spot. She would taste sweet, heady, of chocolate and cream and Annelise.

It would be so easy. Only a small move and she would be his.

Hunger thrummed through him, fierce and undeniable.

He met her gaze and saw something in those sea-foam depths, a little flare of her pupils that made him wonder whether she would push him away if he kissed her.

The realization that she might be as aware of him as he was of her only added more fuel to his desire. As he watched, color rose in her cheeks and she swallowed hard.

He moved slightly, leaning toward her just as he heard the twins giggling in the next room.

The high, sweet sound jolted him out of this strange spell as if he had just been hit by a snowball, like he had that first day back at the ranch.

He had to cut this out. No matter how delectable she was,

how much he enjoyed her company and that of her niece and nephew, Annelise McCade wasn't for him. He wasn't in a good place to start any relationship, especially not with a sweet, kind woman who had her hands full already.

"I should…clean this up," she said, her voice sounding a little distracted.

"I can do it," Tate said. "You go ahead and take care of the twins."

After a moment's hesitation, she nodded and hurried from the room, leaving him there with four empty mugs and a whole load of regret.

Annie still didn't feel like she had caught her breath an hour after she had left the kitchen.

Even after she had tucked both children into bed—blessedly tantrum-free tonight—paid a few bills for the ranch and finally settled down at her sewing machine in the sitting room of the caretaker's quarters, her breathing felt uneven, her pulse faster.

She forced herself to focus on the work at hand, grateful she was almost finished with the last of her Christmas online orders. It had been a mad rush for a few weeks there but she was almost done.

Almost done with that responsibility, anyway. If only that were the only thing on her to-do list.

She pushed down the panic about the gifts she had volunteered to make for the Family Connection. What had she been thinking? She had five days to sew thirty blankets, when she only could usually manage two to three on a good evening.

How would she ever make it?

She had no idea but she intended to try. She might have to pull a few all-nighters but she refused to disappoint any of the children.

It really was a case of all or nothing. If she couldn't finish all of them, there was no sense even delivering *any* of them to the Family Connection. It would be cruel to only have gifts for a few of the children and leave the others out.

She couldn't worry about that now. She would simply put her head down and do the work.

She picked up the ultrasoft material of the baby throw she was working on and returned to her machine.

Within a few moments, she was in the zone, soothed by the rhythm and the familiar motion.

Sewing was like meditation to Annie. It had been since she was a young girl making pillowcases and doll clothes, as well as helping her mother, who had loved to quilt and also took in clothes for alterations.

This had always been a big part of her childhood. Jeanette had a sewing corner in the laundry room of the ranch manager's house where Levi lived now.

During the colder months, Annie's mother would spend many long happy hours sewing and Annie would help her cut out fabric or take the scraps for herself to make crafts or doll clothes. When she was older and a little more technically proficient, she would help sew squares for her mother in whatever pattern of quilt she was making. Log Cabin, Eight-Point Star, Lady of the Lake, Broken Pinwheel. She had sewn all of them.

As an adult now, when she could choose what she sewed, she did it as much to relax and unwind as anything else. She loved being able to put on an audiobook and shut out the world.

Here, all her worries seemed to trickle away.

She didn't have to stress about her poor motherless niece and nephew, about her brother and his stupid choices, about the job she likely would be losing soon and the ranch that probably would have new owners in the new year.

Or the man she couldn't seem to get out of her head.

Somehow Tate pushed his way into her thoughts anyway, despite her best efforts.

Determined to try harder, she turned up the volume on her audiobook, a particularly gripping mystery set in Victorian times at Christmas.

She had just sewn the last stitch in the midst of a tense scene and was clipping the threads when she heard a knock on her outside door.

With a frown, she turned off the audiobook narration and rose from her chair, her back aching from sitting in one position too long.

She assumed it was probably Levi, who sometimes stopped by to chat about ranch business in the evening.

She opened the door, then gasped, completely shocked to find Tate standing there instead of the ranch manager.

"Oh. Hi. I thought you might be Levi."

He raised an eyebrow. "No. Sorry to disappoint you."

She could feel herself flush. "You didn't. I only meant, I wasn't expecting you. Please. Come in."

He stood for a moment on the step before he walked into her sitting room. The space, already small, seemed to shrink more.

"Were you expecting Moran? I was just at his place. He didn't say anything about coming here."

"I wasn't exactly *expecting* him, but Levi sometimes comes over in the evening to catch me up on how things are going on the ranching side of things so I can put it in the report I send every week to Wallace. I've been saving them up since he...well, since he died. I wasn't sure where to send them. I can email them to you, if you want."

"Sure. It would be interesting reading."

"Okay."

That moment earlier when she had been almost certain he

wanted to kiss her seemed to hover between them, as bright as the star on her Christmas tree.

"Is everything okay?" she finally asked when he made no move to explain why he was knocking on her door this late.

That seemed to remind him of his purpose. "Yes. Sorry to bother you but I saw your light on and thought this might be a good time to touch base with you about the plan for tomorrow, when my family arrives. I would have done it earlier but the kids were a little distracting."

"They can be," she agreed.

He took in the sewing machine and the material everywhere. "It looks like I'm interrupting, though."

When she was working hard, she usually only cleaned up after wrapping up for the night, not as she went along, which meant there was thread and bits of fabric everywhere. And, she suddenly remembered, she was wearing her most comfortable sewing clothes. Yoga pants, a loose sweatshirt, her hair in a messy bun and her oversize reading glasses. She probably looked quite a sight.

"It's fine. I was just working on a few things."

He looked at the sewing machine with clear curiosity on his features. "Do you mind me asking what you're making?"

She was always a little uncomfortable talking about her craft, even as she was proud of what she created.

"I'm just finishing a baby blanket for a customer in Vermont to give her new grandson."

"A customer?"

He looked genuinely interested and she nodded, knowing she had no real reason to be embarrassed about her work. She created beautiful comfort items that made people happy. Why feel awkward about telling people about it?

"I have an online store where I sell custom blankets made out of ultraluxurious fabric."

His brows drew together. "I thought you were a hotel concierge before you came here."

"I was. I am. This is my side hustle. Comfort Threads by Annelise."

Surprise flickered in his eyes. "Wow. Good for you. And this is a blanket you've made? May I see it?"

"Um. Sure."

She handed over the baby blanket and felt a little shiver when his big, blunt-tipped fingers smoothed over the purple and yellow material and the silky ruffled border.

"Wow. This fabric is amazing."

"It feels so good wrapped around you, too. Like the best kind of hug."

"I can imagine."

So could she. She could close her eyes and picture him all too clearly, wrapped in one of her creations and not much else.

"Nice work," he said. "So only baby blankets?"

"No. I do all sizes. Adult, babies, kids. The whole gamut. People can choose the fabric for the front and back as well as how they want them bound. They can also have them monogrammed, if they want."

"That's terrific. How many have you made?"

"Counting this one, I've sold more than a hundred since Halloween."

"That is a lot of sewing."

She felt that panic well up when she thought of the commitments she had made in addition to her orders. "Yes. Depending on the size of the blanket, my profit is anywhere from ten to twenty dollars. Not huge, but a nice bit of extra change, especially when I'm sewing in my spare time at night, when I would otherwise be watching TV or reading a book, anyway."

"That's terrific. Good for you."

Her talk of making a little extra money must seem silly to

a man whose family owned multiple companies. She didn't care. She worked hard for every penny, knowing it was going to a good cause.

"I started the company and put my sewing skills to use after I came back to Wyoming, when I realized how much Wes was struggling."

"Your brother has definitely had it rough. I'm sorry he's been dealt such a hard hand."

"He has a great job as a farm implement mechanic and can literally fix anything, but his wife's death left him wiped out financially, between all the medical bills and the funeral and the additional childcare he's having to pay now. Added to that, he and Cassie were in the middle of a big home renovation when she died but he had to use their remodeling fund to cover expenses. I'm trying to help him replenish that a little so he can finish fixing the house."

"You're a good sister," he said gruffly, looking at her with a warm expression that left her feeling slightly breathless.

"Not really," she said, more than a little embarrassed that she was telling all this to a man who had never had to worry a moment about money.

"How can you say that? You gave up your job, moved hundreds of miles away and are working late into the night to help Wes and his family."

"Whatever I do never feels like enough, you know? They need so many things. Money is the least of it. Sometimes it feels hopeless."

He was silent for a moment before nodding. "I know exactly what you mean. During the decade I have spent working for the Sheridan Trust, that has been one of the toughest lessons for me to accept. We can't fix everything. Some of these places we go into have so many needs. Everything from clean water to health care to education to basic infrastructure. It's overwhelming and hard to know where to start. Over time, I've had to accept that while we can't fix everything overnight, change has to start somewhere, right?"

He was such a good person. She wondered if he knew just how much like his father he had become.

"You're so right," she said.

She felt much better about the long hours at her sewing machine. She couldn't fix everything for Wes and the kids but she was doing what she could. That was the important thing.

She smiled at Tate and for a moment something sizzled to life between them again, as it had in the kitchen earlier.

She was the first to look away.

"I saw the program about you and the Sheridan Trust on PBS a few years ago."

She didn't tell him she had watched it over and over.

He winced. "I was so embarrassed to do that. My team had to talk me into it but in the end it turned out to be a good decision. We were able to bring in some great partners on a couple of projects we were working on."

"You've really enjoyed your work there, haven't you?"

"Yeah. You could say that. I wish I could keep doing it."

She didn't need to see the regret in his eyes. She could hear the fervor in his voice.

"Why do you have to leave?"

He was quiet for a long moment, then a sigh seemed to come from deep inside.

"My grandfather's death changed everything for me. I suppose I've known for years that one day I was expected to step into his shoes. Believe me, that is no easy undertaking."

"Why you? Surely there are other well-qualified people who can protect the family's business interests."

"We have some brilliant people on board," he agreed. "Wallace always tried to have a deep bench full of plenty of people who could make the hard decisions when necessary. My grandfather was old-fashioned, though. He built the company singlehandedly and has always wanted someone from the family to oversee things after he was gone. Since my father isn't around to do it, that leaves me."

His voice was grim, almost hollow at the words. She could not imagine the sense of responsibility he must feel, not only to his grandfather but also to the rest of his family.

"Oh, Tate. I'm so sorry."

He gave a small laugh, looking a little dismayed at himself. "I don't think I've verbalized to anyone else just how conflicted I've been about leaving the trust. I have loved working there the past ten years and I'm proud of what we have accomplished."

"You should be."

"It's been such an important part of my life. Walking away from it is turning out to be much harder than I expected."

"You'll still play a role, won't you?"

"I don't know, at this point. Everything is up in the air right now."

"I'm sure you'll figure it out and make whatever decision is best."

"How can you know that?"

She shrugged. "Wallace obviously trusted your good sense or he wouldn't have wanted you to be his successor, would he?"

"I...suppose not."

"Your grandfather was the smartest man I ever met, with an uncanny ability to see to the heart of people. Everyone considered him a business genius. If he thought you were the best person to take over for him, you should trust his judgment, don't you think?"

Tate stared at her for a long moment, then shook his head,

looking astonished at her words. "You're right. I had never looked at it that way. I've been focused on all I have to give up instead of looking at what I might be bringing to the table. Thank you for the perspective. It helps."

She smiled. "I'm glad."

"And thank you for not telling me I'm being an idiot for feeling conflicted about leaving something I've loved and worked hard at."

"I would never do that. Your feelings are your feelings. I know it's not at all at the same level as what you're facing but I can relate a little. I struggled to leave behind a job I loved in San Francisco, but also knew when I came here, I would be exactly where I need to be. You will probably find the same thing."

"I hope so. It helps when I remind myself that by stepping up to keep the business side of things running smoothly, I'm ensuring we can continue on with all the philanthropic projects we've invested in over the past ten years."

"That's a good way to look at it. And that's why I'm sewing a baby blanket for someone in Vermont who I will never meet. Every little bit will help my brother and his twins put the pieces of their lives back together."

He smiled again, this time a warm, soft, infinitely sexy smile that made her heart race.

She had to stop this. She was going to fall for him and Tate would end up breaking her heart. He wouldn't do it on purpose, that wasn't the kind of man he was, but the result would be the same.

He was the first to look away. "So. Tomorrow is the big day when my family arrives. The house looks terrific. You've made it so warm and welcoming for them."

"Thank you, though we both know all I did was follow directions and copy the pictures from last year."

"Not so. You brought an extra element of holiday cheer to the task."

"Everyone is arriving tomorrow at the same time, right?"

"Yes, except my cousin Tom, Lillian's son. He and his family are flying into Jackson Hole next week because of his children's school schedule. Every one else is flying in on one of the Sheridan planes to the Afton airport, planning to arrive around noon. Because it's a private flight without a set time, I wouldn't be surprised if that arrival time is pushed back a little. My aunt Lillian especially tends to run on her own time."

She should probably have a contingency plan in place if that happened and their arrival coincided with the time she usually picked the children up from the bus stop.

Given the circumstances, it would probably be best if they went home with her friend Wendy.

"We can be ready whenever they arrive. You're all set with the personal chef?"

"Yes. She will be here to make lunch and dinner. We're on our own for breakfasts since she had other obligations in the morning."

She almost offered to fix breakfast for his family but did not want to overstep.

"I'll drive one of the ranch SUVs to the airport and I've talked to Levi about driving the other one. He can help me with the luggage."

"I'll be the welcoming committee here. What about the flight crew? Do you need rooms for them? I should have thought to ask that before now."

"No. They're turning right around and flying back to California."

"Sounds good."

"Thank you for all the work you've done over the past few days. I know it hasn't been easy."

"It's been my pleasure. The house has never looked so beautiful, at least not in my memory."

She meant her words. She loved creating a comfortable retreat for his family, especially after the difficult loss they had all endured.

Annie was a nurturer. It was in her DNA and probably the reason she had enjoyed her job as a hotel concierge. Her entire identity involved meeting other people's needs.

She was certainly self-aware enough to know that likely stemmed from her childhood, from the years she had spent trying to paste together her fraying family before her parents ultimately divorced.

She supposed that finding personal joy in making sure other people were happy wasn't the worst trait a person could have.

"You are right. I've never seen it look so good. My family, particularly Irene, will all be thrilled at how good it looks. Thank you."

"You're very welcome."

He looked as if he wanted to say something else. After a moment he gestured toward the door. "I'll let you get back to your side hustle."

"I'm almost done for the night. For the season actually. This is the final order from my store that I'm sending before Christmas. I cut off new orders a week ago."

"Smart."

She didn't want to tell him about the thirty other blankets she was making for a local charity.

"Good night," he said.

Again, she had the feeling he wanted to say something more but he only smiled again and left the way he had come.

9

THE FLIGHT FROM SAN FRANCISCO TO THE SMALL airport in Afton, Wyoming, was every bit as uncomfortable as Brie feared. From the moment she showed up at the runway, she felt awkward and out of place.

She sat next to Catherine and tried to make conversation with her half sister but the teenager put on big, bulky headphones, pulled the hood of her sweatshirt up over her head, nestled against the window of the plane and closed her eyes.

She was quite certain Catherine wasn't asleep, though she was doing a good approximation of it.

Yet one more person in the family Brie had disappointed. In her sister's case, she wasn't exactly sure why. Catherine seemed angry at her all the time. Brie didn't know if that was the girl's default mood or if all the annoyance was aimed specifically at her.

Her sister had been born when Brie was nearly fifteen and

had already been a troublesome teenager. Tate had been on his way to college.

During her difficult prep school years, Catherine had been the one joyous spot in Brie's life. The little girl would follow her around, jabbering about her dolls or the cat or whatever popped into her mind.

As much as Brie had adored her little sister, she had been a mess during those years, full of so many raw emotions she couldn't handle. Guilt, anger, grief. Mix all those with adolescence and the end result wasn't a pretty picture.

Her mom and Stan had tried to get her into counseling but she hadn't been at all receptive. She had partied hard, drinking, smoking weed, staying out all night.

She had finally grown tired of what she considered too many overbearing rules at home and had run off for the first time when she was seventeen.

She had followed that self-destructive path on and off for a decade.

As a result, she and Catherine were virtual strangers now. The girl who once adored her had grown into a teen who barely tolerated her. Brie consoled herself that she wasn't the only one. Catherine didn't seem to like anyone.

But they were stuck together for the next week and a half. She was determined in that time to try to reestablish a better relationship with her younger sister. At the very least, maybe she could keep Catherine from making all of Brie's own mistakes.

She couldn't do much right now, when her sister was clearly shutting her out, but they had endless days at the ranch with little else to do but interact. She would give Cat space now.

At least it wasn't a long flight. Brie tried to focus on her book and was soon caught up in the autobiography of one of her favorite actresses.

Soon enough, the flight crew announced they would be landing soon. Brie stowed her book and looked out the windows. She caught a glimpse of the Tetons in the distance, distinctive and rugged, the Grand Teton shrouded in clouds, as usual.

After they taxied down the small runway of the Afton Municipal Airport, the crew put down the steps and Brie immediately stepped forward to join Stan in helping Lillian and Irene down to the tarmac.

She did love traveling on a private plane but not having an accessible Jetway could be tough on old bones.

"Do you need a hand?" she asked her mother.

"No, dear. I'm fine." Pamela smiled, but Brie was quite certain it was fake.

Despite her mother's assurances, Brie could see something was wrong. Pamela seemed pale and subdued, though she put on a good show.

Maybe she was imagining things. Nobody else seemed to notice anything amiss. Certainly Catherine hadn't said anything and the teenager lived in the same house with Pamela. Wouldn't she know if her parents were fighting?

"Oh. I had forgotten that smell," Irene said, sniffing the air with her regal nose.

"What?" Catherine sniffed. "I only smell jet fuel."

"It's deeper than that. It's the smell of the mountains in winter. I can't explain it. Snow and pine and memories."

Brie knew exactly what her grandmother meant. Memories had poured over her the moment she inhaled.

Not all of them were bad memories, though the pain and guilt always seemed to take center stage.

She had made so many mistakes, trying to run away from that pain. One of the overriding lessons she had learned through rehab and therapy was that running away or trying to bury those memories through alcohol or drugs didn't help. Her only answer was to face them head-on, no matter how tough.

A tall, handsome figure came striding toward them.

"Tate. Darling," her mother said, holding out arms that seemed too thin.

"Hi, Mom." He kissed her cheek, then did the same to Irene and Lillian.

"I had forgotten how cold the wind can be here," Irene complained.

"I've got a vehicle all warmed up for you over there," he said. "Let's get you all settled first and then I'll grab the bags."

"Brie, Catherine, can you help me with the dogs? They're still in their crates on the plane."

Her sister huffed out a breath but followed her up the steps again. They found their grandmother's two sweet little bichon-poodle mixes, Simone and Jean-Paul, waiting patiently.

"Hey there," Catherine crooned, with far more affection than she ever gave to Brie.

By the time they carried the dogs down, all the bags and people had been loaded up into the two vehicles.

"There's room right here on the seat for the crates," Irene said.

As Catherine climbed in, Brie quickly did the math and realized they were short one passenger spot.

As usual, she was the odd one out.

Her grandmother seemed to know what she was thinking. "We could fold up the crates and you could hold the dogs on your laps."

As cute as the dogs were, she wasn't particularly thrilled about that option. Still, it was a short ride.

"No need," Tate said before she could reach back inside

for the crates. He gestured to the second vehicle, a late-model crew cab pickup truck.

"This is the ranch manager, Levi Moran. He's bringing the bags. He can give you a ride, too, if you don't mind. We were planning to split the group between two SUVs but we discovered the other one had a flat tire just before we were supposed to pick you up. A truck will have to do. Do you mind?"

Brie glanced over at the truck and the cowboy who was standing by the tailgate. He definitely looked like trouble. Wavy dark hair, blue eyes, wearing a black Stetson, cowboy boots, a tan ranch jacket and Wrangler jeans riding low on his narrow hips.

He smiled politely and she felt something stir deep inside, something she didn't want to feel. She was done with troublemaking men, whether they were surfers, musicians or cowboys. She wanted someone safe, reliable. Not a man who looked like he could be starring in a country music video.

She glanced between the packed SUV and the pickup truck. Dogs on her lap or a dangerous cowboy in the driver's seat. She preferred the dogs at this stage of her life but couldn't admit that to her family.

Brie forced a smile. "Sure. No problem."

"I'll ride with Brie," Catherine said, jumping out of the Suburban quickly.

Brie had to blink. Where had that come from? Her sister had just spent an hour pretending they were on different hemispheres instead of sitting next to each other on a small airplane. What made her want to be with her now?

The answer was pretty obvious when Catherine gave the cowboy a broad smile and tossed her hair as she climbed into the front seat of the pickup truck, leaving Brie to sit behind them.

"Sorry the pickup is a little muddy. No time to wash it

after we used it to haul some hay down to the pasture this morning."

"A little dirt never hurt anybody," Brie said.

She climbed into the back seat, setting the battered leather backpack she had picked up in a market in Marrakech on the seat beside her.

A moment later, they were on their way.

"So. Levi, wasn't it?" Catherine smiled at him, tossing her blond hair.

"That's right."

"I'm Catherine."

"I know. Your grandfather had a picture of you on his desk. And you must be Brianna."

He said her name with a bit of a Western twang she found ridiculously appealing.

"Yes. Most people call me Brie."

"Nice to meet you both," he said as he drove out of the airport onto the road that would lead them north to Holly Creek and the Angel's View. "I'm sorry about your grandfather. He was a good man. One of the best men I ever knew. I'm going to miss him."

Emotion welled up in her throat. To her chagrin, Brie had to swallow it down before she could trust her voice.

Catherine jumped in before she could respond. "We're all really going to miss him but I still don't know why Grandma Irene insisted we come all the way out here to remember him."

"I guess maybe she thought he would appreciate knowing you were willing to make the effort to come to the back of the beyond for him," Levi said mildly.

"I guess."

Catherine apparently didn't pick up on the ranch manager's dry tone. Brie did and she didn't much like it.

"How long have you been at the Angel's View?" Catherine asked.

"Going on five years now."

"That long?" From the back seat, Brie could see her sister's eyebrows raise.

"Yeah. And before that, I worked at an operation up in Montana for several years. That was after I graduated from college in Utah with a degree in equine studies and a minor in range management."

"You must have graduated early." For the first time, Catherine began to look a little uneasy, as if she had jumped on a horse she couldn't quite handle. She must have thought Levi was younger, maybe early to midtwenties. Still far too old for her but maybe young enough for a flirtation.

It was hard to tell under that cowboy hat but Brie would have guessed he was closer to her age. Maybe even a year or two older.

Too bad she wasn't interested in a flirtation.

"Nope. The usual schedule. I actually took an extra year because I got married and was working full-time and couldn't always fit my classes in."

That seemed to shut Catherine down once and for all. She sat back with a deflated kind of look.

"You're married?"

"Was. Divorced now."

"Any kids?" Brie asked.

He glanced in the rearview mirror, almost as if he had forgotten she was there. Somehow she knew he hadn't. Brie couldn't have said exactly how she knew it. Women's intuition, maybe. But she sensed Levi Moran was as aware of her as she was of him.

"One. A boy, eight. Tanner. He lives with his mom in Jackson. What about you?"

Catherine, apparently thinking he was talking to her, giggled a little. "I'm only fifteen. And I'm never getting married, anyway. I'm going to take off like Brie did and travel around the world. I might at least wait until I'm done with high school, though. Only losers and stoners drop out."

She turned around in her seat. "No offense," she said in all seriousness.

Brie would have laughed if she could have taken a breath around the knife in her gut.

"Oh, none taken," she lied, trying for a cheerful tone. "I was both of those things when I was your age. I hope I've grown out of that. And also of being a bitch."

The cowboy gave a laugh that he covered with a little cough. He caught her gaze in the rearview mirror again and the amusement in his expression made butterflies jump in her stomach.

She really shouldn't find him so darned good-looking.

"What about you, Ms. Sheridan? Any significant others in the picture?"

"Not currently," she answered, her voice cool. She couldn't let him think she was here to play around with the staff. That was something she might have done when she was a teenager but she had come too far for those kind of games.

She had too much at stake now.

"How many horses are there?" Catherine asked him. "My mom wasn't sure."

"Your grandfather kept around ten for himself and guests and we're currently in various stages of training ten more. One of the ranch mares is due to foal next month, so it will soon be eleven. We also have about a hundred head of Scottish Highland cattle."

Catherine didn't seem interested in the cattle side.

"Can we ride any of them? The horses, I mean. Not the cows, of course."

"Sure. We have an indoor arena you can always use when the weather's poor as well as trails around the ranch we try to keep groomed in the wintertime."

"I love horses," she told him. "I compete at home in dressage."

"I'm afraid you won't find any English saddles here. Wallace wouldn't hear of it."

She looked upset at that but finally shrugged. "I'll adapt. I can use a Western saddle, I just don't like to."

"What about you, ma'am? Do you ride?"

If she was right about his age, they were contemporaries. She appreciated good manners but wasn't crazy about him calling her *ma'am*.

"Not in years, I'm afraid."

"We can change that, if you want. All of the horses in the stable here are sweet-tempered. A good temperament in a horse is the one thing Wallace always insisted on."

She felt a spasm of pain at his words. She knew exactly why her grandfather insisted on sweet horses. Because of her.

Wait. I'm coming with you.

Stay here. We're riding on a trail that is too steep for you, with a hard drop-off. I promise, tomorrow I'll take you for another ride.

I can handle it, Daddy. Please let me go with you. It's not fair! Tate always gets to go.

Tate is fourteen and has been riding longer than you have and his horse isn't as easily spooked.

The words played over in her head, as clear as if the conversation had happened on the way to the airport that morning. Her father, kind but firm as he told her she couldn't go on a fishing day trip into the mountains with him and her brother. Brie, just as stubbornly convinced at eleven that she could ride as well as Tate and her father.

She closed her eyes, wishing she could shut off the terrible memories of what happened next.

She realized after an awkward moment that the ranch manager was waiting for her to respond. "No, thanks. I don't ride."

He looked as if he wanted to push the matter but something seemed to make him change his mind. Maybe he could see some trace of those dark memories in her tense shoulders and the hard line of her mouth.

"What else is there to do besides riding? Do you even have internet?" Catherine asked.

Levi Moran gave her a sideways look. "We definitely have *fishing* nets. Does that count?"

She made a sound of disgust that would have made Brie smile if she wasn't still battling her personal demons.

"Yes, we have internet. Your grandfather insisted the whole ranch have the techiest tech available."

"Is techiest tech a thing?" Brie asked.

He smiled again. "I don't know. I just take care of the horses and the cattle and leave the rest to somebody else."

"This is going to be the most lame Christmas ever," Catherine muttered.

"I remember there being plenty to do when I was a girl," Brie said. "Winter here was always so peaceful. Skiing, snowshoeing, skating."

"Anything I can do *indoors*?" Catherine said with an exaggerated eye roll.

"I'm sure we'll find plenty to do. Tate probably has a whole list for us."

Catherine sighed, not thrilled at that idea, but lapsed into silence for the remainder of the short drive to the ranch, in the foothills of the Star Valley.

Though she hadn't been here for decades, the terrain was beginning to look familiar. When Levi turned through the small, quaint town of Holly Creek, memories crowded in fast.

She remembered staying out late on release day at that bookstore with Annelise McCade so they could buy the newest *Harry Potter* the moment it came out.

The café reminded her of going to breakfast once with her father and grandfather and eating so many pancakes that she was almost sick.

How many trips to the feed store had she made with her dad or with Annie and Scott McCade?

She sighed. This was going to be a long Christmas holiday if she couldn't figure out how to come to terms with those memories.

"What about you?"

It took Brie a moment to realize the ranch manager had said something to her.

"Sorry. I missed the question," she admitted. "I was thinking about something else."

"Catherine was telling me she would rather be spending Christmas in Hawaii, like her family has always done. I was wondering if you feel the same."

She didn't know how to answer. She had no choice but to come back to the ranch. She owed Wallace that and much, much more. He, more than anyone else in the family, had believed in her.

He had helped her through rehab, had encouraged her to finish the degree she had worked on here and there over the years, had even given her a job at Sheridan International she enjoyed.

Besides honoring her grandfather, Brie had another reason for coming home. She wanted desperately for her family to see her as something more than the Sheridan screwup. The problem was, she had no idea how to prove that.

"Brie never came to Hawaii with us for Christmas," Catherine answered for her. "She hardly came home to visit at all."

The outright bitterness in Catherine's voice startled her. Was that the reason Catherine seemed so hostile? Was she angry at Brie for all the stupid choices she had made over the past decade?

Brie couldn't blame her. She was angry enough at herself for both of them.

"Well, she's here with you now. That's the important thing, isn't it?" the ranch manager asked in that sexy drawl. "No point wasting today by being mad about yesterday, right?"

He said this just as he pulled under the arch reading Angel's View Ranch and headed up the long driveway to the house.

As they drove past a paddock filled with gorgeous horses toward the house and outbuildings, Brie felt paralyzed by the memories.

The ranch was the same and different than she remembered. Some of the outbuildings were new, including the indoor riding arena he had talked about. So many things were familiar, though. She had memories in nearly every corner of the ranch, many of them wonderful.

The big SUV was already there in the driveway and she saw Tate helping everyone out.

Levi pulled in behind it. "Here you go," he said cheerfully. "Safe and sound. The Angel's View might not be Hawaii but we're not so bad."

"There's a glowing endorsement," Catherine said with another eye roll. "Maybe you should make some T-shirts like that."

She jumped out and headed for the front door before Brie could tell her to take some luggage with her.

She would have to work to find common ground with her sister. And with her mother and stepfather. And with Tate.

Face, it, she had her work cut out for her during the holiday season just trying not to screw things up. With all that on her plate, she shouldn't even be giving this sexy cowboy a moment's thought.

After Tate set down his grandmother's bags in the main bedroom where Wallace always slept, he followed voices and found his grandmother and Lillian admiring the Christmas tree in the office.

"It looks very nice in here, Tate. The staff did an excellent job of making the place feel festive and welcoming."

He wanted to tell her the staff consisted of only Annelise McCade but she didn't give him the chance.

"The house seems different somehow." She looked around the well-appointed office. "In my memory, it was cold and drafty and rather shabby."

"This is anything but shabby," Lillian agreed. "My room is quite luxurious and I love how warm it is."

"I understand Grandpa had the whole place redone about five or six years ago."

"It's been at least that since I was here," Irene admitted. "I do remember him showing me pictures but it looks better in person than the pictures."

Tate was glad Annelise had suggested turning up the fireplaces in each room so everyone would feel comfortable. She was excellent at that sort of thing.

"Let me know if you need anything else."

"We're fine for now. Thank you, my dear," Irene said with a sad sort of smile.

How difficult this must be for her, coming here to the place her late husband had loved more than any other, to spread his ashes alongside those of their only child.

He had been so busy resenting her demand that the family come here for the holidays that he hadn't given a great deal of thought to how emotional this visit must be for Irene, who had lost the love of her life only a few months before.

He gave his grandmother a hug, thinking how fragile she seemed lately, this fierce woman who was approaching eighty.

All the bags had been taken to their respective rooms, he saw when he returned to the great room, so Tate headed for the kitchen to meet the personal chef he had hired.

Before he could reach it, Brie came in from outside, her cheeks and nose a little pink from the cold.

"Hey," she said when she spotted him. "Stop. I need to talk to you."

She had ridden with Levi by necessity and had also carried her own bag inside to her designated room, the one she had always used when they were children, so this was his first real chance at a conversation since they arrived.

"Sure. What about?"

She stomped a little snow off her boots, shoved gloves into her pocket and untwisted her scarf.

He had to admit, Brie seemed more centered these days than he had seen her in years. Her eyes had lost that haunted look and she no longer had the edge of restlessness about her that seemed to have defined her for the past decade.

"Mom. What else," she said. "Now that you've had a chance to talk to her, what do you think? I'm right, aren't I? Something is going on with her.

He gave a rough laugh. "I've barely exchanged two words with her. On the drive, Lillian and Irene dominated the conversation, as they tend to do."

"No surprise there."

Now that he thought of it, his mother *had* been unusually quiet. Was that coincidence or was there something to Brie's concerns?

"For what it's worth," she went on, looking around as if to make sure no one else was within earshot, "she hasn't once looked me in the eye since we boarded the plane in California. I've been watching. And Stan isn't acting like himself, either. He's usually friendly and warm to me but he's hardly said a word."

He didn't want to give credence to her speculation that their mother and stepfather might be having marital problems. He still wasn't convinced it was any of their business.

"If anything, he was overly solicitous in the car. He kept asking if she was warm enough and telling her to turn on the heated seats on the way here."

"Maybe he was trying to make up for something. Classic guilt syndrome. I wonder if he had an affair."

He didn't want to think that of a man he had always liked and respected. Stanford was the chief legal counsel for Sheridan International, a man Tate had to work with closely as he transitioned to running the family financial interests.

"If anything is going on, Mom will tell us in her own way. Keep in mind, it's not easy for any of us to come back here after all these years."

Brie's features tightened. "You're right. That could be it."

"What were you doing outside just now?" he asked.

She shrugged, looking a little guilty. "I've been traveling all morning, surrounded by people. I just needed to stretch my legs so I took a walk around to see what I remember about the place."

"And?"

"Like any place you haven't seen for twenty years, I guess.

A few things are familiar, plenty is new. The setting is still as beautiful."

"Isn't it?"

"I would still rather be having Christmas at Irene's place at the coast. Or Hawaii."

"Same. Next year, for sure."

Unless their grandmother wasn't around, either, the next year. Tate didn't want to depress his sister by bringing that up.

The sound of clattering pans from the kitchen drew his attention. "I was just checking on lunch," he told her. "It should be ready soon. I'll text and let everyone know."

"Sounds good. I guess I'll go unpack."

He waved her down the hall and pushed open the door to the kitchen.

To his surprise, instead of the personal chef he had hired, he found a frantic-looking Annelise stirring something on the stove.

There was no sign of the meal he expected.

"What's going on? Where's lunch?"

"I'm working on it. Your fancy personal chef never showed up."

"What are you talking about? She was supposed to be here an hour ago. I thought everything would be ready by now."

"I know. I've been calling her since about ten minutes after she was supposed to be here. I don't know how many times I've tried. Now my calls are going straight to voice mail. I finally decided about twenty minutes ago that I should probably come up with a contingency plan. I'm making vegetable soup to go with cold-cut sandwiches on ciabatta bread. I didn't know else what to do."

Feeding his family was turning out to be a harder job than helping an entire village in Sudan build a new irrigation system.

"Maybe if you called, she would pick up," Annelise said, though she didn't sound very hopeful.

He dutifully dialed the number. His call immediately went straight to voice mail, as hers had done.

"That's not good. I got a message that the mailbox is full."

"Probably from all my frantic messages cluttering the in-box."

"Thank you for trying." He shoved his phone back into his pocket. "And for stepping in to save the day. You are once again a lifesaver."

"I didn't want your family to go hungry."

"We wouldn't have starved. There's always takeout. But this is much better. How can I help?"

She gave him a surprised look. Did she really think he was going to leave her to figure it all out by herself?

"The soup is almost done. There are a few more vegetables left, if you would like to cut some up some carrots and celery for a relish tray."

He washed his hands thoroughly, then went to work, grateful he had spent enough time in third-world countries that he could fend for himself in most circumstances. And help feed a house party apparently.

"What are we going to do about dinner if she still doesn't come?"

"We can worry about that later. For now, let's get everyone fed and settled and then I'll try to track her down again."

He glanced around the kitchen. "Where are the twins? It's suspiciously quiet in here."

She made a face. "School for another hour, then I've asked the mom of one of their friends if she can pick them up from school. She's on the list of approved people who can take them."

He didn't want to admit that the house seemed a little less bright without them there.

While he cut vegetables, she set the table in the dining room and carried out the tray of sandwiches as well as soup bowls and a salad she must have also thrown together.

The woman was a genius under pressure, which probably made her an excellent concierge in a busy city hotel.

He was arranging his cut vegetables on the platter when Brie came into the kitchen. She stopped dead when she caught him working at the kitchen island.

"What's going on? When you didn't text me, I thought I had better see if you needed help."

This was not the sulky, angry sister of the past. She would never have thought to pitch in without being asked.

"The private chef I hired is a no-show, so Annelise is pinch-hitting."

Annelise turned around and smiled at Brianna, whose eyes lit up. "Annie. Hi!"

Brie crossed the kitchen and hugged Annie, who gave a little laugh and hugged her back tightly. When they both emerged from the embrace, he thought Annie looked a little teary-eyed.

Brie might be also but she was better at hiding her emotions.

"You look fabulous!" his sister exclaimed.

Tate couldn't have agreed more. Though she looked flustered at the unexpected meal drama, Annelise glowed with an inner light that drew his gaze again and again.

"You do, too. Gosh, Brie, it's so good to see you. It's been *forever.*"

"I was so shocked when Tate told me you were back working at the ranch. I would love the chance to catch up. Let's make time while I'm here, okay?"

"Definitely."

"How about not right now, though, when we're in the middle of a crisis," Tate suggested.

"Right." Annelise turned once more brisk and business-like as she scooped the soup into a tureen with a slotted lid.

"Everything is ready, if you want to notify your family."

"I'll go knock on all the doors," Brie offered. "Grandma will probably appreciate that more than a text."

She headed out of the kitchen and Tate turned back to Annelise. "Let me carry that out for you. It looks heavy."

"I'm stronger than I look," she told him. "I've got it."

He didn't want to argue when she was basically saving his bacon so he carried his relish tray into the dining room.

"This looks wonderful," he said as he set the vegetables down near the tray of sandwiches. "I can't believe you pulled this off entirely in the past half hour."

"There's a selection of soft drinks, iced teas and bottled waters," she said. "If one of you wants to play bartender or sommelier, there are adult beverage options, as well."

"Got it," Tate said, though he doubted there would be much need of that. Nobody in his family was a big drinker, barring Brie in her most rebellious days. He hadn't seen her drink since her return.

"Let me just check to make sure everything is ready, then I'll get out of your way," she said.

He suddenly wanted to invite her to sit down and eat with them. He followed her into the dining room, about to do exactly that when his grandmother walked in.

Her gaze immediately landed on Annie.

"Annelise McCade. Is that really you?"

Annie gave his grandmother a flustered smile. "Hello, Mrs. Sheridan. It is a pleasure to see you again."

"Wallace told me he hired you away from the Lancaster San Francisco to be the caretaker at this old place."

"Yes. Going on a year now." Her eyes softened. "I'm sorry for your loss, ma'am. I truly admired your husband."

Raw grief spasmed across Irene's wrinkled but still lovely features. "He was a good man. And I must say, he did nothing but sing your praises."

She looked at Annelise's apron. "I don't understand. I thought you were the caretaker, not the chef."

"Today I'm both," she said.

"The caterer I hired fell through," Tate said apologetically. "Annelise is helping out until we can come up with a plan B."

"Oh, how kind of you. I hope my grandson is not taking advantage of you."

For some reason, that made color seep across Annelise's cheekbones. She sent him a swift look he couldn't read. "No, ma'am," she said to his grandmother. "He even cut up some vegetables for you all."

Irene blinked. "Is that right?"

"Yes," Tate said quickly. "And lunch is ready as soon as everyone gets here."

"I believe they're all coming in now."

Lunch was more pleasant than he might have expected, possibly because his family members were all tired from traveling. Even Catherine was suspiciously quiet.

The food was delicious. Annie's soup was rich and layered, more complex than a simple vegetable soup should be, and she had added some kind of fresh condiment to the sandwiches that made the simple cold cuts tastier than usual.

The meal did give him a chance to assess his mother more closely than he had been able to do during the drive.

He realized as he looked at her that he hadn't actually seen her since his grandfather's public memorial service the month before.

He saw Stanford often at the offices but should have made time to visit his mother.

In contrast to the ride from the small airstrip, she was almost chatty with Catherine and Brie about some of the places they should go shopping in Jackson Hole. He saw Brie frowning, as if she didn't quite know what to make of the situation.

"While we're all here, let's talk about what we're going to do tomorrow to remember Wallace," Irene said.

"What did you have in mind?" Tate asked.

She picked up her napkin and twisted it through her fingers. "Now that I'm here again, I'm not sure. I should have come out with him at least once or twice over the past few years so I could know more about what drew him back again and again."

Tate had wished the same more than once over the past few days, that he had taken the chance to come here with Wallace when his grandfather was alive.

"Levi, the ranch manager, was telling me the other day how much Wallace liked to ride into the mountains east of here. Apparently there's a beautiful little meadow back in about a half mile from the house where the creek comes down the hillside in a series of small waterfalls."

"Oh, that's right. Cascade Springs. I remember that place." Irene's expression grew distant, as if she were seeing it now instead of the comfortable dining room. "In the early summer, it was always covered with wildflowers of every possible color. They were breathtaking."

Tate remembered having picnics there with his family and his father taking their picture almost every summer in exactly the same spot in one place where the river rippled over rocks, making a series of small waterfalls.

"Do you think we can make it up there this time of year?" Stanford asked, his voice serious.

If Tate remembered his geography, Cascade Springs wasn't that far from where he, Annelise and the twins had cut down the Christmas tree. They had been able to drive there quite easily but since then a series of small storms the past few days had dropped more snow in the backcountry.

He wasn't sure it would be safe now to drive regular vehicles up the steep, snow-packed road.

"I don't know," Tate admitted. "Let me talk to Levi and see what he would suggest. He might know of somewhere closer."

"Now that you've reminded me of it, I think Cascade Springs is exactly the place," Irene said. "We can have a small memorial there and say our own private goodbye to him, just the family, in a place he loved."

He knew his grandmother well enough to know that now she had her heart set on a thing she wouldn't be swayed.

Now Tate only had to hope he and Levi could come up with a way to make it work.

10

THAT COULD HAVE GONE MUCH WORSE.

Annie had been in a serious panic when she couldn't reach the personal chef Tate had called. At least the kitchen had been well stocked with vegetables and herbs and she had been able to throw together a few easy recipes.

She wasn't sure how she had done it but somehow she had managed to pull off a halfway decent lunch.

She was washing the large Dutch oven she'd used to cook the soup when her phone rang.

She dried her hands on a towel and answered.

"Hello. Is this Annelise McCade at the Angel's View Ranch?"

"Yes," she said warily at the unfamiliar voice.

"Oh, good. This is Leslie Bingham returning your call."

She drew a blank for a few seconds until she remembered

how she knew the name. "Leslie. Hi. Is everything okay? Where are you?"

"Actually, no. Things aren't okay. I'm so sorry I dropped the ball this afternoon. I would have been there except I was in the back of an ambulance."

"An ambulance?" Annie exclaimed. "Oh my word. What happened? Please tell me you're okay."

"I wish I could." Leslie sounded apologetic but resigned. "I was in a car accident on my way through the canyon, unfortunately. A potato chip truck hit a patch of ice in the other lane and slid right into me."

"Oh, no! I'm so sorry."

"I think I have more places on me that are bruised than not." She made a small pain-filled sound. "I have two broken ribs and a separated shoulder. I'm going to need surgery to repair my broken nose and I'll likely have to stay in the hospital at least another day or two. Right now I'm hopped up on painkillers, which is probably the only reason I can make it through a phone call."

Annie didn't know the woman but just hearing her litany of injuries made her ache.

"I am so sorry."

"Not the way I expected to spend Christmas. That's the reason I didn't call earlier. Somehow in all the craziness after the accident, I left my phone in my vehicle. My husband just brought it to me from the impound yard where they towed what's left of my car. It ran out of juice. As soon as I plugged it in, I got hit with all your messages."

She winced, remembering her messages that had grown increasingly frantic as the afternoon wore on. "You can ignore those. Things were a little stressful here, as you can imagine. Though it sounds like your afternoon was much worse."

"I was so looking forward to the job, too," the woman said

mournfully. "I've always wanted to see inside that beautiful house and cooking for a family is so much more fun than a business event. I wish I could help Mr. Sheridan but I just don't see how I can. I tried to call his number but the call didn't go through."

Sometimes the house could have random dead zones where cell service didn't work. Annie expected that was the reason she couldn't connect with Tate.

"I can let him know. I'm so sorry about your injuries. I hope you're on the mend soon."

"Thank you."

Leslie was fortunate to be alive. Annie was happy the woman had survived a head-on collision without worse injuries.

Still, the ramifications began to sink in. Tate didn't have anyone to cook for his family now, the seven people and two dogs who were staying at the house until a few days after Christmas.

"If you would like, I can send you all the menus I worked out for the week along with the shopping list for each one. I'm really sorry about today particularly. Tonight's dinner was my special chicken and caper pasta. I'm afraid it's all over my wrecked car now."

"Please don't worry. You have more important things to focus on. We'll figure something out. You worry about getting better. We can handle this."

"Thank you."

Annie had just ended the call with the other woman when Tate walked into the kitchen carrying the empty salad bowl and the sandwich tray, now covered in dirty plates.

"You shouldn't be doing that. I can take care of it," Annelise scolded.

"Why? I can certainly clear a table full of dishes. Catherine is helping."

A moment later, a teenage girl who would be pretty if she didn't look so dour came in carrying some silverware and the vegetable tray.

"Where should I put this crap?" she asked with a definite note of resentment in her voice.

"Anywhere is fine. Thanks so much. I'm Annie, by the way. You must be Catherine."

Tate's half sister gave her a bored look that immediately made Annie feel stupid for introducing herself as if they could be friends.

"Annie and her family were the original owners of the land around here. Her father was the ranch manager when Brie and I were kids."

"Cool," Catherine said, though it was obvious by her tone that she meant exactly the opposite.

"Sorry about that," Tate said after his sister turned and walked back out of the room. "She's not very happy about being here for the holidays. Apparently Hawaii was her destination of choice."

"I can't blame her for that. I would rather be in Hawaii, too. Some sand and surf would be just the ticket right now."

"I, for one, am glad you are here. I would have been completely lost without you today."

"I have some bad news. I just got off the phone with Leslie. Apparently she was in a traffic accident in the canyon between here in Jackson."

"Good Lord!" He looked dismayed. "Is she all right?"

"It sounds horrible. She's got broken bones and contusions but it could be much, much worse. The bottom line for us, at least, is that she won't be able to do the job."

He groaned. "I thought I had the food situation all figured out finally. What are we going to do now?"

"Don't worry. We can muddle through for a few days while you look for someone else."

"If we have to, I guess we could always order in every day."

Annie didn't want to pierce his optimism but as she had already told him, there were very few quality restaurants in the area that would be available for delivery or takeout through the holidays. That might work for one or two meals but she could almost guarantee his family would tire of the limited options quickly.

"We can handle this," Annie said, more as a pep talk to herself than to him. "I'll work on coming up with a menu for the next few days. I'll arrange for a grocery delivery to stock up on some things, especially with a storm coming in over the weekend."

"That's brilliant. Good idea. We can order pizza tonight, if we have to. Everyone likes that, especially if I grab a veggie with cauliflower crust for Brie and Catherine."

"Let's save that as an emergency option. I have a couple of go-to recipes that are relatively easy. I'll start there."

"Thank you. Seriously. Thank you."

For a moment, he looked as if he wanted to kiss her. Annie caught herself before she could lean forward and let him.

"This is my job, caring for those staying at the Angel's View." Her brisk words were intended as a reminder for herself more than him.

"Cooking isn't in your job description, but I would be very grateful if you would be willing to help a little longer, until I can figure something else."

"I'll help as long as you need," she said.

The smile he gave her left her slightly light-headed. She actually felt herself sway toward him and checked herself for the ridiculous response just as his sister Catherine came in carrying another load of dishes.

While the rest of her family rested in their rooms—or, in Catherine's case, hooked up a video game console in the media room and played some kind of island-hopping adventure game on the giant TV—Brie found herself restless.

Her bedroom was vastly different from the one she remembered, now decorated in rich, mature colors of umber and a deep wine.

A Christmas tree twinkled in the corner and more lights gleamed on the mantel, hidden behind greenery and three or four thick white candles.

She sent an email to check in with her sponsor, tried to read a bit, caught up on work. Finally, as the afternoon dragged on, she decided to go for another walk.

She had found when she was trying to beat her various addictions that walking was the perfect therapy for her. It became almost like meditation, soothing the wild turmoil of emotions inside her.

She walked down the long driveway to the arch over the road. The Highland cattle looked gorgeous, with their wide horns and the long shaggy hair hanging in their faces.

She admired them for a moment before heading back toward the ranch house.

On impulse, she didn't go inside. Instead, she headed back to the barn, not really sure why. Seeing the cattle got her in the mood to talk to a few horses.

While she didn't ride anymore, she still loved horses. Maybe she could at least take a look to see what kind of animals Wallace kept.

She pushed open the barn door and looked around. Sunlight poured in from high windows near the roofline, spilling over the floor.

Instantly, the smell transported her back to her youth. Hay, animals, life. She had spent many happy hours in this barn. Somehow, she had allowed the dark memories to completely obscure the good ones.

If she closed her eyes, Brie could picture her father there, admiring the horses, talking to his father, looking completely comfortable in a Western-cut shirt and jeans.

Oh, she missed him. How different would her life have been if they all had not lost Cole Sheridan so early?

No one seemed to be around. She could hear a few horses nickering but couldn't see anyone. She headed down through the row of horse stalls. Only a few animals were inside. Most, she assumed, would be outside in the paddock attached to the barn. She saw a beautiful mare that looked ready to foal and another gelding that had its forelegs wrapped, indicating it had an injury.

Nearby, another mare watched her with interest. The mare had soulful eyes. She trotted to the entrance of the stall when Brie approached and stuck her head over the railing for attention.

"You are a pretty one, aren't you," Brie said.

The horse seemed to nod her head, which made Brie smile. She enjoyed petting her for a moment, wishing she could spend the whole Christmas holiday here in the barn with the animals who didn't judge her or remember all her past mistakes.

As she turned to go, she caught a faint whimper from a stall at the back of the barn. Curious, she followed the sound, where she found a scene she didn't expect.

Levi Moran was sitting in the hay with his back to her. A dog's head was in his lap and he was crooning soft encouragement to her.

"You've got this, Luna. You can do it. You're going to be a great mom. Come on."

The dog was having puppies, she realized. Two puppies were already nursing at her teats and she was still straining for more.

"You are the best. Good girl, Luna. You did so good. Keep going. You've got more in there. Come on."

The dog's sides contracted suddenly and as Brie watched, entranced, she bore down. A puppy emerged from under her tail, wrapped in a clear membrane.

"Good job. Good job. You've got this."

The mother dog licked away at the covering until the puppy emerged, looking like a little rodent with its eyes closed and its paws moving wildly.

"That was beautiful," she couldn't resist saying softly as Levi moved the puppy closer to the dog to nurse.

The cowboy jerked his head up. "How long have you been there?"

"Long enough," she said. "That was amazing. You're a good midwife. Dogwife. Whatever you would call it."

He gave her a rueful look. "It's her first litter. We're all a little protective of Luna."

"She's a good mama."

"She's not done yet. I figure she's got two or three more in there."

"Is there anything I can do to help?"

He looked surprised that she would offer. "You could grab some more paper towels. There are some in the supply cabinet up by the office. And maybe a water bottle out of the fridge in the office. That's for me, by the way. Not Luna here."

"Sure."

She hurried that way and found several utility cabinets lined up along a wall. One was labeled Paper Products. She found the paper towels easily.

Next, she headed into the ranch office, which she would always associate with Annie McCade's father. She found a full-size refrigerator that was as neat and orderly as the supply closets had been.

She pulled out a water bottle for him and took the liberty of snatching one for herself. When she returned to the stall, she found the dog straining again, panting hard.

"Looks like the next one is coming faster than the first three did," Levi said.

"Is it okay if I watch?" Brie asked. "I don't want to disturb her but I've never seen anything like this before."

"I don't think she'll mind. I guess you've seen enough by now to know it's not a very elegant process. It can get pretty messy."

"Sounds like life," she murmured.

He gave her a long look. "True enough."

She pulled a bench over from a nearby stall. "What kind of dog is she?"

"Australian shepherd. This is the fifth generation born on the ranch."

"She's beautiful. You're beautiful," she said to the dog, who flapped her tail weakly on the blankets she was resting on.

For the next two hours, Brie completely lost track of time as she watched the dog give birth not one more time, but three.

It turned out to be one of the most moving experiences of her life, something she would never forget.

Levi Moran talked gently to the dog the whole time, murmuring what a good girl she was.

The three additional puppies came in their own time. When each puppy was delivered, Tate would wait for Luna to clean it off, sniff it, nudge it for a few moments, then he would take the puppy and weigh it on a small scale she hadn't noticed before on a small table of the stall.

He recorded information about the puppy and put a different colored collar on each one. He also directed Brie to take pictures of each one for further identification purposes, then he returned each puppy to Luna.

Finally, right after Levi said he thought maybe she was finished, Luna delivered one more puppy in a rush of fluid.

"I think that's it," he said after cleaning the last puppy and returning it to Luna.

"That's what you said the last time."

"This time I mean it." He gave her a tired-looking smile she felt clear to her toes.

"That was amazing," she said. She meant the delivery, of course. Not the smile. Or at least that's what she told herself.

"She is pretty impressive," he agreed. "Whelping can sometimes take hours for dogs, especially a first litter. Most of the time they prefer to be by themselves but Luna has always loved being part of a pack. She's a natural mama."

"She had a good doula. Thank you for letting me stay. I've never seen anything like that."

"I was glad to have the company and the help."

"What are you going to name the puppies?"

"I don't know. They'll all be sold and the new owners will pick their final names but we have to call them something in the meantime. I'll let Annie and the twins help me figure that out."

He paused and gave her another smile. "Though I think for all your help today, you ought to have naming rights to at least one of them."

"The little girl with the white feet," she said immediately. That had been the first puppy she had watched being delivered. "I'll pick her name."

"You say that like you already know exactly what to call her."

"She-Ra," she said promptly.

He raised an eyebrow. "As in She-Ra, the Princess of Power?"

She flushed. "Sure. I used to watch reruns of that show when I was a kid and always liked it."

"You got it, then. She-Ra, it is."

"I guess I'd better go back to the house and get cleaned up."

She didn't want to, though. She wanted to stay here with him and the puppies.

Impossible, she reminded herself. She was not in the market for a fling with a handsome cowboy, no matter how gentle he was with a dog having puppies. Or how he made Brie wish she didn't have such a long and tangled history.

11

"CAN WE GO DOWN TO THE BARN?"
Annie looked up from the recipe she was studying to find the twins gazing at her with matching expressions of entreaty on their cute little faces.

"The barn?" she said blankly.

"Yeah. We can't wait to go see the puppies! I can't believe Luna had six puppies. That's three for each of us to hold."

Annie wanted to see the puppies, too. She had a sudden intense yearning for the peace and comfort she always found at the barn.

This was the worst possible time, though. She had entirely too much to do. Nor did she want to send the twins down there on their own. Levi was probably busy and wouldn't be able to keep an eye on them and she shuddered to think of the trouble they could get into at the barn without close supervision.

Now that the rest of the Sheridans were here, she would have to keep a much tighter rein on them.

While she had never given them free access to the house or the grounds, she did sometimes send them down with Levi to play with the ranch dogs. She couldn't do that now with Tate's family in residence.

"So can we?" Henry pressed when she didn't immediately reply.

"I know we're all excited to see Luna's new puppies but it will have to wait until after dinner. I'm sorry. I have too much to do right now. When he texted me about them a little while ago, Levi told me Luna and the puppies are all sleeping, anyway. We should let them rest."

"We won't bother them one bit," Alice assured her. "We just want to see them, not touch them. That's what Levi said we have to do for now. Look with our eyes, not with our hands."

"We'll go see them after dinner, I promise," she said. "Meantime, why don't you bring my laptop in here and I'll find a movie for you both to watch."

She felt like the world's worst aunt, using TV as a temporary babysitter when the joy and excitement of new puppies beckoned, but right now she did not have another choice.

She was making chicken cordon bleu, wild rice and homemade rolls. It wouldn't be the most glamorous or exciting meal but was the best she could come up with on short notice.

"You promise you'll take us to see Luna and the puppies later?" Henry asked.

"Cross my heart," she said.

She wished she could have left them longer with her friend but Wendy had told her one of her other kids had a piano recital later that afternoon.

"The twins are welcome to go with us," she had said.

Annie knew perfectly well what a disaster that could turn

into, with poor Wendy trying to force two active six-year-olds to sit politely and listen to an hour of piano music. Wendy already had her own six-year-old to wrestle. She didn't need two more.

"No, it's fine," she had lied. "I'll come get them before you leave for the recital."

"Don't even think about it. We'll drop them off on our way. Besides, it might give me a chance to see that sexy Tate Sheridan in real life."

She had dropped them off a half hour ago. Too bad for Wendy, Tate hadn't been anywhere in sight.

While the twins watched an animated movie on her laptop, sharing one earbud each, Annie prepped the chicken breasts and then started working on dessert using raspberries from the freezer that she had picked that summer from the canes that grew against the barn.

When she finally put the cake into the oven, she realized the twins were nowhere in sight.

Oh, shoot.

They must have escaped when her back was turned.

After washing her hands, she went in search of them. Unfortunately, they weren't in her apartment, the first place she looked. Which meant they must have wandered somewhere else in the house, despite her firm instructions for them to stay put.

Maybe they had gone to the barn, after all. Those puppies were a seductive draw. She was about to put on her boots and coat to go check when she heard giggling coming from the great room.

Annie shifted direction and hurried toward the sound just as Irene Sheridan, Wallace's formidable widow, walked down the hall using a cane.

Irene reached the children first; they were standing holding hands and admiring the Christmas tree they had helped Annelise and Tate decorate.

Irene stopped in surprise. "Well. Hello. Who are you?" she asked before Annie could say anything.

The twins turned to look at her with matching looks of curiosity. "I'm Alice Jane McCade and this is my brother, Henry Martin McCade. We are six years old. How old are you?"

Annie winced at the rude question and stepped forward. "I'm so sorry, Mrs. Sheridan. This is my niece and nephew. They're staying with me through the holidays. Alice and Henry, this is Mrs. Irene Sheridan. She is Tate's grandmother."

"You're pretty," Alice said.

Irene blinked, her blue eyes startled in her wrinkled features. "Thank you," she said rather warily.

"Your white hair looks like an angel cloud," Alice went on, her voice matter-of-fact.

"Well." Irene gave a little smile. "Isn't that a lovely thing to say?"

"We're looking at our tree," Henry told her. "We helped Tate kill it and bring it here and then we put the ornaments on it. Tate gave us piggyback rides to put the high ones up. He's nice."

"Is that right?"

"Do you know where Tate is?" Alice asked, looking around as if her friend was hiding somewhere behind the tree. "I have to tell him about what happened at school today. My friend Abbie fell over right in the middle of singing 'Jingle Bells.' We were practicing for our Christmas show next week. My teacher said she probably locked her knees. I don't even know what that means. I thought maybe Tate would. Do you know what that means?"

"Come back into the kitchen, kids," Annie said quickly. "We don't need to bother Mrs. Sheridan."

"They're not bothering me," Irene said, her voice firm.

"Are you sure?"

Even when Annie had been a little girl, she had been a little frightened of Irene. The woman had seemed old to her then. Unlike Wallace, she hadn't smiled a great deal and had seemed much more proper and maybe a bit stuffy.

"The older I get, the more I find myself missing the presence of children," Irene said now. "My youngest granddaughter is a teenager, more interested in her friends and her phone than talking to her grandmother. It's been ages since I've been around little ones."

"Do you know what it means to lock your knees?" Alice pressed. "Why did that make my friend faint?"

"Believe it or not, I do know. It causes the blood to pool in your feet, reducing blood flow to your brain. Your brain uses blood to breathe and think and sing. Without it, a person can faint. Was your friend okay?"

"Our teacher made her rest with her feet up for a while and she was fine by the time we had recess."

"There you go." Irene sat down in the chair closest to the fire. "Do you children enjoy playing games? I seem to remember there's a whole cabinet full of board games over there in the corner and it's been ages since I've played some of them. See if you can find one you like. I'm partial to Yahtzee myself. Have you played that one?"

"Oh, yes. We love that one," Henry said. "I'm really good at it."

Nobody was really good at Yahtzee. They either had luck in their dice rolls or they didn't. Annie had tried to explain that to Henry but he still thought he had some kind of magic touch.

While the twins were distracted, rushing to the cabinet to

look through the board games there, Annie hurried over to speak with Irene.

"I'm sorry about the twins, Mrs. Sheridan. I'll try to keep them out of your way in the future. I was busy in the kitchen and lost track of them."

"Please. Call me Irene. And no need to apologize. They weren't hurting anything, only looking at their Christmas tree."

She looked over at the twins and then back at Annie. "Are they your brother's children? Wesley, wasn't that his name?"

"Yes. That's right."

"And they're staying with you for Christmas? Where are their parents?"

She sighed, wishing she had a better explanation to offer. "Their mother died last year and Wes is…struggling after her death. He was drinking too much and ended up in jail after starting a bar fight. He'll be in the county lockup until after the holidays. I didn't have any other choice but to bring them to the ranch to stay with me. I'm sorry I didn't let anyone in the family know. I should have."

Irene waved a hand. "Don't be silly. You're taking care of your family. That's the most important thing. If I've learned anything in my eighty years on the planet, it's to cherish my family while I have them. Nothing else matters."

Pain flitted across her regal features, making Annie's heart ache for her. "I agree," she said softly.

The timer in the kitchen went off, letting Annie know the cake was ready.

"I've got to run and grab that."

"Go ahead. The children and I will be completely fine. We will sit here by the fire and play board games on a snowy afternoon. It will remind me of being a girl myself again."

She truly hoped that was the case and that the children behaved themselves. Other than dragging them to the kitchen with her, she didn't know what else to do but leave them. And why on earth would they want to sit and watch a video they had already seen a dozen times when they could play one of their favorite games with someone new?

She couldn't blame them for finding Irene far more interesting than a movie.

The timer beeped again.

"Go," Irene said again. "We're fine."

Annie hurried to the kitchen, hoping that leaving them with Tate's grandmother wasn't a huge mistake.

This day was quickly going from bad to worse.

Tate hung up the phone on yet another personal chef who was completely booked for the holiday season. Everyone in the world seemed to be coming to the Jackson Hole area at exactly the same time and each one of them needed a personal chef.

He had called caterers, too, and their schedules were all full.

He supposed the busy holiday season was not the ideal time to hire someone at the last minute.

What were they to do? They couldn't rely on Annie for every meal. It wasn't fair to her, especially as she had other responsibilities around the house.

He should have come up with a backup plan before now.

Really, they could all cook. Everyone in his family was relatively self-sufficient. Irene had a personal chef who came in a few times a week to deliver premade meals and he thought Lillian shared the same service, but his mother and Stan didn't bother. They both enjoyed cooking and also ate out often.

Maybe they could take turns. He could come up with a rotating schedule, assign everyone a meal and make them responsible for preparing it for the rest of the family.

It was definitely an option.

In the meantime, he had promised Annelise he would help with dinner and instead had spent the afternoon trying to find staff.

He shoved his phone in his pocket and headed to the kitchen, where he found her slicing tomatoes for a green salad.

She gave him a distracted smile when he walked in. She had a little flour on her cheek and he had to curl his hands into fists to keep from brushing it away.

"Hi. Any luck finding someone to replace Leslie?"

He sighed. "I'm afraid not. I've called every number I can dig up, from Jackson to Idaho Falls. I can't find anyone. Everyone seems to be booked."

He had to give credit to Annelise. She didn't flinch, only nodded calmly. "Okay. I kind of expected that. Don't worry. I'm adequate in the kitchen and can handle it. We will figure out a way to make it work."

"I can't ask you to do that."

"I don't mind. Honestly. I like to cook and I will enjoy feeding your family. As long as they don't expect gourmet meals, everything should be fine."

"I had the idea that maybe we could all pitch in. We're not helpless."

"If that's the way you prefer to handle it, that's up to you. I'm happy to help but I could also step back."

Given that his mother and Stan were acting so strangely, having Annelise take care of meals would help, Tate had to admit. "I will be happy to compensate you for taking on the extra work. What if I paid you what I planned to pay Leslie?"

He named an amount that made her mouth sag a little.

"Wow. I didn't realize personal chefs made that kind of money."

"They do when the situation is desperate."

"You don't have to pay me that much. It wouldn't be right.

I don't have the expertise of an actual personal chef. But even half that amount would help Wes and the kids finish their house."

"Deal," he said immediately. What else could he do? He fully intended to pay her the full amount, anyway.

"Speaking of the twins, are they still at your friend's house?"

He had not seen them all day and didn't want to admit that he missed their mischievous smiles and constant conversation.

"I'm surprised you didn't see them when you came in," Annie said, giving him a sideways look. "They're playing games in the great room with your grandmother."

He stared. "My grandmother?"

"Not my idea, believe me," she said quickly. "They were out looking at their Christmas tree when Irene came in and she asked them if they wanted to play Yahtzee with her. You know Alice and Henry. They were thrilled to have someone new to talk to. Someone who wanted to entertain them, even better."

His grandmother had always loved to play board games with him and Brie. Occasionally when he was small and his parents were out of town for an event or working on a project for the Sheridan Trust, he would stay with his grandparents. He remembered spending hours at their elegant dining room table with his grandmother teaching him how to play cribbage and the occasional game of Texas Hold'em.

He had forgotten all about that. His grandparents had never let him win, either. Or at least if they did, they weren't obvious about it. When he did beat them, he knew it was because of his skill alone, which made the victory even more sweet.

"I hope you don't mind." Annelise looked nervous. "When she invited them to play, I didn't know how to refuse."

"There's no sense in even trying to refuse Irene. She's a force of nature when she puts her mind to something."

Annelise smiled. "If you want the truth, I was grateful to have someone distract them. There are new puppies at the barn and they want to immediately rush down to see them."

"Who wouldn't? I do, too."

She laughed and he wanted to bask in it. "Same. I told them I would take them down after dinner. That is one potential complication about me handling the meals. Henry and Alice and their schedule can be a lot to work around."

"There are plenty of us to help you entertain them and to help you in the kitchen. You won't have to do everything by yourself."

She gave him a grateful look. "They're in school until Thursday next week, which will help."

"I cannot tell you what a relief it is to have you on board." He meant the words wholeheartedly. "My grandfather was a genius about people. Hiring you was a brilliant decision on his part."

"I really hope your family isn't expecting gourmet fare."

She looked so worried he wanted to hold her close and assure her everything would be fine.

"We will be grateful for anything you fix. Trust me. You're talking to a man who has spent the last several holidays eating humble fare in poor villages and was happy to get it. I'm not picky and neither is my family."

She nodded, though she still looked anxious. "In that case, I will work on coming up with the menu for the remaining days of your stay. Leslie emailed me the menu the two of you had discussed so I'll start there, making a few substitutions for things I don't know how to make."

"Thank you, Annelise."

She gave him a sidelong look. "You know you can call me Annie, right? Everyone else does."

"Maybe I like being different. Annelise is a lovely name. I've always thought so."

"Oh." She gazed at him for a long moment, color dusting her cheekbones along with that enticing smudge of flour. Heat seemed to crackle between them again, pushing away the chill of the December afternoon.

She was the first to look away.

"How is everyone settling in?" she asked. "Does anyone need anything?"

Tate jerked his attention back to the conversation instead of those cheekbones he would like to kiss, flour or not.

"I believe everyone is fine. They seem content to hang out in their suites. Everyone except my grandmother apparently. I haven't seen Brie for a while. I think she might have gone for a walk. She does that a lot."

"Maybe she went down to the barn and found the new puppies."

"Speaking of the barn, I need some advice from Levi."

"Oh? Anything I could help with? I was a concierge, remember."

He smiled. "Maybe. Tomorrow would have been my grandfather's eighty-second birthday, so that's the day we were planning our family memorial. Irene wants to honor him in a place he loved. We were talking about Cascade Springs."

"Oh. That is a beautiful spot. And you're right. That was one of Wallace's favorite places on the ranch. He has a picture of it in his office here."

"The trick is, how do we move seven people up there safely this time of year, especially when two of them are elderly women? Irene and Lillian obviously can't snowshoe and I doubt they would be comfortable riding on the back of a snowmobile."

Annelise seemed to find that image amusing. "I don't know.

Your grandmother strikes me as someone who would be willing to do whatever was necessary."

Tate laughed. "Good point."

"The snow machine we use to groom trails would seat three or four people. You could split up and have some on the snowcat and some on snowmobiles."

"That might work."

"Or what about a sleigh?"

"The Angel's View doesn't have one, does it? I remember we did when I was a kid but I haven't noticed one while I've been kicking around this week. Unless it's in some outbuilding I haven't seen yet."

"No. Wallace sold it several years ago." She paused. "You could rent one! I have a friend whose husband has a big sleigh along with a team of Percherons to pull it. Nick does sleigh rides around the area for restaurants or the downtown businesses. He's as busy as everyone else with Christmas next week but I can see if he might be available sometime tomorrow."

A sleigh would solve everything, especially if it were big enough for his entire family to fit at the same time. "That would be terrific!"

"I'll text them right now to ask," Annie said. "What time were you thinking?"

"We are flexible, honestly. Whatever time works for his schedule, at this point."

She picked up her phone from the built-in desk in the kitchen and thumbed the screen for a moment. "Okay. I asked her. I'll let you know what she says."

"Thank you," he said. The words were hardly out when her phone pinged an almost instantaneous reply.

"That's her now." She read the text for a moment, then smiled. "Betsy says Nick is totally free tomorrow all day until about six, when he's doing a couple of private family parties."

Yet another relief off his mind. Annelise was going to solve all of his problems. "Why don't you share his contact with me and I'll give him a call to coordinate times? That way you don't have to be in the middle of it."

"Great idea."

"I'll go call him now," he said when his phone notified him of the incoming text from her. "Once more, you saved me unnecessary stress."

"I'm glad to help."

She was. He knew she meant it. Annelise liked helping others. He had seen her features glow the night before when she was telling him about her Etsy store, not only because she was helping her brother but also because she liked bringing comfort to the strangers who bought her blankets through her store.

By the time this visit to Angel's View was over, Tate was going to be deeply in her debt.

He headed back toward his office to make the call. As he walked through the great room, with its cheerful fire and the tree that put out its lovely pine scent, he heard singing that made him stop in his tracks.

It was the twins, putting on an impromptu concert apparently. They had an audience of two now, Irene and his great-aunt Lillian, who each held one of Irene's fluffy little dogs on her lap. They looked captivated by the children.

When the twins finished singing, the elderly women both clapped. "Oh, bravo. Bravo," Irene said.

"Tate! Hi, Tate!"

He was a little unnerved when Alice jumped up and hurried toward him, arms out for a hug.

"Um. Hi," he answered, hugging her back.

"I was looking and looking for you today," she told him.

"I'm right here."

"I know." She hugged him again as if she hadn't seen him in ages. Over her head, he caught Irene's raised eyebrow.

So much for his worries about Irene being annoyed by the children. She and Lillian both looked like they were completely enjoying themselves.

"Guess what? I like your grandma and your aunt Lillian," she informed him.

"Yeah. Me, too," Henry said. "They're funny."

Now it was his turn to raise an eyebrow. Though both had sharp senses of humor, that wasn't the first thing that came to mind about them. Lillian had built a fashion house from the ground up that was now worth millions and Irene had been at Wallace's side every step of the way as they built Sheridan International together.

"They can both be quite entertaining," he said.

The women made matching scoffing noises. "Do you hear that, Lil?" Irene said.

"Yes. We're just like a barrel of monkeys, aren't we?"

He had to smile. "You are, my dears. You just hide it well, usually. What are you playing?"

"We were playing Go Fish and I won," Alice announced.

"Congratulations."

"You can play, if you want," Alice said. "You can be my partner. Sometimes that's what my auntie does."

Annelise was so sweet to these children. "I'm afraid I can't right now. Maybe we can catch a game another time. I have to go make a phone call. You have fun with my fun grandmother and great-aunt."

The children's giggles followed him down the hall. It was a lovely sound, he had to admit.

12

"AND PLEASE, JESUS, BLESS THAT SANTA WILL help our daddy come home for Christmas. Amen."

At Alice's earnest prayer, Annie opened her eyes with a sigh, peering down at the girl who knelt beside her bed.

No matter how many times she told the twins their dad wasn't going to make it home before the holidays, Alice and Henry clung tightly to the hope that some miracle would happen.

"Amen," she said, opting not to have the same argument again tonight.

What would be the point? They wouldn't listen to her and she was too exhausted, anyway—and still had to clean up the mess she had left in the kitchen after dinner, prep for the next day's meals and try to sew some of the blankets she had promised to the Family Connection.

"Good night, darlings," she said, kissing each one on the forehead, then slipping out of the room.

The twins were two little bundles of energy during the day. Fortunately, that usually left them quick to fall asleep at night.

She waited a few moments until she could be certain they were asleep. When their breathing was even and their eyes closed, she returned to the kitchen to clean up from dinner.

Her first foray into being a personal chef hadn't gone badly. All of the Sheridans seemed to enjoy the chicken cordon bleu and her lemon raspberry cake had definitely been a hit.

She wished she had an assistant in the kitchen who could clean the dishes, though. She definitely wasn't looking forward to that part.

When she walked into the kitchen a moment later, she stopped and stared. All the counters were empty of dishes and Brie was loading the last pieces of cutlery into the dishwasher.

"Oh," Annie exclaimed. "You weren't supposed to clean up! That's my job. I'm sorry. I was just putting my niece and nephew to sleep."

Brie gave her a smile over her shoulder. "I didn't mind. I like washing up. You might not believe this, but I actually spent six months washing dishes at a Michelin-starred restaurant on the coast of Spain."

"Really?"

Brie shrugged. "I was seeing one of the sous chefs at the time and that was about the only way I could spend any time with him."

Annie couldn't imagine taking a job washing dishes in order to be closer to a man, but maybe he was fabulous in the...kitchen.

"I suppose that's one solution."

"The relationship broke up eventually. I was actually more

sorry about leaving the job than I was about leaving the guy, if you want the truth."

Annie stepped forward to dry the dishes draining in the sink.

"So, Annie McCade. What brings you back to the Angel's View Ranch?" Brie asked.

"It's a long story."

She explained about Cassie and the baby and about Wes and his propensity for bar fights.

"That stinks. What judge would sentence a single dad to be in jail over the holidays?"

"I think one who was tired of seeing him in her courtroom and wanted to shake some sense into his thick skull."

"When does he get out?"

"Probably about mid-January, according to his attorney."

"How are the kids doing with it all? It can't be easy on them."

"They seem to be okay. Other than they still seem to think Santa is going to deliver their father on Christmas morning."

Brie chuckled. "Do they think he's going to be wrapped up under the tree?"

"Maybe. Who knows what goes on inside the head of a six-year-old?"

"Do you remember when we were six? We both got bikes for Christmas and convinced my grandfather to let us ride them around inside the house."

Annie had completely forgotten that. The memory made her smile.

"It's so good to see you again," Brianna said after a moment. "Believe it or not, I've wondered about you over the years. Where you were, what you were up to. I should have tried to connect on social media. I'm embarrassed that I didn't."

"I could have reached out to you," Annie said. "I just assumed your time here was something you had put behind you.

No one would blame you for wanting to forget everything here after...after your father died."

Emotions flickered in the other woman's eyes. "You're right. That's what I tried to do. I never wanted to come back to the ranch. There were always too many memories of the summer when everything changed."

Brianna had never talked about what happened that day on the mountainside. All Annie knew was that Cole had fallen down a steep incline and Tate and Brie had to ride down for help.

She also knew her dearest friend had changed in an instant. The happy, cheerful, funny girl who went up the mountainside had disappeared. The Brie who came down had been a completely different person.

"Do you know you have new puppies in the barn?" Brie asked. "I helped the ranch foreman deliver them. It was amazing."

"Levi texted me earlier to let me and the twins know they had finally arrived. I took Henry and Alice down about an hour ago. They're in love."

"It's easy to love those puppies. I wish I could take every one of them back to the city with me but I'm afraid they probably wouldn't enjoy my one-bedroom apartment."

"Probably not."

"I'm tempted to try sneaking one in my suitcase, though."

"Thanks for the warning. If one goes missing, we'll know where to look."

Brie smiled and Annie had to smile back. She was tired and had so much to do, but right now she wanted to talk to this friend who had once been so very dear to her.

"The twins are busy coming up with names for them all."

"Except for She-Ra. The one with the white boots. I named that one."

Annie laughed. "I remember watching that show with you on Saturday mornings! Levi told me that was her name but he didn't tell me you picked it."

"It was an obvious choice, because of the boots. And because she was fierce."

"I love it," Annie said. She had so much to do right now but decided she could put everything on the backburner for a little while longer so she could catch up with an old friend. "Would you like some hot cocoa? I might even have some Baileys to add to it."

"I'll gladly take the hot chocolate, but without the Baileys, please. I'm sober these days, after a decade of bad decisions."

"How's that going for you?" she asked, truly interested in the answer.

"Hard every damn day."

Annie quickly heated the milk and melted the chocolate squares into it before pouring some into a mug and handing it over to Brie.

The other woman took a sip and gave a happy sigh. "Oh, that is too delicious."

Annie smiled, sipping at her own.

"Sugar is my lingering vice these days," Brie admitted. "I can't seem to quit that."

"So you spent six months working in a restaurant kitchen and you're currently clean and sober. What else have you been doing for the past twenty years?"

"How much time do you have?"

"Plenty for an old friend," Annie assured her. It was a blatant lie. Her to-do list was higher than the Christmas tree in the great room. Right now, she knew this was where she needed to be.

As a hotel concierge, she had become good at reading people. She sensed that Brie wanted to talk. Maybe she *needed* to.

Brie sipped again at her chocolate, her mouth suddenly flat and her eyes filled with regret. "I wish I could say I've spent my life feeding the hungry and comforting the sick. I can't. Mostly, I've been partying. More concerned with having a good time and twisting myself into knots to please whatever man I'm with than figuring out who I am or what I want out of life. Now I find myself approaching thirty without much to show for myself. Pretty pathetic, wouldn't you agree?"

"What would you like to be doing?"

Brie gave a rough-sounding laugh. "That's the irony of it. I've spent all this time trying to figure that out but the answer was right in front of me all along. I'd like to feed the hungry and comfort the sick. Or at least provide clean drinking water and build schoolhouses."

"The Sheridan Trust!"

Brie looked rueful. "I want to take over Tate's job now that he's moving to the corporate side of the family enterprises. But I've spent so much time burning bridges over the past decade, disappointing my family over and over again. Why would they ever trust me with something so important?"

Annie could hear the pain in her friend's voice and didn't know how to answer.

"Does Tate know that's what you want to do?" she finally asked.

Brie shook her head. "Every time I start to talk to him about it, I chicken out. He sees me as the family screwup. How can he think otherwise? I ran away with a guy when I was seventeen. I've been through rehab three times. I burned through every penny my family sent me and then some. Why should he ever trust me with the important work he's been doing? There is too much at stake."

Annie knew she should keep her mouth shut. None of this

was her business. She didn't know all the history between Brie and her family.

She did know what it was to see someone she loved in turmoil. Her brother was in deep pain and she felt helpless to pull him out of it. If she could help Brie, wasn't it worth the effort?

"You're probably right. Tate probably won't be able to trust you," she said softly. "At least not until you learn to forgive and trust yourself."

Brie gazed at her intently over her cocoa for a long moment, until Annie was certain she had gone too far. She should definitely have kept her mouth shut.

Finally, when she was about to excuse herself and escape to her room, Brie laughed. "You always were a smarty-pants, weren't you?"

"I was an insufferable know-it-all as a kid. At least that's what Wes always told me. It's funny but being a know-it-all actually came in really handy in my previous job as a hotel concierge."

Brie smiled and reached across the table to squeeze her fingers. "In this case, you're right. Absolutely right. I know it's me. I feel weighed down, like I'm constantly carting around all the things I've done and the hurt I've caused."

"Nobody can help you put those things down. You have to do it yourself."

"I know. I'm working on it." She smiled and squeezed Annie's fingers again. "I'm so glad you're here. I didn't realize how much I missed you until I saw you again. No matter what, we can't lose track of each other again, even after..." Her voice trailed off.

"After your family sells the Angel View?" Annie finished for her.

"Did Tate tell you Irene is planning to put it on the market?"

She nodded, trying not to show how the idea of that hurt.

"I'm sorry. It doesn't make financial sense to hold on to it for sentimental reasons when no one left will use it and love it like Wallace did."

"I'm sure the new owners will," Annie said.

"Yes. If it makes you feel any better, Wallace insisted on writing a conservation easement into his will. The land will never be developed. It will always be protected."

"That does help," Annie said.

"I hope you'll still talk to me after the family sells the Angel's View."

"Don't be silly. You are my oldest friend. My dearest friend, for the first ten years of my life. Nothing will change that."

Brie gave a watery smile. "I wish we had stayed in touch. I had forgotten until now how good I always felt around you."

"We've reconnected now." Annie smiled, thinking this was truly a gift for her this Christmas.

"Thank you for the cocoa and the advice."

"Any time. You know where to find me."

She gestured down the hall, where her sewing awaited.

13

TATE HAD BEEN LUCKY ENOUGH TO SEE SOME beautiful scenery in the years he had traveled around the world for the Sheridan Trust.

The awe-inspiring temples at Angkor Wat, the breathtaking savannas of Tanzania, the raw splendor of the Amazon rainforests.

He felt extraordinarily fortunate to have been able to experience so much in his lifetime. Still, Tate wasn't sure there was a prettier spot anywhere than the Angel's View Ranch. No wonder Wallace had loved it so much.

The mountains had a rosy glow in the morning light as he walked, breath puffing, from the ranch house to the road, then turned around to walk back.

One of the ranch dogs walked alongside him. Though he had asked Levi their names, he couldn't remember which was which. The smart cow dogs all looked similar, with the same merle coloring and piercing blue eyes.

This one was a friendly guy who came up frequently for pats and kept pace right alongside Tate.

He was glad of the company and the exercise.

Today the family would memorialize Wallace and say their final goodbyes to the man who had been so influential in all their lives.

The sleigh and horses would be there in a few hours to take his family up the hill to Cascade Springs, where Irene wanted to spread a few of Wallace's ashes overlooking the ranch.

Tate wasn't ready to say goodbye to the old man.

Wallace had not only been his grandfather but also his friend. As a teenager, he had welcomed his grandfather's advice and leaned on him for emotional support. After Tate's father died, Wallace had willingly stepped in to fill the role of father figure. He gave him advice about girls, he talked to him about college, he was always willing to lend an ear.

Tate considered it the greatest honor of his life that his grandfather had trusted him enough to let him take over running the family foundation.

He still had a hard time believing the man was gone. He kept thinking that any minute Wallace would come striding down the path from the barn, looking bluff and hearty and confident, as if he could conquer the world.

He had almost reached the house when he saw Annelise and the twins walking out of the private entrance of her apartment.

"Good morning," he called.

Annelise jumped but the twins turned with matching looks of delight.

"Tate! Hi, Tate!" Alice waved enthusiastically.

"Hey there. Where are you three off to?"

Annelise held up a plate. In the crook of her arm was a

thermos. "There were plenty of leftovers from breakfast so we were running some coffee and cinnamon rolls down to the barn for Bill and Levi."

"And we're going to see the puppies," Henry informed him, a gleeful note in his voice.

"That sounds fun. Here, let me take something."

She handed over the plate of cinnamon rolls, steaming in the cold morning.

"What time are the sleigh and driver coming?"

"Noon. A few more hours. I hope we make it back down the mountain before the storm hits."

She looked up at the sky, blue right now with only a few puffy high clouds. "You should be fine. I don't think it's supposed to start snowing until after dark."

"We'll be back in plenty of time, then."

"It's supposed to be a big one, though. By this time tomorrow, you probably wouldn't be able to make it up to Cascade Springs except on snowmobiles."

"The timing worked in our favor."

"It still will be cold. I'll send along plenty of blankets and I'm planning to have potato-and-ham soup and fresh rolls when you come back."

"That sounds delicious. Thank you."

"I wish we could ride in the sleigh," Henry said glumly.

"So do I," Alice said with a pout. "Why can't we?"

"I have explained this to you several times already this morning," Annelise said, a note of frustration in her voice. "They're not taking a sleigh ride for fun, like we do during the winter carnival. Tate and his family are traveling up to his grandfather's favorite place to say goodbye to him. It's like a funeral."

"I don't like funerals. They're sad," Henry said.

"We had a funeral for our mom last year," Alice told Tate. "I cried and cried. So did Henry."

"Only a little," her brother said defensively.

"It's okay if you cried a lot," Tate said. "When my father died, I was a lot older than you two and I feel like I cried for a whole year. I still miss him every single day."

Annelise gazed at him, her eyes soft with compassion.

"I miss my mom, too," Alice said, reaching up to grab his hand in shared sympathy.

"Yeah. Me, too," Henry said with a sigh.

Annelise threw her arm around the boy and hugged him close.

These poor children. What a tough thing for two little kids to have to face. He wanted to do something for them. Something more than a sleigh ride.

But he could at least start with that.

"How about this," Tate said. "When my family is all finished going up in the mountains for my grandfather's memorial, I'll talk to the driver about taking you two and your aunt for little ride, wherever you want to go."

Alice tugged at his hand with both of hers, eyes wide with astonishment. "Do you mean it? Can we?"

"Sure. Why not? I've hired the driver and sleigh for the entire afternoon. I don't imagine it will take us longer than an hour to drive up to the meadow, say a few words and then head back to the house. As long as the horses aren't too tired, you could easily go for a little ride around the ranch. Or farther, if you wanted."

Both children whooped and Alice dropped his hand long enough to clap both of hers together before she reached for his fingers again.

"Thank you," Annelise said, her voice as soft as her expression. "You just made their day. They've been moping all morning about not being able to go along with you all on the sleigh ride."

Tate loved her smile and had a sudden wish to do whatever necessary so she would look at him with that approving look all the time.

He wanted to kiss her right there, but that had become so commonplace he was used to it by now.

They reached the barn before he could do anything foolish, like act on the urge.

The twins were chattering with excitement as they headed into the barn.

The ranch manager was inside, scooping feed from a large container into a bucket.

"Hey, Levi," Henry exclaimed. "Guess what? We get to go on a sleigh ride today!" Henry exclaimed.

"Wow. That sounds fun."

"I know! Maybe you can come with us," Alice said.

"Maybe, but I'm pretty busy here right now, especially since we're getting ready for a big storm."

"We brought you some leftover cinnamon rolls and coffee," Annelise said.

His eyes lit up. "That's about the best news I've had all day. Thank you. I'm sure Bill will appreciate it when he comes in from feeding the cattle."

"Can we see the puppies?" Henry asked. "We've been waiting and waiting."

"You sure can. I checked on them a little while ago."

Puppies and sleigh rides. The kids looked as if they couldn't hold any more excitement. They were just about vibrating with joy as they hurried to the rear of the barn. Tate could tell Annelise was eager, too.

Inside the last stall, a whelping box contained the mama

dog lying on her side and what looked like about six or seven pups nursing.

"Oh, Luna," Annelise breathed. "Look at you, Little Mama. You're such a good girl."

The dog's tail slapped the blankets she was lying on.

"They're noisy," Henry exclaimed.

The puppies were nursing with little squeaks and grunts.

"Can we hold them?" Alice asked.

"Not yet," Levi said. "I told you that last night and it's still too early. We don't want to give them any of our sicknesses or germs. It's better to wait two or three weeks before you hold them much."

"That's forever!" she moaned.

"Yeah. We won't even be here then. We'll probably be at our house," Henry said.

"I'll make sure you get the chance to come back and visit," Annelise promised.

"I want to hold one really bad, but we don't want to make them sick," Alice said sadly.

Levi smiled at the kids. "That's right. Thanks for being good about this. I appreciate it and I know Luna does, too."

"And Santa," Henry said.

"Yes. Santa probably appreciates it, too."

They watched the puppies nurse for a few more moments, then Annelise finally spoke. "We should get back, kids. I need your help in the kitchen today, remember? We've got a whole bunch of potatoes to scrub."

"Yay! I love scrubbing potatoes!" Henry said.

"Me, too," Alice said.

Tate laughed. "That's not something you hear every day."

"What's not to love? Water, dirt, scrub brushes. It's got fun written all over it."

"Can we come see the puppies again tomorrow?" Henry asked the ranch manager.

Levi shrugged. "Probably, but we've got a pretty good storm coming tonight. You might need another sleigh ride to get through the snow down to the barn."

"Will the puppies be okay in the cold?" Alice looked worried.

"They're toasty as can be in here," Levi assured her. "I've got a warming light and plenty of blankets, plus their mom will make sure to keep them warm."

"Come on," Annelise told the twins again. "Tell Levi thanks for letting you take a look at them."

"Thanks, Levi," they chorused.

"You're welcome, kiddos. Thanks for the cinnamon rolls and the coffee. I might even leave some for Bill, if he's lucky."

As they walked back to the house, Tate was startled to realize he felt much better about the day.

Yes, Wallace was still gone. He would miss his grandfather deeply and from losing his father, he knew he always would. But the morning walk and the excursion with the twins to the barn had helped center him.

Wallace would have been thrilled about the new puppies, about new life coming to the ranch again.

Tate felt even better when Alice slipped her hand in his again as they walked back to the ranch house.

How had these twins wormed their way into his heart so easily? He was going to miss them when he returned to the city.

And Annelise.

He didn't like thinking about the void that would remain long after he left the Angel's View for good.

"Everybody ready?" Nick Dawson called back to them.

"Ready!" Alice and Henry shouted in unison.

"As we'll ever be," Annie said with a rueful smile.

Tate sat across from her beside Henry while Annie shared a blanket with Alice.

Annie leaned across to speak to him in a low voice.

"You know you really don't have to come with us. You've already been on a long sleigh ride today, after the memorial for your grandfather."

"Are you kidding? I've been looking forward to this since we talked about it this morning. This and seeing the puppies earlier will be the highlight in my whole day."

"Where are we going?" Henry asked, his eyes bright as the horses started off down the snow-covered driveway, tack jingling.

The twins really couldn't be more excited. They had talked of nothing else all day.

"Wherever you want," Nick said. "We can go anywhere there's snow."

"Can we go past our friend Lucy's house?" Alice asked.

"Is that Lucy Walker?" Nick asked. "I know where she lives."

"Yes. Right by our regular house," Henry said.

Nick considered. "That would actually be perfect. The main roads are mostly clear of snow so we can't take a sleigh on them but there's a good back road along the creek that has enough snow for the runners."

"Let me text her mom to make sure she's home," Annie said.

She pulled off her mittens, found her phone and quickly sent a message to Wendy.

"We're in luck," she said a moment later when she received an answering text. "Looks like Lucy and her brothers and sister are home. Wendy says she'll have them keep watch for us."

"Yay!" Alice said. "This is so much fun!"

Nick turned the team down the small road that led through

a wooded area along the creek toward Wes's house. In the summertime, Annie often rode one of the horses this way because she loved the quiet and serenity of it, with the creek bubbling beside the road and hawks soaring overhead.

"This is the most fun I ever had!" Henry said, just about bouncing out of his seat.

Tate grinned at the boy. "I'm glad you're having a good time."

"Me, too," Alice said, never one to let Henry have the last word.

It was fun, Annie had to admit. With the sleigh bells jingling, it was like something out of a movie.

Tate was so sweet with the twins. Seeing him now, laughing and joking with them, Annie couldn't believe she had ever worried about how he would handle having them at Angel's View temporarily.

She should have known he would be wonderful with them. He had been a kind boy who had grown into a good man, much like his father.

She supposed it was inevitable when the twins started singing "Jingle Bells," which they kept up the ten minutes it took them to reach their destination.

"There's Lucy's house!" Alice called, pointing ahead to the two-story farmhouse.

"They have a snowman," Henry said. "Can we build a snowman at your house, Tate?"

"Sure. I think we'll have enough snow tonight that you should have plenty for a whole army of snowmen, if you want."

"No. Just one. Or maybe two, so he has a girlfriend," Alice said.

As they passed by the Walkers' house, the twins were excited to see their friend Lucy standing on the porch, along with her two younger brothers and their older sister.

"Hi, Henry! Hi, Alice!" the children all called, waving frantically.

Henry and Alice waved like they were on a parade float, their features glowing with excitement.

"Now where?"

"Can we go past our house?" Henry asked.

"Maybe our dad is home from jail!"

Annie sighed at Alice's excited voice. "He's not, honey. You know that. He has to stay for three more weeks."

"Any reason you need to stop at Wes's house?" Nick asked from the driver's bench.

"Yes, actually, if you don't mind," Annie said quickly.

She had three boxes of material in the basement she intended to use for the Family Connection gift blankets.

"I have been storing a few things there that I need this weekend and was planning to come over later tonight, after dinner. This will save me a trip through the snow. Are you sure you don't mind?"

"Not at all. There's plenty of room back there for a few boxes."

It was a large sleigh, which the team of gorgeous big-boned dappled Percherons seemed to pull without much effort at all.

Wes's small farmhouse looked even more forlorn now that nobody lived in it, with no lights on inside and no cheerful Christmas decorations.

Seeing it like this, cold and empty, hurt her heart, especially because she knew what might have been. Her late sister-in-law had showed off all her mood boards, the designs she wanted during the renovation they were both excited about. When they bought the house three years ago, Cassie would call her constantly, asking her advice about this kind of tile or that flooring, as if Annie had answers for any of it.

She knew just how beautiful it could be, once Wes was able

to finally turn his attention away from his grief and back to where it needed to be, caring for his children.

The sidewalks had been shoveled and the driveway was clear, thanks to neighbors looking after the house and property in Wes's absence.

Many people in town wanted to help her brother, if only he would let them.

Nick pulled up in front of the house.

"This won't take long."

"Take your time," he answered. "Mack and Jerry will appreciate a coffee break."

"Horses don't drink coffee." Henry giggled.

"Do they?" Alice asked.

"No. I was just teasing," Nick said. He pulled out a thermos. "But I do. Seriously, take your time. It's fine."

"Can we go in and visit our house?" Alice asked.

Annie forced a smile, though she wanted to throw something. Darn her stupid brother all over again for putting them in this situation where his child had to ask if she could visit her own house.

"Yes, but we can't take long. We don't want to leave the horses and Mr. Dawson out here in the cold."

Tate stepped down first so he could lift down the children. He reached a hand up for her. Annie put her hand in his, glad she was wearing mittens and he had on gloves. She wasn't sure she would have much willpower, if he was touching her with bare skin.

Tate came with them as they headed up the walk. "I figured I could help you carry stuff back to the sleigh," he explained when she gave him a look of surprise.

"Thank you," she said, though she really didn't want him to see the state of the house. Still, it would save her a few trips, she supposed.

Though she hadn't brought a key along, she knew the code to the attached garage. She punched it in and then unlocked the door into the house with the extra key Wes kept hidden under a paint can on a utility shelf.

The place had that strange, musty smell of unused houses. She checked it a few times a week to make sure the pipes hadn't burst or anything. It always seemed so sad without inhabitants.

The twins ran into their bedrooms, which at least had carpeting, though the windows showed insulation where the trim was unfinished.

"You don't have to say anything," she muttered to Tate. "I know it's a mess."

"It's not as bad as you led me to think. It looks to me like it only needs some finish carpentry and a few coats of paint."

"And new floorboards and tile in the bathrooms and the carpet laid down in the bedrooms. I know. If he put in a few weeks of hard work, Wes could be done with the whole thing. I told you he's been in survival mode for the past year, though, trying to be a single dad while dealing with his own grief. I think finishing the renovations just felt like too much for him."

"Understandable."

He seemed very interested in walking through each room. Annie just wanted to find her fabric and leave this sad house.

"I've got a couple of boxes I've been storing in the basement."

Tate followed her down the uncarpeted stairs that she worried would give the children splinters.

Her boxes were stacked neatly in a corner of the utility room. "I need all four of those. If you take two, I can grab the other two. Do you think we can fit them on the sleigh?"

"Sure. There's plenty of room." He picked up three of them in a big stack, leaving her only one. "What are they?"

She sighed, not wanting to get into a long-winded explanation but not seeing any way around it.

"It's material for more blankets."

He sent her a surprised look over the top box. "I thought you said the other night that you were done with your holiday orders for your online store."

"I am. I'm done with my paid orders. I didn't tell you the rest of it, that I offered to make some for a charity in town. They're having a Christmas party next week. A friend of mine—Nick's wife, Betsy, actually—is the director. She asked me if I would make a few blankets for them to give away."

"What kind of organization?"

"It's called the Family Connection and offers services for any family in crisis. Foster families, families with members seriously ill or incarcerated, those who might be dealing with job loss or food insecurity. Really, any family that needs help."

"Sounds like a good cause."

"I made the commitment before I knew you and your family were coming for Christmas," she admitted.

"You mean before I roped you into cooking for us, in addition to watching over your niece and nephew and taking care of all your other jobs."

"I'll be fine," she said, though she wasn't at all sure of that.

"You're an amazing woman, Annie."

He gazed down at her with so much warmth she felt as if she wouldn't need any blanket when they were back in the sleigh.

She knew if she stayed here with him, she might do something foolish. Like throw the boxes into the air and jump into his arms. Instead, she turned abruptly and headed for the stairs.

When they reached the top, the twins were waiting for them.

"Tate, do you want to see my room?" Henry said. "I have a Thomas the Tank Engine train table with a whole track."

"You can see my bedroom, too," Alice said. "I have a tent on my bed that is my favorite color, which is purple."

"Sure thing. I can't miss that. Let's take a look." He set the boxes down beside the door.

"We should hurry, though," Annie said. "Remember, we can't keep the horses waiting too long in the cold."

"We can be quick," he said.

With a sigh, she set her box down atop his and followed them all down the hall, where he first dutifully admired Alice's purple bed tent and her full collection of Winnie the Pooh stuffed animals and then followed Henry to his room.

The bedrooms were mostly done at least, except for the finish carpentry and the carpet. They had remnants on the floor now.

"My dad made the bed," Henry said. "I helped him sand the corners by myself."

"That is really cool," he said, running his hand over the wood. "Look how smooth those corners are."

"I know," Henry said proudly.

The twins were completely enamored with Tate. Annie shouldn't have been surprised. Their father had been so absent from their lives over the past year. Even when he was with them, Wes was mostly going through the motions.

Was it any wonder they latched on to the first male to pay them the attention they should be getting from their own father?

She let them admire the bedrooms for a few more moments before she reminded the twins again that Nick was waiting for them.

"We're staying here Christmas Eve, though, right?" Alice asked.

Sometimes she felt like she was talking to a couple of snowmen, for all the attention they paid what she told them. "No," she said, trying for patience. "We talked about this. You're staying with me at Angel's View until after you go back to school."

"What about Santa?" Henry asked, his features suddenly distressed. "How will he know how to find us?"

"Santa is a smart guy," Tate said. "He's pretty good at figuring out that kind of thing."

"I guess if he sees you when you're sleeping and knows when you're awake, he knows *where* you're sleeping, too," Alice said thoughtfully.

"True enough." Tate smiled down at her and Annie let out a breath. Much more of this and she would be head over heels for the man.

If she wasn't already.

"We really do need to go," she said.

"Your aunt is right. Turn off all the lights in your room."

As they headed out through the garage again and she locked the house up in reverse, Annie took the time to remind herself of all the reasons why this ridiculous crush on Tate was never going anywhere.

Christmas would be here in a week and he would be leaving with his family soon after. It wouldn't be long after that before she would probably receive word that the sale of the Angel's View had gone through and she was out of a job.

Tate was like an impossible Christmas wish. He was fun to dream about but she was old enough to know that Christmas wishes didn't always come true.

14

HE COULDN'T SEEM TO GET THE IMAGE OF THAT half-finished renovation at Wes McCade's place out of his mind.

The kitchen in need of cabinet doors, the unpainted dry-wall mud, the unfinished woodwork.

God knows, it wasn't the worst conditions he'd ever seen for a family home. The furnace worked, the electricity had come on, the house had running water. By many standards, it was luxurious.

Still, he hated the idea of those sweet kids having to live in what was basically a shell of a house.

A dedicated crew could finish things up there in only a few days.

The thought continued to run through his head all after-noon and evening.

After dinner, as the snow began to fall harder outside, Lillian and Irene were in the mood to play poker and enlisted him and Brie to play with them.

While playing cards with a couple of octogenarian card-sharps wasn't exactly his favorite way to spend a winter evening, he was willing to make the sacrifice. It seemed to be helping Irene through her grief over the family saying its final goodbyes to Wallace, anyway.

The service really had been lovely, with each of them saying a few words about how Wallace had touched their lives. He had been moved by everything they said. Brie had sobbed quietly and even Catherine had shed a tear when Irene, mouth quivering, scattered a few ashes next to the river.

Wallace would have loved the memorial. He would have loved having them all here this holiday season in the place that had always been his refuge.

Tate had to admit, it was kind of cozy to be safe and warm by the fire while the storm outside grew in intensity.

Catherine and his mother and stepfather had decided to watch the latest Marvel movie in the media room instead of playing cards. He probably would have preferred that but had committed to poker and didn't want to leave them short a player.

Even as he tried to focus on the cards in front of him, his thoughts turned to Annelise and the twins again and again.

He had seen her briefly at dinner but then she and the twins had disappeared into her apartment.

What was he going to do about this growing attraction to her?

"Well, that's it for me," Irene said with a yawn when it wasn't yet ten. She set down her cards and rose to stretch. "It's past my bedtime."

"It's not even nine thirty," Brie exclaimed.

"I guess I just can't party like I used to," Irene said.

Brie sent Tate a sidelong glance that had him biting his lip, trying to picture their formidable grandmother dancing on tables and closing down the bar.

"Yes. I'm pretty tired, too," her sister said. "This is about as late as I can stay up these days. Why don't we leave the late-night shenanigans to you night owls?"

"I think I'm ready to settle in with a good book and listen to the storm," Irene said.

When Lillian stood, the two hooked arms, both of them stooped and wrinkled but still lovely.

"Thank you both for the game."

"Don't you find it funny that they've suddenly decided to leave now that we're starting to catch up to them?" Brie mused aloud, which made both women laugh.

"Pure coincidence," Irene said.

Brie made a disbelieving sound but didn't call her on it. Instead, his sister rose and kissed both women on the cheek. "Good night, both of you."

Irene hugged her. "It's been lovely to spend time with you," she said gruffly.

"Right back at you," Brie said.

After she stepped away, both women held their cheeks out for Tate to kiss. With an inward laugh, he stepped forward to oblige.

"Good night."

"Thank you for arranging everything so perfectly today," Irene said, her voice soft. "I cannot imagine a better way to send off your grandfather than to take a sleigh ride up to a place he loved."

He hugged her. She seemed more fragile than ever, like a precious glass angel atop a tree.

Losing Wallace had been hard enough. He didn't want to think about Irene's limited time with them.

"It really was a nice afternoon," Brie said after the two women walked down the hallway to their rooms. "It was hard to say goodbye to Grandpa but having everyone there helped. Almost like we were all sharing the burden of grief instead of having to carry it alone, you know?"

"I do."

"I mean, I'm still sad about losing him. Nothing will change that. Things will never be the same, of course. But today helped. The sleigh ride was exactly what Grandpa would have wanted."

Brie finished putting away the deck of cards and the poker chips and slid them in the game cabinet. "We've been here a day and a half and so far nobody seems to be dying of boredom."

"Except maybe Catherine."

"I don't think she's completely hating it. She seemed to have fun swimming in the heated pool earlier when it started to snow. It will help when Cousin Tom and his family arrive next week so she doesn't feel like she's the only young person here."

"Hey. We're young," Tate protested.

"We're not teenagers anymore," Brie pointed out.

"Thank the Lord. I hated being a teenager."

"Yeah. Not my best years, either," she said wryly.

It was the first time he had heard his sister joke about that difficult time in her life, when she had been depressed, angry, reacting to everything from a place of pain and loss.

"Anyway, Catherine is good friends with Tom's oldest, Quinn. She'll enjoy the company."

"I hope so."

Angel's View really was a cozy place to be during a blizzard, with the Christmas tree that the twins had decorated twinkling merrily against the storm.

He hoped the power stayed on. He had memories when he was a kid of the power going out at least once during the holidays nearly every time they stayed here. Wallace had tried to explain it was something about the power grid but he hadn't paid much attention.

He wished now that he had listened better to his grandfather—about power grids and so much more.

"That wind seems to be picking up," Brie said after a moment.

Without his attention focused on the card play, the sound of the storm seemed magnified. The wind moaned outside, strong enough to occasionally rattle the windows.

Brie took a sip of her drink, which he knew was sparkling water with a splash of cranberry and mint.

"So. I don't mean to nag but I was wondering if you had the chance to talk to Mom yet?"

He sighed. "I tried. As everyone was putting on their coats and scarves to load up the sleigh this afternoon, I had a minute with her and asked if everything was all right. I told her we were both worried about her because she had been so quiet since she arrived."

"What did she say?"

"Basically nothing. She deflected and assured me she is perfectly fine, simply taking longer than she would like to recover from the flu she had after Thanksgiving."

"Do you think she's telling the truth?"

"It's a plausible explanation."

"You're just going to leave it at that?"

"What do you want me to do? Interrogate her? Tie her to a chair, shine a light in her eyes and bring out the rubber hose?"

"I should have known you wouldn't take this seriously."

He regretted his flippant answer as soon as he said it. He always seemed to say the wrong thing around Brie.

"I am not saying I don't share your concerns," he said carefully. "If something is wrong, she will tell us in her own time. She's a grown woman. She has no obligation to confide in her adult children if she doesn't want to. If we keep pushing her, she's only going to be angry with both of us for worrying too much."

"You're right. I know you're right. I seem to be hypersensitive these days."

That was understandable, given her tumultuous history with the family.

"I think I'll go work out. Maybe I can go hit the bike in the gym. I haven't done enough physical exercise today."

"You mean trying to keep your head in the game with Irene and Lillian doesn't count?"

She managed a smile, though still seemed upset about their mother.

Tate sat for a moment in the great room after she left, enjoying the flickering flames in the fireplace and the increasing storm.

He had plenty of things he should be doing right now, including his endless study of the inner workings of Sheridan International.

He decided to follow his aunt Lillian's advice. Quarterly reports wouldn't be so bad if he were settled in by the fire in his room while the storm blew outside.

He decided to refill his water first and was refreshing his glass in the kitchen when he heard a sound behind him.

He turned around in time to see Annelise draw up short when she spotted him.

"Oh. I'm sorry," she said. "I thought everyone had gone to their rooms."

"I'm headed that way but needed hydration." He held up his glass.

"Same." She held up a water bottle of her own. "My refrigerator tends to run out of ice quickly when the kids are here, for some reason. Maybe because they can't have a drink of water without filling it up to the brim with ice. I was going to borrow some from the freezer in here."

"Let me help you."

"That's not necessary," she started to object.

"I know. I'd like to, though. It's a little thing when you've been doing a hundred things to help me."

After a moment, she handed over her water bottle and he used the scoop inside the freezer ice bin to fill it for her. "Do you use the filtered water from the refrigerator?"

"Yes. Thank you."

When her bottle was full, he handed it back for her to screw on the cap.

"Thank you."

"You're welcome." Tate gestured out the window. "Quite a storm we're having. I keep thinking the power is going to go out any minute now."

"Oh, don't say that," she exclaimed. "I still have work to do tonight."

"You're sewing blankets now? You put in a long day already. Dinner was delicious, by the way. I didn't have a chance to tell you. I came into the kitchen after we finished but you had disappeared."

She shrugged. "The twins were tired after their big day on the sleigh ride. Any time they actually want to sleep, I am never going to argue."

"You should rest, too, while you have the chance."

"Christmas will be over before we know it. It's no big deal to burn the midnight oil for a few weeks while your family is here. I only hope I can stay awake to sew for another hour tonight."

She held up her water bottle. "This should help. Sometimes when I think I'm exhausted, I'm really only dehydrated."

"You're amazing."

She made a face. "Because I know a little about dehydration? That's not any great epiphany. It's common knowledge."

"I meant how you're doing everything. Taking care of the twins, cooking for all of us, sewing blankets for needy families. You're bringing Christmas joy to all kinds of people."

Her cheeks seemed to turn pink. "Not so amazing. I'm just really good at overcommitting myself."

He smiled, fiercely drawn to her. He didn't want to say good night to her, he found. Not yet. "Would it help you stay awake if I keep you company?"

Her eyes widened at his offer. "Keep me…company?"

He didn't want her to say no. The offer was more for his benefit than hers.

"I'll admit I have absolutely zero skills when it comes to sewing. Less than zero. But I'll be happy to help you cut out fabric or I'm handy with a tape measure. If all else fails, I can tell you stories about places I've visited or some of the projects we've done. Or I can always read my quarterly reports to you."

She laughed. "That would be guaranteed to put me to sleep. I would sleep-sew and probably sew my sleeve to my project."

"Is that a thing?"

"I may or may not have done it before," she admitted ruefully.

"There you go. You need me to help you avoid that sort of catastrophe."

"While I do appreciate the offer, why do I get the feeling you are only looking for an excuse to avoid reading those quarterly reports?"

She definitely had him pegged. "Is it that obvious?" he asked.

She didn't answer, only gave him a pointed look.

"Okay. You're right. I'm having a hard time wrapping my head around all the Sheridan International stuff."

"I'm sure you are. That's because you're happy where you are at the Sheridan Trust."

He didn't want to hear that right now, mostly because he knew she was absolutely right.

To his relief, she didn't wait for an answer.

"I would be glad to have company," she said instead. "I'm afraid it won't be very exciting for you. Binding blankets is my least-favorite part of the process but it has to be done."

He was quite certain he wouldn't find her work at all boring. He was fascinated by everything about Annelise McCade.

Yeah. He had it bad.

"Great. Let me grab my laptop and I'll be there shortly."

After retrieving his laptop, he headed back to her apartment. She had left it open ajar for him, so he wouldn't wake the kids by knocking, he assumed.

He poked his head inside. "Are you sure I won't be bothering you?"

She shook her head. "Come in. You might even be able to find a place to sit, around all the toys and fabric."

He did, in a plump, comfortable easy chair that gave him a great view of her bent over her sewing machine.

Her little Christmas tree twinkled merrily in the corner and the entire apartment smelled like heaven, of cinnamon and clove and vanilla.

He inhaled deeply. "What smells so good in here?" *Besides you*, he wanted to add but didn't.

She pointed at the tree. "Isn't it delicious? The kids and I baked cinnamon ornaments this morning."

He looked closer at the tree and saw them now, little brown ornaments shaped like stars and hearts that looked as if they were made out of gingerbread.

"Wow. There's a memory. I made those once in school when I was a boy. Maybe second or third grade. I had completely forgotten all about that until right this moment. I made a little snowman that my mom kept on the tree for years. She might still hang it, for all I know."

"You don't visit your mother's house during the holidays?"

"I haven't been home for the holidays in years, if you want the truth. I'm usually in the middle of something overseas. The Sheridan Trust relies on a lot of volunteers who tend to have more time off during the holidays so it's always been a good time to schedule projects."

"That makes sense."

"What about you? Where do you usually spend the holidays?"

"My most memorable holidays were spent here at the ranch, until my parents divorced. Divorce makes it hard for kids to build consistent traditions. My parents split custody for the holidays so I spent half of them here and half in California. After I went off to school and could choose for myself, I came here most of the time. My mom had my stepdad and her new family and I figured I saw her more often the rest of the year, since we were geographically closer. My dad didn't really have anyone else, plus Wes was here, too."

"I'm sorry about your dad. I always liked him."

He wasn't sure if he had said that to her since he had been back, a grave oversight on his part.

She looked surprised. "Thanks. I miss him a lot, especially this time of year."

She pointed at his laptop. "If you want to get to your reports, I promise, it wouldn't bother me."

"They can wait," he said.

He wondered if she picked up his underlying message, that he would much rather talk to her than read financial reports.

He was beginning to realize he would rather talk to her than do just about anything else.

Annelise was a delight. She had a funny sense of humor and listened better than just about anyone he knew.

While she sewed, they talked about their respective apartments in the Bay Area, about her journey to becoming a hotel concierge, about some of the memorable projects he had worked on and the people he had met.

Through it all, awareness seemed to swirl between them, much like the snow outside the window. He found himself trying to make her laugh, simply because the sound of it enchanted him. And he liked watching her work, the little frown of concentration when she was working her machine and the skillful way she turned the fabric.

It was soothing, in a way he couldn't have explained.

Finally, she snipped some thread on a blanket in contrasting shades of purple and lavender, turned off her sewing machine and stood. "I think that's all my eyes can handle tonight."

He glanced at his watch and saw it was a few minutes past midnight. He had been here for more than two hours.

"I didn't realize it was so late. I'm sorry to keep you up so late."

"Don't be sorry. You helped me more than I can say. I probably would have quit an hour ago if you hadn't been here keeping me awake."

He stood as well. "I'm not sure that's a good thing. You need your sleep."

"Yes. But I have a deadline, too. Right now I need to focus on that. Six blankets down, twenty-four to go."

"How are you going to make it before next week?"

"Don't remind me. I can't stress about that right now. I just have to put my head down and keep going."

"It's very sweet of you to go to all this trouble for children you don't even know."

She came around the machine to fold the blanket carefully and set it on the small stack next to her sofa. "I might not know them personally, but I know the pain they're going through. I've seen it firsthand this past year in my niece and

nephew, who have struggled with grades, with emotional out-
bursts, with just about everything since their mother died."

"It must help them so much to have the stability you're
providing."

"I hope so, but I'm not so sure." She paused. "I have to
help, Tate. Not just because of Alice and Henry but because
I know how it feels to be lost and alone."

He sensed that wasn't something she shared with many
people and felt deeply honored. "When was that?"

She shrugged, not meeting his gaze. "After my parents' divorce,
I was a mess. For several years as a young teen, I struggled with
depression and anxiety. I hated leaving my father when my mother
took me to California. I wanted my family back and would have
given anything to be able to stay here at Angel's View."

"I'm sorry. That must have been so hard." He didn't want
to think of the sweet girl she had been, trying to find her way.

"I got through it eventually. Time heals and all that. I understand that a blanket isn't much in the scheme of things,
but if it provides comfort and warmth to even one struggling
child or teen, it's worth all the effort."

Her words brought back a memory he had shoved deep into
the recesses of his subconscious.

"I think I understand what you mean. After my dad's death,
Aunt Lillian sewed me a throw pillow out of one of his favorite
shirts. I took that thing to college and never told my roommates
what it meant to me. Even as a young adult, there were times I
just wanted to hold it close to me after a bad day or whenever I
ached to tell him something. It helped me feel closer to him."

"Your dad was a pretty amazing person."

"So was yours."

"I guess we're lucky to have had them as long as we did,
weren't we?"

"It still doesn't take the sting away, though."

She shook her head a little sadly and he couldn't help himself. He did what he had been aching to do since nearly the moment he arrived at the ranch. He reached out and pulled her into his arms.

With a sigh, she wrapped her arms around him as if she had been waiting just for this.

It seemed totally natural, the most comfortable thing in the world. She fit against him as if she were made just for that spot. He closed his eyes, aware of a quiet, seductive peace stealing over him.

She was perfect.

And perfect for him.

He held her for a long time while the wind howled outside and all the stress and chaos inside him seemed to quiet.

She smelled better than her cinnamon ornaments. Of peaches and vanilla and other things that made his mouth water.

The awareness that had been simmering inside him for days seemed to flare, until he couldn't focus on anything else.

He wanted to kiss her. Desperately. At the same time, he didn't want to ruin this moment, when he felt more at peace than he had since his grandfather died.

He might have been able to withstand the impulse if she hadn't lifted her face to his.

"Tate."

She said his name. Only that. But it was enough. He lowered his mouth to hers and felt a shiver ripple over her shoulders.

He couldn't tell if she was momentarily shocked or appalled, until she made a soft little sound in her throat, tightened her arms around his waist and kissed him back with a warmth and tenderness that made him catch his breath.

15

ANNIE COULDN'T QUITE BELIEVE THIS WAS happening.

What a surreal evening it had been. She never would have expected Tate to offer his company while she sewed. Nor would she have expected to have enjoyed having him in her apartment so much, chatting with him about everything under the sun while the storm raged outside.

Now, here she was in his arms, his mouth firm on hers and every part of her aching for him.

Was this really happening or was it some exhaustion-fueled dream?

Annie wasn't quite sure. It seemed too unbelievable. Tate Sheridan, the man she had woven all those ridiculous dreams about when she was an impressionable girl, was actually kissing her.

This was too vivid, too intoxicating, to be a dream. She

could feel the heat of him, could smell that delicious masculine, slightly exotic scent of sandalwood and sage, could taste his mouth, warm, delicious with a hint of berries and mint.

She shouldn't be doing this, for a hundred different reasons—chief among them was the overwhelming certainty that she would end up with her heart shredded like old rags when he and his family sold the Angel's View and he returned to his life as a high-powered bazillionaire.

What did she have to offer a man like him?

She was an ordinary woman who loved her family and whose superpower was making other people comfortable. She wasn't some glamorous, beautiful heiress who could offer him fascinating conversation and valuable connections.

She knew all that. Still she kissed him. How could she resist, when he kissed her like she was something dear and precious to him?

She might have stayed there all night if the sound of a small whimper didn't intrude into the delicious haze surrounding them. A whimper that was coming from the twins' bedroom.

Reality crashed in.

She was standing in her living room, kissing Tate Sheridan. What in the name of Kris Kringle was she thinking?

She wasn't thinking at all, she realized. She had thrown all warning to the wind and had acted purely on visceral need, driven by silly daydreams about this man that she should have left behind in childhood.

The time for that was past. She had to focus on the twins right now. When she heard the whimper again, she managed to untangle her mouth from his and take a slight step back, her breath coming fast and shallowly.

"I... That sounds like Alice. She must be having a bad dream. I need to..." She gestured weakly toward the twins' door.

"Right."

Tate ran a hand through his hair, a stunned look on his face.

Annie rushed into the bedroom, where she found Alice making those tiny mewling sounds in her sleep.

Her niece moved her head restlessly on the pillow. "Mommy. Don't go, Mommy. Please don't go. I'm sorry. I'll be good, I promise."

Annie's heart shattered all over again. The poor thing. Most of the time, the twins seemed to be coping as well as could be expected to losing their mother.

Every once in a while, their raw grief seemed to creep out of the depths of their subconscious.

Pushing the memory of that disastrous kiss away for now, Annie sat on the edge of the bed. This wasn't the first time one or the other of the twins had had a bad dream while she was caring for them. She was never quite sure what to do. Should she wake them up to the reality of all they had lost or let them sleep and try to ease past the misery of the dream to something better?

When Alice whimpered again, Annie knew she had to do something. She ran a hand over the hair she had braided after her bath, fighting the urge to pull her niece into her arms. "Don't cry, sweetheart. I'm here."

"Mommy?" Alice's eyes fluttered open slightly.

"No. It's Auntie. I've got you, honey."

To Annie's relief, Alice closed her eyes, and after a moment, her breathing started to slow again.

Annie stayed there, hand on Alice's shoulder, for a long time. The quiet sadness of the moment, comforting this grieving child, brought her to her senses more than jumping into cold Holly Creek might have.

She should not have kissed Tate Sheridan, even if he had been her childhood crush and maybe her idea as an adult of the perfect man.

He was her de facto boss, now that his grandfather was gone. More than that, he was completely out of her reach. He was the head of a powerful conglomerate of companies, part of an extraordinarily wealthy, respected family.

What did she have? A family in crisis, her brother in jail and a couple of twins who needed her right now to be completely focused on them.

And a job that she would probably lose within weeks, when his grandmother sold the ranch.

If she wasn't careful, she would wind up making a fool of herself over him, falling hard and ending up bruised and broken.

He would only be here another week, until Christmas was over. She only had to keep her distance until then, then they would both go their separate ways.

Unfortunately, it was impossible to completely keep her distance. They lived under the same roof and she was cooking for his family twice a day.

How was she going to face him? Simple. She would be casual, would act as if the kiss was only one of those things.

It wasn't as if it had just rocked her to the core. Much.

She had only a few hours before she had to get up the next day to make breakfast. And while Tate had talked about only fixing lunch and dinner for the Sheridans, saying his family could take care of their own breakfasts, people might be looking for something a little more substantial than yogurt and fruit with the storm on the horizon. She had found there was something about a winter storm that seemed to make people ravenous, as if they were following some biological need to hibernate.

She had some thick-cut bacon in the refrigerator and also could make blueberry pancakes.

How on earth would she be able to sleep after that kiss? She had no idea but she had to at least try.

After making sure the twins were asleep, Annie walked back to the living to turn off the lights.

To her utter shock, Tate was once more sitting in her favorite easy chair, looking big and gorgeous and delectable.

He frowned when she walked out. "Is Alice okay?"

He had stayed because he was worried about her niece, not for any other reason, she told herself.

"Yes. She never really woke up, was mostly mumbling in her sleep. She seems to have settled now."

"Is that normal? For her to have nightmares like that?"

"I don't know if it's normal or not. They both have them but it's not that often. Maybe once a week or so, they will wake up. They've been through a lot of chaos and trauma this year."

"Those poor kids."

She couldn't help but be touched by his concern for her family. "Once in a while, I think the sadness bubbles over into their dreams."

"It can't be easy, having their father in jail."

"Right. I'm hoping things will settle down for all of them once my brother gets his act together and steps up to take responsibility for his children."

He was quiet, gazing into the fire. "Wes must have loved his wife very much."

"Yes."

Wes and Cassie had fallen for each other in high school. They had only ever looked at each other once they started dating.

"She was everything to him," she said. "My heart aches for his loss. I'm not unfeeling. I know he grieves. But Cassie is gone and we can't change that. Meanwhile, there are two children in there who need him right now. He needs to suck it up and grieve on his own time. The rest of his time and energy should be devoted to caring for those children."

She didn't realize how passionate she must sound until she saw Tate's surprised expression.

She winced. "You probably think I sound like an unfeeling monster."

"Hardly. I think you sound like an aunt fighting to look after the best interests of her niece and nephew."

"Someone has to," she said quietly. The approval in his voice warmed her and she wanted to bask in the glow. She couldn't do that. Hadn't she just been telling herself all the reasons she couldn't bask in anything?

"Listen, Tate. About earlier…"

He sighed and reached for her hand. He twisted his fingers through hers. "I'm sorry, Annelise. I should never have kissed you. The moment I did, I knew it was wrong but I couldn't seem to stop."

She had just been telling herself the same thing. Why did hearing it from him hurt so much?

"It's late, we're both tired and it's been a strange few days. We probably should both forget this ever happened."

"Right," he murmured, looking as if he didn't believe that was quite possible.

She didn't either, but they had to try.

"Thank you again for keeping me awake," Annie said briskly. "Because of you, I was able to finish a whole extra blanket than I would otherwise."

"Glad I could be of service," he said, his voice dry.

He rose, looking as if he wanted to say something more. He gazed at her for a long moment, then finally seemed to shake his head.

"Good night, Annelise."

She tried not to shiver at the way he said her name. "Good night."

After she closed the door behind him, Annie shut off the lights on the Christmas tree, then headed into her bedroom.

She knew that kiss, stirring and emotional, would haunt her dreams.

How would she be able to keep her growing feelings for him under control?

She never thought she would be able to admit this, but maybe it was a good thing the Sheridans were selling Angel's View. She easily could see herself falling for Tate and then having to go through the motions for potentially *years*, pretending she didn't care. If the Sheridans kept the ranch, Tate would probably one day bring a wife, children, to the ranch. Annie wasn't quite sure she was strong enough for that.

One more week. She could make it through Christmas, then he would be gone. She only had to focus on her niece and nephew, her work and the blankets she had agreed to make for the Family Connection.

No problem at all, right?

Nothing made a six-year-old child more excited than waking up to find the world buried in snow.

"Snow day! Snow day!" Alice, still in her pajamas, jumped around Annie's living room doing a little dance of celebration. Outside, the storm still raged, flinging giant flakes against the window.

All Annie could see was white and more white. She had peeked out earlier and found at least two feet of new snow, possibly more.

"Yay! We don't have to go to school!" Henry dabbed, his new favorite dance move since learning it from his friends.

Annie smiled and rubbed his head. "Hate to break it to you,

honey, but today is Sunday. You wouldn't have had school, anyway."

His shoulders slumped. "That's totally not fair! Why does it always have to snow on the weekend? We're never gonna have a snow day!"

Annie chuckled. She remembered lamenting the same thing when she was his age. School was rarely canceled in this part of Wyoming, mainly because Star Valley had a well-organized battalion of plows that always seemed to be able to clear away the white stuff for the buses to run, along with individuals who had tractors to plow the secondary streets.

"Why do you want a snow day? You love school! Anyway, you only have four days left of school before you're out for two whole weeks. Plus your last day is the Christmas program you've been so excited to perform."

That seemed to cheer him up. Or at least distract him with anticipation for something else.

"Oh, yeah. Our program is Thursday. And then Santa is coming in only two more sleeps after that!"

Annie had so much to do before then. She tried not to panic. One minute at a time. Right now she was focusing on breakfast for the Sheridans.

She took the twins into the main kitchen with her and was busy mixing pancake batter when Brie came down wearing a thick fuchsia robe and UGG slippers. She went straight for the coffee maker.

"Have you seen how much snow fell last night? Holy sh…" Her voice trailed off with a guilty look at the twins. "Holy cow," she quickly amended.

Annie wanted to assure her Alice and Henry had heard much worse from their father but decided not to.

"It's a *ton* of snow but we don't even get a snow day because it's already Sunday," Alice informed her in an aggrieved tone. "Do you think that's fair?"

"Um. No."

Annie realized this might be the first time Brianna was formally interacting with the twins. She might have seen them in passing but Annie didn't think they had ever talked.

"Brie, have you met my niece and nephew?"

"I don't believe so. Hi."

"Henry, Alice, this is my good friend Brianna. She was my very best friend when I was a little girl and lived here with your dad and your grandparents."

"Hi, Brianna. I'm six years old and go to first grade," Alice said. "I like your robe. Pink is one of my two favorite colors."

Brie looked down at her robe. She didn't seem to know what to say. "Um. Thanks. I like yours, too."

"I have a bathrobe, too. Mine is purple. That's my other favorite color."

"Brianna is Tate's sister," Annie told them.

Both twins seemed thrilled to know that information. Apparently, that was all they needed to hear before completely warming to Brianna.

"Tate is our friend," Henry told her. "He took us on a sleigh ride yesterday."

"So I hear."

"Do you think we have enough snow to build another snowman now?" Alice asked.

"Honey, I think you could build a whole village of snowmen," Brianna told her.

The twins continued chattering about the storm and Christmas and their program. Finally Brianna seemed to clue in that they really didn't need much of an audience. They were happy talking to each other. She made her way over to Annie.

"Can I help you with breakfast?"

"I'm not doing much. Some bacon and blueberry pancakes, in case people want them. You can wash and cut up some fruit, if you'd like. There are cantaloupes, pineapple and strawberries."

"Yum."

She made pancakes for the twins, shaped like Mickey Mouse, with chocolate chips instead of blueberries for eyes.

They tucked in with delight.

"I'm a little surprised you don't have kids of your own," Brie said when Annie returned to the stove to turn the bacon. "You always talked about having two girls and a boy. I even remember what you were going to name them. Cheyenne, Katie and Justin, wasn't it?"

"Your memory is apparently better than mine. I have no recollection of that."

Annie did know she missed the ten-year-old girl she had once been, full of hope and anticipation for the future.

"Do you still want kids?" Brie asked.

"I don't know if that's in the cards for me."

"Why not? No special someone in the picture?"

Annie shook her head. "Not currently. I had a long-term engagement until about a year ago to an attorney but we broke things off after I moved here to help out my brother."

"Long-distance relationships can be tough."

Annie gave a mirthless laugh. "Agreed. So can discovering the man you're on the brink of merging your life with is a selfish jerk who doesn't understand grief, loss or family responsibilities."

Brie looked startled. "Sounds like you had a lucky escape."

"Good thing I figured that out so I didn't waste three more years hoping I could turn him into something he wasn't," she said dryly.

Brie laughed and hugged her. "I have missed you, Annie. I had no idea how much."

She completely agreed. How lucky she was to rediscover an old friend for Christmas.

"What about you? Any current relationships on your end?"

"Not currently. I told you, I'm swearing off men and I meant it. I'll see your selfish attorney and raise you about a half dozen asses. I've had a string of disasters over the years. I seem to go for men who are emotionally unavailable, unstable or worse. I've had some doozies. I finally decided when the last one put thousands of dollars of debt on one of my credit cards that I should probably figure out why I keep picking gorgeous losers, time after time."

"Did you come up with an answer?"

"When I do, I'll let you know," Brie said with a laugh as she continued cutting up the cantaloupe.

A moment later, there was a knock on the back door and a bundled-up and snow-covered Levi walked in.

"Look, kids," Annie said with a teasing smile. "It's the abominable snowman!"

"Grrr." Levi held up his arms like Frankenstein's monster and advanced into the room.

"No, it's not." Alice giggled. "It's only Levi."

"You're traipsing snow everywhere," Annie chided.

"Sorry. I just came in to see if I could grab some coffee for Bill. The coffee maker down at the bunkhouse is on the fritz. We've got a full day of shoveling ahead of us and you know what a bear he can be without the juice."

"Yes. I do know."

She found a thermos in the cupboard and poured some from the coffee maker. "Do you want some bacon? It's almost done."

"Do you have enough?"

"More than enough. I bought out the grocery store in town."

She would have to arrange another grocery delivery before Christmas. She added it to her mental list.

"How about a couple slices for me and a couple for Bill?"

She drained the bacon onto paper towels and then slipped a few pieces into a bag for him along with some toast and two bananas and handed it all over to him.

"Thanks, Annie. That will definitely hit the spot while we're shoveling."

"You're welcome."

"How are the puppies this morning?" Brie asked him.

"They're good. Cute as can be," he answered. "When the snow lets up, you need to come visit them. They're staying nice and warm. They're all mostly eating, sleeping and pooping right now."

"Sounds like plenty of guys I've dated," Brie said, which made Levi break into a wide smile.

"You obviously haven't been dating the right guys."

"Exactly what I was just telling Annie," she said.

For one unguarded moment when Brie's back was turned, Annie thought Levi looked at the other woman with an expression she could only describe as hungry.

Really? Levi and Brie?

Annie frowned, not completely comfortable with the idea. Levi had dealt with a broken heart once already. He was still dealing with it. Every time he and his ex traded custody of their son, she knew the pain felt just as fresh.

He didn't need to fall for a woman who had just said she was taking a break from men.

Not her business, she told herself as she added a couple of napkins to the bag. Brie and Levi were both adults. It was nothing to her how they looked at each other.

Anyway, she was probably imagining things.

"Thanks for the fuel." Levi held up the bag and the thermos.

"You're welcome."

"Bye, kids. Annie. Ms. Sheridan."

"Be safe," Annie told him.

He nodded and headed back out into the cold.

Brie was the first to speak after he left. "So. You and Levi. Is that something?"

She thought of the kiss she had shared with Brie's brother the night before, the one that had kept her tossing and turning all night long. "Um. No."

"Is there a reason why not? Just curious. I mean, he's hot in a sexy cowboy kind of way and you're both here alone most of the time."

Annie made a face. "He's become a good friend over the past year since I've been back, but that's it. He feels the same way. There is no spark between us."

Unlike with your brother, she wanted to add. With Tate, there were enough embers to start the whole house on fire.

Something in Brie's expression made Annie's gaze sharpen. Was *Brie* interested in Levi?

On the one hand, she thought the two of them would be terrific together. She was enough of a romantic that she loved when two people she cared about found each other.

On the other, she didn't want to see either of them get their heart broken. "Levi is a good guy. A really good guy."

Brie was quiet for a minute. "I think I'm beginning to see that. He was so sweet when Luna was having her pups."

"He's great with horses. An amazing trainer."

"He said he was divorced and has a kid. What's the story there?"

"You should ask him." Annie didn't feel right gossiping about a friend. But if Brie was seriously interested in him, she should probably know a little background.

"I know he married young and they had a son together. He's from Montana and worked on a ranch there until he got divorced. His ex-wife lives in Jackson Hole with her new husband, who is older and made a lot of money selling a tech company."

"What's his son's name?"

"Tanner."

"Tanner is my friend," Henry said, refilling his glass of water at the sink.

Annie smiled. Tate's son was a few years older than the twins but whenever he came to the ranch for Levi's visitation, she tried to arrange playdates. They always had a great time together.

"Tanner is a great kid," she said to Brie after Henry returned to watch TV with his sister. "He comes every other weekend to stay with Levi. The mother, on the other hand, is a real piece of work."

"How so?"

So much for not gossiping. Here she was spilling everything. Annie was annoyed with herself. On the other hand, she wasn't saying anything about Levi, only about the mother of his son.

"I shouldn't have said that. I'm sure she's very nice in some social circumstances," she said. "But she makes things so tough on Levi, who is doing his best to be a good dad. For instance, this is supposed to be Tanner's year to spend Christmas with Levi. He had all kinds of fun things planned, especially after we found out the twins would be here, too. A few weeks ago, his ex dropped a bomb and told him she had last-minute booked a big getaway in the Caribbean for the holidays. When Levi got upset about it, she acted like *she* was the injured party and he was being unreasonable, even though this is the second year in a row he won't be with his son at Christmas. I only know because I happened to be in the barn when she called."

"That's tough."

"He's a good guy," Annie said again. "He just…doesn't need more drama in his life, you know?"

Brie sighed again. "Yeah. I get it. Warning duly noted."

"That wasn't a warning!" Annie exclaimed. "I didn't mean that. I was only telling you some of what lies beneath his smiles and good humor."

"I appreciate that. Thanks."

Brie gave another pensive look out the window where Levi was riding the tractor now, shoveling some of the heavy snow out of the driveway, then turned away.

Annie wished she had kept her mouth shut about the whole thing.

16

"SO WHAT IF IT'S SNOWING? WHY DOES THAT have to mean we can't go skiing today? Correct me if I'm wrong, but don't you need snow for skiing?"

Tate tried not to roll his eyes at Catherine. She might be fifteen but sometimes she acted about as emotionally mature as Henry and Alice. Maybe even less so.

"Yes," he said patiently. "You definitely need snow. But you also need to be able to drive to the ski resort. It's an hour away through a treacherous winding canyon along the river, which is currently closed to all traffic. Even if we wanted to brave the storm to make it there, we can't, unless you want to drive about four hours out of the way."

"So what are we supposed to do all day? This place is the *worst*. I knew it was going to be lame here but I didn't expect to be trapped in a freaking snowstorm. It's like *The Shining* all over again."

"There are a hundred things we can do." Pamela gave her daughter a chastising look across the breakfast table.

Tate didn't miss the circles under his mother's eyes or the way her skin seemed stretched over her bones.

What was going on with her? And why wouldn't she tell him or Brie?

"No way are there a hundred things to do. There are like five," Catherine muttered.

"We can watch another movie. Your grandfather has a huge collection, plus the house has all the streaming services."

"With crappy internet that will probably get worse in the storm."

Pamela's patience sounded like it was beginning to fray. "You could swim or sit in the hot tub. You could play a game with your grandmother and Great-Aunt Lillian. You could bake cookies. If all else fails, you could go back out in the snow with your brother and help him shovel."

Tate was pretty sure she would nix that idea in a hurry.

He glanced through the doorway of the dining room to the kitchen, where he could see Annie washing dishes. The idea that had been brewing since the moment he woke after a restless night to find several feet of snow seemed to wriggle its way to the forefront.

He couldn't shake the image of an exhausted Annie, working at her sewing machine until her eyes crossed.

"Or we could help someone else."

Catherine did her patented eye roll, with all the drama he might have expected from Alice. "Why is that your answer to every single problem in the world?"

"Because it's a good one," Stan said mildly. "The world would be a much better place if more people thought about others first before themselves."

Tate gave his stepfather a grateful look. The man was wise

on so many levels. Stan was a good guy who had always treated all of them with respect and love. What more could Tate want for his mother?

"What did you have in mind?" Pamela asked, her eyes more engaged than he had seen since she arrived at the ranch.

He looked at Catherine, who was slouched in her chair with her arms crossed defensively. "You're always wanting to go with me on one of the projects for the Sheridan Trust, right?"

His baby sister had been begging him to take her along since she was around the twins' age.

Circumstances had never quite aligned. Either the timing didn't work out with her schedule or Pamela and Stan deemed the location too unstable for a young sheltered girl who could be kidnapped or worse.

Knowing the work they did in communities with great needs could be life-changing for the volunteers and would be certain to help Catherine lose any sense of entitlement, he had promised he would take her the next summer. He had been looking for an appropriate project when Wallace died unexpectedly.

Now that probably wouldn't happen, since he was leaving the work to someone else.

Tate pushed away the sadness that always hit him at the thought. Now who was acting entitled?

"I was thinking we could maybe help someone closer to home."

"I'm not mucking out horse stables," Catherine warned. "Mom and Dad make me do that at home in exchange for riding lessons."

"It's not the horse stables. Maybe we build to that," he said with a grin.

"Then what?" she asked.

He glanced through the doorway at Annelise, who wiped a soapy hand across her forehead.

"Annelise," he called. "Would you mind coming in here for a second."

She looked up, startled and a little wary, but wiped her hands on her apron and walked into the dining room.

"Does somebody need more pancakes?"

"No," Pamela told her. "Everything has been so delicious. Thank you for all your hard work."

"You're welcome," she said. "It's really my pleasure."

He appreciated that she didn't point out that his mother had hardly eaten anything for breakfast or for any of the other meals Annelise had served since she arrived.

"Annelise. Tell them what you've been doing."

She blinked. "Right now, washing dishes."

"I'm not talking about right now. I'm talking about what you've been doing at night. The blankets you're making for families in crisis."

She sent him a suspicious look. "Why? Is there a problem? Is my sewing machine making too much noise?"

"No," he assured her quickly. "Because I think it's a great thing you're doing and I thought they should know."

"Yes, dear. Tell us. What sort of blankets?" Irene asked.

Annelise shifted, clearly uncomfortable with having all the combined force of the Sheridans turning their attention to her. "It might be easier if I grab one to show you. I find it's hard to explain how comforting they are unless you can touch one and feel the weight of it."

She hurried away to her rooms but returned in a moment carrying the lavender-and-purple one she had been working on the night before.

"Oh, how lovely," his aunt Lillian exclaimed. "May I see?"

Annelise handed it over to Lillian, who ran her experienced hand over the fabric.

"That is wonderful. Feel that, Irene."

Irene did the same, running her hand over the soft blanket.

"I have an online store where I sew and personalize these ultrasoft blankets for people. They're great for babies, new mothers, older people, people undergoing medical treatment, etc."

"It's heavenly," Pamela said when Irene handed the blanket to her. "What a perfect thing on a stormy day like today."

"I find they're a real comfort item," Annelise said. "When the rest of the world feels dark and scary, you can always cuddle up under a blanket and things feel better for a moment. That's why I volunteered to sew thirty of them for a local group that serves families in crisis."

"Thirty?" Irene exclaimed. "My word!"

"In my defense, this was before I knew your family was coming to Angel's View for Christmas. I thought I would have plenty of time to sew them in the evenings, around my other responsibilities."

"As you would have, before you ended up having to cook for the lot of us," Irene said.

Annelise looked embarrassed. "It will be fine. The party where they will be given out isn't until Tuesday night. That gives me nearly three days to finish them."

"How many more do you have to make?" Pamela asked.

"She has six done," Tate said. "Counting that one that she finished after midnight last night."

"They are lovely, my dear," Lillian said. "Your stitches are perfect.

"Thank you."

"And if anyone would know about stitches, it's Lillian London," Irene said.

Tate could see Annelise's eyes flare as she suddenly connected the dots. "Lillian London. The fashion designer. Is that you?"

His great-aunt smiled. "Guilty."

Annelise looked completely astonished by that revelation, so shocked that Tate almost smiled. He sometimes forgot his beloved aunt Lillian was formidable in her own right, with a fashion house in San Francisco and another in New York City.

"Oh, my word. I had no idea."

"I'm retired now and have turned most things over to my capable team. But retired or not, I know good work. And yours is very good. What a wonderful project. Almost makes me want to get out my old sewing machine."

"I was hoping you would say that." Tate stepped forward. "I was thinking since we're all snowed in, anyway and can't do much except shovel snow, we all could pitch in and help Annie with her project."

"Except I suck at sewing," Catherine pointed out. "We had to sew these cooling bandannas once at summer camp a few years ago and this total mean girl named Chelsea said she thought her cat could do a better job than I did."

"I only have one sewing machine," Annelise said, still looking as if she was trying to process what was happening. "That could be a problem."

"Maybe. But there are other things we could do to help you. Catherine, for instance, could possibly help entertain the twins today and keep them out of your hair while you sew."

"You want me to babysit a couple of little kids?"

"It's for a good cause. And they're pretty funny, too. I'm sure they'd love to watch a holiday movie with you and maybe play some of your more kid-friendly video games. If the snow stops, you might even be able to walk down to the barn to see the new puppies."

She shrugged. "Sure. I guess. That could be fun."

"I might not be able to sew like I used to," Lillian said, "but I'm still pretty good with a pair of scissors, if you have material that needs to be cut."

"And don't worry a thing about lunch or dinner," Pamela said. "Brie and I can handle that."

This was exactly what Tate had hoped would happen, that his family would get into the spirit of the giving season and rally behind the project to take some of the burden from Annelise's shoulders.

She looked completely overwhelmed. And not entirely enthusiastic, he realized.

"This is so very kind of you all. Honestly, I'm grateful. But I wouldn't feel right about taking your help. You're here to relax for the holidays, not to help out someone foolish enough to overcommit."

His mother touched Annie's hand lightly. "Too often, I find the word *overcommit* has become synonymous with the holidays, hasn't it? In this case, you were doing a good thing and we threw a wrench in your plans by showing up and piling more work on you. It only seems right that we help you meet your commitment."

"We insist," Irene said. "Now the only thing you have to do is give us some guidance on where to start."

Annelise looked as if she still wanted to argue but was helpless in the face of his determined family.

"We want to help you," Tate pressed. "You know Wallace would have wanted this. He was the first one to use his gifts and his resources to help other people. You owe it to him to let us pitch in."

"No fair, using your grandfather to win an argument."

He only smiled, completely unrepentant. "Whatever it takes."

She shook her head, though he could see she was touched by his family's willingness to help. She gazed at him for a moment and he was once more standing in her small living room, his arms wrapped around her, her curves pressed against him and her mouth softening under his.

He couldn't get that kiss out of his head. Even shoveling snow all morning hadn't done the trick. Something told him he would be remembering the embrace for a very long time.

"What about you?" Irene asked. "You started this. How are you going to help out?"

He kissed the top of his grandmother's white curls, grateful beyond words that she and Wallace had taught him from a very early age to think about others. They might be richly blessed in material wealth but service and philanthropy was the most valuable thing they had ever given him, first instilling the lesson in their son and then in him.

"For now, I'm going to go out and keep clearing snow with Bill and Levi. I'll come back in when we're done and help out where I'm needed."

"You'd better," Annelise muttered. He wanted to kiss the top of her head, too, but managed to refrain. He could just imagine what the female relatives in his family would say if he did that.

Annie couldn't quite believe it but with the entire Sheridan—and London—team on board, she felt much less panicky about finishing before the Family Connection Christmas party.

Yes, it might be only three days away, but she was making serious progress. With Lillian and Irene cutting out fabric for her, she had already completed three blankets by noon and fully expected to do at least ten more by day's end, at this rate. That would bring her remaining blankets down to a much more manageable number.

They made the work fun, too. Lillian and Irene chattered as they helped cut out fabric, telling stories about parties they had attended in years past and the gowns they had worn and the men they had dated.

Annie was quickly coming to adore them. The two women had a zest for life she only hoped she could duplicate when she was their age. How wonderful that even though each had lost her husband, they had each other to help them through their remaining years.

Though it had been difficult, she had been able to put aside her reservations eventually. The combined force of the family was difficult to resist and they all seemed genuinely eager to help her out.

It would be so lovely to be able to relax and enjoy the rest of the holidays without this burden on her shoulders.

This had taught her a valuable lesson about not promising things she couldn't deliver. Yes, she had been doing a good thing by offering to donate the blankets. But she needed to temper her generosity with reality.

"So. Annelise," Lillian said while they were working. "Surely there's some handsome cowboy in your life."

She remembered Tate kissing her just about exactly where Lillian was sitting right now. "I'm afraid not. Unless you want to count my six-year-old nephew."

"A pretty girl like you ought to be fighting them off in droves."

She hated to argue with the great Lillian London but she had to. "I'm afraid not. I had a fiancé but we broke up when I moved back to Wyoming to help out my brother."

"What about since then?" Irene asked.

"Star Valley is not exactly a bachelor paradise. I date here and there but nothing serious. That's okay for me right now. I have other things that are more important than my love life."

"Your family," Irene said with an approving nod.

"That's right."

"I was sorry to hear about your father's death a few years ago. He was a good man. I know Wallace always respected him."

She managed a smile. "He was."

"And your brother. What's going on with him?"

"He's making a mess of his life right now but I have high hopes he'll be able to turn things around soon."

"Then will you go back to working for the Lancaster hotel company?" Lillian asked. "The matriarch of that family, Winnie Lancaster, is a friend of ours."

"Yes. Winnie's a character. We could put a good word in for you to make sure they hire you back," Irene said.

Annie smiled, enchanted by both of them. "Right now I'm focusing on finishing these blankets and then helping the twins make it through Christmas. I'll worry about the rest later."

"Smart girl," Irene said. "No need to borrow worry. That's what I always say."

"Do let us know when you need us to talk to Winnie, though," her sister said.

After a lunch of cold cut wraps, leftover potato-and-ham soup and a delicious broccoli salad that Tate's mother and stepfather put together, the afternoon passed in a flurry of sewing and binding.

She found something so fulfilling about working together with a group for a common purpose.

Annie checked on the twins a few times and found them having a great time with Tate's youngest sister, who actually seemed to be enjoying herself, as well. She hoped the twins were behaving themselves and not being too rambunctious.

She knew they had watched Christmas movies on the bigscreen TV in the media room and that Pamela had fixed them all a big batch of buttered popcorn, which they had devoured.

After lunch, the ferocious storm seemed to calm and the sun even peeked out from behind the clouds. She was busy sewing away when the twins came to the door and asked if they could go outside and play.

"You'll have to bundle up."

"I can help them put their snow clothes on," Catherine said.

"Cat says we can build a snowman bigger than the house! She says she'll help us!" Henry said.

"It might not be *quite* as big as the house," the teenager temporized.

"But still big, right?" Alice demanded.

"Sure thing, kiddo."

After Annie pulled out their snow pants, parkas, gloves, hats and boots, she helped the twins into them and sent them on their way with Catherine, who came out from her room similarly attired.

When she returned to her sewing machine, Annie found Lillian stifling a yawn, which sparked one from her sister.

"I caught that," she teased them.

"We're old ladies," Irene said. "All this excitement is a lot for us."

"You are far from old," she said. "But you both have worked so hard today. I can't believe you cut out the fabric for the rest of the blankets. I can take it from here, if you would both like to take a rest before dinnertime."

"I wouldn't mind a nap, to be honest," Irene said. "Being old stinks. I wish I had half the energy I did when I was your age."

"You've both been amazing today. Without you, I would never have made it."

"Even with us, it's going to be a push," Lillian warned.

"Yes, but you've given me hope. Thank you."

Irene looked at her sister, who was smothering another yawn. "Maybe we can take just a quick nap before dinner, then later tonight we could come in and help you with the binding."

"Sounds like a plan."

The sisters helped each other up, which she found adorable. She loved Wes and her two younger half brothers but sometimes wished she had a sister of her own.

Cassie had become the sister of her heart. Her death had been tragic on so many levels.

After Irene and Lillian left, Annie threw herself into the work, sewing feverishly until she had finished three more blankets.

Eyes burning and her shoulders tight, she finally lifted her head in time to see it was beginning to darken outside her window. With surprise, she realized it was nearly five. She had been sewing for three hours nonstop since Lillian and Irene had left her to it.

Surely the children hadn't been outside for three hours! They would have frostbite! She was the worst aunt ever. She hurried outside but couldn't see anything but a giant snowman. While he wasn't as big as the house, he had to be at least eight feet tall.

When she returned through the mudroom, she found the children's coats and snow pants hung up to dry and their boots lined up neatly.

She finally tracked them down in the media room, down the hall from the great room. They were curled up on pillows on the floor, watching what looked like the stop-action movie of *Rudolph the Red-Nosed Reindeer*. She was just in time to hear the song about misfit toys.

"This is my favorite part," Catherine was telling them. She was on pillows between them and seemed to be having a grand time. "I always wanted to take all those misfit toys home and give them a place to live in my bedroom."

"Me, too," Alice said, settling closer to the older girl, which warmed Annie's heart.

Tate had been a genius to suggest this, she thought. He had managed to distract his sister and keep the children occupied at the same time.

"Everything okay in here?" she asked.

Catherine looked up in surprise and paused the movie with

the remote. "We're fine. Just watching Rudolph and the misfit toys."

"Great show."

"Yeah. One of my favorites. I haven't watched it in a long time."

"Neither have I. Mind if I watch with you for a minute?"

"I thought you were sewing all the blankets," Henry said.

"I still need to sew more but we made good progress today. I need to rest my eyes for a minute."

"You can sit by me," Henry said.

"My bones are too tired for the floor. Why don't I take a recliner? You can sit with me if you want."

"Okay."

She settled into a recliner and her nephew hopped up next to her.

The warm room was so cozy and the chair so comfortable that Annie later didn't remember much of the show. She must have fallen asleep the moment Catherine started it again.

She awoke in a darkened room, lit only by the blue color of the screen.

No kids. No Catherine.

Only a man standing a few feet away, she realized in shock. Tate.

"Hey there," he murmured.

She scrambled up, embarrassed. "Where did everybody go?"

"Dinner is ready. I've been sent to wake you."

She sincerely hoped she hadn't been snoring.

She glanced at her watch and saw that she could only have been asleep for less than an hour.

"How embarrassing. I was only planning to watch the show with the twins for a minute but I must have fallen asleep. I should have set an alarm on my phone."

"I'm sorry I had to be the one to wake you. I wish I could

have let you sleep but I have a feeling you wouldn't have thanked me for that."

She yawned, blinking away the last vestiges of sleep. "You're right. I wouldn't have been happy. I have too much to do."

"Has my family's help made any difference at all or have we only complicated things for you?"

"They've been wonderful," she exclaimed. "If nothing else, Irene and Lillian have kept me laughing all day. Those two are quite the characters."

He smiled down at her, looking so male and gorgeous that she couldn't seem to look away.

He wasn't for her, Annie had to remind herself.

"They have big personalities, don't they?" he said. "It was great to see them staying busy. I think they probably got more out of today than you did."

"I highly doubt that. They both worked hard and saved me hours of work."

"I'm glad."

He smiled again and she was supremely conscious of her bedraggled state. The messy bun she had pulled her hair into was probably lopsided and falling out and she hadn't given a thought to her makeup all day long.

She had a tough time remembering any of that while Tate was gazing down at her with a warm light in his eyes that made her want to curl up and soak in it like one of the barn cats in a patch of sunlight.

"I think Irene and Lillian had a great time. They were more animated than I've seen them in a long time," he said.

"I'm so glad."

"It was also great to see my mother and Brie working together in the kitchen. When I walked in from shoveling, they were laughing about something and neither one could stop."

"Oh. That makes me happy."

"Same." He smiled and took her hand to pull her out of the chair. "When I suggested my family help you this morning, I was thinking about what you needed. It has occurred to me that *we* were the ones who needed it most. Pitching in to help you finish your blankets has probably benefited my family far more than you. Thank you."

He wanted to kiss her again.

She wasn't sure how she knew. Maybe the way his gaze flicked to her mouth, then away, the slight parting of his lips, the curling of his hands around hers.

She caught her breath, wanting him to tug her toward him. The memory of their kiss the night before seemed to swirl around them.

She almost leaned toward him but caught herself just in time.

She really had to do something about this. It had been one thing to have a crush on him when she was eleven. It was something else entirely now that she was an adult who knew nothing could ever come of this attraction but heartache.

Didn't she have enough stress in her life right now, trying to hold things together for the twins before Christmas?

She did not have time or energy to fight off this yearning for more than Tate would ever be able to give her.

"What did I do wrong?" he asked. "That's a pretty dark look you're giving me."

Oh, curse her expressive features. She was the worst poker player in the world. People could read any emotion on her face like a billboard.

"Sorry. I was, um, thinking about the storm and wondering if it's still going to be snowing on Tuesday when I have to take the blankets down to the Family Connection."

"I can take you, if you want. We can go in one of the ranch Suburbans, if you think there's enough room for all the blankets."

"I don't know. We're talking about thirty fluffy blankets, which take up a lot of real estate in a vehicle. I don't think I really considered the delivery dilemma when I volunteered to make them."

"We'll figure something out. We can make multiple trips or we can always take multiple vehicles. If we had an enclosed horse trailer, we could take that. Judging by the state of everything else I've seen around the ranch, I can guess Levi keeps them immaculate."

"You are so right. He scrubs them out every time he uses one of the horse trailers. That definitely might work. Thank you. I never would have thought of that."

He smiled. "I love to solve problems. I think I inherited that from my father. He used to love finding more practical or efficient ways to do things through the Sheridan Trust."

"I'm sure it's a skill that comes in handy."

"Yes."

He was definitely skilled in many ways. She remembered that kiss again and felt a shiver ripple over her shoulders.

"Um, you said dinner was ready, right? We should probably go. Everyone will be wondering what we're doing in here."

As soon as she said the words, Annie wished she hadn't, especially when his gaze sharpened. Again, he seemed to look down at her mouth and then back up. She could swear she saw a hunger in his eyes that matched her own, but maybe it was only the reflection of that blue screen.

"What would you like to be doing in here?" he murmured.

Heat flared between them and she swallowed hard.

That seemed to be enough of a signal for him. With a small groan, he pulled her toward him and his mouth met hers.

If she thought last night's kiss was exhilarating, this one left her literally weak in the knees.

"I've been thinking about that kiss all day, wondering if

your mouth could possibly be as sweet as I remembered," he murmured.

He kissed her again, his mouth slanting over hers again and again. "It's not, in case you were wondering. It's a hundred times sweeter."

Deep in her bones, she knew kissing him was a mistake. But how could she resist when his kiss felt so perfectly right, as if she had spent her entire life waiting for him to find her again?

She lost herself in the kiss, forgetting everything. His family. The twins. The dinner waiting for them. All the work she still had to do that night.

Nothing else seemed as important as this man, this moment, this fragile tenderness she could feel taking root in her heart.

She was falling for him. As she kissed him, Annie acknowledged the truth to herself. This wasn't simply a childish crush. This was far more than that. She was tumbling hard and fast for Tate Sheridan.

What was she going to do?

Nothing, she told herself. At least not right now. For now she was going to savor this stolen time with him. She would worry about the rest later.

She wasn't sure how long they kissed. Probably about ten seconds too long. She was vaguely aware of the door to the media room opening. Tate must have heard it, too, because he jerked his mouth away from hers an instant too late.

"What are you doing in here?"

Annie heard the suspicion in a certain six-year-old's voice and turned to find Henry standing in the doorway, eyes narrowed as he took in the scene.

"Um. Just talking," she managed, though her heart was beating loudly enough she was certain her nephew must be able to hear it from ten feet away.

"You were talking really close to each other."

"Um. Yes. I was, er, telling Tate a secret and I didn't want anybody else to hear it."

One beautiful thing about Henry, he seemed to take just about everything at face value. Alice would never have accepted such a lame excuse but Henry only grinned at both of them.

"Was it about a Christmas present? I love secrets at Christmas. Alice has a bunch. I know what she's getting you for Christmas. Want me to tell you?"

"No," she said quickly. "Secrets should stay secrets, unless the secret involves someone hurting someone else. Then you should always tell a grown-up."

"Is that what you were telling Tate? About a Christmas present?"

"No. Just an ordinary secret," he answered. "No big deal. Did you come in here for something?"

"Yeah. I was supposed to find you and tell you everyone is waiting for you for dinner."

"Right. Good. Thanks a lot."

"We'd better go, then." Though her heart was still racing and she was quite certain her breathing must sound ragged, Annie forced a smile and reached for Henry's hand.

She walked out with her nephew, telling herself she was glad of the interruption.

Somehow she didn't quite believe it.

17

SOMETHING WAS GOING ON BETWEEN HER brother and Annie McCade.

Brie wasn't sure how she knew, she just did. They had both come from the media room with weird overly casual expressions that didn't fool her for a moment.

She also thought Annie's lips looked suspiciously swollen.

Had they been kissing or arguing?

She couldn't quite tell.

Annie tried to excuse herself and the twins to eat in her room but Brie's mother and grandmother wouldn't hear of it.

"After today, you feel like one of the family," Irene had said. "Sit down, all three of you. I'm starving and can't wait to see what Brie and Pamela fixed for us."

It wasn't any glorious meal, only a simple creamy chicken pasta she and her mother had thrown together, but everyone seemed to find it delicious.

As for Tate and Annie, Brie noticed that while they were seated near each other, the two of them quite scrupulously avoided looking at each other.

They seemed to focus on everything but the other person. She noticed that even when passing the salad she had made, they were careful not to touch each other.

Brie found the whole thing fascinating. It seemed impossible but she couldn't deny the energy that seemed to spark between them like a live wire downed by the storm.

Nobody else seemed to overtly notice anything, though she did wonder if her grandmother wasn't looking between the two with a curious expression.

Because their lives had taken such different paths as adults, it occurred to Brie that she really didn't know much about her brother's romantic history.

She had met a few of his girlfriends over the years when she had dropped home for random visits or he had connected with her while they were both overseas. They had all been nice, she supposed, but nobody was particularly memorable and none of them had lasted more than a few months.

Tate hadn't seemed invested in any of those relationships. She had never felt this kind of vibe between him and any of those women.

Brie didn't quite know what to think about it. On the one hand, she adored Annie and would love to see her and Tate together.

On the other, she would hate to see her old friend hurt and Brie suspected Tate wasn't in a place right now where he could seriously pursue a relationship, as he navigated the process of taking over for Wallace.

Still, it was none of her business.

She glanced down the table at Levi Moran. Irene and Brie's mother had insisted on inviting both him and Bill for dinner to repay them for spending the day out in the storm clearing snow. It was what her grandfather would have done, she knew, but Brie still wasn't completely comfortable with it.

Bill, the grizzled old ranch hand she had met briefly, had declined but Levi was there, his hair still a little wet and curling on the ends where he must have showered before coming.

She didn't want to think about him in the shower.

He was chatting easily with both Catherine on one side and Lillian on the other about the horses at the ranch and about the interesting Scottish Highland breed of cattle Wallace had favored.

More than once, Levi would shift his attention in her direction and catch her looking at him. Brie could feel herself flush as she tried to focus again on the food. When was the last time a man had made her blush? She couldn't remember.

When dinner was over, she was the first to stand. "I'm cleaning up," she announced.

"You and your mother did all the work of cooking the food," Annie protested. "The kids and I can clean up."

"You can clear the table but I'm doing the washing up. I like to, remember?"

"I can help dry."

Levi stood up as well, tall and rangy, and she felt herself flush again. She wanted to tell him he had done enough that day, out on the tractor clearing the driveway several times, but she couldn't seem to find the words.

This was her own fault, she thought a few moments later when she found herself alone with him in the kitchen.

Maybe she shouldn't have insisted so strongly that she could take care of the dishes without help.

Everyone had retired to their rooms. Annie was probably going back to sew after she got the twins to bed. Brie's mother looked exhausted and Stanford had walked with her down the hallway. She thought Irene and Lillian might be in the great room chatting by the fire or maybe playing poker again. It was hard to tell with those two.

Fortunately, there weren't that many dishes. They could be done quickly, she told herself.

"I like your family," Levi informed her as he dried a large serving tray. "I'll be honest, I didn't think I would."

"Why not?" she asked, stung. "My family is great."

His features were pensive as he picked up the pan she had just washed. "I never understood why Wallace always came here by himself, month after month. I found it sad, if you want the truth. I figured the rest of his family thought they were all too good to get, er, *dirt* on their boots."

"It wasn't that. All of us loved this place. Most of my happiest memories were here when I was a girl. You should have seen some of the things Annie and I got up to."

She smiled at the memories. Singing karaoke, horribly off-key. Trying to teach one of the ranch dogs to dance on her hind legs. And of course horseback riding together. She had loved doing that any chance she had.

"So why did you stay away?"

She scrubbed hard at a piece of baked-on food on a pan. "All of my worst memories are here, too."

Or at least the one memory she couldn't bury.

"After my dad died, coming back here was painful for all of us. Except Wallace, I suppose. He wouldn't have kept coming back if he didn't find some kind of peace here. The rest of us only had pain. My mom and Tate and I came back the Christmas after my father was killed. It was so hard on us that my mother made some excuse the next year. And then she married Stan a year or so after that, so we stopped coming."

"Are you sorry you came back this year?" he asked.

"The jury is still out on that one," she said.

He nodded and she had the strangest feeling he didn't like her answer. He was quickly becoming the best part of coming back but she couldn't tell him that.

She opted to change the subject. "Annie told me this morning about your son, that he's spending Christmas with his mother. I can't imagine how tough that must be for you. I'm sorry."

"It sucks," he said after a moment. "Tanner and I were both looking forward to having some time together. How can a boring old dad compete with Christmas in the Caribbean, though?"

"You're not boring. Or old."

He must be a wonderful father. She wasn't sure how she knew. Judging how calm and sweet he had been with Luna when she was delivering her puppies, Brie could imagine Tate was a fun, caring father.

"What were you going to do with Tanner this year?"

He looked surprised at the question. The dishes were done but neither one of them seemed in a hurry to leave this quiet, peaceful room. He leaned against the kitchen island and she perched on one of the kitchen stools.

"Nothing that exciting. On Christmas Eve, we always grill steak and shrimp—that's his favorite—then we go to church service in town. Afterward, we come back to the ranch to play board games until he gets tired enough to fall asleep. Early Christmas morning, we usually go for a horseback ride in the snow. That's one of his favorite things."

"Where do you ride?"

"Just along the creek below the ranch. There are some river otters there, if you know where to look. He loves seeing those. Then we watch a movie or play with the things he got for Christmas. Nothing special."

"That sounds lovely," she said softly.

He gazed at her for a long moment, his expression unreadable. "We like it. I guess we can do all that next year. Although maybe his mother will take him somewhere else next year for Christmas. Maybe the Azores or Tahiti."

"I spent a Christmas in Tahiti. It was beautiful, but I mostly wanted to be home with my family."

She had never admitted that to anyone before. She had spent so many years running away, avoiding the disappointment and sadness she hated seeing on her mother's features.

Levi glanced at his watch. "I guess I'd better take off. Tanner was going to call tonight if he got the chance."

She was touched, thinking about Levi arranging his schedule around his son's phone call that might or might not come. She hoped for his sake it would.

"Thank you for your help with the dishes."

"You're welcome. Have a good night, Brianna."

She shivered a little when he said her name in that slight drawl.

His gaze sharpened and he looked down at her, a peculiar light in his blue eyes.

He wanted to kiss her.

She wasn't sure how she knew but it was clear in his expression.

She wanted that, too. She ached for it. She had been thinking about it since that first day in the barn with Luna.

She even leaned toward him and parted her lips.

To her dismay, he shoved on his Stetson and turned away. "Good night," he said again, more abruptly this time.

He turned and headed out of the house, leaving her filled with a deep yearning that mortified her.

"You can argue all you want but I'm coming with you."

Annie frowned at Tate, who stood outside the ranch crew

cab pickup truck with a deceptively mild expression on his features.

She had only seen him in passing over the past two days as she worked frantically to finish the blankets. His grandmother and aunt had helped her Monday, as well, with his sister and mother taking over the cooking for the family.

He had been right. Even with their help, finishing all the blankets and sewing on all the names had taken everything she had.

She was thrilled with the finished product, especially after Brie, Catherine and Pamela had volunteered to wrap them all. The three of them had done a marvelous job. The gifts looked like something out of a high-end boutique and she knew the children served by the Family Connection would be so thrilled with them.

She had to get them to the organization's office first, for the party that night. Apparently she was going to have to get past Tate to do it.

"I appreciate your offer, but it's really not necessary. I can do this on my own."

"I know you *can* but there's no reason you should. It took us a half hour to load them up without crinkling the gift bags. It's going to take at least that long on the other end to unload them."

She sighed. As hard as it was for her to admit, he was right. She could use help unloading them at the Family Connection office.

"I feel like your family has already done so much to help me with these. I hate to take you away from a day when you could be skiing with your sisters."

"I can ski with them another day during the holidays. I would rather be helping you."

How could she argue with that?

"Thank you," she said. In truth, she was grateful for his help and some part of her looked forward to spending time with him, even as she knew she shouldn't.

"Do you want to drive?" he asked.

She shrugged. "Go ahead. The seat is already set for you."

He held the door open for her and she climbed into the cab. She had to brush past him and tried not to be too obvious while she inhaled the scent of him.

"Where are we heading?" he asked as he drove down the long, winding driveway to the road.

"The south end of Star Valley. It's about twenty miles."

"Got it. Okay. You'll have to give me directions when we get closer."

"I will. It's not that far from the county jail. I was thinking about stopping for a moment while I'm there. Would you mind? It's visitation day at the jail and I missed last week."

The previous Tuesday seemed like a lifetime ago, when Tate had only just arrived the day before and the two of them worked together to decorate the house and then had driven up into the mountains with the twins to cut the big tree for the great room.

Had it only been a week? She could hardly remember what the Angel's View was like without him there.

When he and his family left, the place would feel so empty. She didn't even want to think about it.

She did know she wasn't doing a very good job of protecting her heart from him. With every day, he seemed to wriggle in deeper.

"I don't mind at all," he assured her. "We can swing past after we empty the trailer at the center."

"Thank you. I'm not sure when I'll have another chance to come for a visit while the kids are out of school for Christmas vacation."

"The kids can't go visit their dad?"

"They can. It's totally allowed, especially where he's only serving a short sentence in the jail. But Wes doesn't want them to see him while he's incarcerated so I've tried to honor his wishes."

"That's got to be tough on all three of them."

"It is. The kids miss him. He does talk on the phone to them a few times a week but it's not the same. But he's only in there another short while. If it were months or years, that would be a different story. I would take them, whether he wanted me to or not."

"Makes sense."

"Don't get me wrong. They know their father's in jail. If they didn't know, some of the kids at school would be sure to tell them. I don't know how other kids always seem to know those kinds of things but they somehow find out."

"Parents talk, I suppose."

"Yes. Unfortunately. Henry and Alice obviously know their father had to go to jail and I think they have some understanding of why. Still, Wes doesn't want them to actually see him there in his prison orange."

"I get it. I'm not sure I would, either. It's a tough situation for everybody."

"A few more weeks. I just have to keep holding on for that."

And pray that her brother would finally wake up and take charge of his life so that he didn't end up with a longer prison term, to be served in the state penitentiary in Rawlins.

They drove in comfortable silence for several moments, until Tate seemed to sigh as he looked out the windshield at the mountains.

"It's so beautiful here. I'm not sure why that keeps taking me by surprise. That's just breathtaking out there, with the sunshine gleaming on all that new snow, isn't it?"

"I guess there were reasons your grandfather loved the Angel's View so much."

He sent a sideways look across the vehicle. "I wish we could hang on to the ranch, Annie. You know that, right?"

There it was, the topic she absolutely did *not* want to discuss with him.

"I get it," she said. She might understand but it still hurt to think of it passing to new ownership.

"It doesn't make financial sense to keep paying the huge outlay to keep it running when none of us will use it as much as my grandfather did. The horses or the cattle have never brought in enough to justify the overhead."

"You don't have to explain anything to me, Tate. I get it."

He looked as if he wanted to argue but she was glad they were approaching the small town where the Family Connection was based.

"We're getting closer," she said. "You're going to turn left in about a half mile. You'll see a little drive-in restaurant and it's a redbrick building directly after that."

"Thanks."

He focused on driving the rest of the way, until he pulled into the driveway of the large building where the Family Connection offered respite babysitting, play groups and parent education classes.

Betsy Dawson, Nick's wife, came out of the building before Tate could turn off the engine.

Annie climbed out and the director rushed over to hug her. "You're so good to do this. Everyone is thrilled to have your gorgeous blankets to give the children. We have two or three other gifts for each child, small toys and books and things, but yours will definitely be the highlight of the night."

"I was happy to do it," she assured her friend. "Where do you want them?"

"My office for now. We were thinking we would pile a few of them under the tree but there are too many—they'll take up all the room. We'll figure it out, though."

For the next few moments, she, Tate and Betsy carried several loads each of blankets into the office and set them in neat rows. Annie had to admit, it was an impressive group of gifts.

"I wish you would reconsider and bring the twins to the party tonight. We have enough other gifts to give them. I would love for you to see all the thrilled faces of the children as they unwrap their blankets. That should be your reward after all your hard work."

Annie wasn't sorry. As wonderful as the Family Connection was and as wholeheartedly as she supported their mission, it didn't feel like the right decision for the twins right now. They were in a fragile state and didn't need another reminder that their family was in crisis.

Besides that, for the past two nights, she had basically abdicated her responsibility as temporary chef for Tate's family. She had dinner preparing already and wouldn't be done in time to go to the party.

"I'm sure it will be wonderful. You can take plenty of pictures and send them to me."

"I will. I still think it's too bad you won't be there. I know the children will be sorry they won't have the chance to thank you in person."

Annie didn't want to tell her friend that was another big reason she did not want to attend the party with the twins.

She didn't need praise or thanks. She had not made the blankets for that reason, only in hopes of making someone's day a little brighter.

Her parents had always taught her the act itself should be the reward for a kindness, not any reaction from the recipient.

"I'm sorry we won't be able to make it but I am sure it will be a wonderful success."

"With your help, it definitely will be," Betsy said. "The kids are going to love these. I can't thank you enough."

"You should know it was a team effort. I couldn't have done it without the help of the Sheridans. Everyone pitched in."

"Oh, how kind. You know, that doesn't surprise me a bit," Betsy said. "Wallace was always doing good things for the entire Star Valley."

"He was a good man," Annie agreed.

A few moments later, they said their goodbyes and Tate once more helped her into the pickup truck cab.

"Seems like a great organization," Tate said as he drove out of the parking lot.

"They try really hard to meet a wide variety of needs. Unfortunately, as is the case of most nonprofits, the needs usually outstrip available resources."

"I took Betsy's business card. Maybe the Sheridan Trust can help her pursue some grants or target specific donors who might be able to assist."

Oh, he was a dear man. She wondered if he knew just how similar he was to his grandfather and father. "Thank you. That means a lot, Tate."

How could she help falling for him? She closed her eyes, already feeling the faint warning of her impending heartache.

"Which way to the jail?" he asked. "You said it wasn't far."

"Are you sure you have time to stop? We could always return to the ranch and I could drive myself back."

"It's not a problem at all. Which way am I going?"

She gave him directions to the local jail that was about a mile away from the center.

When they reached the low-slung concrete building with its razor-wire recreation area, Tate pulled through a double parking space that provided enough room for the now-empty horse trailer.

He turned off the engine again but Annie made no move to climb out. She knew she needed to but it always took her a moment to gather her courage.

"You okay?" he finally asked.

"Not really," she admitted in a small voice. "It's so hard to see Wes behind bars. I know he deserves everything the judge threw at him. He needs to wake up and take care of his responsibilities. Nothing else was getting through to him so maybe a month in jail is the only way for that to sink in. Knowing that doesn't make it any easier to see him through a wall of glass."

"I'm sorry." He reached out and covered her fingers. "How can I help?"

She swallowed hard as emotions burned in her throat at his compassion.

"You've already done so much, bringing me here and of-fering moral support. Believe me. It helps."

He squeezed her hand. "I'll come in with you. I can at least wait in the reception area for you."

He walked around the truck and helped her out, then reached for her hand. To her astonishment, he held her hand the entire time they walked into the jail, offering comfort and encouragement just by his touch.

18

WITH EACH STEP TOWARD THE SQUAT, UGLY jail, Annelise seemed to withdraw inside herself.

It was a physical thing. Her steps became slower, more closely spaced, her shoulders hunched. Her hand in his began to tremble.

Tate could tell she hated this.

He wished he had some way to make it easier for her. Other than packing her back up into the truck and driving away with her, he didn't know how he could.

While he might want to spare her the ordeal, he was fairly certain she wouldn't appreciate that kind of Neanderthal tactics.

The inside of the jail reception area was a utilitarian space with rows of plastic chairs and a couple of nondescript lamps. Someone had at least tried to make it a little festive, with a small artificial tree in an unnatural dark green color taking up one corner and a bare string of blinking lights around the glass enclosure where a deputy sheriff watched them approach.

"Hey there, Miss Annie." The balding deputy sheriff with the huge handlebar mustache gave her a wide smile.

"Hi, Jim."

"We missed you last week."

"Yes. I had other commitments."

"Looks like you brought a friend with you today."

Tate was both touched and charmed to see her color a little. She quickly dropped the hand she had been holding.

"Yes. This is Tate Sheridan. Tate, this is Jim Harris."

The deputy looked him up and down. "Any relation to Wallace?"

"My grandfather," he answered.

"He was a good man," Deputy Harris said, his voice gruff. "I'll miss him. A group of us old-timers used to meet up when he was in town for breakfast at the café in Holly Springs. Wallace was always a character. He could keep us all laughing through breakfast clear up until they started serving lunch. I'm sorry for your loss."

"Thank you."

"I believe I also knew your father," the deputy said. "Well, he was a friend of a friend. But he and I and our mutual buddy once spent three or four days on a fishing trip together into the Wind Rivers, back in the day."

His father had loved fly-fishing. Some of Tate's most priceless memories involved fishing trips into the mountains around the ranch when they would come out for the summers.

His worst memory did, as well.

"Did you want to go back with Annie to see Wes? If you do, you'll have to fill out some paperwork and I'll have to make copies of your ID."

Tate was torn. While he sensed that Annelise would appreciate his support and he dearly wanted to offer it, he also suspected Wes might be uncomfortable, having him barge into their visit without advance notice.

He debated his options before shaking his head. "I'll wait out here so you can talk to your brother," he told her. "But if you need me, I'm happy to fill out the paperwork."

She sent him a grateful look that made him want to hug her.

"I'm okay," she assured him. "But thank you. You can wait here. I won't take long. Or you can go back out to the truck, if you prefer."

"Take as long as you need. I don't mind waiting. You're here. You might as well visit your brother as long as possible, especially if you won't be back before Christmas."

He could not imagine how grim it must be to spend the holidays incarcerated.

"Thanks. It won't be longer than fifteen minutes. That's the time limit. Anyway, Wes never has all that much to say."

She gave a smile that looked sad and nervous at the same time. She didn't bring a purse or bag inside with with her. The deputy opened the door for her and she walked through, where he assumed she would have to go through other security measures before meeting with Wes.

After she left, Tate stood for a moment, hating this feeling of helplessness.

He should be used to it by now after spending the past decade traveling to the most poverty-stricken or war-torn countries in the world with the Sheridan Trust.

With all his experience, it never grew easier. He wanted to sweep into any given situation and start solving all the problems.

The grim despair in Annie's expression haunted him. She was usually so upbeat, jumping right in to help him make the holidays brighter for his family. From decorating Christmas trees to housekeeping to cooking for them, she was always willing to help with a ready smile and a positive attitude.

Knowing that her attitude was only a thin, crackly veneer covering the deep worry she had for her family made him wish he could help in some significant way beyond driving her to deliver some blankets.

What could he do? He had no power in this situation. Wes McCade's own grief and poor choices had led to his incarceration, leaving his sister to pick up the pieces and care for his children.

He knew how grief could destroy a family. Hadn't he seen it firsthand? He remembered his mother after Cole's death, so lost and numb with sorrow. Pamela had become a shell of herself for at least a year after. She might have been there physically, still trying to be a mother to him and to Brie, but she had struggled hard with depression and grief.

Eventually, she had begun to heal. She had started engaging more with them, had begun smiling once more and seemed to start finding new reasons for joy.

A few years later, she had started seeing Stan, an old family friend.

Each of them had been severely impacted by the loss of Cole Sheridan.

Brie had only been eleven when he died and a teenager when Pamela remarried. She hadn't handled gaining a stepfather and eventually a half sister at all well. She had rebelled in the typical ways of teenagers. Alcohol, weed, staying out all night.

Tate had been at university the first time she had run away and his mother had called him frantically. He had gone looking for her and found her crashing with a guy nearly twice her age.

He knew she had been acting from a place of pain, just like

Annie's brother. That didn't excuse her out-of-control behavior but it did help explain it.

The next decade had been more of the same, with her disappearing for months at a time, then emerging when she needed money or was in trouble.

His heart had ached for that lost girl Brie had been, just as he was filled with admiration for all her hard work the past year to pull her life together.

It had been hard to watch from the outside, knowing he couldn't make it better for her.

Just as he could not erase the pain and loss endured by his family, he couldn't fix everything for Annie and her family.

Some tough roads just had to be walked.

"So, Tate Sheridan," the deputy sheriff said after taking a phone call. "You fish much like your grandpa and dad did?"

"A little," he said, feeling guilty for reasons he couldn't have explained. "It's been a few years."

"You won't find any better fishing on earth than along Holly Creek there where it winds through the Angel's View Ranch. It's blue ribbon trout habitat."

"It's a great resource." His grandfather used to talk so much about the horses he loved on the ranch that Tate tended to forget he also went there for the fishing.

"I don't think your grandpop was as happy anywhere else than he was on that stream with a fly rod in his hand."

"Unless it was when he was on horseback, riding through the mountains he loved."

Jim nodded his agreement. He glanced toward the door where Annelise had passed, then back at Tate.

"Shame about poor Wes McCade, isn't it? That guy just can't seem to catch a break."

"It's a sad situation," he agreed. "From what Annelise says, it sounds like things have gone from bad to worse for him."

"No doubt. Though he's bringing plenty of it on himself."

Tate rose and walked over closer to the bulletproof glass enclosure so the deputy didn't have to raise his voice to communicate with him. "In what way?"

"My house isn't far from his. My wife was friends with his wife and we still attend the same church. Everybody in Holly Creek wants to help the man. He's one of our own and we care about his family. But Wes is a stubborn son of a gun, just like his father was."

"So I understand."

"Don't know if you know this but he was in the middle of a big home renovation when Cassie died. The whole house is torn up."

"I've seen it."

"Then you know what I'm talking about. He's done some of the work but can't seem to finish. A few months back, before these latest legal troubles, a bunch of us neighbors and fellow parishioners offered to help him finish the house for the kids before Christmas. Kind of a gift from all of us who care about them. He turned down every offer of a helping hand. Pure stubbornness. That's all it was."

Tate gazed at the deputy as the seed of an idea that had been simmering in the back of his subconscious suddenly exploded into life.

It was impossible, wasn't it? Christmas was only four days away. It would take a miracle to pull it off and Tate hadn't believed in those in a long time. Not since he was fourteen, praying his heart out beside a mountain trail while trying frantically to find his father's motionless body far below.

He studied the sheriff. Despite working in a challenging job and having the appearance of a tough, wiry old-time lawman, Jim had kind eyes and a friendly smile.

And he liked to fly-fish and shoot the shit at the local café with the old-timers.

Tate was inclined to trust him.

"Any chance you might be willing to give me the names of those people who wanted to help Wes and his family?"

The deputy gave him a speculative look. "I can do better than that. I can hook you up with our pastor. He's a part-time contractor. I tease him that if he's not thumping the Bible, he's pounding nails."

Excitement coursed through Tate. A pastor with construction experience was exactly the sort of person he needed. Someone who knew the area and the people and might be willing to hook him up with those who could help.

"That would be terrific." He pulled out his phone to write down the contact number.

The deputy studied Tate, eyes narrowed. "I'll give it to you on one condition. I want in, whatever you're thinking about doing. In his better days, when he had his head on straight, Wes was a good man who would give you the shirt off his back in the middle of a blizzard like we had this weekend. I want to help and I know I'm not the only one in town."

"It's Christmas. It might be impossible. People are busy this time of year."

"Not too busy to reach out to one of our own who needs a helping hand," the deputy assured him.

Warmed by the man's surety, Tate outlined some of the thoughts that had been racing through his mind since the day he, Annelise and the twins had taken the sleigh ride and had walked through that sad shell of a house down the road from the Angel's View.

"That just might work, especially if you can get enough personnel, " Jim said. "It will be like one of those home renovation shows on TV my wife gets me watching, where they come in and fix things up, top to bottom, in only a few days."

"Right. The bones are there and, like you said, most of the hard work has already been done."

"I can get you twenty men from our church who have just been waiting for the chance to step in and help. We've got everything. Electricians, painters, carpenters, a guy who does flooring."

"Give me your pastor's name and I'll give him a call."

"You got it. His name is Patrick Morris. I've got his number right here, since he also acts as the jail chaplain."

He gave it to him and Tate dutifully entered it into his phone. Before dialing, he looked at the door back to the cells. "I need you to be my lookout and let me know when Annelise is done in there. After everything she's been through, I would really like this to be a Christmas surprise to her and the kids, too."

"You got it," the deputy said with a grin.

Tate returned to his seat, dialing the number as he went. This was what he did. He solved problems.

A sense of anticipation and excitement pushed out all the grim helplessness he had been feeling.

He might not be able to pull this off but he sure as hell planned to try.

19

S HE REALLY HATED THESE VISITS.

Annie sat in the uncomfortable visitor's chair waiting for a guard to let her brother in from his cell. Though Wes was considered a minimum-security prisoner, Annie still had to speak with him through glass. She couldn't touch him or hug him.

He wore the same orange jumpsuit as all the other jail prisoners but at least he wasn't in handcuffs. She was grateful for that.

The deputy led him into the visiting room.

"Fifteen minutes." The deputy, Paul Sanchez, nodded to Annie. They had gone to school together before she moved to California with her mother. He had been a bully in school, and as far as she could tell nothing had changed.

Wes looked gaunt compared to when he had come to jail, his features sharp and circles under his eyes.

He apparently hadn't shaved that day. Dark stubble covered his jawline, giving him a disreputable outlaw look.

He was still handsome, looking enough like their father to make her wish Scott was there to talk some sense into his son.

Those eyes were what always haunted her after these visits, filled with a complex mix of sorrow and guilt.

"Hi," she said, forcing a cheerful smile she was far from feeling. "I'm so sorry I missed last week. It's been a hectic time."

"You're not obligated to visit me."

His voice was hoarse and she got the feeling he didn't do much talking in here.

"I want to visit you. How else will you stay in touch with what Henry and Alice are doing?"

At the mention of his children, she saw his hard expression ease a little. "Are they staying out of trouble?"

"Not really," she admitted, which earned her a half smile. She would take it.

"What are they up to?"

"Mostly practicing for their program tomorrow. They couldn't be more excited for it. I had to promise them a hundred times that I'll video it so you can watch later."

"Thanks. I appreciate that."

His fingers tapped on the table, a habit he had picked up while in jail, probably to give his hands something to do instead of holding a whiskey bottle.

"How are things going with the Sheridans? I hear the whole family is back at the ranch for the holidays."

"How did you know that?"

Her brother was in the county lockup but somehow managed to hear all the gossip in town.

"My attorney stopped by to visit and mentioned it. She says that everyone in Holly Springs is buzzing about them."

"That's right. They've been here since last Friday. Tate has been here longer. They all went up to Cascade Springs on Saturday before the big storm to do a family memorial for Wallace. Tate said it was nice."

"That's good."

"That's the reason I couldn't stop last week. I was helping Tate get the house ready for his family."

To her dismay, she could feel her cheeks heat. Curse her complete lack of poker face. She had to hope her brother didn't notice. He probably wouldn't. He didn't seem to notice much these days.

"He was always a standup kind of guy."

"He's been really great about me having the twins staying at the house. Everyone has. Irene, Brie. Pamela. They've all been wonderful."

"You can always go back to our place, if it's an issue. Do they really need a live-in caretaker when the family is staying there?"

"Probably not. But right now the house does not have either a housekeeper or cook since Deb Garza retired, so I've been filling in."

"And taking care of the twins. That's a lot."

"I don't mind. It hasn't been bad. Actually, for the past three days, I've been mostly sewing."

She told him about the blankets she had offered to make for the Family Connection and how all the Sheridans had stepped in to help.

"Wow. That was kind of them."

"I never would have made it without them. But the blankets are all delivered and I'm back to fixing dinner tonight. We're having roast and baby potatoes."

"Sounds delicious. Just be careful you don't let the Sheridans take advantage of your willingness to help. That's my job," he said, his voice edged with dark humor.

Though she knew he was joking, his words still bothered her. "I don't know why you say things like that. No one is taking advantage of me. Tate is giving me a bonus to my already very competitive salary, which is going to your house fund."

"You should keep it. You've earned it."

"I'm saving it so you can fix the house. Not just for you but for Henry and Alice, too. You know I would do anything for the twins."

He sighed. "I don't have enough words to tell you how much I appreciate it."

"I hope so." She did not want to pour salt in his wounds but still wasn't sure he understood the gravity of the situation. "If I weren't here, they would have to go in foster care. You get that, right?"

"Yeah. Loud and clear."

Feeling bad for contributing to his clear self-disgust, she softened her tone. "How are you getting by?"

A muscle flexed in his jaw. "It's not all bad, believe it or not. I'm doing a lot of reading. A couple of the guys in here are decent company. Pastor Morris comes in a few times a week and I've been talking to him a lot."

"That's good."

His sigh was deep and heartfelt. "I hate being away from the twins, especially at Christmastime. I don't know how they'll ever forgive me."

The despair Annie heard in his voice was painful to hear. "Henry and Alice are fine. Don't you worry about them. They miss you and wish you could all be together but they're resilient. This is one Christmas. Better to be without you for one Christmas while you get your head back on straight than run the risk of losing you in a drunk-driving accident and missing every future Christmas with you."

His jaw seemed to harden and she worried for a moment

that she had been too blunt. On the other hand, maybe he needed a little more tough love.

"You sound like Judge Parker. That's basically what she said when she sentenced me."

"She wants to help you, just like everyone else does."

"I know."

"Don't worry about Henry and Alice. They'll have a joyful Christmas. I plan to make sure of that. They're looking forward to their program this week and I have other fun things planned for Christmas Eve and Christmas Day."

"Thank you."

She smiled. "I have assured them over and over that Santa will still find them, no matter where they're staying."

He raked a hand through his hair, managing to appear guilty and grateful at the same time.

"I won't forget how much I owe you."

"I wish you would. I've told you. You don't owe me anything. We're family. This is what we do."

"I'm glad one of us, at least, hasn't forgotten what family means. I've been a poor excuse for a father and a brother. I don't know how you can even look me in the eye, after the choices I've made."

She wished so much that she could hug her brother and had to fold her hands together on her lap to keep from reaching out and encountering cold glass.

"You're on a better track now. Things will look up from here on. I know they will."

"I will have to take your word on that."

"My word isn't what matters here. It's yours. You're the only one who can make those necessary changes."

"Yeah. That becomes painfully obvious when you're staring at the walls of a six-by-eight-foot cell."

They chatted about the children and the few presents he had

stockpiled throughout the year for them for Christmas until Deputy Sanchez walked over to stand directly behind Wes.

"Time to go," he said gruffly.

"Right." Wes stood up. He met her gaze and she saw sadness there but also a new determination that had been missing since Cassie died.

"Thanks again," he said.

"Your attorney told me you could have a video visit with the kids on Christmas. We'll call you," she promised.

He shook his head. "I still don't want them to see me in here."

"I get it. I've supported you in that but it's Christmas. I think they need to see you, even for a moment, to make sure you're okay."

"Time to go," the deputy said more forcefully.

"We'll call you," Annie said firmly.

She sat for a moment after Wes was escorted out of the visitor's room and returned to his cell.

He was making progress. She had to believe that. She knew he loved his kids. She had to hope that he would focus on that when the grief and despair became too much to bear.

With her heart heavy and sad, she left the visitation room and walked back down the hall, where she buzzed for Deputy Harris to open the door.

He usually could open it remotely from his desk but this time he stood to greet her. "Done already? That seemed like a quick fifteen minutes," he said with a warm smile that contrasted sharply with his coworker's.

Over his shoulder, she saw Tate was on his phone. He had his back to her and she couldn't hear what he was saying.

While she was always in a hurry to leave this place, she didn't want to rush him after he had been so kind to wait for her.

"Your brother doing okay?" Jim asked.

"As well as can be expected for a guy who has to spend Christmas in jail."

"I don't know if it makes you feel any better, but our inmates get a real Christmas dinner. Turkey, mashed potatoes, homemade rolls and pie. We try to make it delicious. I think they look forward to it."

"That does make me feel better. Thanks." She forced a smile, not wanting to tell him that somehow seemed even worse, to enjoy some of the trappings of the holidays without the family connections that went along with it.

For a few more moments, they chatted about the twins and what they were asking Santa to bring them. Finally, Tate ended his phone call and turned around. She saw him exchange an odd look with Jim but thought she had likely imagined it.

"Hey. Sorry about that. How did it go?" Tate asked.

She made a face. "Hard. As always. I hate seeing him in here just about as much as he hates being in here."

"I'm sorry." He didn't touch her but his sympathetic look still made her feel like she was on the receiving end of the warm hug she had so wanted to be able to give her brother.

"Thanks."

"I'm sorry you had to wait for me. I should have just gone back to the ranch and driven myself back to visit after we finished dropping off the blankets."

"I didn't mind at all," he assured her. "Anyway, it was great for me. I was able to take care of some things that have been on my mind lately."

She waited for him to tell her what those things were but he only smiled again. "Should we go, then?"

"Right." She turned back to Jim. "Thanks for watching out for Wes."

"No problem. Sheridan, it was nice to meet you."

"Yeah. I'll be in touch," Tate said, which only confused Annie further. Why would Tate be in touch with Jim?

She felt nosy for being curious. Tate didn't give her a chance to ask, anyway. He quickly ushered her out of the jail, into the crisp December air.

As soon as she walked outside, Annie paused on the sidewalk and inhaled deeply of air that didn't smell like disinfectant and misery.

"That bad?"

Fresh air and freedom. She had never been so grateful for them as she was each Tuesday afternoon when she left the jail.

She and Tate headed for the ranch pickup truck. He helped her inside, then climbed in himself and started the engine. The heated seat immediately made her feel better.

"You know, I was so angry at Judge Parker when she sentenced Wes to serve time over Christmas. Why Christmas? He's a single dad with two little kids at home. I felt like she was only being punitive because she was tired of dealing with him. He had three drunk-and-disorderly charges in only a handful of months and maybe she just wanted him out of her courtroom."

"You don't think that now?"

"No. I think I'm finally beginning to understand why she took that drastic step. She recognized that Wes needed this smack in the face with reality. Nothing else was getting through to him. Maybe he needed to be away from the kids at Christmas, as hard as that has been on all of us, so that he had the time and space he needed to dry out and reorder his priorities."

"I totally get it," Tate said. "I don't want to betray confidences but someone I love was in a similar circumstance until about a year ago. Substance abuse. Addiction. Self-destructive behavior. The whole thing. She didn't have children to be impacted, but it was hard on those who love her to watch her go through it. This past year, she's worked like hell to turn things around and she's doing great now. I'm incredibly proud of her."

She smiled softly. "Brianna is amazing, isn't she?"

He looked horrified that she had made the connection. "I never said it was Brie!"

"You didn't have to. She has already shared with me some of her journey."

"Our dad's death hit her hard. I think harder than my mom or I realized. She lost her way for a while. I will always regret that I was too wrapped up in my own life to truly see how troubled she was."

"Have you told her what you just said to me? About how proud you are of the efforts she's making?"

He gave her a startled look across the cab. "Maybe not in so many words."

"You should tell her in exactly those words. I think she really needs to hear them."

He seemed to consider that. "You're right. I need to. She's been an inspiration, not just to me but to others who are battling similar demons."

He paused. "Thank you for the advice. Once again, I thought I was helping you by providing support while you visited your brother. You've turned the tables on me, helping me realize I haven't been as forthcoming with my sister as I should have been. I appreciate it."

"You're welcome."

He was quiet for a long moment and, to her astonishment, he picked up her hand and entwined his fingers through hers. "You're a remarkable woman, Annelise. In case no one has told you that lately."

She felt herself flush. "I don't feel like it most of the time. But thank you for the encouragement."

He looked down at her and she thought for a moment he was going to kiss her again. She held her breath, knowing she couldn't let him. As much as she desperately wanted him to.

She was already struggling to remember all the reasons she would be smart to protect her heart against him. With each kiss, those reasons seemed to shrink to nothing.

"We should probably go," she said quickly, before she could do something supremely foolish like throw herself into his arms. "The kids will be getting home from school shortly. I need to be there when they arrive."

He seemed to collect himself. "You're right," he said, though she was certain she heard regret in his voice as he put the truck in gear and drove out of the parking lot.

20

THE PUPPIES KEPT CALLING BRIE BACK TO THE barn.

That's what she told herself, anyway, as she traipsed in her thick, clunky snow boots on the well-worn path between the ranch house and the outbuildings.

Catherine had only wanted to ski for a few hours, which was fine with Brie. She liked skiing but never could spend all day doing it.

As soon as they returned to the ranch, Brie had been compelled to see the puppies, wondering if they had opened their eyes yet.

It certainly had nothing to do with a certain cowboy she couldn't seem to get out of her mind.

The place was empty of humans, as far as she could tell.

One of the barn cats watched her, tail swishing through the

hay, as she walked past the stalls on the way to Luna's whelping pen. The mama dog was sleeping and so were all of her puppies. Brie watched them for a long time, finding a funny kind of peace in the sweet way they nestled together for warmth.

When she headed back through the barn, one of the horses nickered. It was one of the mares she had noticed that first afternoon she had helped Levi deliver the puppies.

She had to say hello. It would be rude not to, she told herself as she moved closer to the animal. "Hi there," she murmured. "You are a pretty girl."

She stood patting the horse for a long time, inhaling the familiar scents of hay, dust, horses.

"She's a sweet one."

The voice out of nowhere had her whirling around to find Levi leaning against a nearby stall.

"You scared the life out of me! Where did you come from?"

"I had to run to town to pick up some vaccines from the vet. I made enough noise when I came in but you were busy communing with Lacey here."

"Lacey. Is that your name?" she crooned, rubbing the horse's jawline.

"Wallace loved her. Never rode her, but always stopped for a visit when he was here. I always wondered why your grandfather bought a horse so perfectly suited for someone much smaller than he was, especially since your grandmother never came with him to the ranch."

"Maybe he just wanted a gentle-natured horse for visitors."

"Could be. But we have a few other all-around horses who are good for that." He stepped closer and Lacey batted her long eyelashes at him.

"Do you want to know what I think now? I think he bought her for you."

His words made her chest burn. She had disappointed her

grandfather so much over the years with her reckless, wild-child behavior. He had reached out in countless ways to help her and she had rejected every single overture.

"I doubt that," she muttered.

"The only way you'll know is to take a ride."

"I don't ride," she said, her voice clipped. "I told you that."

"Don't? Or won't?"

"What difference does it make?"

"None, I suppose. You just don't strike me as the sort of woman who gives up something she loves for no good reason."

He reached into a bucket nearby and pulled out an apple, which he handed over to Brie to feed Lacey. The horse lipped it from her and seemed to think it was the most delicious treat in the world.

"I did love riding," she said softly as the apple disappeared. "It was something my father and I shared together, from the time I was younger than the twins."

"Seems strange to me that you completely gave it up after he died. I would have thought you would have kept at it as a way to connect with him."

"Well, I didn't," she said shortly.

He didn't understand all the guilt and pain wrapped up in her memories. How could he?

"Why don't we take her for a little ride?" Levi pressed. "We can head over to the arena. She could use the exercise."

She felt a sudden vast yearning to saddle up the horse and gallop away, to experience that joy she had always found while riding.

She closed her eyes and focused on shoving the urge back down. "I can't."

Levi looked disappointed in her, which made her feel even worse. "I never knew your father, but from what everybody has told me, he was a stand-up guy who tried hard to make a difference in the world."

"He was."

"Do you really think a man like that would have wanted his daughter to give up something she loved so much, as some misguided way to honor his memory? That makes no sense at all."

She hitched in a breath. "That's not the reason I gave it up."

"Then why? Because he died on a horse? That's an even more asinine reason, if you ask me. Just because people die in traffic accidents doesn't mean we should give up riding in cars."

"I didn't ask you," she snapped. "You don't understand. Not about this. Not about anything. Just leave it alone, Levi."

"I would like to understand. Tell me why you stopped riding, Brie. I can see by the way you look at Lacey here that you love horses. Why sacrifice that?"

His quiet words seemed to open up the box she kept padlocked inside her, the one where the worst of her memories stayed.

"I can't," she whispered, her voice breaking on the words.

"Why not?" he asked, his voice pitched as low as hers.

She closed her eyes, not able to look at him while she finally told him the ugly truth.

"He died because of me. It was my fault. That's why I can't ride."

He froze, his eyes wide with shock. "Your father was bucked off a spooked horse on a steep trail and fell down the mountainside. That's what Wallace told me. He even showed me once where it happened."

"Wallace wasn't there. No one was there but Tate and he was ahead on the trail and didn't see what happened."

Once she started talking, it was as if all the words she had shoved down for years came spilling out, raw and ugly, and she couldn't seem to dam them up again.

"I shouldn't have been there in the first place. That's the

worst part. If I hadn't disobeyed, if I hadn't been so furious about being left behind and followed him and Tate up that trail, none of it would have happened. I killed him, as surely as if I had shoved him over that drop-off."

To her horror, she began to cry. They were huge tears, as if they had swelled and grown inside her all these years, just waiting to come out.

She wiped at her eyes with her coat sleeve, wishing she hadn't said anything. She didn't want to tell him. She didn't need to see the disgust in his eyes when he heard everything she had done.

"What happened?" Levi asked in that same low calm voice that she had heard him use for horses and puppies.

It worked on her, too. She took a breath, fighting for control. She had told him this much. She might as well tell him the rest.

"One morning Dad and Tate decided to ride to Hidden Lake up in the backcountry above the ranch so they could go fishing. I begged and begged to go with them but my dad said no. Not this time. The horse I usually rode when I was at the ranch had turned up lame the day before and there wasn't another one I could handle, even though I was a good rider. The only other available horse was a mare who had only been at the ranch for a week or so and Scott McCade, Annie's dad, said she was too skittish and nervous for that steep ride. He was working with her but she wasn't ready yet."

She closed her eyes, remembering everything about that day. The slant of morning sun, the June air, alive with birdsong, the steely determination inside her to show she could do hard things.

"I hated being left behind. I had just turned eleven and felt like Tate was always the one who got to have all the fun. Annie had gone somewhere with her mom and wasn't around for me to complain to so the moment Scott left to go get something in town, I snuck down to the barn and saddled up the new horse. Her name was Molly. I was maybe a half hour behind them so I pushed her hard up the trail. Harder than I should have."

The trail was a treacherous one, with several areas where the path cut across a tumble of rocks with a steep drop-off of hundreds of feet on the other side.

One misstep by Molly and both of them would have tumbled over the side.

"Somehow I caught up with them after less than an hour. I still don't know how. They must have stopped somewhere along the way, maybe to fish for a few minutes in the nearby creek."

The scene was crystal clear to her now. Her father and brother must not have heard her approach. She could see her father ahead, riding across a thin section of trail with a steep drop-off to his left.

"I couldn't see Tate. The trail was only wide enough for single file so he must have ridden ahead and turned a bend, but I did see my dad, who was just starting across a scree. At that moment, my horse got spooked by something. I still don't know what. A ground squirrel, a bird, a mosquito, a snake slithering nearby. I don't know. Molly whinnied and started bucking. I was…was holding on for dear life. My dad turned in the saddle and saw me having trouble but the trail was too narrow for him to safely turn the horse around. I could see he wanted to help me and I guess he figured the only way was to get off his horse and run back."

"Makes sense."

She closed her eyes, trying to block out those horrible images. Her father stopping his horse, climbing out of the saddle, jumping down so he could come help her…then losing his footing on the unstable rock surface.

"I wish he had just ridden the horse past the scree and then turned around to come back. I don't know why he didn't. Instead, he slid off. I'm not sure if his horse bumped him, if his boots slipped on the rock, if he just lost his balance, but the next thing I knew, he was tumbling down. I screamed and that was the last straw for my horse, who bucked me off and took off back down the trail."

She let out a sob now, remembering the sheer terror of that moment. The wind had been knocked out of her and she had laid there for a moment, crying and scared, then had managed to climb to her feet just as her brother came riding back fast.

Levi reached for her now and though she knew it was a mistake, she sank gratefully into his arms. For a long time, he held her, his body warm and solid against her. Finally she dug for strength to tell him the rest.

"Tate must have heard both of us cry out. He didn't know what happened at first and I was hysterical by this point. It was horrible."

At first they couldn't see Cole, then Tate had spotted him far below, because of his red bandanna.

"When we found him, he was at least three hundred feet down a steep slope, not moving. We screamed to him but he didn't answer. Tate wanted to go down to help him but we didn't have a rope long enough and I was afraid he would fall, too, and I would be left there alone. I… I begged him not to."

It wouldn't have made a difference. She knew that now but she also knew Tate had been upset that she had made him have to choose between her or going down to help their father.

"We didn't want to leave him there but had to get help. Tate finally decided the best thing would be to go down the trail until we had cell service, so he could call 911."

His arms tightened around her and she was glad she didn't have to see his expression. "That must have been hell for two kids."

She nodded against his chest. It was unbelievably hard to share these details she had never told anyone else, not even in therapy, no matter how the therapists pushed. Still, there was an odd sort of comfort in the telling, somehow.

"My horse was long gone by now and Dad's horse was too big for me to handle. We left it there and I rode with Tate."

She shivered, though she wasn't cold. "It was a horrible ride down. I was crying and sobbing the whole way and poor Tate had to try to comfort me, deal with his own shock and handle the horse at the same time. I sometimes forget he was only fourteen. Just a kid himself."

Had she ever told him what a rock he had been that day? How much she admired the steady strength and comfort he had offered her?

"We were nearly to the ranch when our grandpa came riding up the trail. By that time, Molly had made it down by herself. He knew something was wrong so he was coming after us."

She could still remember Wallace's howl of pain when they had told him what had happened. She had never seen her grandfather express that kind of raw emotion, before or since.

"By the time they were able to get a rescue crew down to our dad, it was too late. He was gone and it…it became a recovery effort. He had severe head trauma, multiple broken bones and a punctured lung from broken ribs. They said he probably died within minutes of falling. We couldn't have made it to him in time to help him, so I guess it's better Tate didn't risk his life to go down to him."

"I'm so damn sorry you had to go through that," he said.

She lifted her gaze to meet his finally. Instead of the disgust she expected to see, all she saw was compassion and concern. He obviously didn't understand what she had done.

"I could have made so many different choices that day. I should have stayed at the ranch like he told me to. And I took a horse without permission, a horse I didn't have the skill to manage. I knew that trail was dangerous but that didn't stop me from being reckless."

He frowned. "You said you were eleven, right?"

She nodded.

"A baby. Just a baby." He stroked her hair, as if he were comforting that eleven-year-old girl she had been. "We make decisions as children we would never make as adults who have the ability to see the full picture. You can't blame yourself for that."

"We could have both died that day! I've thought often that we should have. Or at least that it should have been me."

"I'm glad you didn't," he said simply. "That's a whole lot of pain for one person to carry around, especially when it's all for nothing. And it still doesn't explain why you gave up riding."

She eased away and stared at him. "Didn't you hear anything I said? My father would have been here, all these years, if not for me. I killed him!"

"That is far from the truth. You didn't kill your father. Nobody who heard what happened could ever think that. I know your grandfather didn't hold you responsible and I'm willing to bet Tate doesn't, either."

Why couldn't she make him understand?

"I shouldn't have been there. I disobeyed and took a horse I wasn't supposed to."

"You acted like plenty of other kids would have. I probably would have done the same. I hated being left behind worse than anything. It was a tragic accident."

She shook her head. "We are going to have to agree to disagree."

"I can't agree to disagree when you're obviously wrong about this. I've worked around horses my whole life. Even the best-behaved horses can be unpredictable and stubborn under the right circumstances. And even the best rider can make a mistake in the heat of the moment. Your father should have moved off to a safer spot where he could dismount safely. The fact is, you were not responsible for what happened that day, and from everything I've heard about your father, I think he would be the first one to tell you to stop blaming yourself for something you didn't do."

"Except he can't tell me that. Because he's dead."

"If he were here, I'm willing to bet he would tell his daughter it's long past time she stops letting decisions she made as a child control the rest of her life."

"You don't know what you're talking about," she snapped. "I'm not doing that."

"Aren't you?"

Yes. She had been submerging her feelings since she was a teenager, burying them first in alcohol and marijuana and then harder drugs.

All that running and here she was back where it all started.

"I'm sorry as hell your dad died. And I'm even sorrier you had to be there to see it. But I am certain he wouldn't be happy to know you've spent all this time blaming yourself. Don't you think he would want you to squeeze every drop of joy out of the gift of life we all have?"

She pictured her father, always laughing, always happy, always up for an adventure as he dedicated his life to helping others. How she would have disappointed him, just as she had let down everyone else in her family.

"In a way, you owe it to him," Levi said.

"You're saying I'm betraying my father's memory because I gave up something I loved after he died."

"Yeah. I guess I am."

He moved to the stall door. "You definitely need to take Lacey for a ride. She's a sweet horse. She would love to take you. What do you say? Just a few times around the arena."

She gazed at the little mare and that yearning tugged at her again.

Levi was right about one thing. Cole Sheridan would have hated knowing his death had such a lasting imprint on every decision she made. It would hurt him to know how she still struggled, after twenty years, to find peace.

"I don't have the right boots."

She couldn't actually be considering this, could she?

Triumph flashed in Levi's gaze for just an instant. He knew he had her, blast the man.

"I'm sure there's a pair around here that will fit you. Wallace always liked to keep some in various sizes, just in case he had guests here who didn't know any better and tried to ride in flip-flops."

He left her there with the horses. A moment later, he came out of the office with a pair of tooled red boots with black flowers on them.

"I don't know if these are an exact fit but they are probably pretty close. He bought them about a year ago."

She closed her eyes. When she finished rehab this time, her grandfather had invited her many times to come to the ranch to ride with him.

She should have done it, damn it. Why hadn't she? She had allowed fear to rule her decisions and, because of that, she had missed out on truly reconnecting with Wallace in the last months of his life.

Going through addiction and recovery had taught her many

valuable lessons about herself. A big one was that she tried everything possible to run from her problems. It never worked. They always caught up with her eventually.

It was only a short ride around an arena. She could do it, if only to get this stubborn cowboy off her back.

"Fine," she said. "I'll ride a few times around the arena. Will that make you happy?"

"Yeah," he drawled, cinching on the saddle. "And more importantly, I think it will make you happy, too."

She wanted to throw something at him. She settled for holding the reins and talking to the horse while he put on the necessary tack.

A moment later, they were leading Lacey outside the barn to the arena next door. Brie's heart was pounding so hard she thought Levi could probably hear it but he said nothing as he turned on the lights inside the large space.

She hadn't been in here yet. It was the perfect size for training a horse, with a dirt floor and even a little spectator area.

Levi led the horse over to a concrete mounting block. It was now or never. She could still always back out.

No. She was tired of giving up on things just because they were hard. She could do this.

With renewed determination, she grabbed hold of the pommel and swung herself up into the saddle, a motion that felt painfully familiar and yet foreign at the same time.

It felt so strange, after all these years, to be on a horse again. She didn't know what to do for a moment and then her muscles started to relax and lean into it.

The horse knew what to do. Lacey started walking around the arena, her gait easy and natural, leaving Levi behind at the mounting block, watching them.

She caught the horse's rhythm and could feel her mouth stretch into a smile.

Oh. She remembered this. The feeling of wonder. Of freedom. Of flight.

She let out a little laugh and urged the horse to a trot. Lacey was a sweetheart, following all her commands, and after a moment Brie completely lost herself in the remembered joy.

The joy reminded her a little of the happiness she had felt over the past few days at reuniting with Annie, discovering a central piece of her childhood—of herself—she had thought was gone forever.

In the end, she rode much longer than a few minutes. At least a half hour passed with Levi leaning against the wall, watching her conquer this fear.

Every time she passed him as the horse circled the arena, he would grin and she would feel as if a shot of pure energy coursed through her veins.

Finally, she knew she would have to get off. Already, her muscles were beginning to ache at the unaccustomed exercise. She pulled the reins the next time she got close to Levi and slid out of the saddle.

Somehow, she wasn't sure how, he was there to catch her and she tumbled into his arms.

"That was amazing!" she exclaimed. "I had forgotten. All of it came back the moment she started moving. It was incredible. You were so right."

She hugged him tightly, deeply grateful he had pushed her.

How had this man become so important to her in such a short time? She felt as if he were the only one who truly saw past the mistakes she had made and the pain she had caused her family to the heart of her, the woman who ached to be held and comforted and loved.

"Thank you," she said, suddenly feeling shy as he smiled down at her.

"You are so welcome. That was the best thing I've been part of in a long time."

It seemed inevitable when he leaned down and his mouth found hers.

She was so caught up in the exhilaration of the moment, she kissed him back with all the fierce hunger she had been fighting since she came to the ranch.

His mouth tasted sweet, delicious, like cinnamon and sugar. She wanted to lick every drop of him. She wanted to shove off his Stetson, push him back against the railing and explore every single taut muscle.

He kissed her with the same kind of intensity, his hands pulling her tight against him.

Where could they go? Surely there was a soft surface somewhere nearby where they could sink down and she could start taking off his denim jacket, his boots, his Wranglers...

She froze as reality poured over her like a bucket of mash.

She couldn't do any of those delicious things she wanted to. Not with Levi. Not now.

She had far too much to lose.

She was supposed to be showing her family she was someone they could count on. If she wanted Tate and Irene to consider her to run the Sheridan Trust, she had to stay focused on the goal.

Having a fling with the ranch manager would definitely distract her from that and would probably show her family that she hadn't changed all that much.

She had run away at seventeen, dropping out of high school to go with her much older and completely inappropriate boyfriend, backpacking through Europe. He had stolen all her cash and left her in a hostel in Greece, forcing her to call her mother for help.

Unfortunately, Paulo wasn't the first or the last bad decision.

Brie didn't want to be that woman anymore. She had vowed that until she felt like she had her head completely on straight, until she was either working at the Sheridan Trust or she had proved herself in the public relations department at Sheridan International where she worked now, she couldn't afford the distraction of a relationship.

Levi wasn't at all like the other men she had dated. She knew that instinctively, which might be why she was so fiercely drawn to him.

He was a good man, a hardworking father, a compassionate friend.

But he was still very much a distraction. Having him work for her family didn't help the situation at all.

She didn't want to stop kissing him but somehow Brie found the strength to ease away.

"We… We can't."

"Pretty sure we just did."

Oh, that drawl. She could listen to it all day.

"No. I mean, we shouldn't."

He hesitated and seemed to withdraw a little. "Probably not."

The heat in his eyes cooled slightly and she ached at the loss. She wanted that warm, laughing smile again, the one that made her feel like she could do anything.

She sighed, knowing she couldn't just leave things at *no*. After his kindness to her that day, he deserved more than that.

"Look, Levi, I'm fiercely attracted to you. I don't want to be, but there it is. The thing is, I'm not going to do anything about it. I can't."

His jaw seemed to harden. "I guess that's clear enough."

She was making a mess of this. As usual.

She reached for his hand, trying her best to find the right words. "I'm attracted to you and I… I like you. I think I could probably fall in love with you without too much effort on my part."

Some of the heat flashed back in his expression. "Ditto," he murmured. "You fascinate me more than any woman I've ever known. Smart, funny, kind, beautiful."

She wanted to take those words and tuck them close against her heart. He didn't know the truth, though. If he did, he wouldn't say all that.

She sighed. "I would like to be all those things. But I'm not. I'm an alcoholic and an addict."

She expected him to be shocked. Instead, he only nodded. "Your grandfather was thrilled when you made it through rehab. He was so proud of how far you have come."

The words almost made her cry all over again.

"If you know about my…about my past, you have to see what a mistake this is. Right?"

"It didn't feel like a mistake."

"Not to me, either. But here's the thing. I've spent a decade making bad decisions about men. I don't trust myself yet to… to make the good ones. I need time."

He studied her, his expression intense. What did he see when he looked at her? The Past Brie, the hot-mess party girl?

Or the woman she was trying to become?

"That's fair," he finally said. "How can a guy argue with that?"

"I do appreciate everything today. Thank you for pushing me out of my comfort zone."

"Glad I could help." He paused. "Come on. Let's get her back to the barn."

She walked with him, wishing with all her heart that things could be different.

21

TATE WAS IN THE GREAT ROOM WORKING ON HIS laptop when he heard his sister come in. Brie walked down the hall toward her room without saying a word. He wasn't sure she even saw him.

She almost looked like she was in some kind of weird trance.

She wasn't using again, was she?

"Brie."

She looked up. As he saw her gaze sharpen on him, he winced at his own first instinctive thought.

She was trying so damn hard to turn her life around and here he was ready to jump to dire conclusions.

"Oh. Hi."

What had her so distracted? "Got a minute?" he asked.

"I… Sure."

She walked over and sat beside him and it was clear something heavy was on her mind.

"Everything okay?"

"Why do you ask?"

"I don't know. You seem upset about something."

"I don't… I'm not. I just… I just went riding."

"A horse?" he asked, shocked. She had been quite adamant in her refusal to ride again after that terrible summer day when their father died.

"No. A lawn mower. Yes, a horse. A sweet mare named Lacey."

"That's a shocker."

"Tell me about it. You're not as shocked as I was. Levi Moran can be pretty persuasive."

If the man could convince Brie to break her long-standing vow never to ride again, Tate needed to give him a raise.

"How was it?"

"I only went around the riding arena for a half hour or so." She paused and lifted her features to his and he saw her eyes were radiant, glowing with happiness. "It was incredible. I've missed riding. So much."

She had loved it through their childhood and was never happiest than when she was on horseback.

"If you loved it so much, why did you stop? I've always wondered."

She was quiet for a long time, gazing at the big sparkly Christmas tree, with the ornaments Tate had hung with the twins.

"Guilt. Regret. Sorrow. All kinds of thing. At the heart, I think I have always felt like I didn't deserve to find joy in riding horses anymore when I was responsible for Dad's death."

He stared. "Oh, Brie. That's not true. You know it's not."

She gave him an impatient look. "I've just been arguing with Levi about this for the past hour. Yes, I was a child. Yes, it was an accident. But it would never have happened if I hadn't thrown a fit about you and Dad going fishing without me. If I hadn't ridden after you on a horse I couldn't handle, he would still be here."

It had been twenty years but the wound was still as fresh as if it had happened last week. Neither of them had ever gotten over it, he suddenly realized.

"I'm sorry you've felt that way all these years. I never have blamed you. Not for a minute. If anyone was responsible, it was me. I am the one who begged and begged him to take me up to Hidden Lake to go fishing that day. He didn't want to. He had work to do at home but I wouldn't let it rest. I've regretted that every day since."

They had never talked about this, he realized. Not even right after the accident. Both of them had turned inward, shutting out everyone else who might have wanted to help them.

"It was an accident, Brie. You were a child. You weren't responsible."

"That's what Levi tried to tell me. I'm still not sure I am buying it. I've spent my whole life missing him so much and knowing it was my fault he wasn't around."

"I miss him, too," Tate said gruffly. "You know Dad wouldn't have wanted you to blame yourself for a second."

"I know. But it's tough to shift gears in one afternoon and change an internal belief I've held for nearly twenty years."

He took her hand. "Maybe it's time we both let it go."

"I don't know if I can," she whispered.

"I think we have to. I think that one single cataclysmic event has damaged both of us long enough. Don't you?"

She gave a short laugh. "You are so right."

He hated thinking of her blaming herself all these years. If he could have spared her all that pain, he would have.

"For what it's worth," he said quietly, "I'm proud of you. I should have told you that a long time ago. What you've done, working so hard to rebuild your life? That's an amazing accomplishment and takes extraordinary strength and courage."

She sniffled and wiped at her eyes. "Thank you. I don't think I realized how very much I needed to hear that from you."

Maybe this holiday season could be the chance for them to forge a new closer relationship out of the wreckage of the past. He hoped so. He had missed his baby sister.

"How did things go with delivering Annie's blankets to the Family Connection?" Brie asked.

"Good. They were thrilled. The kids should be receiving their blankets right about now. I wish I could have been there to see their faces."

"That's great." She paused, giving him a sideways look. "Annie is pretty terrific, isn't she?"

An understatement. Annelise had become infinitely precious to him since he had returned to the Angel's View.

What was he going to do about her?

The thought of going back to the city and leaving behind the joy and happiness he found around her had him feeling bleak.

He wasn't going yet, though, Tate reminded himself. He could still enjoy the moments he had left.

"Can you keep a secret?" he asked.

"That depends. How juicy is it?"

He had to smile. "Not juicy at all, I'm afraid. It's a good one, though."

He told her about his idea of helping Wes and his family and the plans that were already in motion. Pastor Morris turned out to be the perfect partner in crime and was already at work trying to organize everything so they could hit the ground running the next morning.

When he finished, she stared at him, mouth open. "Wow.

You seriously did all that in one afternoon? You do not mess around."

"I had help. There are many people in Holly Creek who want to lend a hand to Wes and his family. I'm just organizing the effort. It's kind of what I do."

"Do you really think you can finish all that before Christmas Eve? That's only three days."

It seemed impossible but if they had enough people, he thought they could pull it off. "We're going to try to finish as much as we can."

Annelise spent her whole time helping others. He wanted to do this for her. Yes, Wes and the twins would be the primary beneficiaries but Tate hoped it would put her mind to rest to know this was one less burden off her brother's shoulders when he was released from jail.

"I'm in. One hundred percent. How can I help?"

Tate beamed at his sister. "The crew we've set up can take care of the basics. Drywall, painting, finish carpentry. It's the softer things I'm not good at, the details that make a house into a home. Rugs, dishtowels, accessories. That sort of thing. They probably have most of what they need but maybe we could freshen things up a bit. How do you feel about going shopping tomorrow?"

She laughed. "Silly question. I'm always down for shopping. Especially if you're paying."

"Thank you. I was hoping you would say that. I've been working on a shopping list. I can email it to you. You might be able to buy some of it online and rush deliver it."

"We're in the middle of nowhere Wyoming. It might be faster for me to fly back to California, go shopping and bring everything back with me."

"Okay. If you think that's best."

She laughed. "I was joking, Tate. I can run over to Idaho

Falls to the box stores and probably find everything we need. I'm on this. Maybe Mom and Catherine will want to come with me. We can split the list."

"That would be perfect. I'm trying to keep it a secret from Annie and the twins, though, so you'll have to be sneaky."

"Send me the list and I'll go through it. This is going to be great. I'm so excited."

To his surprise, she kissed him on the cheek before walking the rest of the way to her bedroom.

He watched her go, struck by the thought that while they were all grieving Wallace and none of them had wanted to come to Angel's View for Christmas, the best gift of this season might be the chance to heal old wounds and make fresh starts.

22

CHRISTMAS WAS DEFINITELY IN THE AIR AROUND the Angel's View Ranch.

The entire Sheridan family seemed consumed with secrets. The day after Annie delivered the blankets, everyone in the family disappeared. She wasn't sure where they all went; they were all oddly secretive about it. The house was empty except for Irene and Lillian, who stayed in their rooms.

When they returned from wherever they went that evening around suppertime, everyone seemed in a happy mood but not necessarily talkative. At least not to her. Maybe she was imagining it but Tate and Brie, at least, seemed to be avoiding her.

She didn't have time to think about it much. If all the Sheridans seemed more cheerful, the twins were the exact opposite. The approaching holiday seemed to be bringing out the worst in both of them. They bickered and whined all evening long, from having to do their nightly reading practice with her to not liking the pasta dinner she served them.

Their crankiness came to a head at bath time when they each fought about who got to be the first one in the tub. Henry ended up pulling Alice's hair and she pinched him in retaliation. They both ended up in tears and Annie, at the end of her rope, forced them to sit side by side on her small sofa until they apologized.

It probably wasn't the best way to handle it, she was certain. But she was doing her best, especially for someone who had never had children of her own.

She thought the situation had calmed down a little bit and that their moods had improved. After she read them their bedtime story, a holiday favorite about a reindeer named Snowball, she saw by Alice's furrowed brow that she had something serious on her mind.

Her niece didn't say anything until Annie was tucking in her covers, when it all came blurting out.

"Do I have to go to school tomorrow? Can't I stay here with you?"

Annie sat on the edge of the bed. "Oh, honey. Why would you want to stay home? Tomorrow is your program you have been so excited about. You've been talking about it for weeks. You have a solo and everything. Why don't you want to go?"

"I just don't." Alice's chin wobbled and a few tears welled up in her eyes.

"Why? I can't help if you won't tell me what's going on."

"I don't want to do a stupid program if Daddy can't be there."

"Oh, honey."

Annie hugged her and that seemed to be the catalyst for more tears. Alice sniffled, wiping her nose on her pajamas. "I said a prayer that Daddy could be out of jail to come but

Henry told me that was stupid and God won't let him out of jail just for a dumb first-grade program. And since Mommy is dead and won't be there, either, I don't want to go. We won't have *anybody*."

Annie's heart seemed to shatter in her chest. She had no idea how to navigate this.

"Sure you will. I'll be there," she said, hugging her niece again. "And all your friends and their moms and dads."

Alice pulled away a little so that she could meet her gaze. "Will Tate be there?"

Henry, watching this scene from his bed, sat up. "He said he would try but I bet he doesn't."

"I'm not sure," she answered honestly. "I haven't had a chance to talk to him about it again. I haven't seen him since yesterday. He seems to be pretty busy right now but I will ask him."

"I know. I didn't see him today, either. I kept looking and looking but he didn't come home all day," Alice said.

"I can't make any promises for someone else, but I will talk to him and remind him about the program tomorrow."

That seemed to calm Alice a little. She sniffled again. "It still won't be the same as having Daddy there. But Tate is my friend, too."

"I hope he can come," Annie said. "But here's the thing you need to remember. You've been practicing your show for weeks. You have a solo and people are counting on you. You should go and have fun and enjoy doing the show, regardless of whether anybody is in the audience at all. It's not really about who's there to see you, right? It's about doing your best and having fun."

"I guess." Alice yawned. "But you're going to ask him, right? You promise?"

She sighed. "I'll do my best."

While it sounded like she was trying to wriggle out, that was all she could offer.

She wasn't sure if she would have the chance to even talk with Tate that evening, since he had been making himself scarce all day.

She held Alice close, loving the sweet, strawberry smell of her shampoo and soap.

"One more thing before you go to bed, honey. It's easy to be unhappy about the things you don't have. I get that way, too, sometimes. It's natural to miss your mom and wish your dad hadn't made some bad choices and could be with you at Christmastime. That's totally understandable. But life is never exactly perfect, as much as we might want it to be. We have to figure out how to find the joy, anyway."

"Sometimes it's so *hard*."

"I know. And I'm sorry about that. What if I gave you a cookie that broke in half right before I gave it to you and some of it fell on the floor and a dog ate it?"

"Ew."

"Would you throw away the rest of the cookie you *did* have because it wasn't perfect?"

"No. That would be stupid. I'd still have some of the cookie."

"That's right. You won't have your mom or dad at the program tomorrow and I'm sorry about that but you will have other people there who love you and you can still have a great time doing the show."

"I guess."

"Can I have a cookie right now?" Henry asked from his bed, obviously listening to every word.

"No. You just brushed your teeth. There are no cookies, anyway. I was just using that as an example."

"Oh."

Alice gave her one more tight squeezy hug around her neck, then settled back against the pillow. "I love you, Auntie."

"I love you, too. And I can't wait to see your show tomorrow."

She turned off their light and walked out of the room, not sure if she had made any impact.

She waited until she was sure they were asleep, then headed into the kitchen of the main house to make sure everything was ready for the next day's meals.

To her surprise, Tate was standing at the refrigerator looking at the contents. He had missed dinner and was obviously rummaging for something to eat.

"Oh. Hi."

He looked tired and his shirt had sawdust on it. Maybe he was making something for his mother or Brie for Christmas. The idea that this man who was extraordinarily wealthy might be making a gift with his own hands charmed her completely.

"We had chicken enchiladas for dinner. They're on the second shelf, in that foil container. Can I heat some for you?"

He shook his head, reaching in to pull out the enchiladas. "I can do it. You don't have to wait on me, Annelise. You're doing enough as it is."

She wanted to argue with him but it didn't seem worth the effort.

"This looks really good," he said, dishing some onto a plate.

"Your family seemed to enjoy it. Those who were here, anyway. Even your mom ate a few bites."

Worry flitted across his expression. "That's good."

He started the microwave for about thirty seconds less than she would have but she refrained from suggesting he increase the cook time. He could figure that out.

"Thank you again for feeding my family. I don't know what we would have done without you."

"You would have been fine. Nobody starved earlier this week while I was working on the blankets."

He smiled. "Good point. I know everyone has enjoyed your food, though."

"I'm glad to hear that."

The microwave dinged and he pulled out his enchilada, took a bite, then put it in for another thirty seconds.

When he finally had his food, he sat at the island. Her promise to Alice rang in her ears and Annie sighed. She wouldn't have a better chance to talk to him about it.

"I feel weird about this but I was wondering if I could ask a favor."

"What is it?" he asked immediately. "Anything you need."

She blinked, touched by his alacrity. "It's not huge. I don't need a liver transplant or something. It's just… Do you remember when Alice and Henry told you about their school program? Well, it's tomorrow and they would really like you to come. Al had a bit of a breakdown tonight and was in tears about neither of her parents being able to come. She wanted me to ask if you would be there so I promised I would."

"She really wants me there that much?" he asked, clearly astonished.

She shrugged. "She said that would make her feel better. I completely understand if you can't. It's a first-grade Christmas program. While it's bound to be adorable, it won't exactly be top-shelf entertainment, if you know what I mean. I'm not sure why you would even consider it. You probably have far more important things to do."

She was rambling, she realized, and quickly clamped her jaw shut.

"I would love to go," he said instantly. "My schedule is a little packed tomorrow but I will sneak away somehow. You'll have to text me the address of the school. What time should I plan to be there?"

He was such a kind man. A wonderful, caring person.

Was it any wonder she was in love with him?

The undeniable realization made her instantly grateful she was already sitting down.

She didn't want to be in love with Tate Sheridan, especially when she knew it would bring only heartache and loss.

Too bad for her. It was far too late. She was completely gone. She had probably been in love with him since she was eleven.

"Thank you," she managed, shoving down her feelings until she could take them out and deal with them at a more appropriate moment. "She'll be thrilled. They both will actually. Henry wanted you there, too. I could tell."

"It will be my pleasure."

He smiled and she swallowed, wishing with all her heart she could reach across the table and kiss him.

His pupils widened suddenly, as if he knew what she was thinking.

Awareness suddenly seemed to shiver between them, sparkling in the air like glitter.

"Annelise."

The low, throaty way he said her name sent heat pooling in her belly.

"Yes," she murmured. Only that. What else could she say? *Yes. Kiss me.*

He leaned forward, but before their mouths could connect, some sixth sense warned her someone else was coming into the kitchen.

She eased back in her chair just as his mother appeared in the doorway.

Pamela looked between the two of them, her gaze suddenly sharp. Could she sense the sudden tension crackling in the air?

"I'm sorry. Am I interrupting something?"

Tate picked up his fork. "Not at all. I'm just grabbing dinner. Come in."

Pamela approached them, looking fragile and pale but still ethereally lovely. "I'm on a bit of a quest. I'm…having a hard time sleeping and was wondering if there's any tea in the house that might help me sleep. I meant to buy some when we were shopping earlier but I completely forgot until now. Any chance there's anything like that here in the kitchen?"

Annie stood up. "Yes. I think so. Wallace favored a chamomile blend and Deb Garza would make sure the cupboard was always stocked with the kind he liked. I haven't checked lately but I know where she used to keep it. Let me see what I can find."

"I don't want to trouble you. I can look."

Annie made a shooing motion with her hand. "Please. Sit down. I'll find it and heat some water. You can talk to your son."

Pamela didn't look especially thrilled by Annie's suggestion. She sat rather nervously at the island across from Tate.

Was something wrong between them? She had noticed an odd awkwardness between Pamela and both of her older children. Maybe that was just in her imagination, though. Annie had hardly had a conversation with the other woman.

Pamela kept to herself, for the most part. Annie had wondered if she had some kind of food allergy or eating disorder. During mealtimes, she picked at her plate, eating mostly soft vegetables and fruits, and she often seemed distracted, as if her thoughts were a thousand miles away.

Annie added water to the kettle and set it on the range to

heat and was looking for one of the nicest teacups when Tate spoke.

"So," he said to his mother. "Here we are. Now is probably a good time for you to finally tell me what's going on."

Annie sent a swift look at the pair of them and found Pamela sitting stiffly across the island from her son, her features tense.

"I've told you. I'm fine."

"You're obviously not," he said gently. "Please don't keep lying to me. We're worried about you. Brie has been beside herself. I am convinced she's right. You're keeping something from us. What is it? Are you ill?"

Annie shouldn't be here for this intensely personal conversation. She wanted to slip out of the kitchen and leave them to it but she had already started the tea and couldn't just abandon it.

At his question, Pamela seemed to deflate. Her shoulders slumped and she dropped her head into her hands as if her neck couldn't support the weight of it any longer.

"I didn't want to tell you and ruin your holidays. I was planning to tell you next week before we leave but I can see I was foolish to think you wouldn't notice something was wrong."

"Tell me. What's wrong?"

She sighed and lifted her head. "There's no point in trying to pretend, is there? Yes. You're right. I'm ill. It must be obvious. I feel like I have a big *C* tattooed on my forehead."

Annie saw Tate's eyes widen with dismay. He reached for his mother's hand. "*C*. As in cancer?"

She let out a little sound that wasn't quite a sob and nodded. "Yes. Breast cancer. Stage 2. I found a lump earlier this month and had a biopsy a few days before we came here. It was malignant. This entire time, I've been trying to figure out a way to tell you and your sisters. I suppose I should have just come right out with it from the beginning."

★ ★ ★

Cancer.

His worst fear.

He closed his eyes, wishing he could rewind the last few seconds, that they had never happened. It seemed so much harder to have her say it out loud.

Breast cancer. Now that it was out in the open, it all made so much sense. Her lack of appetite or energy. Stan's overprotectiveness. Her abstraction.

Damn it. His mother had already been through so much. She didn't deserve cancer, too.

Unfortunately, cancer was a cruel, indiscriminating monster.

"Catherine doesn't know?"

His mother shook her head. "She's only a child. I wish I didn't have to tell her. She's going to be so frightened."

"She's tougher than we think."

Pamela gave a small laugh. "You could be right. It could be that *I'm* the frightened one. I haven't told anyone. Not Irene, not Lillian. Stan knows, of course. He's been a rock."

At the stove, his gaze found Annie. She was looking at his mother with compassion and sadness, then her gaze shifted to him.

He could tell she wanted to flee. Somehow he knew without words that she didn't want to intrude on this moment with his mother.

He didn't want her to go. He needed to lean on her strength. Needed it more than he knew he should.

"What is the treatment plan?"

"We don't know that yet. I insisted that the oncologist give me through Christmas to come to terms with everything before we start talking about the path forward. I'm meeting with her next week on Wednesday. That's the reason we aren't staying through the New Year."

"You need to tell Brie."

"I know." Her features seemed to crumple and he squeezed her hands for comfort. "I've been trying to, believe me, but the words just…aren't there. She's come so far. I don't want to mess that up."

He thought of his sister the night before, showing a vulnerability and steely resolve at the same time.

"I think we both may have underestimated Brianna. She might be the toughest of us all."

Pamela gave a shaky smile. "You might be right."

"The important thing is to remember you're going to get through this. We will get through it together. You'll have the best doctors anywhere and all the family support you need."

"Thank you, my dear. That means so much to me."

Annie at that moment handed his mother the teacup. "I'm so sorry you're facing this, for what it's worth," she murmured.

His mother looked touched. "It's worth a great deal. Thank you for saying that."

Before Annie could respond, Brie came into the kitchen in her fuchsia bathrobe and slippers. She stopped, obviously picking up on the serious vibes at the table.

"What's this? A family meeting without me?"

Pamela sighed. "Oh, darling."

Brie gave Tate a look, a question in her eyes. He gave a little head gesture, indicating she should sit down first.

She sank into a chair, looking nervous. "What's going on?"

Pamela sighed. "I've been lying to you for a week and I shouldn't have."

"I knew it," she exclaimed. "What's going on? Are you and Stan getting divorced?"

Their mother looked horrified at the very suggestion. "No! Of course not."

"Then what is it?"

Much as she had with Tate, Pamela took Brie's hands and released a heavy breath. "You have been asking me if I was sick and I lied when I told you I was still struggling with the flu I had around Thanksgiving. That's not it, I'm afraid."

"Tell me."

"There's no easy way to say it. I have breast cancer, Stage 2. I don't know the plan yet. I've had a biopsy that confirmed it. I am likely looking at surgery and then radiation and/or chemotherapy. I won't know that until next week."

Brie somehow gasped and sobbed at the same time. "Why try to keep it from us?"

"I was wrong. I'm sorry. If you want the truth, I think I was just trying to pretend none of it was happening. I planned to tell you before leaving the ranch next week. I just…didn't want to ruin your holidays, which seems silly now when I say it out loud."

"Yes. So silly."

"Honestly, I thought there would be plenty of time to discuss it after Christmas, when we're back in the city."

"Tell me everything. What the doctor said. What treatment you're facing. What they've told you to expect."

Except for those first few tears, Brie held it together. Tate couldn't help being impressed that she wasn't falling apart, that she was handling the shock and dismay and fear far better than he would have predicted even a few months before.

23

"ARE YOU READY FOR THIS?"

Wendy Walker slid into the hard plastic chair next to Annie in the elementary school gym. Rows of chairs had been set up facing the stage and the closed curtains.

"I hope so." Annie was a little nervous that the twins, who tended to become silly when they were in crowds, might do something to distract from the show. They had been calm that morning but she knew their moods could turn on a dime.

Something told her that even if they did act out, they wouldn't be the only distraction onstage. When you have sixty first-graders appearing together in a show two days before Christmas, a sedate, low-key performance was likely not on the program.

"I think the kids are ready. Alice and Henry have both been practicing the songs nonstop."

"I know. So has Lucy. If I have to listen to 'Rockin' Around the Christmas Tree' one more time, I should not be held responsible for the consequences."

"I'm sorry to break it to you but you're going to hear it at least one more time, since they'll be singing it shortly."

"One more time. That's my limit."

Wendy glanced at the curtain, which seemed to be twitching suspiciously. "Did you hear about the kid who locked knees this week during rehearsal?"

"Oh, yes. It was all the buzz with the twins."

"That reminds me of when I was a kid and was lucky enough to be a tree in our Christmas show. I couldn't see the edge of the stage over my costume and completely fell off."

Annie smiled and settled in to chat as they waited for the show to start. During the year she had been back in Holly Creek, she had come to treasure the woman's friendship, along with several others here in town. Some were old friends she had reunited with, others like Wendy were new.

She and her husband lived not far from Wes's house and Wendy often took the twins after school.

"Is Adam going to be able to make it?" Annie asked.

Wendy looked away. "I'm not sure. I'm saving a seat for him just in case. He's hoping to run over but he and his crew are all busy right now on a, um, last-minute job."

Wendy's husband was an electrician who always seemed busy.

"Oh, I hope he doesn't miss it."

"If he does, it won't be a big deal. Principal Gallegos is taping it and will have CDs available after Christmas, so we can all watch it later."

Annie made a mental note to order one. She had planned to video it on her phone but it would be far better to have a better, more professional copy for Wes.

"Wow," Wendy said after a moment. "Look at the hot guy who just came in. Wonder whose kid he's here to watch."

She wasn't interested in any hot guy but couldn't resist turning around to see.

She should have known.

A vast rush of gratitude washed over her when she saw Tate walk in, helping two elegant older women.

Behind Irene and Lillian came both of his sisters, his mother and even his stepfather, Stanford, whom Annie had hardly seen except at mealtimes.

"Oh," she exclaimed, emotion welling up inside her. She stood up to get their attention and pointed to the row of empty chairs next to her. Tate helped his grandmother and great-aunt to their seats.

"You came." Annie felt completely at a loss for words, touched to her core. "You *all* came."

"Of course we did," Irene said briskly. "What's more delightful than a children's holiday program?"

Annie didn't have to think very hard to come up with many things but she wasn't about to argue with the formidable Sheridan matriarch. "There's plenty of room. Sit down."

There were exactly enough seats remaining on the row for his family. Somehow, she didn't know whether by accident or design, Tate ended up sitting next to her.

She caught Wendy's gaze and saw her friend looking with interest at the newcomers. "Um, Wendy, this is Tate Sheridan and his family. Tate, this is my good friend Wendy Walker. She is one of Wes's neighbors and her daughter Lucy is best friends with the twins."

The others were talking among themselves and she did not want to interrupt them to make introductions.

"Nice to meet you," he said. "I think we rode a sleigh past your house last weekend."

"Yes. That's right. Lucy was so excited about that. All my kids were."

"Is your husband an electrician, by any chance?"

"That's right. Adam Walker. Walker Electric."

"Good man. I've met him."

"I'm pretty crazy about him," Wendy said.

Before Annie could ask Tate how he could have met Adam Walker in the few short days he had been in town, the principal came out onto the stage.

"Welcome to the Holly Creek Elementary School first-grade holiday spectacular. This is a beloved tradition here and we are thrilled to have so many of you in attendance. Just a reminder to mute your cell phones. Also, be sure to sign the sheet on the way out with your child's name, grade and teacher if you would like to order a copy of the recording we're making of the performance. Only five dollars for a priceless memory and all proceeds go to the PTA. Without further ado, let me introduce the entire first grade, under the direction of Mrs. Celeste Wan, our school music teacher."

The curtains slowly opened, got stuck, then slid open the rest of the way, revealing sixty children standing on risers, all wearing white sweatshirts decorated with stenciled Christmas lights.

They launched into a jubilant rendition of "Rockin' Around the Christmas Tree." Annie had to smile as Wendy, far being annoyed, sat up and beamed at her daughter.

The program was short, only about forty minutes, mostly music but a few very cute skits. Annie saw that both Lillian and Irene were smiling throughout and even Catherine seemed to be enjoying the cute kids.

Adam Walker missed the first number but managed to squeeze in next to his wife as the first-graders were enthusiastically singing "I Have a Little Dreidel."

When they finished, including Alice's solo, the Sheridans were among the first to stand to give them all a standing ovation.

"Bravo," Irene called. "Bravo."

The principal got up and announced that there were refreshments at the back of the gymnasium and parents could find their first-graders and visit with them.

Annie rose and was thanking all of Tate's family for coming to support the twins when Alice and Henry came rushing over.

"Hi, everybody! You all came to see us?" Alice looked astounded.

"Isn't that wonderful?" Annie said.

"We are so glad we did, too. We would have hated to miss such a grand show," Lillian said kindly.

"Yes. You did a marvelous job," Irene said. "I especially enjoyed your solo. You have a lovely voice, young lady. I hope you'll consider singing something for us on Christmas Eve tomorrow."

"I will."

Annie wanted to protest that the Sheridans should be having their own celebration, which didn't need to include the ranch caretaker and her temporary charges, but it didn't seem appropriate to argue right now while the twins were glowing from their performance.

"Do you want a cookie, Tate?" Alice asked. She slipped her hand into his as if to tug him to the refreshment stand. Her niece was definitely smitten with him. It would have made Annie smile, if only she didn't feel the exact same way.

"I think I'm good right now. I have to, er, get back to a project I'm working on. But thanks. You really did a great job. You, too, Henry."

"Thanks. Auntie, can I go get a cookie?"

"Yes. Only one."

"But they have tons!" Henry protested.

"You have to make sure they have enough for everyone else who is here."

When the twins both rushed off toward the refreshment table, Annie turned to Tate. "Thank you again for coming. You made their day. They forgot all about being sad their parents aren't here."

"I wouldn't have missed it for anything and was touched to be invited."

He looked as if he wanted to say more but Adam Walker drew him away. The two men moved to an edge of the gymnasium, talking intently.

Something was definitely going on. Annie was intensely curious to know what, but reminded herself it wasn't any of her business.

She was only the hired help. She needed to remember that. The Sheridans were so kind and inclusive of her and the twins but she had to remember the family would be leaving in a few days.

Soon enough, life would return to the way it had been before Tate showed up at the ranch. Predictable. Safe. Boring.

And empty.

24

ON CHRISTMAS EVE MORNING, BRIE WOKE feeling restless and wasn't sure exactly why.

Her mother was definitely part of it, of course. Learning about Pamela's cancer diagnosis had definitely sent her into a spiral.

In the old days, she would have had a drink—or two or three—to help take off the edge of anxiety. The trouble was, spending her life drunk or high took the edge off everything.

Joy, happiness, excitement. It was all filtered through substances.

She didn't want that anymore. Part of her journey this past year had been learning other ways to calm her emotions.

She couldn't remember a time when she had so many emotions vying for control at once.

Her go-to was walking. She didn't know if it was the physical activity, the rhythmic, almost meditative movement or just breathing fresh air, but it always calmed her.

Needing it more than ever, Brie threw on her boots and parka and headed out into the December morning.

With no clear destination in mind, she headed down to the mailbox again. She had clocked the distance on her phone as a quarter mile down and a quarter mile back. It wasn't that far but at least it was enough to get her blood pumping.

One of the ranch dogs joined her on the walk, sticking close enough to let her pet him a few times before racing ahead.

What a beautiful day. A little more snow had fallen in the night, just a skiff. It clung to the tree branches and covered the fence posts.

She was going to miss this place.

She shook her head, astounded at the realization. She had not wanted to come, would have preferred to spend Christmas anywhere else but here. She never would have guessed that the past week she had spent at the Angel's View would be so pivotal in her life.

Her family was closer than ever. Those days she and her mother had cooked for everyone while Annie finished making her blankets would remain seared in Brie's memory. They had laughed together more than she remembered in a long time.

Even then, she had known her mother was hiding something from her but had decided she wouldn't let it bother her. Now that she knew the truth, it only made her admire Pamela more for being able to find joy and humor while confronting fear and uncertainty.

Brie did not know what the future held for her mother and she had still not found the courage to talk to Tate about working for the Sheridan Trust.

Whatever happened would happen. That was the greatest gift she had received so far, this new serenity. Whatever happened, she would deal with it.

She was heading back to the house when she spotted someone coming out of the barn, leading two horses.

Her heart began to pound. She hadn't seen Levi since the day he had convinced her to take Lacey for a ride and they had shared that stunning kiss.

She had avoided going down to the barn, needing space and distance to figure things out. She also knew he had been busy helping Tate with the renovations at Wes McCade's house.

Now here he was, leading a big bay and the smaller horse she recognized as Lacey. Both were saddled.

She didn't have time to be nervous about seeing him again.

"Morning," he called.

"Hi. Merry Christmas Eve."

His smile was a little wary. "Same to you. I saw you out walking this morning and wondered if you might want to take a little ride."

"You're crazy. It's freezing!"

He inclined his head. "You've got a warm coat on."

"And the wrong kind of boots again."

From behind his back, he pulled out the boots she had worn when she'd ridden Lacey around the arena.

"It would be a short one. I've only got an hour before I'm meeting Tate and a crew at the house to finish moving all the furniture back in from the garage."

"I'll be there right behind you. My mom and sister and I are staging the house, with all the accessories we bought. We even picked up a little Christmas tree. That was Cat's idea."

"Your family has done a nice thing for Wes and his kids. He's had a rough time of it the past year."

"I can certainly relate a little to what he's going through. I've had plenty of experience trying to escape through drinking or pills or whatever. What we've done won't take away his pain by any means but I hope it brings a little light to the darkness and helps him remember a whole town cares about him."

"I'm sure it will help. So, what do you say? Quick horseback ride? There's a trail that goes along the creek bottom."

"The one you told me about, where you go with Tanner to see river otters."

"They might be out this morning. Want to check it out?"

She did, suddenly. She couldn't imagine a better Christmas Eve morning than a short horseback ride to see otters.

She grabbed the boots from him and sat down on a bench outside the barn to change from her clunky, fake-fur-lined snow boots to the cowboy boots. She set her own boots inside the barn so they wouldn't be completely frozen when she put them back on, then let him help her mount the horse.

Once they started across the ranch, Brie realized there was a vast difference between riding a horse around an indoor arena and being outside in the cold morning air.

This was a million times better.

She leaned into the moment, trying to record every detail so that she could take it out of her memory to relive when she returned to the city. The horses' breath, steaming in the morning air, the clink of the tack, their hoofbeats on the snowy road.

It was all perfect, especially the cowboy riding beside her.

Levi smiled at her. "Doing okay?"

"Better than okay," she said, adjusting her weight in the saddle.

They passed some of the shaggy Highland cattle, who turned to follow their progress with interest, watching through their long bangs. Brie gazed up at the mountains, filled with a deep love for this place.

She didn't want to sell.

The truth settled over her, as warm and comforting as a crackling fire.

Her grandfather had loved this place and now Brie did, too.

Yes, it held painful memories. It always would. But perhaps she had not given the wonderful memories enough weight. She had far more of those. This week had given her even more.

What were the chances she could convince the rest of the family to keep the property for a little while longer?

A week ago, before she had come here to the ranch, Brie would have thought she didn't have a chance of convincing her family of anything.

Now she wasn't so sure. Tate listened to her and so did her mother. Even Irene seemed more inclined to give her an opportunity to speak her mind.

Did she have the courage to talk to them about keeping the ranch in the family, as Wallace would have liked, at least for now?

She had to try.

"The otters are usually right there where the creek bends," Levi said. He drew in the reins and she did the same. They stayed on their horses, peering through the bare branches of some brush along the riverbank.

"There." He pointed.

She craned her neck, trying to see.

"You might have a better view off the horse, if we go a little closer. Be careful in those slick boots," he said.

He helped her down to the ground and took her hand. They moved a little off the road, to a spot where she had an unobstructed view of the river, steam rising up in the cold air.

After a moment, she finally saw movement.

"Oh. I see them!"

They were adorable, a family of three dark shapes wriggling through the creek, two large and one smaller. They would huddle for warmth for a while, then one would dive away to find something to eat and bring it back to the others.

That is what a family did. They took care of each other.

They watched the otters cavort in the water for a long time. This was another memory she would sear into her mind.

"Ready to go back?" he finally asked.

She didn't want to leave, but he had to go meet Levi and her feet were going to be frostbitten in the cowboy boots if she stood much longer in the snow.

"I guess."

As they headed back toward the ranch, Brie realized she felt more and more comfortable on the horse.

She wanted to come back in the summer and take Lacey up into the mountains. It would be tough going back on the trail where her father had died, but for the first time in her life, she thought she might be strong enough to handle it.

Especially if she had Levi by her side.

She glanced behind her where he rode, this good man she was coming to care about so much.

She thought she was done running from things that threatened her. So why was she running so hard from Levi?

He helped her off the horse outside the barn, then quickly stepped away. "I can see to the horses. You're probably freezing."

"I'll help. My father would have grounded me for a week if I let someone else take care of my horse."

He looked as if he wanted to argue but he finally shrugged.

"Thank you for this morning," she said after they had brushed the horses and returned them to their stalls. "It was magical."

"I'm glad. I hope it's not twenty years before you do it again."

"It won't be."

He smiled and she saw sadness there again. She suddenly remembered how tough the holidays were for him, not being with his son.

"How are you doing? I should have asked. Are you talking to Tanner today?"

Pain spasmed across his face. "We're planning a video call later today and again in the morning, assuming Santa finds him in the Caribbean."

"Santa is pretty good about that kind of thing."

"So I hear. I also sent some presents along with his mom for him to open down there."

"You're a good father, Levi. And a good man."

He gazed at her for a moment and she saw sadness in his eyes. She longed to wipe it. Without thinking it through, she stepped forward and kissed him.

She meant the embrace only as comfort but heat instantly sparked between them, pushing away the last of the chill from their ride.

Now *this* was the perfect way to spend Christmas Eve morning. A horseback ride, cute river otters and a kiss she felt all the way to her toes.

She felt so right in his arms, perfectly safe and filled with joy. Nothing else mattered but this.

She wanted the kiss to go on forever but one of the horses down the row of stalls neighed and the sound seemed to drag Levi back to awareness.

He wrenched his mouth away and gazed down at her, his eyes dark and unreadable. "I can't do this with you, Brie," he finally said.

Apparently it was only the perfect Christmas Eve morning for her. Pain sliced through her. "I'm sorry," she said, wishing she had never acted on the impulse. She turned to leave the barn, to escape the awkwardness and embarrassment of the moment, but he reached out a hand to stop her from going.

"When I kiss you, I only want more. It's hell, knowing I can't have it."

She swallowed, gathering her nerve. "Do you know when I said the other night that I don't trust myself to make the right choices?"

He nodded. "Has anything changed?"

"Not really. I still have a long way to go before I trust myself." She paused and stepped forward, her heart pounding. "But I trust you. Completely."

He stared. "You hardly know me"

She shrugged. "I trust you because my grandfather trusted you. Because Tate does and Annie does."

She smiled, feeling more right about this than anything else in her life. "And because I've seen what a good man you are. The man I'm falling in love with. That's all that really matters, isn't it?"

His gaze darkened and he kissed her again. This time, she let all her growing feelings for him filter into the kiss.

It was soft, tender, earthshattering.

When he lifted his head, both of them were smiling and Brie knew she would never forget this bubbling joy shooting through her veins, better than anything else she had ever experienced.

It was real and right and perfect.

She didn't know where this would lead but they had time to figure it out.

He was everything she had ever wanted and never thought she deserved. In his arms, she began to realize maybe she was wrong all this time.

Levi saw the best in her. The person she wanted to be. The person she was finally beginning to accept that she could be.

What more could she ever want?

25

TATE HAD NEVER WORKED SO HARD IN HIS LIFE, but by early afternoon on Christmas Eve, Wes McCade's house renovation was complete.

A crew of Levi, Pastor Morris and three more guys from Wes's church had helped move back all the furniture and Brie and Catherine were making the bed in Alice's room. He could hear them laughing about something, though he didn't know what it was.

Brie seemed in a giddy mood. He suspected he knew why, especially when he had caught her and Levi Moran stealing a kiss when they were supposed to be carrying in some throw rugs from the garage.

They didn't know he had seen them, as he had shut the door quietly and returned to the house, trying to figure out how he felt about that.

Levi seemed like a stand-up guy. He had worked every bit as hard as Tate during this hurried renovation. Tate also knew his grandfather had had nothing but good to say about the man and Annie considered him a good friend.

The bottom line was, he trusted Brie's judgment.

A year ago—hell, even a few weeks ago—he might not have been able to say that. But he knew how far she had come. He wanted his sister to be grounded, to be happy. If Levi Moran could provide that, Tate was all for it.

Still, he was aware of a niggling envy.

He wanted the same thing.

He wanted to be able to steal kisses with Annelise, to share all his hopes and his dreams and his troubles with her.

The weight of all his new responsibilities had never felt as onerous. How could he ask her or any woman to be part of his life when he knew he would be spending years trying to fill his grandfather's shoes?

Tate glanced at his watch as the last lamp was turned on and his mother put the final ornament on the Christmas tree Catherine had insisted on.

"That looks terrific."

Pamela smiled. She was still too thin but no longer seemed quite as fragile and breakable as she had earlier in the week. Maybe sharing the news with them had given her some additional strength. He wanted to think that perhaps she had found new energy through helping with this project.

"Thank you, everyone," Tate said as they all stood admiring their work. "The place looks amazing."

"I can't wait for them to see it." Wes's pastor, who had done most of the organizing and coordinated the volunteers, looked around the house with satisfaction.

"I only wish we could be here for the big reveal," his wife, Sara, said.

"Don't worry," Catherine said. "I videoed all the before and after stuff and everyone setting things up today. I'm going to make a movie out of it. When I'm done, I'll send it to you."

That was all news to Tate, though he had wondered why she was hanging around so much, asking the workers questions and videoing what they were doing on her phone.

"Thank you," Sara said. "Maybe when Wes gets home, we should have a big party at the church and show everyone the video. I hope you can all make it."

They would only be here until Monday, two days after Christmas. That was the day the Sheridan jet was coming to pick up the family and fly them all back to California. His mother had a doctor's appointment and he knew both he and Brie wanted to be there for her.

Tate knew that was where he needed to be but the thought of leaving Annie and the twins was tearing him apart.

He shook the pastor's hands. "Thanks again for all your help. I'm sure you had plenty to do tending to your flock during this busy season without me throwing a last-minute service project your way."

"We were all doing exactly what we needed to be doing. What's the point of talking over the pulpit about how a baby changed the world if you're not willing to help be that change yourself?"

Tate smiled. "Merry Christmas, everybody."

"Thank you for making it memorable," Sara Morris said with a smile.

It was, he thought. He had spent every holiday for the past ten years in far-flung corners of the globe working with the Sheridan Trust. He had loved all of that work and the end result and remembered every person he had met along the way.

Something told him this year, coming back to the Angel's View Ranch, would be the most momentous Christmas of his life.

★ ★ ★

Annie expected to spend a quiet Christmas Eve with the twins. They had talked about what they wanted to do and had agreed that before church they would have their own simple dinner of the twins' favorite, pigs in a blanket, then after church they would play games and read some favorite stories together before bed.

Maybe if they had time, for a special treat they would walk down to the barn and see the puppies, who had opened their eyes that very afternoon, in what the twins viewed as a holiday miracle.

Irene Sheridan wouldn't hear of it.

She accosted Annie in the kitchen while she was putting the finishing touches on the ham and mashed potatoes for the family's dinner.

"I completely understand that you have your own traditions," she said when Annie explained her and the twins' plan. "Is it possible for you to rearrange them? We would love to have you join us for a special treat this evening before dinner."

Annie stared at the woman who had become so dear to her this week. "What sort of treat?"

"My grandson thought it would be fun to take another sleigh ride with that nice man who helped us the other day for Wallace's memorial. He's coming in an hour and we thought we would take a short ride around the neighborhood to look at Christmas lights."

"You don't need two very energetic children along with you."

"We absolutely do. Why do you think Tate arranged the whole thing? What's the fun of a sleigh ride if you don't have some children along to enjoy it?"

"Lillian has her son and his family now."

Tom and his wife, Carrie, had arrived early that morning

with their young teenagers in tow, adding to the festive feeling inside the ranch house.

"Yes, but the more, the merrier. That's what I always say."

Annie suspected Irene had never said those words before in her life. This all seemed so odd. Why wouldn't Tate have asked her himself? Why send his grandmother to do it?

And where was he? Annie had hardly seen him all week, since the day he took her to the Family Connection and then to the jail. Only that brief encounter at the twins' program.

She missed him.

How ridiculous. In a few days, he would be flying back to California for good.

"Those children have been such a bright spot for all of us during this holiday season," Irene said. "It would mean so much to me if you would let us enjoy their company a little longer."

"I suppose I could send the twins on the sleigh ride," she finally said. "But I should probably stay here so I can finish taking care of dinner."

Irene would not hear of that. "Not at all," she said firmly. "You have to come, too. I insist. Dinner can wait."

Annie was mystified by her insistence but didn't know how she could possibly refuse.

She didn't want to go with them. Every moment she spent with Tate and his family only endeared them all to her more. The twins would be delighted, though, Annie knew. It might help distract them from all they were missing this year.

Just as the sun was sliding behind the mountains, she bundled the children up in their winter gear and they all headed out to the great room.

"I can't believe we get to go on another sleigh ride!" Alice exclaimed when they all walked outside to the waiting rig.

"And on Christmas Eve," Henry said, all but vibrating with excitement. "Do you think we'll see Santa?"

"Well, our driver is named Nick," Catherine pointed out.

"And I'm lively and quick," he said from atop the sleigh, earning groans from the teenager and her cousins.

Soon they were all loaded up, even Levi. Everyone except for Tom and his wife, who said they had some unpacking still to do and offered to stay and keep watch on the ham.

Annie was among the last to climb in. Wasn't it just her luck that the only spot was next to Tate? She squeezed in, heart pounding at being so close to him.

She glanced across the sleigh and was startled to see Levi and Brie sharing a blanket. She couldn't be sure but she thought they might be holding hands under there.

Brie must have caught her looking. She shrugged a little but sent Annie a smile so filled with joy it seemed to light up the twilight.

"Yeah," Tate murmured, following her gaze. "I'm not sure when that all happened. But good for them."

Annie felt a sharp pang of jealousy under her breastbone. She didn't begrudge them any happiness. She cared about both of them and wanted the best for them.

No. She was being selfish, aching for the happy ending she knew she couldn't have.

The sleigh set off down the ranch access road that ran along the creek bottom.

"We should sing something," Catherine said.

She was sitting across from them and seemed to be in an almost giddy mood, videoing the whole thing on her phone. Her cousin, who was a few years younger with glorious ebony hair, also had her phone out and seemed to be videoing the ride.

"Tate, can we sing the burrito song?" Alice was sitting on his other side, never letting him far out of her sight. Annie wasn't sure whose heart was going to be most broken when he left. Hers or her niece's."

"I'm not sure everybody knows that song," he said.

"We know it, though. Me and Henry have been practicing. They can sing the 'tuqui tuqui' part. That's easy."

"Hey! I learned that song at school," the younger London girl piped up.

She started singing in Spanish and the twins and Tate joined in. Annie was sitting close enough to hear each word, as if he sang only to her. She tried not to shiver.

Nobody else knew the song but they all joined enthusiastically on the chorus and the twins giggled madly when they were done.

After that, Henry wanted to sing "Jingle Bells" and then Pamela suggested "Away in a Manger."

Annie was so busy singing along and trying her best not to be pushed onto Tate's lap by the jostling sleigh that she didn't realize their destination until they pulled up in front of Wes's house.

Her voice trailed off as they sang the last words of the song. "What are we doing here?" she asked, completely baffled.

Why did she suddenly have a feeling she was the only one on the sleigh who didn't know a secret?

Catherine aimed her phone camera at her. "What's this place?" she asked in a voice that suddenly sounded entirely too innocent.

"This is our house," Alice said in excitement. Henry also looked confused.

Okay. At least three of them were completely out of the loop.

There was a suppressed energy suddenly. Even Nick was grinning.

"Just a little Christmas surprise," Irene said.

Annie was baffled. What on earth was happening? Had they arranged some kind of special gift for the children?

"Look, Henry," Alice said. "We have a Christmas tree in our very own house!"

Annie could see it gleaming in the window, bright colors against the December night.

Was that the surprise? It seemed an odd thing to do, especially when the children weren't living here right now, but she wasn't going to argue.

"We should go in," Catherine suggested, still aiming her phone at Annie.

Annie looked around the sleigh, not sure she liked being out of the loop.

"Yes, everybody out," Irene ordered.

This was so strange. She felt a little dizzy, her heart pounding as Tate helped Annie out of the sleigh and lifted out the twins while Levi helped Irene and Lillian to the ground.

"What's going on?" Annie demanded.

"You'll see," Brie said with a reassuring smile.

"The door should be open," Tate said.

Why on earth was the door open? She knew she had locked it the last time she was here, when they had come after Wallace's memorial.

"The twins and Annie should probably go first," he said.

She didn't want to suddenly. It was childish and silly but she sensed something significant waited for her inside. They were all watching them with that same giddy delight and she knew she couldn't linger out here in the cold, especially not when Lillian and Irene must be freezing.

Heart pounding, she gripped the twins' hands—they suddenly seemed as nervous as she was—and together they walked into the house.

Somehow when she pushed open the door, she found Catherine and her cousin already inside, phones out. She wasn't sure how they managed it.

But she suddenly knew why.

She looked around in shock at the old farmhouse, which was completely transformed.

This was her brother's house, but not her brother's house.

Annie's mouth dropped. This was the house he and Cassie had wanted to create for their children, exactly like the mood boards her late sister-in-law had showed off so excitedly as they were working on the renovation.

It was done. Every bit of it.

The woodwork was finished and stained, the floors had been refinished, carpet had been laid down the stairs to the basement.

Shock reverberated through her and all she could do was stare.

"How? When?" The words tangled up inside her. Her gaze found Tate. "Did you do this?"

Tate smiled. "No. Not really. I may have started the ball rolling by making a few phone calls but the community of Holly Creek took that ball and ran. We had volunteers working on everything from flooring to painting to finishing the cabinets. Brie picked up all the accessories and she and my mom and Catherine staged it all for you."

"It's incredible. I… I don't know what to say."

"You don't have to say anything," Brie said gently. "We loved doing it."

"I had to turn down a lot of people who wanted to volunteer," Tate said. "We didn't have room inside the house for them all to work at the same time."

"This doesn't even look like our house," Henry exclaimed.

"I *love* it!" Alice twirled around in a circle, hands clasped to her chest. "I really, really love it."

"Go see your bedrooms," Catherine said, still videoing. "They're really cool."

Annie was completely overwhelmed. The idea of all these people working behind the scenes to help her struggling brother and his children brought tears to her eyes. She wiped them away and let out a sound that was a cross between a laugh and a sob.

"Thank you all so much. I just... Thank you."

Her gaze met Tate's and she found him smiling at her with an expression that stole her breath.

"You should have a tour," Brie said. "Come on. Let me show you everything."

She linked her arm through Annie's and tugged her through the house, pointing out gorgeous details Annie knew it would take her a long time to absorb.

"How on earth did everyone pull this off?"

"Tate gets things done," Brie said simply. "He has worked tirelessly calling people, organizing volunteers, ordering supplies."

Annie felt tears trickle out all over again. She had never been given such an incredible gift. Even though the real recipient was her brother and the children, it was priceless to her.

"What do you think Wes will say?" Levi asked as Brie and Annie returned to the living area.

That was an excellent question. People had tried to help him with the renovations before and he hadn't been receptive to their offers. What could he do about it now? The work was done. The entire town had come together to show him that life had to go on after his terrible loss.

"His pride might get in the way at first," Annie admitted. "He has been stubborn about wanting to do the work himself. But I think once he realizes this was done out of concern and love for him and the twins, he will come around."

She hoped, anyway. She could only pray his time in jail had helped him see he didn't have to carry his pain alone, that the entire town wanted to help.

This was a beautiful, comfortable, warm place for him to heal—for Wes to see that life could once more be filled with grace, with beauty.

With love.

Later that night, after dinner and a church service where Annie had cried as she hugged friends and neighbors who had helped out with the renovation, she was still glowing from the magical Christmas Eve.

Even so, Annie was aware of a tiny thread of sadness weaving through all the joy.

This night had been so wonderful she didn't want it to end. Christmas Day was one step further to the moment when Tate and his family would leave.

"And please bless that Santa will be able to bring home our daddy so we can go home for Christmas and I can sleep in my new bedroom," Alice finished her prayer.

Annie's throat felt tight but she swallowed down the tears. She decided not to argue or tell Alice her dream was impossible.

"We get to talk to your dad tomorrow on the phone," she said. "Won't that be nice? And he'll be home soon."

"Can we still sleep in our new house?"

"Maybe," Annie said, not wanting to commit. There was really no reason they couldn't have stayed there tonight, other than convenience as all the children's gifts were here at her apartment, tucked under her bed.

"Merry Christmas, Auntie," Alice said, hugging her tight.

"I love you, sweetheart."

"And me," Henry said.

She smiled, going to his bed to hug him also. "And you. Now go to sleep or Santa can't come."

After she closed the door to their room, Annie tidied up her sitting room while she waited for them to fall asleep. She had never done the whole Santa thing but assumed it would take some time for them to be deeply enough into slumber that she would feel safe about setting their gifts under the tree.

She had a few more last-minute things to wrap so she did that in her own bedroom with the door locked, in case they wandered out for a drink of water.

Finally, she decided enough time had passed. She peeked in their room and found their eyes closed and their breathing deep and even. They were either both asleep, miracle of miracles, or doing a very good impression of it.

Setting out their gifts and filling the stockings didn't take long. She took a picture to save for Wes to see later.

As she admired the little tree with its homemade ornaments, Annie knew she wouldn't need pictures for her to remember this year always. It had been the single most memorable Christmas of her life,

How would she ever go back to the routine of her ordinary days?

After the excitement of the day, Annie was too restless to sleep yet. She settled into her favorite easy chair by the fire with a book of her favorite holiday short stories.

She finished one and had started another when she suddenly remembered she had one more gift for the twins—two sets of new markers she had bought at the grocery store and had hidden in a drawer in the kitchen when they were helping her unload the groceries.

The ranch kitchen was dark when she walked out to grab them. It was late and apparently all the Sheridans—and Londons—had settled into their suites for bed.

She almost wished she had something to do in the kitchen to calm her racing thoughts but she couldn't think of anything. That morning, Annie had prepped a couple of make-ahead farmers' breakfast casseroles and planned to throw them into the oven first thing, to go with a creamy pecan French toast dish. It was something people could eat at different times of the day, whenever they finished their holiday celebrations.

She quickly found the markers and was about to head back to her apartment when she noticed a glow coming from the great room.

Oh. The big Christmas tree lights were still on and they shouldn't be at this hour.

Tate and Levi had set them to a timer that automatically turned off at midnight but maybe they had malfunctioned. Or perhaps someone had accidentally turned off the timer.

She frowned. Should she leave them on?

No. If it were an artificial tree, she might consider it but a real tree could catch fire, especially if the lights were left on too long and overheated.

In her capacity as the Angel's View caretaker, she would be remiss not to turn them off.

Leaving the markers on the counter to grab on her way back to her apartment, Annie headed into the room and then froze when she realized why the lights twinkled on the tree so late.

They hadn't been left on by accident. Tate was there, sitting in the chair by the fireplace, a book open on his lap. He must have turned them back on.

She wanted to sneak back the way she had come, not sure she had the emotional energy to face him right now, but he looked up when she walked out and she saw a mix of emotions cross his features in rapid succession, so quickly she couldn't identify them.

"Hi."

She hesitated, wishing she had stayed in her rooms where she was safe from these emotions that felt too big, too overwhelming.

She walked forward, not sure what to do. She had not had the chance to talk privately with Tate since that incredible moment when she had walked into her brother's house to find the amazing renovation job he had spearheaded.

She didn't know what to say to him.

How could she express how very much he had touched her heart, without spilling out everything else she felt about him and embarrassing them both?

"I thought everyone had gone to sleep," she said.

"They have, I think. Everyone but us. You should be exhausted. Why are you still up?"

"I suddenly remembered a couple of gifts for the twins I had hidden in the kitchen. I was grabbing them so I could stick them in their stockings."

"Ah."

"And then I saw the lights out here and was worried the tree would catch on fire if they stayed on all night."

"I'll make sure I turn them off."

She had to say something. She couldn't leave things hanging between them when her heart was so very full of gratitude.

She swallowed. "Tate. Tonight. What you did. I don't have words to thank you for the gift you gave my brother and the twins. It was…life-changing."

"I hope it helps," he said gruffly. "I also hope Wes doesn't think it was charity. Remind him, will you, that he had almost all the supplies already. We only had to pick up a few things. And everyone donated their labor."

"I'll tell him. Believe me, he will love it, after the initial shock wears off."

"I hope so."

"We're having a video call with him tomorrow. I thought about having the twins show him around the house using my phone, but maybe the big reveal should wait until he's actually out and can see for himself. What do you think?"

"Either way would work."

Yes. She was leaning more toward the latter idea. When he was released in a few weeks would be soon enough.

"He will love it," she repeated. "You've given him something far beyond the house renovation. You've given him and the children a chance to start fresh. Renewed hope. I cannot overstate the value of such a gift."

The words seemed to catch in her throat and all the emotions of the day poured through her again. Annie was helpless to hold them back this time. A few of the tears she had been holding inside trickled out and she gave a single sob and then another and then she was weeping.

They were tears of gratitude and of joy, yes. But also of sorrow.

She did not want Tate to go.

Through her tears, she saw he looked lost for a moment, his eyes filled with distress, and then he stepped forward and pulled her into his arms.

She froze. This was not what she needed. She should escape to her own room where she could cry in peace. She couldn't seem to make the rest of her limbs cooperate. How could she leave the warm, enticing comfort of his arms?

"Don't cry, sweetheart," he murmured. "Please don't cry. I'm sorry. Whatever I did, I'm sorry."

She shook her head and managed a watery laugh. "Please. Don't be sorry. You did nothing wrong. What you did. It was wonderful."

"If it was so wonderful, why are you crying like your heart is breaking?"

Because I love you. And you're leaving.

She couldn't tell him the truth, of course. She could never take those words back.

"It's a lot to take in," she said instead.

She rested her head against his chest, savoring every single impression. She knew she wouldn't forget this holiday season.

This moment, here beside the Christmas tree they had cut down, with a fire in the hearth and Tate's arms around her? This would be a memory to make her ache for years to come. When she was Irene's age, feisty and formidable, she knew it would still feel as fresh and painful.

"Why did you do it?" she finally asked. "I know the twins are sweet and everything, but why go to so much trouble for someone you haven't seen in years? This was supposed to be a time for you to enjoy being with your family. Instead, you organized a home renovation almost from the ground up in what had to be an insanely short amount of time. Why?"

26

TATE DIDN'T KNOW HOW TO ANSWER. NOT without revealing things he was certain she didn't want to hear.

His arms tightened and he closed his eyes, trying to find the words.

He knew the reason the project had come to mean so much to him. He had known since the afternoon of the children's program, when he had returned to the renovation.

He had been in the middle of helping to paint one of the bedrooms when someone asked him a question. He didn't even remember what it was now. He did remember they had to ask him three times because his mind was not there in that house.

It was here. With Annie.

He had been thinking about her nonstop the entire time he

worked on the house. Wondering if she would like the paint color, the backsplash in the kitchen, the bathroom tile pattern.

The truth had come to him then.

He hadn't organized the renovation for Wes or for the twins. They might have been the ultimate recipients but Annie had been the catalyst.

It was all for her.

He wanted to see her smile, to take some of the burden from her shoulders.

"Why?" she asked again now.

He gazed down at her, this woman who had become so vitally important to him in such a short span of time.

No. It had been longer, he realized. She had meant something to him years ago. This week had only renewed a bond that had always been there.

He had to tell her.

All the reasons he had been fighting these feelings pinched and prodded him like needles from the Christmas tree. The problems were still there between them, things he didn't know how to conquer.

He was still about to take on responsibilities that overwhelmed him where his presence would be required at Sheridan International headquarters and she had responsibilities here, with the children, that he would never ask her to forsake.

And his grandmother planned to sell the ranch Annelise loved and he wasn't sure she would ever be able to forgive him for that.

None of that mattered right now. Suddenly Tate was certain they could work through any obstacle, if both of them were willing. He knew he was, with everything inside him.

Was she?

There was only one way to find out.

"It was all for you," he murmured.

Her gaze met his and he saw more tears spill out. "For…me?"

He brushed one away with his thumb, wishing he could take away all her tears. "That's not supposed to make you cry."

She gave a disbelieving laugh that ended in a sob. "Did you honestly think you could tell me that and I wouldn't cry?"

"I don't know what I thought," he admitted. "If you want the truth, I haven't been thinking straight since the day I came to the ranch. You've got me tangled up in knots, Annelise McCade."

"Me?"

"Yes. You." He couldn't resist the pull another moment. He lowered his mouth and found hers.

The kiss was gentle, sweet, overflowing with all the tenderness he felt toward this amazing woman he knew was in his heart forever.

Annelise was the piece that had been missing his entire life. The one who calmed the chaos and made everything else feel right.

"I love you," he finally murmured. The words he had never said to another woman should have felt awkward but they didn't. They felt like the most natural thing in the world.

Apparently not to her. Not yet, anyway.

"You…what?" She stared at him, green eyes dark with shock.

He drew in a breath and kissed her again, unable to resist. "I love you," he repeated. "When I came to the Angel's View, I was dreading every moment of this holiday season. I didn't want to say a final goodbye to my grandfather or deal with the rest of the family or face that my life will change forever when I return to the city."

She opened her mouth as if to argue again that his place was with the Sheridan Trust. This wasn't the time for that discussion, especially because as he had worked on her brother's house, Tate had also come to find a certain peace with the expectations his family had for him.

Some part of him would always relish the time he had spent working for the trust, knowing he had made a difference to countless lives.

He had the opportunity to do the same now in a different way, to continue his grandfather's legacy using all the lessons Wallace had instilled over the years.

He was actually looking forward to the challenge of it now, trying to incorporate all the things he had learned through running the trust into the business side of things.

He could tell her all of that later. For now, this moment beside the Christmas tree, he focused on how this woman had come back into his life and changed everything.

"I was dreading being here at the Angel's View. And then the moment I set foot on the ranch, someone smacked me with a snowball and everything changed in an instant."

Delicious color climbed her cheekbones and she gave an embarrassed laugh.

"I'm still mortified about that."

"Don't be," he said. "I wouldn't change a single thing about the time I've been here. You brought joy to my life, Annie. Laughter and happiness and love, with your kind heart and your generous spirit. I never expected to fall in love. But how could I do anything else?"

"Oh, Tate."

She kissed him this time, her mouth warm and willing and her arms tight around him. She shared his feelings. She couldn't kiss him like that if she didn't.

Joy and wonder soared through him, higher than the tallest pine on the mountain.

He laughed. He couldn't help it. She smiled against his mouth. "What's so funny?"

"Not funny. Just wonderful. You are the best Christmas gift I could ever have. The only one I could ever want."

She shook her head. "I'm the one who feels like someone just handed me everything I ever wanted."

He kissed her again and somehow, he wasn't sure how, they ended up on the sofa together, with her in his lap and everything perfect in the world.

"I have to tell you something," she said after a long moment. "Promise you won't laugh."

"I'll try, but there are no guarantees," he said. "I'm so happy right now, who knows what will set me off?"

She smiled against his mouth. "I think I first fell in love with you when I was around Alice's age."

He stared. "You did not."

"Yes, I did. You were probably ten, the same age as my brother, but you were always so much nicer to me than he was. You all came back to the ranch for Christmas, I remember, and on Christmas Day one of your gifts was a new football. I begged and begged to play with you and Wes. He told me to go inside and leave you two alone, but you were so sweet to me. You showed me how to hold the ball and how to throw it and you never laughed at me when I threw it horribly. I fell in love with you that day and I never fell out. I only realized it this week when you came back to Angel's View, but you've been in my heart all these years."

He brushed his mouth against hers again, touched to the depths of his soul.

"Merry Christmas, Annelise."

"Merry Christmas."

She smiled, her eyes bright with joy and happiness and love, and Tate vowed he would spend the rest of their lives together making sure each Christmas was better than the one before.

EPILOGUE

CHRISTMAS AT ANGEL'S VIEW WAS A MAGICAL time for a wedding.

The great room was decorated in glorious holiday style, with another huge tree and garlands strewn everywhere.

Right now, it was filled with excited family and friends, Pastor Morris was waiting to officiate as they exchanged vows and the caterer had delicious food all ready for the party afterward.

It would be a lovely day, if only the bride could finish fixing her dress.

Annie sat at her sewing machine trying to fold one last tuck that wasn't laying right along the neckline.

"Is this really the best time for this?" Brie asked. "I mean, you do kind of have something else to do right now."

Annie looked up only long enough to see that Brie looked gorgeous in the wine-colored matron-of-honor dress she was wearing. Her dearest friend and the sister of her heart had missed *maid*-of-honor duties when she and Levi had married in a beautiful, quiet ceremony by the river in late summer.

They were currently living in the ranch manager's house where Annie had lived with her family so long ago, but Brie and Levi had recently purchased a plot of land across from the ranch to build their own place.

Annie was so thrilled for both of them, especially for Brie, who had recently taken a position as codirector of the Sheridan Trust along with Tate's previous second-in-command there.

The two women were splitting the travel duties, which worked out perfectly for Brie, who didn't seem to want to be too far from Levi and Tanner these days.

"The ceremony isn't supposed to start for another half hour. This will only take a second," Annie said as she focused on the dress. "I have to wear this thing all day, right? If I don't fix it, that tuck will drive me crazy."

"I didn't see anything wrong with it," Lillian London said, somewhat grumpily.

"The dress you designed is perfect," Annie assured her. "I couldn't ask for a more gorgeous wedding gown and I'm so honored the amazing Lillian London designed an exclusive for me. I love everything about it. It just sags about a quarter inch on the back neckline."

"I knew I should have done the work myself," Lillian groused. "I can't trust anyone else these days."

"I didn't really notice it until today, or I would have fixed it myself after the final fitting last week."

"No one will even see your back, with the veil," Irene pointed out.

"Maybe not, but I'll know it's there. And I want everything to be perfect today."

She was nearly done when the cutest flower girl ever popped

her head into the room, the entwined floral crown on her head listing a little.

"I'm bored," she said. "Henry is hanging out with Tanner and I have no one to talk to."

"You can hang out with us. All the cool kids are in here," Catherine said from her spot on the sofa where she was filming everything, even Annie in her slip at her sewing machine. Annie suspected she was going to be a brilliant filmmaker someday. The video she had done that Christmas Eve a year ago still made Annie cry every time she watched it.

"Also, Daddy wants to know if everything is okay but he wasn't sure if it was okay to come back and ask himself. So I'm supposed to ask you and go back and tell him."

"I'm great," Annie assured her. "I have never been better."

"Okay," Alice said. She skipped out of the room again, hopefully to report to her father that all was well.

Wes would be walking her down the aisle, a task that seemed to make him more nervous than she ever would have guessed.

A year had changed so many things in her world. One of the biggest was her brother, who had made tremendous strides. The twins couldn't wait to spend Christmas with him this year, claiming they planned to have twice as much fun to make up for the previous year when he was in jail.

She had a vivid memory of the January day when he was released from jail. She and the kids had decided to wait and let the house renovation be a surprise to him. She had picked him up from the jail and the kids had somehow managed to keep the secret until they were back at his house.

She could still recall how Wes, completely unsuspecting, had walked through the door of his farmhouse and had stood in shock, looking around at all the unbelievable changes.

When she had told him the entire town had stepped up to do the work in only a few days, organized by Tate—that they were all invested in helping him work through his pain to a new beginning—tears had rolled down his face and he hadn't bothered to wipe them away.

She knew the past year had not been easy for her brother. Still, every month seemed better than the one before. She was incredibly proud at the way he had shifted gears so he wasn't focused exclusively on his own pain but on being present and engaged in his children's lives.

He was even dating again, which thrilled her beyond words. The woman in question was a widow also, with a preschool-age son who adored both Alice and Henry. She was kind and warm, everything Annie could have wanted for them.

It was too early to say whether their relationship would blossom into more but Annie had high hopes that her brother wouldn't screw it up.

She wanted Wes to find love again. How could she not, when her life was so full and rich and beautiful with Tate by her side?

"There. That should do it."

She pulled the dress away from her sewing machine and shook it out and Brie immediately stepped forward to help her into it, careful not to mess up Annie's makeup and her updo.

"Oh, you're right. That's much better," Brie said, smoothing a hand over the back of the dress.

"Let me see," Lillian demanded.

Annie turned in front of the other woman, feeling her scrutiny even if she couldn't see it.

"Okay. Yes. That *is* better."

Her mother came into the room at that moment, along with Pamela. Tate's mother was wearing a gorgeous, colorful scarf to cover her head, where her hair was growing back but still short and patchy from the chemotherapy.

The past year had been hard on her. But Christmas, a time of joy and renewal, had worked its miracle for Pamela, as well.

At her latest oncology appointment just a few weeks earlier, the doctors told her the tests were currently clear.

She wasn't out of the woods and would have to be monitored closely for years but Annie knew the whole family felt as if a dark cloud had parted and light finally was beginning to filter through.

"You're just in time to help with the veil," Irene commanded from her chair.

The two mothers, hers and the mother of the man she loved with all her heart, adjusted the veil, folding the fabric just so around her face.

"Are you ready for this, my dear?" Pamela asked.

"So ready," Annie answered firmly.

Tate was everything she had ever wanted. Despite their respective family trials over the past year, the two of them had leaned on each other for support, for encouragement, for love. She would have been lost without him and she couldn't wait to officially merge their lives together.

He had stepped up to embrace the challenge of taking over for Wallace. While she knew he still missed his work for the Sheridan Trust, he planned to continue scheduling in at least two projects a year where he could get his hands dirty helping other people.

For now, they were going to split their time between San Francisco and Wyoming so that she could still help Wes with the twins, at least until they were a little older.

It wouldn't be easy. Life rarely was, Annie thought as she walked out of the room followed by her wonderful entourage.

Lucky for them, she and Tate had dear friends, a supportive family and a love that shone brighter than a Christmas star.

★ ★ ★ ★ ★

Since nurse Abby Powell is between jobs, she agrees to move to Colorado with her son and care for her best friend's grandmother while the older woman recovers from a fall. She never expected to get roped into helping the woman's prickly grandson, Ethan Lancaster, decorate the historic home for Christmas in time for a town fundraiser.

Turn the page for a sneak preview of New York Times bestselling author RaeAnne Thayne's heartwarming Christmas romance, *Christmas at Holiday House.*

1

ABBY POWELL DROVE THROUGH THE DOWN-
town area of Silver Bells, Colorado, fighting the odd
sensation that she had somehow slipped onto the set of a Hall-
mark movie.

This couldn't be real, could it? No town could possibly look
so festive and charming and...perfect.

On this day before Thanksgiving, Christmas seemed to
have already taken over the ski resort town. Snow was lightly
falling, dusting everything with a soft, pearly powder. The
holiday season was in full view, from the brick storefronts
adorned with colorful Christmas lights twinkling merrily in
the dusk to the wreaths on every door in sight to the crowds
of shoppers in parkas and coordinating beanies who made their
way out of the stores, arms heavy with bags.

If she rolled down her windows, would she hear Christmas

music chiming through the early evening? She was tempted to check it out but glanced in the rearview mirror and decided her five-year-old son probably wouldn't appreciate a sudden ice-cold breeze.

This snow-globe perfection seemed like a different planet from Phoenix, where her apartment complex manager at least had made a bit of an effort to get into the spirit of things. Before they left, she had noticed a new string of lights on one of the saguaro cacti in the common area near the barbecue.

"Are we almost there, Mommy?"

She shot another glance a Christopher. "Nearly, honey. This is the right town. Now I only have to find the address."

"Good. I'm tired of the car."

She smiled at his overly dramatic tone. No one could sound more long-suffering than a five-year-old. "I know it's been a long drive, but you have been such a good boy."

"'Course I have. Santa's watching."

Christopher had been obsessed with Santa since before Halloween. She wasn't exactly sure what had flipped the switch this year. If someone could figure out the inner workings of a five-year-old boy's brain, she wanted to meet that person.

Maybe her son was finally old enough that the concept of a benevolent gift-giver made more sense. Or maybe his friends at preschool had discussed it at length.

"If he is watching," she said now to her son, "I know he has seen a boy who's been a big help to his mom on this drive."

This trip, nearly eight hours, was their longest road trip together. Christopher really had been wonderful. She hadn't been sure how he would be able to entertain himself for the journey. This would be a good test for the longer trip from Phoenix to Austin in a month's time, when she would be hauling a trailer full of some of their belongings.

The only other long road trip they'd ever taken together

had been in February when they had driven the six hours from Phoenix to Southern California. They had spent a long weekend there playing on the beach and spending an unforgettable day at Disneyland, just the two of them.

Everything was just the two of them these days.

Abby ignored the pang that thought always stirred in her. She did her best. She and Christopher took many trips to the zoo, the aquarium, local museums and festivals. She made certain her son had a rich life, filled with swimming lessons, playdates and educational opportunities.

She never felt like it was enough. Did every single mother worry she wasn't hitting some mythical benchmark that defined good parenting?

Probably. Single or not, likely every parent, regardless of relationship status, stressed about the same thing. Why hadn't anybody warned her worry was part of the job description?

Her navigation system instructed her to make a right at the next street. At the stop sign, she signaled, then obeyed and was struck by how the business of the downtown area seemed to melt away, replaced by a serene, tree-lined road bordered with older homes behind iron fences, each more lovely than the one before.

Where was Holiday House, her destination?

She peered down the street through the soft, swirling flakes that had begun to fall harder, obscuring her view.

Navigation system or not, she expected she would know the place when she saw it. During the two years they had been college roommates, Lucy Lancaster had shown her plenty of pictures of the huge, graceful mansion where her friend had spent the happiest moments of her childhood.

Abby could picture it in her mind: three stories, with a wide porch across the entire front, a smaller porch on the second level and three thick Doric columns supporting them.

She drove slowly, peering at each house.

"Will the lady like us?" Christopher asked, his voice worried, as they continued on their way.

Since Kevin's death, Christopher, who had been a precocious, adventurous toddler, had become more nervous around other people.

That was another reason she was moving to Austin—for herself and for her son. Both of them needed to reach outside themselves and embrace the beautiful world around them. Kevin, who had spent his entire career trying to help others, wouldn't have wanted them to be insular and withdrawn.

Abby smiled in the mirror. "How could she not like us? We're adorable."

Chris giggled, his dimple flashing. The sound chimed through the interior of her small SUV, warming her heart. He was a complete joy. How dark and dreary her world would have been without him these past two years. In the early days of grief and shock, he had been the only thing dragging her out of bed in the mornings.

"Don't worry," she said now. "Winifred Lancaster is wonderful. She's our friend Lucy's grandmother, so you know she must be awesome."

That connection seemed to reassure Christopher. "Lucy's funny. She's my friend."

"I know. Aren't we lucky to have her in our life?"

"I like it when she sends me stuff from other countries."

That wasn't an infrequent occurrence. Lucy Lancaster, her best friend and former college roommate, had lived in a dozen countries since they lived together, always trying to make a difference in the world. It helped that Lucy had a freakish facility for languages and probably spoke eight or nine by now.

First she was in the Peace Corps in central Europe, then she worked for a nongovernmental organization in North Africa, focused on improving educational opportunities for girls. For the past two years she had taught English in Thailand. Wherever she traveled, she stayed in touch with Abby, often sending local treats and games or toys made by her students to Christopher.

Her life seemed exciting and fulfilling, though Abby wasn't entirely sure her friend was as happy as she said she was.

"In one hundred feet, your destination is on the left."

The disembodied voice of her navigation spoke through the car, making them both jump.

"Is that it? That big house?" Christopher asked, a new note of excitement in his voice.

Abby swallowed. Holiday House was vast, easily the biggest house on the block—the biggest one in town, from what she had seen driving here. The house and large garden took up almost half a block at the end of the road.

"Oh, my."

It was gorgeous, everything Lucy had said and more, illuminated with tasteful landscape lights as dusk gave way to night. How was it possible that she and Christopher were lucky enough to be able to spend the holidays here? Abby wanted to pinch herself.

"I really hope she likes us," Christopher said.

Abby's cell phone rang with a FaceTime call before she could even turn into the driveway. When she saw it was Lucy, she pulled over to the side of the road and shifted her car into Park so she could safely take the call.

"Do you have spies watching for me or something?" she asked, only half joking when her friend's face flashed on the screen.

"No. I was just checking in, wondering how close you are."

"We couldn't be any closer." She turned her phone camera around so Lucy could see what Abby was looking at out the window—the beautiful pale house that gleamed in the snow.

"Are you just getting there?" Lucy's relief was obvious in her expression. "Oh, I'm so glad. How was your drive?"

"Mostly uneventful. We learned that Jingles isn't a great traveler, but we made do."

Their cat had thrown up at the first stop, then yowled about every hundred miles, requiring a stop. She hadn't minded too terribly, since Christopher always seemed to need a stretch and bathroom break around that same time.

"Hi, Lucy," Christopher called from the back seat.

Abby turned the phone in that direction, where her son waved enthusiastically.

"There's my favorite dude."

"We went on a long car ride, only now I want to be out of my car seat."

"You're there, kiddo. I can't wait for you to meet my grandmother. I think you two are going to love each other."

"Okay." That seemed to put the last of Christopher's worries to rest.

"Thank you so much for doing this," Lucy said to her. "I honestly don't have words."

"Really?" Abby teased. "With all the languages you speak?"

Lucy rattled off a bunch of words that Abby assumed all meant *thank you*. She picked up *gracias* and *merci* but that was it.

"Seriously, I can't thank you enough. I still can't believe you agreed to drop everything to help out Winnie. You're going to love her, too, I promise."

Abby shrugged. "The timing was right. My last day at the hospital was Saturday and we were only going to spend the month kicking around Phoenix before the move to Austin."

The past twenty-four hours were a blur, really, from the moment Lucy had called her, frantic, to tell her that her beloved grandmother had sustained a serious fall. She was in the hospital with a broken wrist, sprained ankle and bruised ribs.

She needed home care in order to stay in her house, and did Abby have any friends from nursing school in Colorado who might be looking for work?

She wasn't sure if Lucy had asked her to come out or if Abby had offered. It didn't matter, she supposed. By the end of the phone call, she had agreed to travel to Colorado for a few weeks to help Winifred, until Lucy could finish her school term and make it home to Silver Bells herself.

It would be a lovely holiday adventure for her and Christopher, she told herself again, as she had repeated about as often as Jingles and Christopher had needed bathroom breaks.

She wanted to give her son the best Christmas ever and couldn't imagine a better place to do that than Silver Bells, a beautiful historic winter resort town tucked into the Rocky Mountains.

"I'm sure I will love her," she said to Lucy. "She's got to be at least as wonderful as you've always said."

"Better," Lucy said fiercely.

"Then we'll all be fine."

Lucy hesitated. "There is one tiny complication I should probably mention."

Her friend was going to offer a complication *now*, when Abby was a hundred feet from her grandmother's door? "Please don't tell me I just spent eight hours in the car with a five-year-old and a dyspeptic cat for nothing."

"No. Not for nothing. But..." Lucy paused again. "I may have misled you about how desperate the situation was. Not on purpose, I promise. I was only going on the information I had."

"Misled me how?"

"When Winnie called to tell me about her accident and asked me to find a home nurse, she led me to think she was in dire straits. She told me Ethan, my brother, was insisting she go into a rehab facility."

"That's often the best place for older patients after a fall, so they can receive supported care."

"She absolutely refuses. Winnie wants to be home and I'll admit, I don't blame her. She loves Holiday House, especially this time of year."

It was not hard to see why, Abby thought, looking at the grand house on display in front of her.

"Where is the part where you misled me?"

"She led me to believe that if I didn't find a nurse, Ethan would have her carted straight from the hospital to a rehab center."

"Have things changed?"

"Not really. But kind of." Lucy looked apologetic. "I thought Ethan was going to be out of town until next week, and by the time he got back you would be there and it would be a done deal. I had arranged with Winnie's friends to get her home from the hospital and for someone to stay with her until you could get there. Unbeknownst to me, my brother rearranged his schedule and ended up flying back to town this morning instead of next week. I had no idea he would be there, I swear."

Okay. So she would have Lucy's brother to deal with, too. No big deal. She had been a nurse for years, with plenty of experience dealing with arrogant doctors and demanding family members. How hard could Ethan Lancaster be?

Unless he had already arranged for Winnie to go to assisted living, in which case she *had* just traveled eight hours in a car with a five-year-old boy and said dyspeptic cat for nothing. "So do you need my help or don't you?"

"We do. Definitely. Winnie and I need you more than ever. She really can't be alone at the house, especially now with a broken wrist. If you're not there, Ethan is sure to move her out of her house."

"If she is in her right mind, he can't make her go."

As much as Abby adored Lucy, her friend's brother sounded

like a jerk. During the two years she and Lucy had been roommates at Arizona State University, before she graduated and married Kevin and Lucy left to work overseas, she had never met Ethan. She knew *of* him, though, and knew he had been living overseas, managing one of the family's hotels in Dubai. She wasn't eager to meet him now.

"He might not be able to force her, but Ethan can be persuasive. He says this is the perfect opportunity, while she is recovering from her accident. He's been saying for years that Holiday House is too big for her and too much work. This latest accident will only reinforce his opinion. My brother can be stubborn. Like all the Lancasters, I guess. Once he makes up his mind, he can be immovable."

The whole thing sounded tangled and ugly, the kind of family drama Abby had always tried to avoid and of which she had zero personal experience.

"Are we going to have to barricade ourselves inside Holiday House with your grandmother and fight off your brother like that kid in *Home Alone*?"

Lucy grinned. "As much as I would pay to see that, no. Just be your amazing self, that's all. I talked to Ethan earlier today and told him the cavalry was on the way—namely you—that you were a nurse and amazing and would be the perfect one to stay with Winnie while she recovers, until I can get there. He's not happy about it, but what can he do?"

What had Lucy dragged her into? She hadn't said anything about her brother throwing a wrench in things during any of their previous conversations over the past twenty-four hours.

"I don't want to referee a fight between you and your brother, with your grandmother in the middle. I can find a hotel for tonight and go back to Phoenix tomorrow."

"I need you there. So does Winnie. Please, Abs. You'll love her and you'll love Holiday House."

Abby had no doubt she would love the house, which might just be the most beautiful structure she had ever seen in real life.

She wasn't crazy about the rest of it. She wasn't good at family squabbles and didn't want to be caught in the middle.

"Everything will be fine. I'll be there in two weeks and you can decide whether you want to stay and spend Christmas with Winnie and me, or go back and finish packing for your big move."

She was here not only to help Lucy with her grandmother's medical needs but also for Christopher, she reminded herself. She wanted this Christmas to be perfect for him.

Oh, she knew her hopes were probably unrealistic. No Christmas could be perfect, but they would have to be better than the past two she had been through.

Two years ago, she had spent the holidays still reeling from Kevin's death, only ten days before Christmas, battling her own grief as well as that of a confused, sad toddler.

Her days had been busy dealing with the police investigation, paperwork and the hospital's hollow apologies for their egregious security lapses that allowed an unstable patient to bring a loaded weapon into the facility and shoot the very resident who had been trying to help him.

The previous year, the hospital where she worked—across town from the one where Kevin had died—had been short staffed in the middle of a local influenza outbreak and she had been forced to work overtime through the entire holidays.

This year, she had vowed things would be different. Christopher had turned five earlier in November, old enough to begin forming long-term memories. She wanted those memories to be good ones, not of a frazzled mom working long hours and too tired the rest of the time to have fun with him.

"I don't want to battle your brother, Lucy."

"You won't have to. Ethan isn't unreasonable. He might

seem overbearing and bossy. Part of that is his personality and part of that is from his position as president and CEO of Lancaster Hotels. But underneath his gruff, he's a reasonable guy. He adores Winnie and wants the best for her. We just differ a little right now on what that is."

The man wanted to move his grandmother out of her home against her wishes. That didn't exactly endear him to Abby.

"I guess we'll see how reasonable he is," she said, more determined than ever to stand up for Winifred Lancaster now.

Lucy's face lit up with relief. "You're staying. Oh, yay. I could hug you right now. I owe you big-time. Seriously. Anything I own is yours. I mean that. Which, okay, isn't much, but I offer it freely."

She smiled. Lucy had never been one to care about material possessions, which was one of the things Abby loved about her. Someone meeting her for the first time would probably have no idea her family owned an entire luxury hotel group.

"I will pay you that back in spades, I promise. Thank you. I'll check in tomorrow to see how you're settling in. Bye. Bye, Christopher."

He son had apparently turned a show on in his tablet while she had been talking to Lucy. He waved but didn't look away from the screen.

Okay. She could do this. Abby turned to pull onto the driveway. Someone inside must have seen Abby's SUV approach. The black iron gates slid open smoothly before she reached them.

Her stomach jumped with nerves as she continued up the long, winding drive and pulled up to the house.

When she climbed out to unbuckle Christopher from his car seat, her son gave her a winsome smile of thanks while their cat meowed from his carrier.

"Can we take Mr. Jingles?" Christopher asked.

Like the rest of them, the cat was tired of traveling, but she didn't want to toss a rascal of a cat into what might be a volatile situation.

"We had better leave him here for a moment until we check things out. He'll be okay in his carrier for a few more moments, since he has his sweater on and we won't take very long."

To be safe, she set a quick alarm on her watch to remind her about Jingles in twenty minutes.

The cat seemed content for now in her carrier. Abby left the dome light on as well so he wouldn't be nervous, then walked up the big steps to the front door, Christopher's hand tightly in hers.

A few pine boughs decorated the window on one side of the front door but not the other, as if someone had started the job of decorating for the holidays and become sidetracked. Winnie must have been in the middle of it when she was injured.

Maybe Abby and Christopher could help her finish. It would be a fun activity for them, in between helping Winnie.

"Can I ring the bell?" Christopher asked eagerly.

"Go ahead."

What child didn't love ringing doorbells? she wondered as chimes sounded in the November air.

A moment later, warmth rushed out as the door was opened by a tall dark-haired man in a white dress shirt and loosened tie. She had a quick impression of sculpted features and blue eyes much like Lucy's. This could only be Ethan Lancaster and he wasn't happy to see her, at least judging by his scowl.

"Hi. I'm Abby Powell. I'm a friend of Lucy's. This is my son, Christopher."

He didn't smile a greeting. "I know who you are. Come in. Maybe you can talk some sense into my grandmother."

He didn't wait to see if they followed before heading back

down the hall. After a moment, Abby walked into a grand foyer dominated by a sweeping staircase.

She didn't know what else to do but close the door behind them and follow him, trying not to notice how his tailored shirt clung to a strong back and tapered to lean hips, or the way his hair curled just so at the nape of his neck.

She was exhausted. That was the only explanation she could find for the instant attraction curling through her.

She gripped Christopher's hand as Ethan Lancaster led her down a hallway lined with artwork she would love to examine in closer detail at a later time.

After what felt like forever, he reached an open doorway where she could hear a game show playing on a television.

Ethan Lancaster led the way into a huge bedroom decorated like something out of a Victorian bordello, with flowered wallpaper, fringe-edged red satin curtains and large dark furniture pieces. Dominating the room was a giant four-poster bed with a canopy that matched the curtains.

In the middle of the bed rested a petite woman with wrinkled features and hair the pink color of cherry-flavored cotton candy.

Perched around her were three little corgis, who lifted their heads long enough to yip a quick greeting in unison, then promptly closed their eyes as if they couldn't be bothered to care.

"Abby. Darling. So wonderful to see you. How long has it been?"

"At least a decade," she answered, walking closer to kiss the woman's cheek in greeting.

She had only met Winifred Lancaster a few times, when the woman came to visit Lucy.

Winnie was unforgettable. Though small in stature, she was the kind of woman who commanded attention wherever she went, mainly because she seemed intensely interested in everyone around her.

Winnie had insisted on including Abby whenever she would do anything with Lucy. They had gone to dinner at several of the better restaurants in the Phoenix metro area. She had even met Kevin when he could break away from his med school classes.

Abby immediately sat down on the side of the bed and took the older woman's free hand in hers. "Well, I have to say, you look better than I had feared," she said, which made Winnie break out in raucous laughter.

"I'm not quite knocking on death's door, you mean."

"Not even walking up the sidewalk, from what I can see. Lucy tells me you had a bad fall."

"She tripped on one of the blasted dogs and tumbled half-way down the stairs," Ethan Lancaster said darkly. "How long did you lie there in pain, Winnie?"

His grandmother sent him an annoyed look. "Not long. Only an hour or so, until I was able to get to my phone and call for help."

An hour. It sounded like an interminable time frame. She couldn't even imagine it, though she knew the woman's injuries could have been much worse.

"Things aren't not as bad as my darling grandson is making them sound. I only broke my arm and sprained an ankle."

"Don't forget the bruised ribs and the pulled muscles in your shoulder," Ethan said darkly.

Winnie pulled a face that made Christopher giggle from halfway behind Abby.

"How can I forget them, when they insist on reminding me every time I breathe?"

She peered around Abby. "And who is this handsome young man? This can't be Christopher."

"Yes, it can," Abby's son answered rather defensively, which made Winnie smile. "My name is Christopher Kevin Powell. I just had a birthday and I turned five."

"I am Winifred Elizabeth Johnson Lancaster. My friends call me Winnie and I regret to say that I am much older than five."

"I like your dogs," Christopher said. "They're cute. What are their names?"

She grinned with delight, though Abby didn't miss the twinges of pain in her eyes. "Thank you. I like them, too. They are Holly, Ivy and Nick. See, Ethan? This is a young man of taste and refinement."

"No doubt," Ethan said, his tone mild and without inflection. He didn't roll his eyes, but he might as well have.

"I'm so glad you're here, my dear," Winnie said. "Thank you so very much for coming to my rescue."

"I'm happy I could help," Abby said.

"I feel so much better knowing you can be here to help me."

Ethan's glower seemed to deepen. "You need to be in a facility where they can care for you properly. You can't even shower yourself here."

"This is my home and exactly where I want to be. Now I can be, since Lucy found a solution all the way from Thailand. Abby is a highly qualified nurse and, with her help for the next weeks until Lucy can make it home, I should be fine. Problem solved. She can help me get around, and you can go back to running your empire."

"I had everything arranged with that nice new facility by the hospital."

"Well, you can unarrange it. You ought to know better than to make plans for me without asking my permission. I might be old, but I'm not senile yet."

His laugh sounded more frustrated than amused. "I'm well aware. You're the sharpest old bag I know."

Winnie didn't appear to be offended by this, at least judging by her hoot of laughter.

Ethan reached for her hand and the sight of that wrinkled, age-spotted hand in his made Abigail's knees feel a little wobbly. Probably just hunger, she told herself.

"I just want what's best for you. You know that," Ethan said.

Winnie turned her fingers over and squeezed his. "I know that, darling. Don't think I don't appreciate it. I do. But right now, spending Christmas in the house that I love is absolutely the best medicine for me."

His sigh held capitulation and annoyance in equal measures. "We need to have a serious talk after the holidays. You live in this huge, crumbling heap by yourself. It's not safe."

"Watch it, young man. This is your family's legacy. Before you call it a crumbling heap, maybe you should remember that without this house, you wouldn't have a hundred hotels spread across the globe, including three right here in Silver Bells. Your ancestor mortgaged this house to buy his first hotel after the silver mines ran out. Without that, we all would have been bankrupt."

She had a feeling this wasn't the first time they had had this exact same conversation.

"Now, Abby," the woman said, turning to her. "You and Christopher have been driving a long way. Ethan can bring in your luggage and show you to your quarters. There's a two-room suite just down the hall, so you'll be close to my room if I need you."

"That sounds perfect."

"Ethan can show you everything."

"Will you be okay?" her grandson asked, undeniable worry in his eyes.

"Fine. Just fine. The dogs will keep me company. When you're settled, come back and talk to me," she ordered Abby.

"Ethan, darling, I'll see you tomorrow for Thanksgiving dinner. I'm planning a late one, 5:00 p.m. You can still make that, can't you?"

He sighed again. "Again with Thanksgiving. I thought you agreed to forget about it. I can bring you a meal from the hotel."

"I didn't agree to any such thing. Don't be silly. Thanksgiving dinner is a tradition."

"Traditions don't matter in this situation. You're injured. The last thing you need to worry about is Thanksgiving dinner."

"I won't be worrying about anything. It's all been arranged. I won't have to lift a finger, trust me."

"I can help," Abby offered.

"I can, too," Christopher said, though he obviously had no idea what he was volunteering to do.

"There you go." Winnie beamed at her. "I have ready-made helpers. We'll see you tomorrow—5:00 p.m. sharp. Will you help Abby with her bags now? Christopher, do you mind staying here and keeping me and the dogs company?"

"I don't mind one bit," Christopher said, plopping into a chair next to his new friend's bedside with an expression of delight.

After another charged moment, Ethan walked out into the hall, all but vibrating with frustration.

Left with no choice, Abby followed him. The man looked even more stern and forbidding up close, his mouth set in a tight line.

He was gorgeous, she couldn't deny that, with blue eyes, lean features and an appealing afternoon shadow along his jawline. He also smelled delicious, some intoxicating mix of expensive leather and a pine-covered mountain.

Not that she noticed or anything.

She had to clear the air between them or she was in for an

uncomfortable few weeks. "I'm sorry. When Lucy asked me to stay with your grandmother, I had no idea I was walking into a family disagreement."

His rigid expression eased slightly. "It's certainly not your fault. You walked into an old argument, I'm afraid. I've been trying to convince Winnie to move for years, but she insists she's fine here. Recent events have proven otherwise."

"Because she fell?"

He nodded. "I can't imagine how terrifying that must have been for her, all alone here. Next time, she might not be able to make it to the phone to call for help. I wish I could convince her she would be safer in a one-level condo somewhere."

She was quite confident that would not be an easy sell. At the same time, she couldn't entirely fault the man for wanting to look after his grandmother.

"Do you want me to leave? I told Lucy we could go to a hotel tonight and return to Phoenix first thing tomorrow."

"That's not my choice. Winnie and Lucy want you here, so obviously I've been outvoted."

"Sorry."

"Again, not your fault." His rigid expression softened further until he looked almost approachable. "You've had a long drive. Let's get you settled for now. You're going to need all your strength to keep up with my grandmother."

Don't miss *Christmas at Holiday House* by RaeAnne Thayne,
available from Mills & Boon